Edge of Night

A NOVEL

CAROL WARBURTON

Cover image . . .

Cover design copyrighted 2002 by Covenant Communications, Inc.

Published by Covenant Communications, Inc.
American Fork, Utah

Printed in the United States of America
First Printing: April 2002

09 08 07 06 05 04 03 02   10 9 8 7 6 5 4 3 2 1

ISBN 1-59156-013-6

Library of Congress Cataloging-in-Publication Data

Last Name, First Name, 1966-
    Title, Subtitle : a novel / Author Name.
        p.   cm.
    ISBN x-xxxxxx-xxxx-xxx
    I. Title
    PS3564.U468A88 1997
    813'.54--dc21   97-18033
                                              CIP

DEDICATION

To Roy
In Appreciation

ACKNOWLEDGMENTS

My thanks to Dorothy Keddington, Ka Hancock and Charlene Raddon fellow writers and friends. Your insightful critiques and unfailing encouragement are gifts beyond price.

PROLOGUE

Massachusetts—1858

The rough voice of a man jerked me out of sleep, my heart pounding so hard it was difficult to breathe. Amos! He'd found me!

I searched the dim interior of the wagon, my sleep-dredged mind clogged with fear. Should I burrow deeper into the sacks of oats or try to scramble out and run. But where?

I was trapped! Amos Mickelson ruled the village. Even if I outran him, no one would believe me when I told them what had happened. My thoughts froze when he climbed onto the wagon. I wedged myself into a cavity between two sacks, certain he would untie the canvas and find me.

Then I heard a deep voice speak of the need to reach Bayberry before nightfall, felt the wagon shift as a second man climbed onto the seat as he mentioned barrels of pickled herring. It was the wagon owners, not Amos, men who knew nothing about a stowaway hiding in the back of their wagon.

"Thank you," I whispered—to God, to fate, to whatever had saved me. I heard the snap of reins, felt a lurch as the wagon moved forward. I was going—away from Mickelboro and fear, away from the cottage filled with both warm and cruel memories.

Exhausted from the past night's tension, my mind ceased to worry while my heart reached out to the future. Would I find a way to join my sisters? Would I find another man to love?

Salt Lake City—2002

Jessica Taylor slowed her steps as she entered the chapel of the temple. It was always a rush to get there, but once seated she could feel the tension slowly slip away. Here was refuge. Peace. It was always here. Jessica let it surround her as she closed her eyes and listened to the soft music that filled the chapel. She wanted that same peace for the person whose name was on the pink card she held in her hand, one she'd promised her grandmother she'd take through the temple.

Tamsin/Yeager
Birth: 26 July 1837

Tamsin. What an unusual name, one that spoke of another time, of a life undoubtably much different from her own. Jessica tried to picture this long-ago ancestor—the younger sister of her third great-grandmother. Had she been tall and dark like Jessica, or more rounded and fair like some of her cousins? What had her life been like?

She tried to recall what Gran had said—something about Tamsin and another sister remaining in the East with their mother after the oldest sisters joined the Church. There was also evidence that Tamsin and her husband had been involved with Quakers in the under-ground railroad, and that their home had been a way station for runaway slaves.

Jessica looked at the name with increased respect. Tamsin Yeager must have been a woman of great courage. Goodness and charity too, if she'd risked herself for unfortunate slaves—strangers.

What frightening events had filled her life? Were there children? More pressing to Jessica, was she in the temple today, waiting for her work to be done?

Are you here, Tamsin? Even as Jessica's mind formed the question, she knew the answer, felt it in a wash of warmth, in the sting of reverent tears. Tamsin Yeager was there, her spirit encircling Jessica with love and gratitude as tangible as a physical presence.

CHAPTER 1

Tamsin Yeager
Massachusetts—1858

The morning when I first saw Caleb Tremayne is permanently etched into my memory, the strokes as bold and vivid as those of the Flemish masters. Although the edges have blurred over the years, the colors and sounds remain, muted but beautiful, like a rich tapestry displayed under old glass. In my mind I see the golden orb of the sun in a cloudless sky gilding leaf-shawled trees so they shimmered and glowed like coins spilling from a leather purse. A soft breeze blew in from the ocean, rippling the leaves and setting the flowers dancing.

I think I knew even then that something that would change my life forever was about to happen. All of my senses were primed as if they were waves about to hurl themselves at the sand.

The cool tang of the ocean was everywhere—salty and lobster-spawned and wonderful. I remember looking down at the cove from the wooded bluff. The tide was out, leaving a sickle of beach fringed with boulders and sun-bleached logs. The sight never failed to lift my spirits, the cobalt blue water stretching to the horizon, its satin sheen flecked with whitecaps.

From the bluff, I had access to the best of two worlds: the cove with its treasures of sea creatures and circling white gulls, and the wooded headland butting into the Atlantic, lush with every kind of tree and shrub imaginable.

I came there often to sit on a knoll, feet bare, the sun warming my tension-knotted shoulders. That day I stood on the bluff, wind tugging my long skirt, the sound of the crashing waves banishing the cloying smell of Mother's sickroom.

Mother had been unwell for the past five years, being taken with a raging fever that so weakened her delicate constitution she was left an invalid. Even so, she remained her sweet self, finding delight in sipping tea laced with cream and sugar out of fine china cups, listening as I described a flight of ducks or the amusing antics of the garrulous squirrel living under the woodshed. But her greatest pleasure was in my younger sister Clarissa and myself. The three of us spent our days reading together, or listening while Clarissa played the pianoforte.

Thus was our life until the morning when we had wakened to find Clarissa gone and only a note to tell us she was eloping with Jacob Mueller, a nearby farmer's son—though he was much more than that to me. The shock of her sudden departure brought on a return of Mother's fever. As her health further declined, so did her mind and pleasant nature.

The past night had been especially bad. She had tossed restlessly, her twig-thin fingers scratching the counterpane quilt while she whimpered and called for Father, who'd been dead for six years.

"Hush, he'll be here soon," I had whispered, rising to take one of her fragile hands and hold it against my cheek. "Rest now. Your Tamsin is here." I sang to her then, the same sweet lullaby she had sung to me when I'd been frightened or fretful. "Hush little baby, don't you cry . . ."

I cared for her throughout the night, and when Betsy, a neighbor's maid, thoughtfully came to relieve me, I took my gray shawl and fled the house, needing sunlight and glittering water more than I needed sleep.

I lingered on the bluff, the wind tangling my dark, unbound hair, reveling in the few moments of snatched freedom. My mind drifted back to the time when we'd all been together—Mother, Father, my three older sisters, Clarissa, and me. We'd lived on a farm thirty miles inland from Mickelboro, Massachusetts. Father wasn't wealthy, but he had provided enough for Mother to have someone to cook and do the heavy cleaning. With a perspective acquired by time and maturity, I can see now that Father pampered Mother. She was the kind of woman who was easy to pamper, with her fragile beauty and graceful movements that made other women seem awkward and plain. Mother's people were upper class, acquainted with good books and schooled in the social graces. Frederick Yeager's people were as common as the rich brown earth—hard-working Germans, stubbornly clinging to old ways and old language. Although Father was born in Pennsylvania, he spoke with a heavy German accent and sometimes forgot his manners and sopped up the last of his supper with a scrap of bread. Still, his blonde good looks made it easy to see why Mother had chosen him, but I think Father always felt like a man who'd won a beautiful bird and didn't quite know what to do with her.

Even so, they were happy. Children know such things, can sense it in nuance and gesture and touch. Father pampered us as well. Instead of milking cows or helping in the fields like some men's daughters, we were allowed the luxury of books and lessons on the pianoforte, both supplied by Mother and augmented by the schoolmaster who sometimes boarded in our home.

I sighed and started down the path to the cove, not wanting to think of the devastating changes that had taken place since then. The sun had burned away much of the fog, though a few isolated patches still hung in gauzy tendrils among the trees. The path was steep and sometimes slippery, passing through a stand of white birches before it twisted between slabs of granite. It was as familiar to me as the rooms of my home, with a scrubby, wind-stunted pine waiting like an old friend at the last curve in the path.

I stopped to rest, leaning against the rough trunk of the pine to gaze out at the sea, whose power to fascinate pulsed through the air like something breathing and alive. The ocean was unusually calm. Gulls and cormorants wheeled and banked close to the water, and the little boat making its way past the breakers hardly seemed to move.

It was then that I saw him: a tall, dark-haired man striding across the sand to the scattered logs and rocks. There was something watchful about him. Watchful and cautious. I crouched behind a boulder, curiosity and surprise my primary emotions. In all my years of coming there, I'd never seen anyone on the beach before. My curiosity melded with shivers of nervousness prompted by the stark isolation of the beach and Mother's repeated warning that going off by myself would one day lead to grief.

Such didn't prevent me from watching the man's approach. Even in his haste there was a catlike grace to him. When he reached a log, he turned to look back at a boat, his stance one of taut concern as he watched its slow progress toward a larger vessel. I strained to identify the boat's occupants, wondering if they were people I knew, but distance and the shimmer of sunlight made it impossible to see. My attention jerked back to the man when he raised his hand in farewell and stooped to pick up a satchel by the logs. Fitting the strap over a muscular shoulder, he started toward me. His legs ate up the distance, brown boots scraping on sand and shingle.

I'd lived six of my twenty-one years along this coast, and I prided myself in knowing everyone in the vicinity. This man was a stranger, with his thick black hair falling over heavy brows, high-ridged cheek-bones, and a squared-off chin. He was a man of the outdoors, perhaps a fisherman or a laborer from a farm, his face and neck tanned to the rich color of rawhide with sun creases at the corners of his dark eyes. He was a man in his prime, perhaps five or six years older than I.

My mind assimilated all of this in the space of a breath, as his black hair blowing in the wind, loose-fitting white linen shirt, and coarse woven trousers were but quick impressions. I crouched lower and felt a prickle of excitement as he hurried by, my heart pounding while questions whirled through my mind. Who was he? Had the boat brought him to the cove, or had he helped to launch it? And why hadn't they chosen the larger town of Lobster Harbor, just eight miles distance, with its wharf and easier access to the sea? Not knowing the answers, my mind returned to the man's wet boots and water-darkened trousers. The stranger and the boat went together. But how and why? The puzzle momentarily banished worry about Mother. I welcomed the change and pulled it around me like a warm quilt on a cold New England night.

—•—

But I had little time to think about the man or the boat. On my return home, while still making my way through the orchard that edged our backyard, Betsy ran to meet me, her hair coming loose and the lines in her scarred face registering worry.

"Hurry, oh, do hurry miss. Your mother's taken bad. Deacon Mickelson sent James for the doctor."

I lifted my long skirt and ran, forgetting the need to be circumspect, my stocking-clad legs bared to the knees, paying no heed to Amos Mickelson and his wife, Hester, standing at the door.

"I never should have left her," I cried, though what more I could have done I didn't know. All of Dr. Field's instructions had been followed to the letter, including the purging and daily doses of nitros. Was it all for naught?

I brushed passed the Mickelsons without speaking, only dimly aware that they followed me into the bedroom. Hester Mickelson's soft, "I'm sorry . . . so very sorry," was scarcely audible above the sound of Mother's harsh breathing.

I dropped to my knees by her bed. Death was all around us, hovering in the morning air, waiting to slip through the glass panes of the window. I wanted to hold it back, flail at it with my hands. *Please God, don't take her. She's all I have left. Don't leave me alone.* My tears made it difficult to see her clearly. Why hadn't I kissed her before I left, told her how much I loved her? As I gazed at Mother's gaunt, sunken cheeks and heard the rattle struggling up through the ropey cords in her throat, I felt a sudden desire to cling to her, laugh with her, love her: all the things in which we had once delighted. What would I ever do without her?

CHAPTER 2

The next days passed in a blur of shock and pain. It was as if winter had suddenly come, freezing me and all that moved in my sphere: robins nesting in the apple trees, the distant sight of Hester Mickelson's clothes hanging in the sun, even the words I spoke to the few friends who came to express their condolences. Everything moved in slow motion, voices and figures stiff and brittle, like ice about to shatter in a winter storm. Never one to make speech easily, I lost what little ability I had in the thick folds of grief.

When the day of the funeral arrived, the service was brief with only a short sermon and the singing of one of Mother's favorite hymns. I wished I had given more thought to the funeral. There had been ample time during the long months of Mother's decline. But I had stubbornly clung to the belief that she would recover so we could leave Mickelboro and try to find my sisters, Harriet and Mary Ellen, who'd gone west with elders from the Mormon Church some five years before. We'd received a letter from them filled with glowing accounts of the Great Salt Lake Valley, and the news that they were now the plural wives of one of the men who had escorted them there. When Mother had let this information slip to Deacon Mickelson, he'd forbidden us to have anything more to do with them.

"Plural wives," he'd snorted. "More likely harlots. They've joined the devil's church, and your daughters are the devil's children."

Mother had started to cry, but since our livelihood after Father's death was dependent upon the deacon's generosity, none of us had dared go against his wishes. Instead, we'd contented ourselves with the one letter. If others came, we didn't receive them, since Amos

Mickelson had taken it upon himself to bring our mail. That single missive had been read so often it was memorized. *Please write and tell us how you are faring. Does Tamsin still enjoy cooking? How is Clarissa doing on the pianoforte?*

Clarissa. Just thinking of her tore at my heart. If only she hadn't left. If only I hadn't been so alone at the funeral.

The memory of my arrival home from the cemetery is still vivid, for it was then that I first came to mistrust Deacon Mickelson. He and his wife, Hester, were our benefactors and closest neighbors. The cottage in which we lived had been ours these last six years only through their good graces. It was the Mickelson buggy in which I rode to the cemetery, and when it finally halted in front of my cottage, it was Amos Mickelson who hurried around to help me down.

"Are you certain you won't come up to the house with us?" he asked. "Mrs. Whiting has dinner waiting."

I shook my head, meeting his eyes briefly as he placed a pudgy hand on my waist. Then I saw it—a quick flicker in his expression, nothing more. I was too unschooled in the wiles of men to understand. But there was an instinctive cringing, a knowledge as ancient as Mother Eve, that told me to take care.

"No, thank you." My voice sounded high and unnatural. Hester turned and looked at me, her long features tightening slightly. "Please don't think I'm unappreciative," I hurried on. "You've both been kind . . . more than kind, but I'd like to rest now."

"I'll send Betsy down to sit with you," Hester said. "She can bring your dinner. It's best that you aren't left alone."

I thanked them the second time and turned tiredly to look at the cottage, grateful the buggy was finally pulling away. I think it was then that I glimpsed what I might become—a lonely spinster forever dependent upon the goodness of others, with no life or purpose of her own. My lips parted in protest. Though I had given up marriage to care for Mother, such wasn't the case anymore. I was still young . . . well, moderately young. And Jacob Mueller had once thought me comely.

Jacob! My heart twisted at his name. I must not think of Jacob or Clarissa. Especially not now.

So it was that I entered the cottage, truly alone for the first time in my twenty-one years. I paused and looked at my home and furnishings with new eyes: the tiny parlor and bedroom occupying the front of the house, with a narrow kitchen and second bedroom running across the back. The parlor had been Mother's pride, with a heavy deal table and two high-back chairs brought from Pennsylvania after she and Father married. Her presence was evident in the touches of lace at the window and the needlepoint coverings on the chairs. Her favorite volume of poetry lay on the table as if she had just set it down. In truth it had been months since she'd left her sickbed. Betsy had placed the book there out of reverence for the dead.

It was the same in the bedroom. The massive oak bedstead with the blue quilted coverlet seemed to await the return of its mistress. I awaited her too, trailing my hand across the coverlet before going to stand at the window, something I'd done each day, describing to her the yard and the splendor of the hollyhocks that grew along the fence.

Are there birds, Tamsin? Have the robins built their nests in the apple trees this year?

I could hear her voice, clear and melodious as it had been before she became so ill. That was how I wanted to remember her, not as she had become—demanding and clinging. Now she was gone, and I would give everything I had to bring her back.

A wave of bone-wrenching loneliness washed over me and sent me to the kitchen in search of the room's homey comfort—the cast-iron stove banked against my return, the cheery pot of red geraniums on the windowsill. Although the parlor and bedroom bore Mother's imprint, the kitchen was mine, more by default than desire at first, the oak table mine to scrub after breakfast along with the chipped mugs and bowls from which we sipped tea and ate porridge.

In time, I had come to enjoy my mornings there. I experimented with herbs and glowed with pride when Clarissa and Mother pronounced my chowder the best they'd ever eaten. Soon my experiments expanded to baking. I learned to knead the dough until it was just the right texture, forming it into loaves and setting them to rise in a sunny spot on the table. Today two loaves awaited my return, the airy mounds lifting the cloth I'd draped over them before I'd left. I added wood to the stove and filled the kettle. With the kettle singing and bread in the oven, I pulled out a chair and sat down.

"You need to make plans, Tamsin." The sound of my own voice shattered the oppressive silence and made me smile. If I were a spinster, I might as well be eccentric. Talking to myself seemed a good place to begin. It would also settle my mind.

"And you must find a way to leave here," I added. This was something I'd already decided, something I'd known without conscious thought. I'd seen firsthand what being dependent on another's generosity had done to Mother, eating away at the little joy she'd found after Father's death. Eternal gratitude is a hard taskmaster, especially gratitude to people like the Mickelsons. Not that they were bad, really. It was more the way in which they went about doing good.

Amos Mickelson was the most prominent man in our area, the village named after his grandfather. He was also the owner of Mickelboro's only store and largest farm. Only the minister of our church wielded more religious authority than Deacon Mickelson, the most prominent member of the congregation. Pride was often the deacon's companion, and he never lost an opportunity to point out all he did for us: the new stove he'd bought, a pump in the kitchen, new dresses for the three of us each Christmas and again in the summer.

"You and your daughters look well," he'd say to Mother as we left the church on Sunday. He'd nod as he took in our new gowns, his round barrel chest expanding as he smiled at those around us. Everyone knew where the dresses came from, just as they knew who'd bought the stove and the pump. He'd beam as if we were his daughters, which he liked to pretend we were since he and Hester had never had children. I'm not sure whose charity was more difficult to swallow—Amos's with his overbearing pride in his good works, or Hester's reluctant giving.

I'd declined the invitation for dinner, knowing Hester preferred that I stay away. Hester had never liked our presence in the cottage. She'd resented the fact that Mother had children, and had been envious of Mother's fragile beauty. It was always there, apparent in empty, fluttering platitudes, in the tightness around her mouth as she strove to match her husband's generosity in a hollow, grudging way.

"I must leave the cottage," I repeated. Fearing I would lose courage, I took paper and pen and wrote the words across the top of the paper. Underneath them I wrote my second resolve: *I will find a way to join Harriet and Mary Ellen.* The third line was added in more tentative strokes: *I will find a husband who loves me.*

"There," I whispered. Buoyed by my resolve, I took the paper and wedged it into the corner of the watery pier glass in Mother's bedroom, the bedroom I would now make mine. With the paper to remind me each time I combed my hair, I would not forget. Somehow I would make it happen.

As I looked at my reflection in the old mirror, my confidence ebbed. My thin, pale face was unremarkable, black hair pulled severely into a bun, hazel eyes red-rimmed and lusterless from grief and lack of sleep. Clarissa said my eyes were as indecisive as I was, sometimes appearing brown, the next minute green. How could anyone so unsure of herself break away from the security of the Mickelson farm? As for finding a husband . . .

"You can," I said to the somber reflection. We both straightened our shoulders. "We can."

———•———

My new resolve helped me through the next days, gave purpose to routine, and made space for thoughts unclouded with grief. Even so, a fortnight later I was no closer to a solution than I'd been on the day of the funeral.

Sensing the need for advice, I set out for the home of Susannah Partridge, which lay some three miles from the cottage. My sister and I used to ride there in the cart with Mother before Clarissa had left us. Not wanting to trouble Deacon Mickelson for the loan of his cart and pony, I kept at a brisk pace, knowing I must hurry if I wished to be back before dark.

It was the loveliest of weather, utterly windless with hazy sunshine and only a few clouds. The road I followed wound inland, past the Mickelson's large farm with neat fields and rail fences, and on to less significant holdings. The Partridge farm lay at the edge of a rise, the house butting close to the hill for protection from the winter storms.

The dog met me with a welcoming bark. I bent to pet him, noticing his limp and the patches of gray that grew behind his short ears. His bark brought his mistress, her ample frame filling the doorway. Susannah Partridge was a big woman, standing taller than many men—big hands, big feet, and as everyone knew, a big and generous heart.

"Tamsin!" Pleasure showed in her face. Wariness too—something that hadn't been there until she and Mother had quarreled a few years before.

Mother never told us why they differed, only that we wouldn't be visiting her anymore. We continued to nod when we saw the Partridges at church or in the village, but we didn't stop to chat. Our questions to Mother met with silence, and in time we stopped asking, though we often wondered. Clarissa believed they'd quarreled because Susannah didn't approve of Mother's manner of rearing us. I was convinced it had something to do with Amos Mickelson, whose name I had overheard during the heated discussion that took place while we'd waited in the cart. There were spots of color on Mother's cheeks when she rejoined us. I remember looking back at Susannah, one of her large hands held to her mouth as if she wished to take back words or hold back tears, I could never be sure. But I was certain she was sorry.

She stood before me now in the open door.

"Aunt Susannah." Although it had been many months since we'd spoken, I used the title she'd asked Clarissa and me to use. My voice was tentative, for I was unsure of my welcome. My fear was foolish, for before the words were out I was enfolded in Susannah's fleshy arms, feeling the softness of her ample bosom, smelling the faint odor of sweat and flour and lye soap. When she released me she took me into the kitchen, inviting me to sit down, smiling as she added water to the kettle and cut thick slices of fresh-baked bread.

The kitchen was much as I remembered it, the scrubbed oak table and ladder-back chairs, a slate sink with a sluice bringing water from the spring. But there were changes too—a baby's cradle being the most noticeable. We'd heard of her son Matthew's marriage to Lydia Hillman and of the arrival of Susannah's first grandchild quickly followed by a second.

"I guess you're wondering why I came," I said after Susannah filled my cup with steaming tea.

Susannah shook her head. "I know why you're here. Since Ellen's funeral I've prayed every day you'd come." She placed fingers to her quivering lips. "I've missed you and your mother . . . and Clarissa." She took my hand. "I wanted to speak to you at the funeral, but the Mickelsons were with you." Tears filled her eyes. "I'm so sorry about your mother. About Clarissa too. But I'm glad you came."

"Thank you." I blinked rapidly, not wanting to lose control. "I needed to hear that . . . to hear another voice. Everything is such a jumble. What to do? Where to go? I can't stay where I am. I refuse to." My voice trailed away when Susannah's fingers tightened on mine.

"Deacon Mickelson?" she asked.

"And Hester. I won't let them run my life like they did Mother's."

Susannah's mouth tightened. "I tried to warn her, but she couldn't see. Perhaps she didn't want to see. No one likes to think ill of their benefactor."

"Betsy said the Milners need someone to help in their cheese room. I was thinking—"

"No." The force of Susannah's voice surprised me.

"Why not?"

"Heaton Milner is a hard man. You'd not be happy there. Besides, I want better for you. A husband. Children. You've cut yourself off from everyone since Clarissa left."

"Mother needed me."

"And she didn't need Clarissa?"

We were on dangerous ground, and Susannah knew it. "I didn't come to talk about Clarissa."

"I know you didn't. But you need to. After Clarissa ran away, I doubt your mother ever spoke of her." Not waiting for my answer, she went on. "It was her way. She could fill an afternoon with talk about flowers or the weather. But to talk about things close to her heart . . ." Susannah shook her head. "You mustn't do the same, Tamsin. Talking heals. I'm here to listen when the time comes."

I looked down at the amber liquid in my cup. How could I talk about Clarissa when I wouldn't even let myself think about her. "No." My voice was a whisper, my throat constricting against months of buried resentment. "No!"

"Then we'll talk about something else." And we did. We talked of Sadie Peterson's new baby, and of Hugh Fleming's run-in with a mule and the resulting broken arm. Anything except Clarissa.

It was late afternoon before I rose from my chair with a promise to return. By then we had explored the possibilities for my future, though nothing definite was decided.

"You can always stay with us." Susannah glanced at the empty cradle. "Lydia and the babies have gone to spend the day with her mother. When they're all here . . ." She shook her head and laughed. "You'll not lack for someone to talk to, that's for sure. But you'll be welcome." She turned serious. "I'm glad you've decided to leave the cottage. That's why I prayed you here, to persuade you to do it. The sooner you get away from the Mickelsons, the better it will be."

———•———

I thought of her words the next week when I wrapped bread and cheese in a cloth and set out for the cove. It was a lovely summer day. Robins sang in the orchard, and the meadow, thick with wild flowers and rimmed with towering oaks, called like the legendary piper. I hurried along, swinging the cloth, a bounce to my step. I felt a stirring of excitement, the first in weeks, as I reached the bluff and looked down at the cove, saw the expanse of water laced with whitecaps, and smelled the sea.

It was as though I'd come home after a long absence. The trees encircled me as I hurried down the twisting path. I leaned against the pine to catch my breath, breathed in the damp smell of the sea and pictured the stranger as he'd come toward me—confident, masculine, purposeful. *Now there's a man,* I thought, and blushed at my boldness, smiled too, even as I wondered what had become of him. Was he visiting someone in the area or had he come on some kind of business? If so, where was his home?

That afternoon marked the beginning of my healing, a turning from grief to acceptance. The sea was part of it, the rhythmic surge of water, the rattle of shale on sand, the unchanging sameness washing like a healing balm. I stood for several minutes, my mind empty, lifting my arms, then my face, letting the sun and the sea and the salt-wind pour into the very core of me. I opened to it like an empty vessel, absorbing slowly until I was filled.

The filling erased the years and turned me into a girl again, one who'd stood in awe at the water's edge when Clarissa and I first discovered the cove. We'd only been at the cottage a few weeks, still exploring and learning about the countryside when we'd stumbled onto the path to the beach. Though I was the older, I'd hung back, letting Clarissa take the lead as she was wont to do, her blonde curls bobbing just ahead. She exclaimed at each new sight, her excitement as contagious as a case of ague.

"Do look, Tamsin. Have you ever seen anything so beautiful?"

Too filled with awe to speak, I only nodded, but I saw and felt. I wished I could live there, looked for the perfect spot to build a home.

We spent the afternoon at the cove, gathering shells, poking sticks at clams trapped in tide pools, staring at the strange beauty of sea anemones. The memory came fresh as yesterday, how we removed shoes and stockings and wiggled our toes in the sand, how Clarissa marched boldly to the water's edge and I held back and waited for the next wave to charge. It made me scurry, but Clarissa waited until the last possible second before she ran, squealing and laughing while water lapped at her pink heels.

The memory jarred and cut, sending me down to the water a woman, not a timid girl. I sat on a water-pocked rock and stripped off shoes and stockings. Like that girl, I wiggled my toes in the sand, feeling the fawn-white granules warmed on the surface by the sun, cool and damp as I plunged my toes deeper. As if bidden by something outside myself, I lifted my skirt and waded into the sea. My breath caught at the coldness—bone chilling and aching and wonderful, like winter's first deep snow. I stood in the pale green water, felt the sand shift beneath my feet as the wave receded, and heard Clarissa's chiding voice from yesteryear: *Don't be a 'fraidy cat.*

This time I did not run, but waited, a grown woman, letting the wave charge toward me, feeling it smack against my knees. It almost buckled them as it rushed past me to spend itself upon the sand. I heard someone laugh. My pleasure swirled when I recognized it as my own, rippling from deep inside, a place turned cold and sterile from months of nursing Mother. Once released, it bubbled like the waves' foamy residue—bubbled joy-filled and wondrous, a sound I'd almost forgotten.

Hitching up my skirt, I waded deeper, twirling as I sang a sailor's chant. The sun shimmered, waves lapped and hissed. I lifted a hand to shield my eyes from the brightness, searched the water for the boat and the dark-haired stranger. Where had he gone? Would I ever see him again?

My mind filled with questions and dreams, and I found a sandy spot between tumbled rocks, unwrapped the bread and cheese, and settled into a little hollow. Sometime after, I closed my eyes and let the sun and wind pour through me again, feeling something hard and tense slowly stretch and relax.

I slept. When I wakened, the sun was hidden by dark, rain-laden clouds, the wind no longer gentle, now gusting and plucking as I pulled on coarse stockings and sand-scuffed shoes. Before I reached the path, the first drops fell, wind-driven and stinging, pelting through the trees as the shower changed to a downpour and turned the path to mud. By the time I reached the bluff I'd slipped twice, my clothes sodden and muddy, water dripping onto my face from lank hair.

I ran, stumbling through the rough grass of the meadow, the orchard and cottage but a faint outline ahead. In my haste, I failed to see a horse and buggy veer from the road to bounce across the meadow and intercept me.

"Tamsin!"

The clatter of the buggy and Amos Mickelson's voice penetrated my consciousness at the same moment. I turned, chest heaving, as the buggy rolled to a stop beside me. For a moment there was only silence as I waited in the drizzle, wiping rain from my face and trying to catch my breath. Deacon Mickelson stared, lips parted, his eyes making me suddenly aware that my wet dress clung to my body. Warmth rushed to my cheeks and I instinctively folded my arms around me, while the rain dripped and the silence stretched until it seemed to scream through the space between us.

"Tamsin." The deacon repeated my name in an uneven rush. I stepped back, wanting to whirl and run, wishing I were home in my cheery kitchen with the stove burning and the door bolted.

Amos's tongue flicked across fleshy lips, and his chest relaxed in a long exhale of breath. Like a man wakening from a dream, his slack face lifted and stretched into its habitual expression of jovial goodwill. "Here." He leaned to offer me his hand. "Climb in."

I hesitated until habit and good manners took over. I'd trusted Deacon Mickelson for years. Surely nothing had changed. But it had. I could feel it in the tension between us, feel it when his hand brushed damp hair away from my face as he wrapped a blanket around me, his breathing strange and ragged.

When the deacon finally flicked the reins and set out toward the cottage, I used the buggy's motion to inch away. My fingers gripped the corners of the blanket and held it like a shield between us.

"It's quite a storm," he said.

I nodded, keeping my eyes straight ahead, willing my teeth not to chatter. *Just get me home,* I prayed, planning to jump down from the buggy before Amos had a chance to touch or help me.

But the deacon was of another mind. As the buggy pulled into my yard, I felt his pudgy hand on my knee. What he tried to pass off as a pat was more. "I don't want you catching cold. Make sure you get out of those wet clothes and into something warm."

I ignored him and jumped down, almost falling in my haste, the blanket clutched tightly around me. "I'll return this to Mistress Mickelson after it's dry."

"No need to bother. I'll stop by this evening to make sure you're all right." His voice sounded like the man I'd always known—friend, benefactor, respected deacon in the village church.

I hurried inside without looking back, closed the door, then leaned against it, my body trembling as I slid the bolt through the hasp. His parting words seemed to echo through the room. *I'll stop by this evening to make sure you're all right.*

"What am I to do?" I prayed, the words echoing hollowly in the room. "Dear God, what am I to do?"

CHAPTER 3

I went to bed before sunset and lay awake for hours with the doors bolted, chairs pushed against them for a barricade, my ears attuned to every sound. I had no notion of what I would do if Amos knocked on the door. Surely with no light in the windows, no answer to his knock, he would go away. A sudden cry from a barn owl, the pop and creak of walls, sounds as familiar to me as my name now seemed fraught with menace. *Don't let him come,* I prayed. *Please, make something keep him away.* Never had a night seemed so black and long.

Amos Mickelson did not come, reinforcing my timid belief that God does hear our prayers. With the coming of dawn, I was able to relax enough to fall into a troubled sleep. When I awoke and saw the sun shining warm and yellow and heard finches chirping merrily from the fence post, my fear began to dissipate. Perhaps I'd misread the look in Amos Mickelson's eyes, mistook his touch for other than it was meant to be. Upon seeing me all wet and bedraggled, might he not have felt surprise, even solicitude? It was easy on such a lovely day to rationalize and set worry aside. The deacon was old enough to be my father. He also had a wife.

After breakfast, I went outside, stopping to pinch the spent blooms from the roses and pull a weed from among the foxglove. Before I knew it, I was on my knees, mounding the rich soil more firmly around the delphinium, then moving to the vegetable garden where rows of beans and potatoes awaited me.

Gardening was as much a part of me as breathing. How else can I explain the pull of soil and humus and seed, my delight when green seedlings push toward the light, the joy of viewing unfurled buds and knowing that in a small way I've had a part in their growing. Mother said mine was a gift from her grandmother, Catherine Hyatt, who came from England before the revolution with starts of lilacs and roses wrapped in burlap.

I passed a pleasant morning, studiously keeping my mind on growing things, not on people. The garden had been my salvation after Clarissa left, the soothing rhythm of rake on soil building a wall against bitterness and betrayal. Not once did I allow thoughts of Amos to intrude through the pastel blooms. Even so, I started at sudden noises and looked with unease toward the Mickelsons' two-storied farmhouse, its brown roof and chimneys visible through the trees.

Go to Susannah's, something seemed to whisper. *She said you could stay with her.* After lunch I set out for the Partridge farm, taking the back way so the deacon wouldn't see me.

Susannah's welcome was warm as she drew me into the kitchen and thanked me for the beans I took to her. "We can snap them outside where it's cooler." She cast a significant look at Lydia, who was nursing the baby. "Lydia's a dear, but she tends to eavesdrop," Susannah continued after we'd settled ourselves on a bench under the hickory tree. She studied me for a moment, her brow furrowing at what she saw. "We need to do something to put the sparkle back in your eyes."

"I'm fine. Just a little tired. I didn't sleep well last night."

Instead of asking me why, Susannah patted my hand. "I've been thinking about you. Have you considered trying to find your sisters?" When I nodded, she went on. "My feelings about a church that teaches a man to have more than one wife haven't changed, but I don't hold with the deacon forbidding your mother to write to her daughters either. Love and family come first." She paused and looked me in the eyes. "There are ways to get around Amos Mickelson you know." She nodded as if the notion pleased her. "You can send letters under my name. Receive them the same way. I tried to get your mother to do that, but she wouldn't."

"No . . . she wouldn't."

"But you could. You must try to locate them. They need to know your mother has passed on."

I agreed, my thoughts on Amos Mickelson instead of Harriet and Mary Ellen. I was uncertain of how to word my request to stay with her—how much to tell her about the incident with the deacon.

"What about your oldest sister . . . Catherine, isn't it? Didn't she and William join the Mormons too?"

"Yes."

"You need to let her know."

"I don't know where she is . . . whether she and William went west as well. We haven't heard from her in several years. I think the deacon intercepted her letters too."

"The old goat," Susannah whispered under her breath.

We fell silent, each wrapped in our thoughts, the snap of beans the only sound to break the afternoon quiet. Susannah's fingers moved quickly, but mine were slow as my mind slipped back to the time before Father's death.

We'd been happy on the big farm, a tight-knit family secure in our love for one another. When Catherine was seventeen, Father's brother came to visit and took Catherine back to Pennsylvania with him, saying it was time the Yeager cousins became better acquainted. Similar invitations for the rest of us were hinted at some future date.

Mother was uncomfortable with her German in-laws, part of the Pennsylvania Dutch community who looked down on her lack of housewife skills as much as Mother looked down on them for their lack of refinement. Even so, Catherine went. A year later she married William Richards, neighbor to our uncle and an apprentice to a printer in Philadelphia.

Later Catherine wrote to invite Harriet and Mary Ellen to live with them.

Please let them come. I'm lonely for family, and a friend has promised positions for both to work in her hat shop.

Thus it was that when Father was killed in a farming accident two years later, Clarissa and I were the only children left at home. I was fifteen at the time, Clarissa a year younger, both of us shattered by the loss of the tall, broad-shouldered man who'd added warmth and spontaneity to our lives.

Mother was more devastated than we were. She wandered from room to room, adjusting the curtains, rearranging bouquets of flowers. Five minutes later she did it again. She was like a ship suddenly stripped of its mainsail—agitated, floundering—with dark pools of fear in her brown eyes. I knew she regretted her estrangement from her family—people who thought she'd married beneath herself.

"What are we to do?" she'd whispered. "I don't want to live with your father's people. But if I don't—" Although she could quote pages of Shakespeare, she had little knowledge of farming and even less notion of how to manage financial affairs.

"Maybe if you wrote to Catherine and William . . ." I had ventured, thinking of the young man who'd stood in church with my sister, confident and sure of himself. "He's a man. He'll know what to do."

Mother sighed and began the familiar pacing. "William knows nothing of farming. He was raised in the city. Their future is there . . . what there is to it. 'Tisn't bright, with the baby and another one on the way. Even if they'd gotten word in time for the funeral, I doubt they'd have had enough money for the trip. As for Harriet and Mary Ellen . . ." Her voice broke and she couldn't go on.

How Amos Mickelson came to be aware of our circumstances, I'm not sure. He arrived in his shiny buggy, a broad-brimmed beaver hat on his balding head, exuding confidence and goodwill.

I well remember the impact he had upon Mother, his stocky presence seeming to stand like a bulwark between her and the gaping cavity of uncertainty. The deacon had heard that our farm might be for sale. He was willing to pay a fair price. There were two more visits. Papers were signed. Before we knew it, we were ensconced in a cottage on the edge of Amos Mickelson's farm, our floundering ship pulled into a safe harbor by the big, good-hearted man.

The cottage was small in comparison to the home we left, but Mother was so relieved she didn't have to turn to Father's people she made it seem a prize. "Just look at the view," she'd exclaim, pointing to the apple orchard. Or, "This parlor is really much more cozy. Now that there's just the three of us, it's all we need."

Overall, I think Mother was pleased with herself. She still had her books and beloved pianoforte and enough money to hire a woman to help with the heavy cleaning. Just as important, she'd found someone to lean on, someone to advise her about decisions.

"I don't know what we'd do without Deacon Mickelson," she said almost daily. "God sent him. How else can one explain how he found us?"

Clarissa and I were quick to agree. Although we missed Father, it was comforting to have someone so big and strong to take care of us.

Each time Mother attempted to thank Amos, he shrugged it off with a wave of his hand. "None of that, Mistress Yeager. The Lord put us here to look out for each other. It's my Christian duty. If I turned my back on you—a poor widow with two daughters—you can be sure I'd feel His wrath."

If Hester were with Amos, she'd nod in agreement. "It's our duty . . . a blessing really . . ." She'd glance at Clarissa and me, a tight smile stretched across her thin face, ". . . since we have no children of our own."

Deacon Mickelson seemed like a gift from God, a jovial, ruddy-faced man who let us feed apples to his pony and taught us to hitch it to a cart and explore the countryside. But his wife was our goad—a spare, unsmiling woman who seemed always to disapprove. She was forever dropping by on one pretext or another, bearing a loaf of bread or a basket of eggs as a means to get inside, pry and ask questions while her eyes darted from the books on the table to Mother's embroidery. *How can you sit idle when there's so much to do?* the look implied.

Mother bore it much better than Clarissa and I. For her, Hester was a small price to pay for security.

"She's a snoop," Clarissa stormed, after Hester had suggested that fewer ribbons for our hair might be a way for Mother to practice economy. "She's always looking for something to criticize."

Mother's fingers plucked at the fringe of her lacy shawl. "Hush. You mustn't speak ill of Mistress Mickelson. Without her goodwill, we might find ourselves sleeping in a ditch or hired out as servants."

Despite her bravado, even Clarissa couldn't bear the thought of losing the cottage. We loved its nooks and crannies, loved the old orchard, and were totally entranced by the cove with its horde of sea treasures. In time we learned to school our thoughts, pasting on polite smiles as we thanked the cheerless woman for her manipulative baskets of charity.

Lost in the past, I barely heard Susannah's voice.

"Amos Mickelson cheated your mother."

"What? . . ." Susannah's voice jerked me from thoughts of the past.

"Deacon Mickelson cheated your mother."

"No." Then quickly, "How?" while my mind spun away from that sun-gilt time to the jolting reality of the present.

"He paid her only a fraction of what the farm was worth. Told her it was a fair price. You know how naive your mother is . . . was. If someone she trusted told her the sky were green, she'd believe it. Ellen trusted Amos. Trusted him completely, at least at first. After that, it was too late."

My mind reeled from the enormity of what Susannah had said, while part of me accepted its validity and placed it beside the Amos Mickelson I'd glimpsed the day before. "How . . . how do you know?"

"My brother is close friends with the deacon's man of business . . . knows Amos too. One night they dined together and your mother's name came up. Something was let slip . . . enough for Oliver to know she'd been cheated. He told Samuel and me about it, but when I tried to tell Ellen—"

"You quarreled," I finished for her.

Susannah nodded, her expression pensive as she relived that afternoon. "Your mother must have said something to the deacon, for we sensed a change in him too. Later when Samuel tried to get credit to buy seed for spring planting, Deacon Mickelson refused to give it to him. It was the same at the smithy. Doors which had always been open to us were suddenly closed." There was an edge to Susannah's voice. "We wouldn't have made it without help from Benjamin and Josiah. They're good sons, both of them, and wise to try to better themselves away from Mickelboro."

"I'm sorry."

"It isn't your fault, nor Ellen's either. She only did what she thought was right. I doubt she had any notion that Amos would seek revenge. He seemed only goodness to her . . . goodness to all who don't speak ill of him."

Anger rose in my throat. "He should be exposed! Cheating Mother. Hurting you. He's a hypocrite, and I've a mind to—"

"No, Tamsin." Susannah's grip on my hand was hard and urgent. "'Twould be foolish and only harm you . . . most likely us too. Amos Mickelson is respected by many. His influence reaches far."

"But—"

"Leave it be, Tamsin." Though her voice was soft, strength ran through it. "I did wrong to tell you about Mr. Mickelson, though perhaps now you understand why I want you to leave his cottage. The man can't be trusted. Who knows what might happen next."

The incident with the deacon jolted through my mind. I opened my mouth to tell Susannah, but something in her eyes stopped me. Susannah Partridge was afraid of the deacon. The knowledge struck at my confidence. Strong as an ox, the villagers said of her. You might as well try to stop a runaway team as get in Susannah's way. Hadn't she taken Horace Smith to task for neglecting his wife and children? Even the minister sought her advice and counsel.

That was before, I suddenly realized. Before her quarrel with Mother. Before the deacon turned people against her. I'd been so wrapped up in myself and caring for Mother, I hadn't noticed. I lowered my gaze to the pile of beans in my lap. "Perhaps you're right."

I have no recollection of what else we talked about that August afternoon. But I remember my thoughts. They came crisp and clear, like dew before it's touched by morning sun. Amos Mickelson was a thief, a biblical wolf in sheep's clothing who, after cheating Mother, passed himself off as our friend and benefactor. I wanted to rail at him, shout the truth down the length of the village. But such action would be foolish. Look what had happened to Susannah.

I masked my feelings from Susannah, putting on a smile to hide my anxiety, stopping to admire her new grandson.

"If no position shows up by the end of the week, you must come to stay with us," Susannah said as she walked with me to the gate. She put her hand on my arm. "In the meantime, take care."

"I will." The promise came easily, but I knew I could not impose on the Partridges. They'd already borne Amos Mickelson's disfavor. If they took me in, they'd be courting it again.

—•—

I did not see Amos Mickelson until two days later, though Hester came to visit me, her eyes narrow with suspicion as if she sensed or knew what had happened during the rainstorm. When I handed her the dry blanket, her mouth tightened into a line that matched her eyes.

"Deacon Mickelson never misses a chance to do good," she said after I explained how I came to have the blanket. She paused and took breath. "Have you given any thought to your future now that your mother is gone?"

"Some." I met her gaze. "I'd like to find my sisters."

Instead of expressing outrage, the corners of her mouth relaxed. "Families can be a great support in times of trial. Although I can't approve of your sisters joining that heathen church, I'm sure you must love and miss them."

"I do."

"If there's anything Mr. Mickelson or I can do in the meantime, don't hesitate to ask." Hester started toward the door. Before she reached it, she turned. "I have a small sum of money put by against a time of need. I think your circumstances qualify as need." Her voice quickened. "There's more than enough to pay your way out to your sisters. I can help make the arrangements too."

I felt a stirring of excitement. This was a solution I hadn't considered. Though it would go against the grain to take Hester's charity, perhaps it was time to set aside pride. "You're very kind."

"I try to help the unfortunate." There was a deliberate pause—another smile. "Why not write to your sisters today? I'll be happy to see that the letter is mailed . . . though of course this will have to be our secret. It will be better if the deacon doesn't know." Her gaze darted around the parlor, settling first on the table then moving to the pianoforte. "Such a long journey will oblige you to sell your furniture. Perhaps I can help there too . . . purchase some of it from you. I've always desired a pianoforte."

"I'll think about it," I said, though I would rather have dumped it into the ocean than have her grasping fingers touch the keys.

When Hester finally left, I slowly looked at the little parlor, saw the portrait of my parents with the oak frame Father had carved. How could I bear to leave it or the pianoforte or the precious books? I had a sudden memory of winter evenings when we'd gathered with Mother by the fire, her voice soft and melodious as she read to us.

Tears that had threatened for days finally came. I covered my face as pain and the realization that my life would never be the same washed over me. When I finally gained control, I wandered around the cottage, stopping to water the geraniums in the window, my mind heavy with indecision. Fear of Amos told me I must leave, yet I was reluctant to accept Hester's offer. Too agitated to stay inside, I sought the garden. Even the flowers could not soothe me that day. Back and forth I paced, my long skirt brushing against the foliage and rustling the leaves. I could not go to Susannah's, and unless I accepted Hester's charity, I lacked the means to undertake the long journey to join my sisters. If only I could find a place out of Amos's reach where I could earn money and make arrangements to join Harriet and Mary Ellen. But where?

The "where" stopped me—that and the fear that if I made inquiries, Amos would hear of it and interfere. Though he had no legal claim on me, after six years as my benefactor and father figure, he still had power to give me pause.

Unease followed me through the day and wakened with me the next morning. Shortly after breakfast a knock sounded on my door. "Please, let it be Mrs. Whiting or Betsy," I breathed.

It was the deacon, his plump face freshly shaven, his generous mouth stretched into a smile. When he removed his broad-brimmed beaver hat, his eyes did not quite meet mine. "Mistress Yeager."

"Deacon Mickelson." His name came out in a rush as I strove to put away concern. He'd stood at this door often, bringing a ham or checking to see how we were doing. Surely I had nothing to fear.

Even as the thought formed, something flickered in his eyes. It was a look of raw hunger, one I'd seen in the eyes of the Mickelson's dog when he gazed into the chicken pen. My fingers tightened on my shawl and I wanted to close the door against him. Then his round, genial face returned to the one I'd known since girlhood: open and wishing to please.

"You've been on my mind. I hope you didn't suffer from the wetting." Amos's eyes left my face and traveled over my person.

I drew the paisley shawl more firmly around me. "I'm well."

"Good . . . good." He turned the brim of his hat in his large hands. I knew those hands—capable, blunt fingers that had patted Clarissa's shining curls and brought me a kitten. Now I feared them and wanted to flee.

Amos waited to be invited inside, but I stood my ground, using the half-open door as a barricade between us.

"I gave the blanket to your wife," I said, while the more incautious part of me wanted to cry, *You cheated Mother!*

"So she informed me." Amos's full lips tightened, and he cleared his throat. "I also got it out of her that you wish to go west and join your sisters. That's another reason I stopped by . . . to tell you that the cottage is yours. Yours to keep for a lifetime. There's no reason to leave. No reason at all. In fact, it would be most unwise. A young woman traveling so far alone . . ."

"I'm hoping to find people with whom to travel. Perhaps a family needing someone to look after their children."

"If your mother were alive she'd be distressed to hear such talk."

"But she's not alive." I made the mistake of meeting his eyes. My pent-up anger must have shown, for his features tightened and a red flush crept upward through his fleshy jowls.

"Then I will act in her stead. You must forget your foolishness."

"Foolish? . . ." Anger boiled through the fear. "You think it foolish to want to go to my sisters—my own flesh and blood? I'd say 'tis natural, the most natural desire and decision for a woman of my circumstances."

"For those without recourse or a home," he conceded. "But the cottage is yours now. As for family—" Amos paused to swallow, his cheeks as ruddy as his jowls. "Your sisters gave up the right to be family when they joined that devilish church. I told your mother she must disown them. You too, if you wish to escape hellfire." His voice gathered firmness. "Mistress Mickelson and I are your family. I am like your own father. There must be no more talk of leaving."

Not giving me opportunity to reply, the deacon stalked away, his broad shoulders rigid with anger and purpose. 'Twas well he did, for had he stayed, I would have lost my trembling control.

I closed the door with a bang. How dare he try to pass himself off as my father! How dare he forbid me to find my sisters! Anger sent the blood to my head. I went to the window and watched his dark-clad figure disappear into the trees. My fingers tightened on the curtain and I became aware of a pulsing fear. Fear of what would happen if I stayed.

CHAPTER 4

I'm not sure what wakened me that night and alerted me to danger. Perhaps fear. Perhaps divine intervention. Regardless of the source, I jolted out of slumber, heart racing, my eyes searching the gray shadows of Mother's room, which was now mine.

Then it came, a noise so slight and stealthy that had my senses not been attuned to just such a sound it might have gone unnoticed. Someone was at the back door, turning the handle, testing the bolt.

The deacon! My worst fears were centered in a muffled thud as he threw his great weight against the bolted door. I was out of bed in a thrice, trembling like a deer ready to take flight. I glanced at the partially open window. A light breeze moved the white curtains. If I hurried I could be gone before Amos realized it.

I grabbed my shoes and cautiously inched toward the window, aware of my pounding heart, listening and searching the pale expanse of yard through the raised sash. Too late I heard the swish of boots on grass as he made his way around the corner of the house.

A force other than myself sent my trembling arms and legs into action. In one quick move, I straightened the coverlet on the bed and plumped the pillows so Amos would think I'd left and the bed had never been slept in. Fumbling for my clothes, I shoved them under the bed. Lying on the bare pine floor, I crawled into the cramped space under the oak bedstead. My nose was just inches from slats and rails and feather mattress, but at least I couldn't be seen. Pray to God, I couldn't be seen.

Amos's approach was audible—furtive footsteps, his clothes brushing the lilac bush outside Mother's window. I heard a cautious scrape of wood as he raised the sash, a muffled grunt when he hefted his bulk through the window.

I held my breath, a hand on my mouth as if it feared I would scream—as well I might, for my fragile control was about to shatter. *Please, God. Please, God.* The prayer became a litany, calming my tensed muscles so they didn't tremble.

Silence. Even the crickets had stilled. Amos was as quiet as I was. I imagined the room, the bed outlined in the moonlight, the deacon's shadowy bulk reflected in the pier glass, his head turning as he inspected the room.

He gave a whispered oath followed by cautious footsteps, the creak of pine boards. I heard the armoire door open, listened to the rustle of clothes; Mother's dresses I hadn't had the heart to pack away. More bumbling, uneven footsteps came, another oath when he stumbled over the foot of the cot. In a rush I realized he had been drinking.

The sound of his heavy shoes moved away and made a slow circle of the parlor, the kitchen, finally the back bedroom where Clarissa and I had once slept. I lay in the cramped confines under Mother's bed, my ears tuned to his every move, little night noises and the ticking of the clock scarcely noted.

"Tamsin!" My heart leaped and pounded at his frustrated bellow, at the crash of something hurled to the floor, at heavy footsteps and an oath.

Silence settled over the house. Was he hoping to lure me from my hiding place? What if he lit a candle and looked under the bed? Time dragged with only the creak of boards when Amos shifted position. I knew he was waiting, listening for any sound. I dared not move, dared not blink.

Another curse rasped through the silent rooms followed by the sound of the bolt being slid from its hasp. He was going. Amos was finally going. I felt a current of air as the door opened and closed, heard boots strike stone paving by the herb garden. Then nothing.

Fear nailed me to my hiding place. Was Amos playing a game, or had he truly given up and gone home? I do not know how long I waited, but it seemed like hours. Unable to lie still any longer, I finally rolled out from beneath the bed and crawled on shaky knees to the window. The moon had slipped behind a cloud, plunging the garden into darkness deep and wide enough to hide a dozen men. He'd gone. I knew it as surely as if someone keeping watch whispered it to me. Amos was gone.

Relief made me weak as a newborn kitten. I sank to the floor, chilled and trembling in the warm night air. My teeth began to chatter, and I felt my face screw up like a frightened child. Leaning my face against the bed, I gave into emotion, sobbing while tears made trails down my clammy cheeks.

I must leave. Leave immediately, before daylight came. I dressed quickly, my fingers fumbling with the buttons. Then I bundled clothes and a few coins into my paisley shawl. At the last moment I snatched the note written earlier to myself from the pier glass.

I went to the kitchen for bread, some cheese, and two hard-boiled eggs and added them to my bundle, feeling my way past the debris of the shattered geranium pot. The need for haste fought with delay when my feet took me into the parlor. All that I held dear was but ghostly shadows in the little room. I could not leave without saying good-bye, first to the pianoforte, then to the table and chairs, lovingly running my hands over their surfaces, caressing wood and fabric. My fingers closed around Mother's favorite book of poetry. It and a volume of Shakespeare lay on the table and called to my heart. Adding them to my bundle, I eased the door open, my nerves primed for any sign of Amos Mickelson.

Seeing nothing, I turned for one last look. My throat tightened as I thought of Mother and Clarissa, our quiet evenings in the parlor, even as a voice in my head clamored, *Hurry! Hurry!*

I ran, keeping to the shadows, anxious to put as much distance as possible between Deacon Mickelson and myself. A dog barked as I passed a house. Heart racing, I glanced back, hoping no one was looking out. I hurried on, past the smithy, a saddler and harness shop, and the brick, two-story mercantile with Amos Mickelson's name above the door, looming like gray sentinels in the quiet night.

The inn lay ahead. Under the trees was a bench where those waiting for the stagecoach could sit. I sat down to remove a rock from my shoe. A nearby stream gurgled and night creatures stirred in the bushes. I lifted the heavy coil of my braid and wiped perspiration from my neck. As I did, I noticed a wagon parked next to the inn. Everything was still, the windows showed no light, the inn yard deserted. With a plan but half-formed, I crept over to the wagon, my senses alerted for a dog or someone guarding the load. Nothing.

Nerves tensed for flight, I lifted the canvas, saw a small space between two kegs, and scrambled inside. I waited in the silent blackness, knees drawn up tight to my chin, listening, my heart clamoring. Silence stretched like a tautly pulled rope. I cautiously pressed back against the wooden staves, searching for give, knowing I couldn't remain long in such a cramped position. The kegs sat solid as boulders, but behind me was space not entirely filled by rough, bulky sacks. I wiggled onto the sacks—oats, by the smell of them—and stretched out, using my bundled shawl as a pillow.

———•———

With the coming of daylight, I left Mickelboro, curled up on a bed of oats. Fear rode with me, my senses primed for my discovery. I braced myself against the wagon's jolt, starting each time I heard the crack of whip and the rough voices of the men who sat but a few feet from my head. I thought they were brothers, young and uncouth of speech, eager to sell the load of goods—kegs of pickled herring and sacks of oats—eager, as well, for money. Their close proximity kept me glued in my place. I feared my slightest movement would alert them to my presence.

The sun had not been up long before I rued my decision to hide in the wagon. Although the stretched canvas allowed room to move and breathe, it acted like nature's own oven, holding in the heat of the September sun and blocking any breeze. It soon became stifling, and the dust sifting through the sides of the wagon added to my misery—not to mention the stench of the pickled herring. Not daring to move, I could only lie on the lumpy sacks and count the minutes, the hours, trying to shut out the rough oaths of the teamsters, their ribald ditties, the nauseating sound when one cleared his throat and spat. I set my mind to other things and planned what to do when the wagon reached its destination. One of the men spoke of Bayberry, while the other held to the plan of getting a better price by going further inland, perhaps even as far as Holyoke.

My heart sank. Though I'd heard of Bayberry, Holyoke lay a good three days away. I closed my eyes and willed myself to stay calm. Perhaps Holyoke might be a blessing in disguise. Hadn't Harriet and Mary Ellen found work in a city? Perhaps like them, I could find a position there. Clinging to this thought, I gave into heat and exhaustion and fell asleep.

Late that afternoon the drivers made the decision to sell their goods in Bayberry. "Old Samuelson has always done well by us. He won't try to cheat us," one man said. "That way we can be home by Sunday and I can walk Zella to church."

As quick as that it was decided; my fate fixed, though I did not know it, only that I was weary to death of heat and the jolting wagon. I sensed a change, a quickening of pace, a lift to the drivers' voices as they called to someone on the road. We were nearing Bayberry. Dare I get out, or should I wait until the men were occupied to make my escape?

Wait! a voice seemed to whisper, one that sounded like Mother's. Too weary to think clearly, I heeded it without hesitation.

Noise and bustle told me we were almost there—other wagons, the clang of hammer on anvil, horses slowing. Voices came too, children's laughter. People were about, people who might become my friends.

"Whoa there, Dolly. Whoa, Hezzie."

The wagon stopped and one of the men got down. "You comin'?"

"In a minute."

Before he could say more, a boyish voice broke in. "Can I watch your wagon for ya, mister? It'll only cost ya a copper."

The driver cleared his throat and spat. "Make sure you watch it good."

"I will. You can depend on it."

My heart sank. How would I be able to leave? I crawled over the sacks to the back of the wagon. When I lifted the canvas, I saw another team and wagon parked near us, the horses' heads deep in nose bags. Knowing I must take a chance, I grabbed my bundle, squeezed through the narrow opening, and jumped down.

"Hey!"

I turned and saw the boy. Placing a finger to my lips, I shook my head. "I mean no harm," I whispered. "I just needed a ride." I tried to smile, knowing I must look a sight, but feeling a stirring of success when the boy winked and grinned.

"I don't see nothin'," he said and looked the other way.

"Thank you."

The boy nodded.

I smoothed my hair and reached for my bonnet. It was crushed like my dress, but I didn't dare venture into the street without it.

"If you'll go to the third house 'round the corner, my ma will let you wash up," the boy said.

I looked at him in surprise, noting his clean, patched trousers, his bare feet and bony ankles. "Thank you." Then quickly, "What's your name?"

"Just tell Ma, Peter sent ya. You're not the first. Won't be the last neither. She's always helpin' people."

"I'll tell her," I promised. "Looks like you take after your mother. Always helping people."

His freckled cheeks flushed. "Better hurry before someone sees ya."

I set off in the direction he'd pointed, no longer feeling quite so alone. I walked briskly, aware of people, several store fronts, a sign announcing the law offices of George Reading. Leaving the board walkway, I stepped into the street, skirted a pile of fresh horse droppings, and turned the corner. The atmosphere was quieter here—wood frame homes set behind picket fences and neatly tended yards.

I paused at the gate in front of the third house. What if Peter had been wrong and his mother turned me away? Knowing how I must look after riding all day in the dusty, cramped wagon, I couldn't blame her.

The house, though neat, was not much bigger than our cottage, but the path was bordered with red and yellow snapdragons and late blooming asters. My heart lifted through its worry. The flowers, like Peter, provided an optimistic message: that people were good and perhaps things would work out.

I went to the back door, stooping to pet a calico cat that circled around my feet before I knocked.

"Yes?" Curiosity rather than surprise showed on the face of the woman who answered my timid knock. She was of medium build, perhaps in her mid-thirties, with delicate, fine-boned features.

"Peter . . . your son told me you might let me wash up. I know it's an imposition, but—" Without warning my eyes filled with tears. *Oh, Lord, please give me courage.*

"Of course. Come in . . . do come in." While I strove to regain my composure, the woman ushered me into her kitchen and pulled out a chair. "You look like you could stand a bite to eat as well as a chance to wash up."

"Thank you." I gratefully took the offered chair, not realizing what a toll the past days had wrought until my legs almost gave way. I took a deep breath and tried to smile. "I'm not usually like this. Please excuse me."

"Think nothing of it, dear. I know what it's like to be at the end of one's rope." She poured hot water into a basin and set it, a bar of lye soap, and a clean towel on the table. "After you wash up, you'll feel more like yourself. Then we can talk." She patted my shoulder, seeming pleased to have me in her kitchen.

"Thank you." It was all I could say. I had not expected to find such warmth and hospitality.

Sensing I needed a measure of privacy, Peter's mother turned and lifted the lid of a simmering pot, stirring its contents. My mouth watered at the savory aroma. Chicken—perhaps chicken stew.

The woman spoke, one hand tucked into the pocket of her brown apron while the other hovered over the pot. "I hope Peter thought to invite you to stay for supper. By the way, my name is Abigail Hamilton. Most people call me Abby. And yours?"

I paused with my hands in the basin, my fingers tingling from the water's heat. "Tamsin. Tamsin Yeager."

"A good name. There's a family by the name of Yeager on a farm a few miles out of town. Are you related to them?"

I shook my head and worked the soap into a lather. "My father's people live in Pennsylvania."

"I see." Abby blew on the contents of the spoon, took a quick taste, and added salt. "It's almost done. When Peter gets home it will be ready."

I washed my face, closing my eyes and letting the warmth seep in. Slowly I relaxed. When I dried my face and hands on the towel, I was embarrassed by the trail of grime on its surface. I felt as if I were not myself. The hand-painted oilcloth covering the kitchen table and the cupboard filled with crockery and utensils seemed slightly out of focus. Any minute I expected to awaken and find myself back home with Mother.

But I could not go back. I must go forward, hold to my last shreds of courage and use my wits if I expected to survive. God or someone—was it Mother?—had sent me to this kind woman. With her help, I could make plans and find a way to reach my sisters.

"Feeling better?" At my nod, Abby smiled. "I thought you would. A good wash and a cup of tea can do wonders for a body. It was a favorite saying of my mother's, and I've never known it to fail."

She took basin and towel from the table, replaced them with cup and saucer and poured the tea, adding a thick slice of bread spread with freshly churned butter. "I made it just yesterday," she said, referring to the butter.

"It's delicious." It took control to keep from gobbling it down in two bites. I hadn't eaten since the night before, the bread and cheese still tucked away in my shawl against future hunger. The tea disappeared as quickly as the bread. Abby, noting my thirst, went to the pump and brought a dipper of water.

"Thank you. I didn't expect to find such kindness."

"I'm sure you would do the same if the circumstances were reversed. You have the look of someone good . . . one who cares."

"Peter does too." When I recounted the circumstances of our meeting, Abby didn't seem surprised. "Have you other children?" I asked.

"Only Peter." A shadow passed over Abby's pretty features and drove the light from her eyes. "There was another son two years older than Petey . . . a baby daughter too. They died five winters ago from diphtheria."

"I'm sorry."

"My husband passed away just a few months after . . . gored by a bull. It took a full week for him to die. His suffering was terrible, and I could do no more than hold his hand. I pleaded with God to let him live . . . to not leave me and Petey alone." Abby swallowed, and her lips quivered. "It wasn't God's will," she went on. "And Peter and I have learned to do much for ourselves."

"You have a nice home," I said into the grief-filled silence.

"Yes." Abby looked around the kitchen, the shadows in her eyes lifting. "It's mine . . . paid for from Thomas's share of the family farm. I wanted no more of it, though it's a nice place. But I didn't want to risk another goring. Peter was small—only five, and always following the men when they tended the animals. I grew up in Bayberry. Town life is more to my liking. So here you see us, Peter and I. Like I told you, I know what it's like to reach the end of one's rope."

"You do." Somehow my own loss didn't seem quite so daunting.

"What of yourself?" Abby inquired. "What brings you here?"

Had I been more myself, I might have devised a story, for I didn't want Amos Mickelson to hear of my whereabouts. But I was not myself, and Abigail already felt like a friend. She was a woman I could trust. I knew it intuitively, just as I sensed she somehow held the key to my future.

I told her all, omitting only the deacon's name and that of the village.

Abby was all sympathy. "What a fright you had. No wonder you fled, though it's a pity you had to leave everything behind."

Peter arrived then, calling to his mother as he burst through the door, the air quickening with his presence. He pulled off his cap when he saw me. "I was afraid you might have gone to the wrong house."

"I found it just as you said. Thank you. I don't know what I'd have done . . . where I'd have gone if you hadn't sent me here."

"It's nothin'." He looked embarrassed, but I could see pleasure in his eyes. Peter Hamilton's heart was as soft as his mother's.

I studied them, mother and son, looking for other signs of resemblance. There was little save a dusting of freckles across the bridge of each nose. Peter was dark, his brown hair standing up in all the wrong places, dark eyes, and skin tanned to butternut by the summer sun. Abigail was fair, her blonde hair—which was pulled into a loose chignon—still lustrous and beautiful, as were her eyes, blue like the palest of asters. As a young woman she must have been beautiful.

Even now, she was handsome, her figure still slender. It surprised me that she was still a widow.

Abby intercepted my gaze. "Peter takes after his father. The Hamiltons are dark. Tall too." She frowned at her son's outgrown trousers. "If he doesn't stop growing, I don't know what I'm going to do."

"Tell Grandpa. He said I was to see we didn't do without."

Abby gave a little sniff. "That man. I've told him a thousand times we're capable of making our own way. It's important for Peter to learn to stand on his own feet . . . not be beholden to kin. It's ready," she said abruptly, referring to the food.

"That's not what Grandpa says." Peter eyed the bowl of chicken stew. "He says we're family, and he promised Pa he'd look after us."

"Only if there's a need."

I looked at Abigail with new eyes, realizing that beneath her softness there was an iron will, rather like that of Susannah. I smiled, liking her all the more.

The rest of the evening passed pleasantly. When we had eaten, I insisted on washing the dishes. Afterward we went outside to enjoy the coolness of the evening on a bench under a little arbor. Abby had her knitting, but I sat idle, watching the sky turn from palest saffron to salmon, listening to the click of needles while Peter filled a bucket at the pump. I tried not to think of Mother or the cove or Amos.

After a while, Abby put down her knitting and took my hand. "Things will work out. Meanwhile you can stay with us. No, it's already settled. Peter prefers sleeping on the porch during the summer. You can have his room. It won't be any trouble."

"I don't know how I can ever repay you."

"God will show you the way. He always does, as you'll see when you've gained more experience with life's twists and turns."

We stayed outside until dark, listening to the crickets, watching the cat stalk a night creature hiding in a lilac bush. For a moment I was at peace. Abby had that ability, to make one believe and take heart. She also had a talent of making things appear as if they were no trouble at all. Much of this I learned during the days I stayed in her home. But that night all seemed to happen as if by magic—the tub of warm water waiting in my room for a bath, and a fresh nightgown smelling faintly of roses lying on the narrow bed.

Before I climbed between muslin sheets I looked at my few possessions. My three dresses now hung on pegs, the stale bread and cheese having been given to the cat. Mother's books sat on the table next to the bed. Only the coins and the scrap of paper still lay in the shawl; the paper which I'd written upon all those weeks before, tucking it into the pier glass so I wouldn't forget my resolve. I picked it up and read the words aloud.

I must leave the cottage.
I will find a way to join Harriet and Mary Ellen.
I will find a husband who loves me.

My eyes lingered on the last. I sensed that Abigail had found such love with her Thomas, and remembering Catherine's glow on the day of her wedding, I thought she had found it too.

So had Harriet and Mary Ellen, if their letter was to be believed, though I could not like the idea of two women sharing one man.

I would not let myself think of Clarissa. Instead, like a familiar image in a favorite dream, I saw the rugged features of the man I'd seen at the cove. Dark hair. Dark eyes. Holding his face in my mind, I slowly relaxed and drifted into sleep.

CHAPTER 5

I slept until noon, my body and emotions so exhausted they made no response to light or sound until the bang of a door jarred me awake.

"Quiet, Peter. Mistress Yeager is still sleeping."

"I'm sorry."

I rolled over and stretched. The strange voices and the unfamiliar bed made me think I was dreaming. Where were the oval pier glass and armoire, the white curtains billowing in the summer breeze?

Reality and recognition meshed as I recalled Abigail's kindness, young Peter's eagerness to help. In the past, disappointment and bitterness had smothered my faith, but that morning I felt God was with me and had led me to those with warm and generous hearts.

I knew I couldn't stay, just as I knew I was neither the first nor the last Abigail had helped. Her kindness must put a serious strain on her limited resources. The bareness of Peter's room attested to that.

Abby's kindness was even more in evidence when I got out of bed. A basin and ewer sat on the table with a towel and a sliver of perfumed soap. When I reached for the more serviceable of my dresses, I saw that the wrinkles had been removed. My soiled shoes were newly cleaned as well. *Bless her,* I thought.

After dressing, I pinned my braided hair into a coil, pausing as I did to look out the window and note that the day was cloudy and that a breeze ruffled the leaves of the sycamore tree.

Abby was in the kitchen, white apron covering her blue gingham dress, sleeves pushed up past her elbows as she placed loaves of bread into the oven.

"Good morning," I said in greeting.

Abby laughed. "More like afternoon. Peter's been worried . . . thought you might be sick."

"I'm sorry. I've never slept until noon before."

"You were exhausted. I told Peter I'd have his hide if he woke you any earlier." She paused and looked me over, nodding as if she were pleased. "There's color in your cheeks. And green becomes you. It matches your eyes, though I'd have sworn last night they were brown."

"That's how they are . . . sometimes green, sometimes brown." I thought suddenly of Clarissa whose fair hair and blue eyes were like Father's, while I more closely resembled Mother.

After we'd eaten and sat with the remains of our meal on the table, I broached the subject of my future. "Do you know of anyone needing help? I can cook . . . sew too, though I'm more comfortable in the kitchen. I've also had experience nursing—attending to my invalid mother."

Abby pursed her lips and studied the shelf of blue and white crockery before her. "Occasionally Mr. Samuelson needs extra help in his store . . . though that's usually supplied by his daughters."

"What about the fair?" Peter asked. "That's where Grandpa finds help."

"You're right." Abby's expression cleared. "They often hire at the fair. Farmers look for laborers, sometimes servants. Others too. People come from as far as Knight's Ferry and Cooperville."

"Grandpa sometimes comes," Peter added. He looked at his mother. "Can we go, please? Mistress Yeager needs to find work, and I can do odd jobs and pick up some extra coppers."

"We'll see." I sensed she was of two minds about the matter, but she didn't say anything until Peter went outside. "There was trouble at the last fair. A knifing that turned into a brawl."

"Please don't feel you must go on my account."

"I'd already considered going. Emma Hawkins invited us to go with their family, though I haven't told Petey yet. He's at an age where I worry. He's too curious by far and thinks he's a man."

"A man with a good heart."

"He does have that." Her face brightened. "If we go early before the heavy drinking begins, we shouldn't come to any harm. Emma's

ped her gloved hand into mine. "As long as I have a
ve one too. Please don't feel you must take just any posi-
so has brought many to regret."

tent stood in the middle of the meadow, poles and stout
ding it taut over booths filled with goods, some for
others to display prize-winning items. Men and women
heir wares—birch brooms, baskets, and home-brewed reme-
ted to cure everything from pinworms to grippe. Food was
n evidence—fragrant smelling pies, cakes, and molasses candy.
uth watered even though I had eaten a substantial breakfast.
mporary pens had been set up to hold the livestock. The nearby
draft horses were attracting the most attention. Peter and the
kins boys ran over to inspect them, ignoring their mothers'
nctions to have a care. Bets were already being placed for the
lling contest.

"Can I go?" Peter asked when we joined him.

"Perhaps." Abby glanced at Micah, who nodded. "You must
promise to stay with Mr. Hawkins though."

We parted company, Micah and the three boys staying with the
animals while Abby, Emma, and I set off for the tent. Numerous
items were on display—quilts, tatted lace, and brightly painted
crockery all exquisitely executed. As I paused to admire a display of
cabbages I overheard two women speaking.

"We hadn't planned to come to the fair this year," the one
standing next to me said, "but Caleb is in need of a housekeeper."

"Again?"

"I fear so. Miss Cooper has gone back to Boston. She missed city life."

"Oh?" The tone of the second woman's voice hinted at mirth.
"Are you certain that was the reason? Remember, I am acquainted
with your brother."

"And what is that to mean?"

"Only that Caleb is not the most mild-tempered of men."

The first woman laughed. "Even I must agree to that." She
paused. "Sometimes I worry about Caleb. It's well past time for him
to marry, time for him to be seeking a wife."

"Perhaps you should find one for him," her friend suggested.

"I've pointed out eligible women . . . just yesterday, in fact. Caleb

husband, Micah, is good ab
too. Perhaps . . ." Abby nodd
think we should go."

Abby slip
home, you h
tion. Doing
A large
ropes ho
purchase
hawked
dies tou
much
My m

shir
Ha
inj
p

———

Saturday dawned bright and fair, w
a good omen. I needed little encou
Something good was about to happen. L
it, the wood thrush on the gatepost sing of i

I dressed with more care than was my ha
and Mother's illness had robbed me of a desire
appearance. For once I was glad my dress had bee
fingers. Its cut and design conveyed simplicity an
deepest claret hue, it brought color to my cheeks,
been Clarissa's pronouncement three years before.

I jerked my mind to safer things, tucking a wayward s
hair into my braid, reaching for my bonnet. I hoped Mo
understand about the dress, that in my haste to leave I'd grab
first came to my hands, all thoughts of mourning forgotten.

"How pretty," Abby exclaimed when I joined her in the ki
She was dressed in her best, a cotton gown of dove gray with a pa
shawl looped over her slender shoulders. "Petey's outside waiting
Mr. Hawkins and his wife. They should be here any minute."

Just then a buckboard pulled up to the gate. Micah and Emma
Hawkins looked to be about forty; both were pleasant-featured
people, leaning to overweight. Micah had a short beard and
mustache, Emma a bonnet with a long feather curling from a nest of
flowers. Their two boys rode in the back. Peter climbed up to join
them while Micah assisted Abby and me onto the vacant seat.

Ours was not the only conveyance out that Saturday morning.
Wagons, buggies, and several buckboards rattled in a steady stream
toward a meadow on the outskirts of Bayberry. The children called
excitedly to their friends while Abby and Emma nodded to those they
knew. Everyone seemed to converge on the site at the same time. I
searched the faces of sedate men in frock coats and beaver hats, farmers
in coarse trousers, women as wide-eyed and eager as their children. Did
someone need a servant? I sat up straighter and whispered a prayer.

just laughed and told me I must content myself with finding him a housekeeper."

The women began to move away. Emboldened of necessity, I followed and touched the taller woman on the arm. "Begging your pardon? . . ."

She gave me a quick glance and made as if to step away.

"Did . . ." My voice almost failed me. "Did I hear you say you were in need of a housekeeper?"

The woman nodded, her expression unfriendly.

I felt the heat in my cheeks. "I . . . I've had experience in housekeeping and am at the present seeking a position."

By now I had the woman's attention—her friend's too. Both of them looked me over, making me feel as if I were on display with the cabbages.

"Have you references?" the first woman asked. She had magnificent eyes, a shade of blue so deep as to seem almost black, with dark-fringed lashes exactly matching her hair.

"Yes. Abigail Hamilton of Bayberry, with whom I now reside."

"Abigail?" The woman's look was more kindly. "I know Abigail Hamilton. Until the death of her husband she lived but a few miles from us." She turned to her friend. "Her husband was killed by a bull. A terrible tragedy."

Abby was as good as her word, vouching for me and making it sound as if we'd been friends for months. By the time we were finished, Melvina Ashcroft, for that was her name, seemed as pleased with the transaction as I was.

"My husband and I will be by for you after church," Melvina said. "If you'll have your things ready, we can reach Glen Oaks before dark. My brother's farm is just north of town. His name is Mr. Tremayne. Mr. Caleb Tremayne."

Abby's fingers closed over mine. It was done. I now had the means to earn money to join my sisters. After that—but I would not let my mind carry the thought any further. For now it was enough to know that I had somewhere to lay my head, a place far away from Amos Mickelson. Glen Oaks, Melvina had called the village.

"We live but ten miles to the west," Melvina said.

My mind would not stay with Melvina, however. Neither would

it remain on the fair. It was already dancing in the direction of Glen Oaks and a man by the name of Caleb Tremayne.

It took us most of the afternoon to reach Glen Oaks. I rode in the back of the buggy with Abby's portmanteau while Melvina and her husband, Hiram, rode in front. Abby had insisted that I take the portmanteau, pointing out that it would enhance my standing with Melvina, who held considerable sway in the community.

"It won't do any harm with Mr. Tremayne, either," Abby had counseled. "First impressions are important. To arrive with everything bundled in your shawl might make both brother and sister wonder."

I folded my camisole and placed it into the satchel. "Do you know Mr. Tremayne?"

"More by reputation than personal knowledge. Mr. Tremayne is not one to socialize—the very opposite of his sister. Other than having a quick temper, I've never heard anything bad of him."

This last did little to assuage my nervousness and curiosity. "What does he look like?"

Abby's brows furrowed. "I only saw him twice, once at his father's funeral, then a few months later when Thomas was gored. He came to help, and spent time outside with Peter's grandpa . . . milking cows, the things men do." The lines around Abby's mouth tightened. "I fear I paid scant heed to Mr. Tremayne that day, but at his father's funeral . . ." She stowed my stockings into the corner of the bag. "I wouldn't call Mr. Tremayne handsome exactly, but there's something about him that attracts. His eyes perhaps, though it's more than that. You'll know when you see him." Closing the satchel, she gave me a steady look. "I'll be curious to hear your impression of him. You must write and tell me what you think."

I carried her charge with me, wondering at the expressions on her face—curious, expectant, perhaps even a little rueful. The man's temper I could handle. Hadn't I put up with Mother on her most trying days? As for what I might think of Mr. Tremayne . . .

I shook myself and looked out at the passing scenery—the frosted blue of whortleberries growing by the roadside, a stand of oaks whose branches towered into the cobalt blue sky.

Melvina's husky voice brought my mind away from the scenery. "Did I mention that my brother has recently built a new home?"

"No, you didn't." I thought it strange for a bachelor to build a new house, but I didn't say it.

"At the time he commenced to build we thought—hoped—Caleb had decided to take a wife. Now . . ." Melvina turned to look at me. "We are of differing opinions. My mother thinks Caleb has been disappointed in love. But since he spends considerable time away from Glen Oaks, I think there's a woman involved, though we all know Caleb is—"

"Melvina!" Hiram Ashcroft's voice, though kindly, held a note of reproof. "Don't you think Mistress Yeager would like to hear of her duties instead of all this prittle prattle?"

Melvina arched her dark brows. "It's not prittle prattle, Hiram. It's woman talk and I've a notion Mistress Yeager is as eager to know what to expect as she is to learn her duties. Am I not right?"

"I'm interested in learning both," I answered, hoping my effort toward diplomacy was successful.

Melvina laughed. "You will do well with Caleb, perhaps even stay out the year, though I do a disservice to Vilate Cooper. I truly think she missed her family and the city, old maid and dour as she was. I think, too, she was intimidated by the two servants. There's Mary, who'll give you a hand with the cooking, and Sally, who sees to the laundry and cleaning. The main thing is to be firm."

"I don't expect to have any problems." I wondered from whence my newfound confidence had sprung. Perhaps it had been there all along, dampened down by Clarissa, who always thought she knew best. Had she?

"My brother seldom entertains," Melvina went on, "so your only responsibility will be to fix his meals and keep the house in order. It's a pretty place. I'll say that for Caleb—it's the envy of many a woman, with big, airy rooms and a long porch on the side to sit on in the summertime." She tucked a dark curl back into her straw bonnet. "We're almost to his farm."

I looked with heightened interest at the countryside—fields of corn already harvested, rolling pastures, a herd of cows bunched near a fence. Abigail said they had once lived near here. "Do any of these farms belong to the Hamiltons?"

"No. They live on the other side of Glen Oaks, nearer our place," Hiram answered. He was a big man, broad of shoulders, with a ruddy face and brown chin whiskers. His face exuded kindness, in guileless gray eyes and full lips that always seemed about to smile. Although by no means handsome, Hiram Ashcroft was a man to whom one was instinctively drawn.

Melvina seemed of the same opinion. Twice I saw her slip her gloved hand into his. A shaft of sadness pierced me and reminded me of my loneliness. Would I ever feel that togetherness . . . the unique oneness shared by those who love?

Before I could think long on the matter, Melvina pointed ahead to where a portion of a house was visible through a stand of trees. "There it is. Isn't it lovely? The fields we just passed are Caleb's too."

I focused on the house, sitting up taller in the buggy, narrowing my eyes to better see. *It's not your home,* part of me chided, but the rest of me paid it no heed, noting the brown hip roof and the white walls rising up to a second story. There were windows, dozens it seemed, though I later found there were only twenty-eight; far more than the cottage, more even than the home of Deacon Mickelson. Pity the poor woman who had to wash them all.

Thoughts of windows were put aside as I took in the rest of the plastered house—the square cupola rising from the roof, steep steps with a black wrought-iron railing leading up to the front door. We approached it by means of a long lane newly planted with saplings, horse chestnuts by the look of them. The yard had only one tree, a magnificent maple rising into the September sky.

"Isn't it nice?" Melvina asked.

I nodded, noting the porch marching along the side of the house, a pleasant haven for hot, sultry afternoons. There were no flowers or shrubs to bid us welcome, though no dogs either, only a small gray-and-white cat, who after a cursory look stretched herself and settled into a patch of sunshine.

"Ho there, Sam," Hiram called.

A gangly boy in his early teens hurried out of the granary.

"See to the horses. They'll need rubbing down. Water too," Hiram told him. "We're not staying long, so don't bother to unhitch them. Just cool them down." He handed his wife from the buggy and gave her a significant look. "There's no time for visiting if you want to be home before dark."

"I know," she responded.

I thought she would have liked to spend the day showing me around and regaling me with tales of her brother.

"I'll go find Caleb," Hiram said. He set off in the direction of the barn, newly built like the house, its walls still unpainted.

Melvina took me to the side of the house. Only then did I discover that the house contained a lower story, half hidden by the sweep of the pillared porch.

"My brother had the stone for the porch pillars brought in from upstate," Melvina said on opening the door. "The kitchen and dining room are on the lower floor . . . a half floor, actually. Since you'll spend much of your time here, I thought you might like to see it first."

The kitchen was spacious, the floor paved with gray stone, the walls whitewashed and reflecting light from three large windows. There was a cupboard for crockery and pans, another holding containers of tea and meal and other staples. I was relieved to see that the slate sink had a spigot for water and the large table looked freshly scrubbed.

"Sally's good to help," Melvina said, "but she needs supervision. There's a cool room off to the side. A cellar too. The dining room is straight ahead."

We passed through the dining room, bare except for an oak table and six matching chairs. Nothing hung at the windows and no rug covered the wood floor.

Melvina seemed chagrined at the room's bareness. "I hoped when Caleb announced plans to build a new home that he intended to bring something of beauty and culture. He's lived a good part of the last fifteen years in Boston where our uncle has a shipping business—a very successful one I might add. Uncle Paul planned to make Caleb his partner. It was all arranged. But when our oldest brother, John, died . . ." Melvina's lips quivered and her eyes filled with tears. "I'm sorry," she apologized, reaching for the handkerchief tucked in her sleeve. "First Father. Now John. The past years have not been easy."

I felt an instant kinship with the woman. "To lose two family members in a short a time is difficult."

"It is." Melvina dabbed at her eyes. "Mother is still not herself, though she and Hannah, John's widow, get on well together. There are three children to keep them occupied. And now that Caleb has returned . . ." Her face brightened at this. "To have Caleb back is a treat we never thought to have. If only . . ."

She turned and led me up narrow stairs to the next level. "Caleb's wife will be a fortunate woman. There are two parlors—both still unfurnished—and two sitting rooms. I managed to persuade him to let me furnish this one."

A door opened, revealing the slender figure of a servant girl, white cap on her lank brown hair, a dust cloth clutched in her hand. "Mrs. Ashcroft," she exclaimed. "I thought I heard someone."

"I've brought the new housekeeper, Sally. Mistress Yeager from over Bayberry way. No doubt you'll be pleased to see her."

Sally nodded as she looked me over, her plain, narrow features bright with interest. "More like Master Caleb'll be pleased to see her. I can't seem to get the hang of cookin'."

"Cooking?" Melvina was clearly puzzled. "Where's Mary?"

"She's doing poorly again. Her feet swelled up something awful. Mr. Tremayne told her to stay in bed."

Melvina's lips tightened. "I hope you had a chance to put the sitting room to rights. In spite of what Miss Cooper might have told you, I want you always to remember to use beeswax on the furniture. It will protect the wood and make it shine far better than turpentine."

"I remembered. And I remembered to air the bedroom . . . changed the sheets too," she added, clearly pleased with herself.

The sitting room, unlike the dining room, was filled with color and warmth: pink-and-green flowered wallpaper, and green striped upholstered chairs. Sunlight streamed through tall windows, burnishing the dark patina of a freshly polished table so that it glowed with a light of its own.

I glanced from the table to Sally, whose skinny figure was still visible by the open door. "You've obviously got the hand for polishing furniture."

Sally's plain face lightened. "I try, ma'am."

The furniture, Melvina informed me, had been purchased when she and Mr. Ashcroft went to Boston.

As we started up the stairs to the top floor our conversation returned to the servants. "I don't know what to do about Mary. She's been with our family for thirty years, but two summers ago she started having trouble with her legs. Dropsy, the doctor calls it. Mother was about to let her go, but when Caleb heard of it, he said she was to come with him, that with only one to look after she'd do better here, though how he thought she'd get by with only Sally to help her . . ." Melvina paused to catch her breath. "Sally is another story and one you should know, though Hiram will say it's prittle prattle."

I smiled, the two of us standing at the top of the stairs, a long hallway stretching the length of the floor. Mother would have called it gossip, not prittle prattle, something a young lady should not indulge in. But I had early learned that that which passed for gossip could sometimes be enlightening.

"Oh?" I put a question in my voice to encourage her.

"Only Caleb knows where Sally came from. He brought her back with him from the coast. Skinny as a waif, she was, her hair crawling with lice, big bruises on her arms and legs. Mary had to cut off most of Sally's hair and douse what was left in turpentine. I didn't see her until she'd been with Mother for a week. By then she was more presentable." Melvina placed a gloved hand on my arm and her forthright manner softened. "Collecting all who are hurt or maimed has long been my brother's downfall. Unfortunately that's what you'll have to deal with: Mary crippled, Sally not quite right—though I'll be the first to say Sally's improving. I fear poor Vilate Cooper was not firm enough and had too little patience. I had great hopes for Miss Cooper, but . . ." Melvina lowered her eyes as if she feared she had said too much, as well she might, for on this last I felt a stirring of apprehension. What had I gotten myself into?

"I have every confidence that you'll do well," Melvina added hastily. "Anyone recommended by Abigail is bound to succeed." A quick smile. "Let me show you to your room."

She led me to the end bedroom, serviceable and airy with touches of blue in the coverlet and curtains. A large braided rug covered a portion of the polished oak floor. As I looked around I noted a blue flowered pitcher and ewer on a stand. A narrow wardrobe and dresser took up the space on the adjoining wall. "How pretty," I said, knowing it was what Melvina wished to hear.

"Melvina!"

The sound of a masculine voice put an end to our conversation. Melvina glanced at herself in the age-stippled mirror. Tucking a wisp of black hair into her bonnet, she adjusted her bright paisley shawl. "That will be Hiram and my brother. I'll take you down to meet him. Then we must be off."

I followed Melvina down the long flight of stairs while unanswered questions scurried through my head.

What kind of a household had I come to, and what manner of man was I about to meet?

CHAPTER 6

As I look back on that golden September afternoon, when I followed Melvina down the stairs to meet Caleb Tremayne, my heart quickens and lifts until it feels light and fragile as air. I picture myself as I was that day: tall and slender with dark hair twisted into a coil under my prim bonnet, the green fabric of my dress reflected in my eyes, nervousness bringing a flush to my cheeks.

I saw Caleb at once; jet-black hair fell over dark, full brows, contrasting with deepest blue eyes, and skin tanned to the rich color of rawhide—it was the man I'd glimpsed at the cove. Near panic and something breath-stopping swept over me. I grasped the rounded newel post at the bottom of the stairs. How could this be? The stranger at the cove and Melvina's brother one and the same? Yet they were. I had only to look, blink, and see that it was so, aware that my heart was beating more quickly than it was wont to.

"I have found a new housekeeper," Melvina was saying. "Miss Yeager from Bayberry. She is a friend of Abigail Hamilton."

I had enough presence of mind to leave the security of the newel post and stand beside Melvina, the four of us in the entry with sunshine streaming in the fanlight above the heavy oak door.

I felt Caleb's eyes upon me, so deep a blue as to appear black—appraising, assessing. And a slight frown set a line between his brows.

"My brother, Mr. Caleb Tremayne," Melvina went on.

Unwelcome heat rushed to my cheeks. "How . . . how do you do."

Mr. Tremayne shot his sister a quick look of inquiry as if he weren't altogether pleased by her choice. He was dressed much the same as when I'd seen him at the beach—white, coarse-woven shirt opened at the neck, with brown, homespun trousers tucked into sturdy leather boots. As I'd thought earlier, he was a man of the outdoors, a man of woods and soil and sunlight. Confident and intelligent too. The qualities were evident in his eyes, his stance, in muscles rippling beneath the fabric of his clothes when he moved.

"I've just shown Miss Yeager her room and explained her duties." Melvina paused and frowned. "I understand Mary is unwell again."

"She is, though it's nothing for you to fret about. Sally and I have gotten along very well."

"But your meals . . ."

"As you can see, I haven't starved."

Hiram moved closer to his wife. "If you have no further need of Melvina, we should be going. The days aren't as long as they were."

"And you're anxious to be home before dark," Caleb said.

Hiram nodded. "Since the Elliotts overturned their buggy, I don't like driving after dark. I don't want the same happening to us."

"Mr. Elliott's wife was killed," Melvina explained to me. "I regret leaving so soon. If you have any questions, you have only to ask Sally or Mary. I'll try to come again in a few weeks. By then you should be settled in."

I assured her all would go well, though I spoke with more confidence than I felt. Seeing Caleb Tremayne had left me unsettled.

Caleb took his sister's arm, and Melvina smiled up at him as they went to the door. When the door closed behind them, I took a deep breath.

A small sound made me turn. Sally was watching me, curiosity bright on her face. When she realized I'd seen her, her gaze dropped.

"I understand you've had to do double duty these last few days," I said, drawn to the girl while I wondered what terrors she'd suffered.

Sally shrugged and studied the half circle of sunlight on the entry floor. "It weren't nothin'." She rubbed one foot with the other in a gesture I remembered from my own awkward girlhood.

"Mr. Tremayne seemed to think it was. He said you did well."

Sally raised her head and smiled. "Master Caleb be my friend," she said, as if that explained everything. The smile transformed her face, making her narrow features seem rounder, her gray eyes appear to have more color.

I wanted to question Sally about her "Master Caleb," but I realized I was probably expected to cook supper. "Have you given any thought to supper?"

"No'm. Mrs. Ashcroft said she'd be back with someone this afternoon. Master Caleb said to let you see to it."

"So I shall, but I'll need an apron. Is there one in the kitchen?"

Sally nodded and continued to look at me, rather like a puppy waiting to be told to fetch a stick.

"I'll need you to help me."

Sally nodded again and led me down the steep stairs to the kitchen, her ill-fitting brown dress brushing each step as we went. I wondered at this and why Miss Cooper hadn't altered it to make her look more presentable.

There was much I wondered about that afternoon while I peeled potatoes and sliced carrots for a vegetable pie. Sally brought vegetables from the cool room and went outside for wood. We said little, Sally being reticent by nature and I having learned from experience that I could not talk and cook at the same time and hope to have success. And I hoped for success that afternoon. Next to my curiosity about Caleb Tremayne was a growing need to please him. He had that effect upon me from the first moment—I wanted to please, to impress, anything to draw those dark eyes to mine. I don't think I realized this at the time any more than I understood the longings that tugged at me as I searched through the cupboard for herbs to put into the pie.

"Have we no basil?" I asked

Sally looked at me as if I were suddenly speaking another language. "I . . . I don't rightly know. Mrs. Tremayne grows all sorts of things . . . taters, beans. We make do with what she sends over from the old house."

"But no herbs?" I asked while I wondered if Mrs. Tremayne was Caleb's mother or his sister-in-law. And where was the old house? With so many questions it took great effort to pull my mind back to fixing supper.

"I . . . I don't know," Sally finally admitted. Her narrow face suddenly brightened. "But Mary does. I'll ask her."

I waited with some impatience while I planned the rest of the meal. There wasn't time to make rolls, so biscuits would have to do— and something sweet, perhaps fruit, and flowers for the table.

Poor Sally did not rest. After showing me where Mary said she'd hung small bags of herbs in a dark corner of the cool room, I sent her outside to pick flowers. "I didn't see a garden, so wildflowers will have to do," I told her.

Sally's eyes grew wide. "Flowers ?" Her mouth curved in a smile. "I know right where to fine 'em. Saw some yesterday. Big yeller ones in the woods, though what Master will think . . ." She paused on this, her head cocked to one side.

"The only way to find out is to try him."

It was late when Caleb finally came in for supper, the sun already down, the kitchen smelling pleasantly of biscuits. I'd taken a few minutes to unpack and tidy myself, comb my hair—the Tamsin who'd given no thought to her appearance only a scant month before.

"Your supper's ready whenever you'd like to eat," I told Caleb when he'd finished washing. I tried not to watch him while I wrapped a cloth around the pie to hold in the heat. But my eyes flitted to Caleb each time they had a chance, noticing that he'd rolled up his sleeves, the dark hair that grew on his sun-browned arms, the long tapered fingers.

Sally had set the big table in the dining room with three places. "'Tain't Master Caleb's way to eat alone. He likes us to eat together."

Carrying the pie, I followed Caleb into the dining room, Sally right behind with the biscuits. I could tell she was excited. The prospect of flowers on the table had unsettled her. "Don't know what Master Caleb will think," she'd said close to a dozen times.

By now I was as anxious as Sally, though my concern was for the food. Would he like the pie? Were the biscuits tender and flaky?

When Caleb saw the table, he glanced at me, then at Sally.

"Miss told me to fetch 'em."

"And very nice they are," Caleb replied, though in truth it was a haphazard arrangement, for Sally had cut the stems too short.

She beamed as she set the biscuits on the table.

When we were seated—Caleb at the head, Sally and I on either side—Sally bowed her head. Caleb did the same. I quickly followed suit, closing my eyes as Caleb's deep voice began: "Dear Lord, we thank thee for thy bounty, and for this food and for the hands that have prepared it. Amen."

No one spoke while Caleb dished up the pie: a large portion for himself, smaller ones for Sally and me. Silence hung around us with only the clink of silver on china.

"You've done well, Miss Yeager. You too, Sally. I won't go hungry with the two of you here." He paused and took a swallow of cider, shooting a quick glance at me as he did. "No doubt you've heard of Mary's trouble. There are days when she has to stay in bed. The rest of the time she does fairly well, though she's getting old and the stairs are a trial for her." Another pause. "I'll leave it for the three of you to work out. I don't require much when I'm at home. Even less when I'm gone. Three square meals . . . clean clothes . . . the house kept to rights so my mother and sister are happy."

"I think I can manage."

"I hope you can." His voice was challenging, his gaze steady as if he waited to be convinced.

"I cared for my sister and invalid mother for several years."

"Indeed?" There was silence while he buttered another biscuit. "You do not look old enough to have had so much experience."

"I'm old enough to know that life does not always turn out the way we plan."

"I see." His expression was curious, and his mouth looked as if he would like to smile. Then he did, making his eyes crinkle at the corners. The smile left as quickly as it came, Caleb's face turning serious as he glanced at Sally. "Someone else has learned a similar lesson. Perhaps one day she'll share her story with you."

Sally sat with her head bent over her plate, not taking part in our conversation. "Shall I take supper up to Mary?" she asked.

At his nod, she went into the kitchen for another plate. Caleb was generous with the portion he dished up, and I wondered about Mary's appetite. I resolved to look in on her before I went to bed.

"I have another requirement of you," Caleb said when Sally had gone. "The child is always to be treated with kindness. She has seen too much of hurt and evil to let anyone add to it. I'm certain your predecessor meant well, but sometimes Miss Cooper lacked patience."

I thought of the times I'd been required to bear Mother's uncertain temper. "You will not find me lacking in such."

Caleb nodded and fixed his dark eyes on mine. "Sally has the potential to learn. In the year she's been with me, she's improved greatly. Given time, I'm confident she'll do as well as any servant." He rose from his chair, his long fingers resting on the edge of the table as he leaned forward. "Tell me Miss Yeager, do you read?"

"I do."

"Would you feel comfortable in teaching Sally her letters?"

"Yes." It was on the tip of my tongue to inform him I was raised on books and poetry, but something in Caleb's eyes seemed to say he knew this and more—about the years of nursing mother, about Clarissa, even Deacon Mickelson. Of course this wasn't possible, but that's how he made me feel, as if he knew me to the very core of my soul, knew me and would take care of me just as he took care of Mary and Sally.

"When you have finished in the kitchen, will you join me in the sitting room? We spend our evenings there. I've begun to teach Sally her letters. The lessons have been irregular. Miss Cooper was too firm while my sister claims I am too indulgent. Perhaps in you we will be fortunate enough to have found someone in the middle."

In this manner I spent my first evening in Caleb Tremayne's home. The three of us sat in the sitting room, the small table whose surface Sally had polished pulled in front of the sofa, slate and chalk and primer fetched by Sally from the cupboard. I did not give much heed to the lesson, my mind occupied instead with watching the interplay between Caleb and the child, for child she was despite her years. That Sally came well-nigh to worshiping Master Caleb was obvious—in her quick darting glances, in striving to please as she recited the letters he wrote on the slate, stumbling in her eagerness, often mistaken. I thought Sally possessed average intelligence, but I doubted she would ever become an adept pupil. Her gaze wandered too often for concentration and I didn't think she understood the written word. If only she had had a mother like mine, one who had fed me on the beauty of Shakespeare and Keats, stringing the words like golden circlets on a chain, her voice a melody as Clarissa and I curled at her side.

I closed my eyes, my fingers absently combing the soft fur of the gray cat who'd slipped in the door with Caleb and now made a nest on my lap. Perhaps reading would be the best way to begin, reading to Sally so she could understand how *A* and *B* joined with vowels and consonants to make words and sentences. My lips curved as I pictured my success, the smile widening as I imagined Caleb's approval, heard his praise—this man I desired to please.

His voice broke into my daydream. "I believe we've put Miss Yeager to sleep."

Sally giggled and I opened my eyes in time to see her exchange a conspiratorial look with Caleb. "Her and Ol' Cat both be sleepin'."

I quickly straightened. "Not anymore." Then quickly, "Would you like me to read to you after you've finished with your letters?"

She lifted the clean slate. "Already finished."

Caleb rose to his feet, his long, booted legs but shadows outside the pool of lamplight. "I've some things to see to in the barn, but there are several books in the cupboard. My study holds more if you should want them, though they may not be on subjects a lady would choose."

I glimpsed something in his blue eyes as he walked passed me, something reckless and at the same time challenging. He was a man of many layers, changeable when it came to his moods, as if he had more on his mind than he wanted me to know.

He walked to the door in long, easy strides, not pausing until he reached it. Caleb was no more than a shadow, but I knew each line and angle of him, having memorized it while he sat with his head bent over Sally's slate. "I'm more than a farmer, Miss Yeager. Before family responsibility brought me back, I was involved in the shipping business. This takes me often from home; my comings and goings are uncertain." He paused and I felt the strength of his gaze. "Miss Cooper was wont to put her nose into things which were not her concern. Though she claimed to suffer from homesickness, it was her curious nature that caused her to leave. Truth be told, I was the instigator of her departure, though both Miss Cooper and I would have my sister believe otherwise. I give this as friendly advice, which I trust you'll take seriously if you wish to remain in my home."

Caleb closed the door, leaving Sally and me to our individual musings, and I realized with a wrench to the heart that what I'd taken as insight into his character might well be nothing more than daydreams and longings of a lonely, spinster heart.

I do not know what Sally thought of Caleb's warning or if she realized it had been intended as such. Her main concern was to take me upstairs to meet Mary, proudly showing me to the room they shared, which was directly across the hall from my own.

Mary was sitting up in bed, a mousy, gray plait hanging over her shoulder. She looked to be about fifty years of age and possessed one of the roundest faces I'd seen, with the beginning of a double chin. Pleasant was the best word to describe her. Pleasant, and looking as if she enjoyed a good laugh—a good gossip too, if her eyes, bright with curiosity, were any indication of her personality.

"You must be Miss Yeager," she said. "I'm Mary . . . though sometimes Mr. Tremayne refers to me as Mrs. Sullivan." She chuckled at this, a wheeze threading through her laughter. "I'm not one to stand on ceremony, so Mary will do . . . and right sorry I am that I wasn't able to help with dinner."

"Mr. Tremayne said you were unwell."

"My legs are like stove pipes and my feet no better." Mary leaned close as if imparting a secret. "Haven't put my shoes on for days." She lifted the covers so I could see her distended legs.

"How dreadful," I said, feeling sympathy for the poor woman.

"They're doing better. Not nearly as swollen as they were. In another day or two I should be able to get around again."

"Has a doctor seen you?"

"My, yes. Mr. Tremayne sent for Dr. Hillman when he heard of my trouble. The doctor gave me some medicine . . ." Mary pulled a face and indicated a brown bottle. "Vilest stuff I've ever tasted. Made from skunk cabbage if you can believe. Told me to take it when they start to swell, and to go to bed . . . which I do, but it still takes several days to run its course."

"You mustn't get up until you're better. Sally will help me."

"Don't know what I'd do without Sally." Mary smiled at the girl. "She's my right arm and both my feet. Always fetching and carrying. Couldn't do more for me if she was my own flesh and blood."

Sally beamed and moved closer to the bed.

"Mr. Tremayne does the same . . . always lookin' out for me and seein' that I get my rest."

"He seems a kind man."

"They don't come any better," Mary agreed. "Rescued Sally from the jaws of hell and me as well, though in my case it wasn't so dramatic. Did you know Mrs. Tremayne was about to let me go? Said it was time I took my ease. She'd talked to Ben about it—that's my son—and he was planning to take me in. Just like that it was settled. I had no say in the matter, though if I'd had the chance I'd have said plenty. Not about Ben, he's a good son. But his wife . . ." Mary pulled a face like the one she'd made for her medicine. "Lucy would have tried to make my life miserable, just like she's made Ben's. Mr. Tremayne knew how it would be. He'd had dealings with Lucy."

"How fortunate for you."

"My, yes. I thank the dear Lord every day and Mr. Tremayne almost as often. He takes care of both Sally and me, and we do the same for him." Mary eased up in the bed, her bright eyes never leaving my face. "Now it's time we heard something about you. Where you come from? Your people? Sitting here all day makes me hungry for talk."

"I come from a town on the coast. My parents are dead . . . my father some years ago, Mother just this summer. The rest of my family moved west, so there's just me. Abigail Hamilton is my friend. She recommended me to Mrs. Ashcroft."

"Abigail Hamilton? Seems I've heard of her. Wasn't her husband killed in an accident?"

Mary looked ready to settle down for a good gossip. At another time I wouldn't have minded, for I was as prone to talk as any woman. But that night my mind was but half with me, the other half having wandered after Caleb Tremayne. I recalled the recklessness I'd glimpsed in his eyes—recklessness tempered with calculation. Hadn't he warned yet challenged me all in the space of a few seconds?

". . . attended the same church, I believe."

With a start, I realized Mary had been speaking. "I . . . I'm sorry. You were saying?"

"Only that Mrs. Tremayne and Mrs. Hamilton attended the same church, all of which don't matter since I can see you're longing for bed."

"I am a little tired," I admitted.

"And me prattling on like a stream in full spate. It's a fault of mine. One you'll soon notice, so don't be afraid to tell me to button my lips. Miss Cooper did it at least once a day, didn't she, Sally?"

The two exchanged smiles.

Curious to know more about my predecessor I wavered for a second. But bed and my room beckoned. Saying good night, I took a candle and crossed the corridor to my room, closing the door behind me. It had been a long day, one of excitement and adventure; all of these and more . . . the "more" being the man I'd seen at the cove.

"Caleb Tremayne." Smiling, I let the sound roll over my tongue. It was a good name, a name of substance, like the man himself. My smile faded when I recalled the warning he'd issued as he quit the sitting room. If I were wise I would heed it and stem my rising curiosity, for curious I was, curious and intrigued by a man who'd already laid claim to my interest.

I lit the glazed china lamp on the dressing table and congratulated myself on my good fortune. It was a pretty room, comfortable too, with a Franklin stove to ward off the chill of winter, a braided rug on the floor, even a small cherry-wood secretary. I would write Abby and let her know of my good fortune. And now, without having to worry about Amos Mickelson intercepting the letters, I could write to my sisters.

My mind wouldn't settle long enough to savor my good fortune. It skittered off in one direction then jumped across to the next, all on Caleb Tremayne. Why had he warned me to keep my nose out of his comings and goings? What did they entail? Shipping, he'd said. If that were the case, why ship from a remote cove? Why not Boston?

I thought on this as I brushed my hair. Though I was drawn to Caleb Tremayne, I knew that to cross him was to invite trouble. A quick temper, his sister had said. Abby had implied the same. Since I didn't want to risk his ire, I would have to concentrate on cooking flavorful meals, running a smooth house, and teaching Sally to read. And I could never let Caleb Tremayne know I'd seen him at the cove. If I did—my mind refused to carry the thought any further. Though it would not let me relax either. Despite my tiredness, it was a long time before I fell asleep.

CHAPTER 7

Thus began my life with Caleb Tremayne, though I use the term loosely, for except at mealtimes I saw little of the man. As he had told me, there were times when he was away from home. Even when he was with us, he spent long hours in the fields or in the barn or reading late at night in his study. This last bit of information I gleaned from Mary, who'd hoarded a variety of tidbits about the Tremayne family and was not shy about sharing them.

"Mr. Tremayne has always been one to read late at night, though what he finds so interesting in all those books and newspapers is beyond me. It used to give his mother fits . . . reading when he should be sleeping. She had no luck breaking him of the practice, so I've not tried, though I'll admit the sound of him coming up the stairs in the middle of the night can give me a start." Mary paused to draw breath. "Mind you, I'm not criticizing. Mr. Tremayne is free to wander around his own house whenever he pleases. But should you waken and hear him, I wouldn't want you to be scared."

"Since I'm a sound sleeper, there's little chance of that." I stretched the truth, sensing it was important for Mary to believe this.

"Miss Cooper wasn't so fortunate. She was always hearing things. Nervous as a cat she was. Like to drove me and Sally crazy." Mary scooted up higher in the bed. She still wasn't feeling well, her distended legs unable to bear her weight for any length of time.

"I hope I won't do that. Drive you crazy I mean."

"My, no. You're a different cut from Miss Cooper. More biddable by far. We'll get on well. Sally's of a similar mind."

I hoped Mr. Tremayne was similarly impressed. It was difficult to know, for he said little at mealtimes, concentrating on the food or the contents of various newspapers. I, on the other hand, was much aware of him. I noted the way he held his fork, his preference for cider over ale, his long-lashed blue eyes. Unused to male company, I was shy and tongue-tied in his presence. Little wonder that in those early days there was little conversation between us.

Thomas Brown and his two sons helped Caleb with the farm work—Sam, whom I'd glimpsed on the day of our arrival, and Parley, a sturdy young man of perhaps eighteen.

"The Browns have lived on the farm almost as long as the Tremaynes have," Mary informed me on the first day she came downstairs. Once in the kitchen she was glad to sit down. I was happy to oblige her, for by now I regarded the kitchen as my domain. Mary had quick hands with a knife, so I set her to peeling vegetables while I measured sugar and cracked eggs, blending them into a creamy batter while keeping an eye on Sally, who was wont to daydream.

"They've lived in the cottage next to the old house for as long as I can remember. Mrs. Brown helps Mrs. Tremayne in the house. Her daughter helps out now. Mrs. Brown and I had our differences . . . some good laughs too." Mary gave me a quick glance. "That's what comes from two women rubbing shoulders too closely in the same kitchen."

I chose to ignore her inference. "Mrs. Brown does the cooking then?"

"She does now." Mary gave a short laugh. "And welcome she is to it. The kitchen, I mean. There's always children underfoot—if not young David, then one of the little girls. Nice enough by themselves, but a handful when they're together. If you ask me, they're the reason Mr. Tremayne built a house of his own."

I hadn't asked her, but I wasn't above encouraging her to say more. "This does seem a large house for a bachelor."

"Many would agree." Mary paused to cut the eye out of a potato. The clock's steady ticking filled the kitchen. I waited, hoping she'd say more—which she did, for Mary liked to talk as much as I liked to listen.

"Why don't you run out and pick some flowers?" Mary said to Sally.

"Flowers?"

"Didn't you say Master Caleb liked having them on the table?"

"Yes."

"Then why not please him by picking some more?"

"All right. That is, if it's all right with Miss Yeager."

I nodded, not certain where all of this was leading.

Once Sally was gone, Mary shook her head. "That child's brain is like a piece of wool—absorbs everything she hears and sees. Trouble is, most times it comes right back out. Don't matter who's around or whether it's the right time or place. Thought you ought to know so you can bear it in mind."

"Thank you."

Mary shifted position in her chair. "Now, where was I?"

"You were talking about when Mr. Tremayne built this house."

"So I was. It caused a terrible row with his mother. She said there was plenty of room at the old house. And there is—five bedrooms. But once Mr. Tremayne made up his mind there was no turning back. Stubborn he is, like his father. It's a Tremayne trait along with their black hair and blue eyes."

"Having such a large house, does Mr. Tremayne have plans to marry?"

"He's never hinted of such, though his family has great hopes." Mary reached for another potato. "Some think he took uncommon interest in his house. Supervised the construction himself . . . brought builders clear from Boston. No local man had a part in it. That caused talk, I can tell you. Some said Mr. Tremayne thought the local men weren't good enough to do his building. 'Tisn't true, of course, but you know how some like to gossip."

By now the cake needed all of my attention, but my lack of response didn't faze Mary. "Since he took so much interest in building it—did some of the work himself—does make one wonder if he had a particular woman in mind. I've never seen any evidence of it though. No letters or nothing." Mary hunted through the peelings for another potato. "With him away so much, he could have a woman friend in another town."

"Mrs. Ashcroft seems to hope that's the case."

"My, yes. She'd have had him married a dozen times if she'd had her way. She's always pushing him to call on this young lady or that one. He doesn't pay her any more mind than he does his mother. Independent he is. Likes to do things his way. Expect that's part of the reason he ran away when he was a boy. Being the youngest with everybody telling him what to do never set well with young Caleb."

"He ran away?"

Mary nodded. "Ran away to sea on his uncle's ship. Must have been close to a year he was gone, and when he came back he wanted no more of farming. Which was smart, since he knew he wouldn't inherit none of it. That's how he came to be in business with his uncle."

I thought on this as I poured the batter into a pan and slid it into the oven. It was a spice cake, the recipe given to Mother by Susannah Partridge. Over the years I'd experimented with it, adding more eggs, a cup of grated carrots and a generous handful of nuts. The cake always brought compliments and I hoped to gain one from Mr. Tremayne. He was home again, having arrived just before dawn. He and the horse and carriage looked to have covered a good distance. At least that's what Sam said, his words overheard by Sally and repeated to me.

She has a mind like a piece of wool, I knew I must remember that and guard what I said when Sally was around.

That evening Caleb was not himself. He ate without thought and certainly without enjoyment. The clam chowder and flaky rolls spread with fresh butter were chewed and swallowed without comment. The last time I served clam chowder, Caleb said he hadn't eaten chowder that good since his grandma made it. I waited expectantly, certain the chowder and spice cake would raise me in his esteem.

Such were my feelings in those days, like a puppy by her master's chair, watching each lift of the spoon, hoping to be slipped a tidbit. None came—not to me, not to Mary, not even to Sally who sat with worshipful eyes, chattering about how she'd seen Ol' Cat catch a mouse down by the cellar.

"What were you doing down by the cellar?" Caleb demanded.

"Just . . . just watching Ol' Cat," Sally stammered.

"Haven't I told you to stay away from there? The ground is still too unstable. You're to stay away. Do you hear?"

"Yes . . . sir." Sally swallowed and blinked as if she wanted to cry. She continued to watch him though, expectancy running through her concern. Was that how I appeared? Always watching and hoping?

"And don't keep staring at me!"

"I'm sorry." Sally's gaze dropped to her bowl of chowder, chin quivering, a hand clutching her napkin.

I darted quick glances at Caleb each time he lowered his gaze. I noticed the dark line of stubble along his jaw, pockets of fatigue under his blue eyes, things I hadn't noticed earlier. *He and the horse and carriage look to have covered a good distance,* I remembered Sam's words. Where had Caleb been? What was wrong?

Sally's sniffle drew my attention back to her. The napkin was raised to her nose, and tears made steady trails down her sallow cheeks.

"You hadn't ought to have gotten after her like that," Mary scolded. "She meant no harm."

I was astounded at Mary's daring. I think Caleb was too. For a second he looked like a boy caught with damp fingers in the sugar bowl. Then his lips tightened and he slammed down his spoon. "Can't a man eat in peace? If you're not all watching me, you're complaining. I don't know why I ever thought—" His jaw clamped down and he arose so abruptly his chair almost toppled. If Caleb noticed he gave no sign, but strode from the room without a backward glance.

The three of us sat in silence, Sally's tears swallowed in a loud hiccup, Mary's plump fingers fluttering at her throat. "Oh, my," she whispered.

"I was . . . only watching Ol' Cat," Sally repeated.

I looked from Mary to Sally and said nothing. This was the first time I'd witnessed Caleb Tremayne's temper. That it had been set off by something so trifling surprised me. "Is the cellar that dangerous?" I asked.

Mary shrugged and patted Sally's shoulder. "It's just one of Master Caleb's bad days."

Determined not to be put off, I continued, "If the ground around the cellar is so unstable, why did he build the house over it?"

Instead of answering, Mary began to clear the table. "It's nothing to worry about. It's just Mr. Tremayne's way." She left the room, her steps slow and ponderous, a slight wheeze to her breathing.

I looked at Sally, hoping she might shed some light on the matter, but the girl avoided my gaze and picked up her bowl. "Don't pay him no mind," she said. The words seemed to be for both of us. "When Master Caleb gets like this, you mustn't pay him no mind."

———•———

Two days later I met Caleb's mother. I had been too busy settling in to pay much heed to anything else, but with the sun shining and the house set to rights, I ventured out. I hadn't realized what a recluse I'd become until I felt the warmth of the October sun on my cheeks, the same sun that shone on the cottage in Mickelboro and on the cove, turning the restless waves to shimmering satin, glinting off granite and fawn-colored sand.

Homesickness washed through me and caught at my throat. I started to walk, scarcely noticing where I went, though part of me was aware of a restless breeze—of tall trees with rust-tinged leaves beckoning in the distance. The lane I followed wound past newly harvested fields with cows grazing in a fenced meadow.

When I reached the trees, I paused and leaned against the trunk of an oak tree. Here, there was no restless sea, only fields and a little stream, and in the distance a farmhouse with a barn and several outbuildings. Was it Caleb's old home? I looked at the two-storied structure with interest. It wasn't far, no more than a mile. Curiosity encouraged me to approach. Would I like Caleb's mother? What of the sister-in-law and her three lively children?

I soon arrived at a yard edged with overgrown roses, a few red blooms almost lost among the leaves. My fingers itched for a pair of shears. The two women evidently did not have any interest in gardening.

A child of perhaps three sat in the shade of a rose bush, attempting to put a doll's dress on an unwilling cat. I heard a yowl, then saw the girl's finger fly to her mouth as cat and dress disappeared into the bushes.

I hurried toward her. "Are you all right?"

The girl held up a finger. "Kitty scratched me."

I blew on the scratch to stop the stinging. "What a naughty kitty."

The child regarded me out of solemn eyes, Tremayne eyes by the look of them—vivid blue, long-lashed, and clearly defined.

A woman of perhaps thirty-five years came to the door. "Are you all right, Becca?"

Becca held up her finger and ran toward the house. "Kitty scratched me." She began to cry in earnest.

The woman gave me a quick glance. "Hush, sweetness. You're getting too big for so many tears."

Becca's loud cries brought an older woman to the door. "What's all the commotion?"

Becca and her mother started to explain. While they talked, I assessed the two women. The younger was likely Caleb's sister-in-law, the tall one with graying hair his mother. I studied the latter with interest. Wasn't that why I had come? To meet her and by so doing come to know her son?

I'd pictured Caleb's mother as an older version of Melvina, warm and garrulous. Instead I found a tall woman, thin to the point of gauntness, and one who exhibited little warmth as she brushed a twig from Becca's skirt. Was this how she'd responded to the wounded animals Caleb had brought to her? How had she treated Sally?

Sensing my presence, Caleb's mother's lifted her head and her gaze met mine. For a second neither of us spoke, her sharp, gray eyes bright and appraising. "I believe we have a visitor," she said after a moment.

The two women and the child watched as I crossed the backyard. None of them smiled. I began to feel uncomfortable. "I'm sorry to intrude. I went for a walk, and when I saw your house I thought I should stop and introduce myself. I'm Tamsin Yeager, your son's new housekeeper and . . ." My voice had grown thin and small like my waning confidence.

"But of course," his mother said. "I've just returned from a stay with my sister. Melvina wrote of Miss Cooper's departure." She paused to remove her skirt from her granddaughter's clutches. "I am Lucinda Tremayne and this is my daughter-in-law, Hannah."

The smile Hannah gave me was tentative, as though it didn't get much practice. Although she was well dressed, Hannah appeared washed-out, her light brown hair without luster and straggling from its pins. She was tired, listless, and widowhood had settled her pleasant features into passive, drooping lines.

"I understand Mary's been poorly again," Mrs. Tremayne said. Unlike her daughter-in-law, she was not listless.

"Actually, she's doing better this week."

"Good . . . good. And Sally?"

"Sally and I get on well."

Mrs. Tremayne continued to study me, her expression revealing nothing of her thoughts. "I suppose my daughter told you Sally's history?" At my nod she went on. "I've tried many times to tell Caleb it won't do. That house is just too large for the likes of Mary and Sally to keep up . . . much too large." Her mouth pulled into a tight line. "There was no need to build the house in the first place. All that money gone for a home that sits mostly empty. If he had a wife and family it would be a different matter."

"Now, Mother . . ." Hannah didn't seem to have energy to say more.

"It's the truth, though saying so to Caleb doesn't make a particle of difference." Lucinda laughed, the act momentarily softening her angular features. "That boy's been a trial to me from the day he was born—always going his own way, doing things no one else would think of. The house is a sore spot between us, but at least it brought him home."

I was under the impression his brother's death had brought Caleb home. Searching for something to say, I grasped at the first thing that came to mind. "Mr. Tremayne seems a busy man. He's always coming and going."

"We don't like it—" A quick jab from Lucinda's elbow brought Hannah's hand to her mouth. "I mean—"

Lucinda's lips tightened and she exchanged a quick glance with Hannah. Listlessness had fled the younger woman's face, replaced by tension.

"It's a busy time of year for all of us . . . so much to do. I was telling Hannah just this morning that I don't recall when I've been more busy. All the vegetables to put by. Apples too." Lucinda launched into a description of all they'd done, her tongue tripping in her eagerness to explain. I knew her mind wasn't on what she was saying. It was on her son and his comings and goings. Caleb Tremayne's frequent trips concerned the women. Why?

The question circled through my mind along with Caleb's warning, cluttering it so that I have no recollection of what we spoke about next. Perhaps the weather, though more likely it was onions, for I returned with a basket filled with them, all freshly dug with soil clinging to the roots.

"I met your mother and Hannah," I told Caleb that evening.

He looked at me, his fork poised midway between mouth and plate, a look of mild surprise on his face. "Did they come to visit?"

"No. I visited them."

"I see." Caleb didn't appear overly pleased at this news.

Like a hound onto the scent of something new and tantalizing, I plunged on. I didn't know what I searched for, only that the women were worried. "I didn't set out to visit them, but ended up there and found Becca crying and—"

The mention of Becca gained his attention. "What was wrong?"

"Only a kitten's scratch, though she shed a good many tears."

Caleb's mouth tightened. "Unfortunately, that's Becca's way. Mother hopes she'll outgrow it, but considering Hannah's state . . ."

"She's unwell?" I prompted, anxious to keep him talking.

"My brother's death has been very difficult for her."

"That's understandable," I said.

Caleb's attention returned to his meal while I, unused to holding conversation with a man, grasped for another topic to hold his interest.

"Would you mind if I planted a garden?"

Caleb stared at me in surprise. "Garden?"

"Yes. Your mother sent a basket of onions with me, and I thought how nice it would be to grow our own—not just onions, but other vegetables too. I've always had a garden with carrots and potatoes . . ."

"And flowers?" Caleb looked at Sally's latest bouquet. They were a motley bunch, the stems of the purple Michaelmas daisies cut too short, the spindly stalks of the meadowsweet well past their prime.

"Those too." Seeing the corners of his mouth lift, I forgot about his mother and reveled in his smile. "It will further Sally's education to learn the names of the flowers, and we will all benefit from the vegetables."

"Don't we have all we need? If not, you can tell Parley or Mr. Brown."

"I know, but . . ." Despite his steady gaze, I hurried on. "Your mother doesn't know what I need each day, so I make do or change my plans or . . ."

"Or grow a garden?"

"Yes."

Something glinted in his deep, blue eyes, filling me again with the notion that Caleb could look into my heart and know of homesickness and my love of soil and seed and sun.

"I'll tell Parley to spade a plot for you. Come spring, after the frost breaks up the clods, it should be ready for planting."

"Thank you." My happiness exceeded what the granting of my request warranted. It also made me forget that I'd been trying to find a clue to the women's worry.

"Have you decided where you'd like the garden to be?"

"As a matter of fact—"

Caleb's deep chuckle filled the room. Hearing it, Sally's narrow face grew animated. "Can Miss Yeager have her garden?" Since Caleb had apologized for his temper, the worshipful look had come back.

"She can. And you can help her choose where to put it."

Sally's cheeks turned pink with pleasure and I wondered if mine had done the same. Caleb didn't speak again until he was leaving the table. "Should you wish to plant flowers around the front steps, I have no objections." He glanced at Sally. "Though maybe that was your plan, and the vegetable garden was only a ruse."

"Why . . . no." Realizing that he was teasing, I laughed. "You don't know what risk you take by giving me full reign like this."

"I think I do." For a moment his eyes locked with mine. "I think I do," he repeated. With that he quit the room.

———•———

The next evening I began my plan to read to Sally. I brought Mother's book of poetry, and after Sally finished copying the alphabet, I opened the book. The impact of seeing the familiar pages almost got the better of me. I blinked rapidly and looked for something that would appeal to Sally.

"This book belonged to my mother," I said. "She read to my sister and me almost every night . . . although there were five girls in the beginning."

Sally gave me a quick look. "Did something happen to 'em?"

"No. Catherine married, then Harriet and Mary Ellen."

"That's only three," Sally pointed out.

"Clarissa . . ." Her name seemed to stick to my tongue. "Clarissa married too," I said, though as to her actual marriage, I couldn't be certain. Only that she was gone. "I thought I'd read to you like my mother did."

Settling myself more closely to the lamp, I began:

"The gentleness of heaven broods o'er the sea

Listen! The mighty Being is awake,

And doth with his eternal motion make

A sound . . ."

My voice trembled and cracked. How foolish to have chosen Wordsworth. How foolish to read of the sea.

"'A sound like thunder—everlasting,'" Caleb's strong voice finished.

I'd been so caught up in reading to Sally, I'd forgotten Caleb was reading at the other end of the room. I remembered him now and looked over at him—his dark head gleaming in the lamplight, blue eyes warm with sympathy, tapered fingers holding the lowered newspaper.

"Forgive me for intruding, but Wordsworth is a favorite of mine."

"Mine too." I cleared my throat. Sally seemed but a blur. "Mary told me you went to sea when you were young."

"Sixteen . . . scarce more than a boy, though I thought myself a man." The corners of Caleb's lips rose. "At the time I thought there was nothing worse than being a farmer, but the first days on my uncle's ship taught me otherwise. My stomach didn't take well to the ship's motion, and being the lowest in pecking order, I was given the most disagreeable tasks." He paused and his voice gained force. "I quickly learned I wasn't cut out to be a sailor, but I continue to admire the sea." His gaze seemed as warm as the lamplight. "What of you, Miss Yeager?"

"Me?" I felt as slow of wit as Sally. "I lived by the ocean. There was a cove and a wooded bluff . . ." The directness of Caleb's gaze made me uncomfortable. ". . . tide pools and sand. My sister and I spent many hours there."

Sally closed her eyes as if to imagine it. "It must have been pretty."

My heart contracted in bittersweet longing. "It was, but Glen Oaks is nice too."

"Oh, it is," Sally exclaimed. "And Master Caleb too." Her sallow cheeks colored and she dropped her eyes. "Him's always nice. But your readin's nice too. Please, can I hear more?"

I chose another poem by Wordsworth, then two by Elizabeth Barrett Browning, reading slowly so Sally could feel the flow of words. I lost myself in the cadence of rhyme, and it wasn't until Sally's head sagged against my arm that I recollected where I was.

Caleb rose from his chair, the newspaper tucked under his arm and an amused expression on his face. "I think you've put her to sleep."

Sally started and sat upright. "I'm sorry, miss. Sorry, Master Caleb." She was the picture of confusion. My heart went out to her. I knew how it was to feel awkward and foolish, knew it firsthand from living with Clarissa, who'd never suffered from the malady.

"It's late . . . well past bedtime." I said, glancing at Caleb, who'd lifted the curtain and was peering out the window with the lamp in his hand.

"I think I'll stay and read, but thank you for reading to Sally," Caleb said in a tone so soft I doubt Sally heard him.

Sally and I took the stairs to the upper floor, the branch of candles lighting our way. As Sally moved ahead of me, I was struck again by her thinness, the childlike body clad in a woman's dress, drab brown and ill fitting. Small wonder she felt awkward and unsure of herself. Why hadn't I done something to improve her appearance? Buoyed by Caleb's parting words, I determined to do so.

"After you undress for bed, let me alter your dress to fit better," I offered.

"Ain't no need."

"I'd like to. I've been meaning to for some time now," I insisted, surprised at Sally's resistance.

"No . . . miss."

We'd reached our bedrooms, the light from a candle flickering over Sally's narrow features as she opened her door.

Still I persisted. "We really need to do something with your dress, Sally."

"No!" Sally's voice rose.

"But, Sally—"

"No!" She slammed the door in my face.

I stood in the hall, not knowing what to do, hearing Mary's comforting voice and Sally's muffled sobs. Dear heaven, what had I done?

Unable to bear the sound of Sally's crying, I went to my room. Everything had been going so well—the promise of a garden, Caleb unbending a little. But now this.

"I'm sorry, Sally. I didn't mean to hurt your feelings," I whispered. Still feeling guilty, I undressed and went to the window where a moon the color of butter cast mellow light down onto the yard— Caleb's yard, Caleb's farm. The farm he'd returned to not by choice, but out of family obligation.

I recalled the passion in his voice when he'd spoken of the sea. Yet here he sat, in a house surrounded by fields instead of pounding surf; like me, positioned out of necessity rather than by choice. Was that the explanation for the frequent trips? Did he miss the sea?

Such reasoning didn't explain his mother's worry and Hannah's concern. Unless . . . my thoughts paused. Unless they feared he might return to Boston. I snatched at the idea and cast my suspicions of illicit business aside. The women were afraid Caleb would leave them. Pleased at my logic, I leaned my forehead against the coolness of the windowpane and closed my eyes. When I opened them I saw the amber glow of a lantern move across the yard and into the barn. I blinked and peered more closely. There were two people. Was one of them Caleb?

Before I could decipher the shadowy silhouettes, the barn door closed, leaving only slits of light between the cracks, slits so narrow that if I hadn't seen the lantern I would have thought I imagined them.

I held my breath, though why I couldn't say. Didn't Caleb Tremayne have the right to walk around his yard at night? Visit his own barn? Logic cried yes, but logic wasn't convincing enough to push me from the window and into bed.

I waited, the minutes stretching, my bare feet growing cold. Then I saw it—the dousing of the lantern. Heard it—the scrape of the barn door opening. My senses came alive at the sound of wheels, the silhouette of driver and wagon emerging from the barn. There was stealth. Of that I was certain. But who was the driver?

I opened the bedroom door. Silence greeted me, Sally's crying having ceased. I carefully made my way down the corridor to Caleb's room. The door was ajar, as was customary except when he was dressing or sleeping. Was he still in the sitting room?

I hesitated at the top of the stairs, chiding myself for roaming around the darkened house, perhaps even stumbling and waking everyone. Was this what Vilate Cooper had done? Was that why she was dismissed?

The questions didn't deter me, though I proceeded with care, each step measured as I clung to the banister, my ears alert for any sound. The sitting room was dark. Not satisfied, I went down the narrow steps to the lower level. Like the bedroom and sitting room, the study was empty too.

A queer dullness closed around my heart when I realized Caleb Tremayne was gone, taking all of my logical explanations with him.

CHAPTER 8

Caleb's absence the next morning was scarcely mentioned, as had been the case on his previous trips from home. "It's his way," Mary told me, just as she'd done the fortnight before. Whether this was something Mary and Sally had agreed to do when they moved to the new house, I didn't know. I only knew that any questions about his trips made them evasive and uneasy.

Sally was uneasy on my account, as well. I was aware of it as soon as I entered the kitchen. Her greeting was without enthusiasm and she made every attempt to avoid me. After breakfast, when she returned from emptying the dishwater, I spoke to her.

"I'm sorry if I hurt your feelings last night."

"It don't matter."

"It does to me." Her skinny body was silhouetted in the doorway and her eyes refused to meet mine. "If you should ever change your mind about your dress, I'll be—"

"I like my dress." Her thin voice quavered, but her eyes met mine, narrow and defiant. "I like my dress just fine." With that she fled the kitchen, slamming the door behind her.

I started after her. "Sally . . ."

"Let her be." Mary's voice was sharp.

I stared at the usually placid woman, noting that her face was creased with concern. "What did I do?" Then before Mary could answer, I added, "I didn't mean to upset her."

"Just let her be," Mary repeated.

"Do you think that's best?"

"I do." Sitting on a stool, Mary returned to the ironing. Silence enveloped the kitchen. I kneaded the dough and Mary ironed, my mind a tangle of concern and frustration as I thought about Sally.

"It wasn't your fault," Mary finally said.

"I only wanted to help her."

"Just as I did . . . and Mrs. Tremayne. Even Miss Cooper."

"The dress . . ."

"'Tisn't the dress. It's Sally."

I looked up from the dough, my fingers moist and sticky.

"It's Sally," Mary repeated, her voice a half-sigh. "Poor girl . . ." Mary set the flatiron onto the stove. "You mustn't tell anyone what I'm about to say. Especially not Sally."

"Of course."

Mary crossed to the table, her plump hands splayed on the floury surface. "She had a miserable life . . . more miserable than you can imagine, and her but a child. Beatings. Her father a drunkard. Never enough to eat. Says her life was no worse than many others. Terrible what the poor have to deal with in the cities."

I nodded and tried to imagine the drunken quarreling and squalid rooms filled with unwashed bodies, though I sensed that what Mary was about to tell me was more than that.

"Sally looks on me as her mother," Mary went on. "We've grown close, she and I. She's told me things . . . terrible things. I don't like to think about them, let alone repeat them. But this . . ."

Mary sniffled and rubbed her nose, leaving a smudge of flour across the tip. "What happened . . ." She struggled for the proper words. "When she started to grow up woman-like, her father tried to do things with her. At first she was able to fend him off, but later . . . later he did horrible things to her . . . things no father ought to do with his daughter."

The image of Deacon Mickelson flashed through my mind. "No . . . oh, no."

Tears glistened in Mary's eyes. "Hell's burning is too good for him. Sally tried to get away. Run out the door with her clothes half ripped off. Her father came after her with nothing on but his shirt. Mr. Tremayne saw them . . . jumped out of his carriage and grabbed her father. Knocked him flat. Mr. Tremayne came away with a black eye." Mary paused and wiped the corner of her eye. "That's how he rescued Sally, how she came to be here. But it's left her marked. Afraid of men, she is, except for Master Caleb. That's why she wears her dresses too big. Doesn't want anyone to know she's a woman."

"How awful," I breathed. My mind made its way through a maze of dreadful pictures while my heart cried. "How old is Sally?"

"Don't know for sure. Doubt Sally does either. Fifteen, maybe sixteen. It's hard to say, small as she is and her mind a bit slow." Mary paused to brush flour from her hands. "She binds herself, you know. Wraps her chest with a piece of old sheet. Like she don't want no part of bein' a woman."

"She's probably afraid."

Mary's round head nodded. "Does her best to avoid Mr. Brown and his boys. Stays clear away from them, though she's not above eavesdropping on their conversations."

I sighed and placed a cloth over the dough. "Poor Sally."

"She's that, all right . . . though to my thinking, calling her such does more harm than good. If we always call her Poor Sally, that's all she'll ever be—someone to pity. So I've taken to calling her My Sweet or sometimes Sweet Sally. Seems to me she needs our love more than our pity. Leastwise that's how I look at it."

"What a clever idea," I said, and meant it. Children needed someone to fuss over them, slip them sweets, give hugs and kisses. I doubted there had been much of that in Sally's life, but it was never too late to try.

"I think Mr. Tremayne explained some of this to his mother, enough for her to understand. After last night, I thought you should know too, so you won't press her about fixing her dresses."

"Did you tell Miss Cooper?"

Mary shook her head. "Miss Cooper would'a held it against Sally and think it was her fault, though how she could believe such a thing is beyond me. Some women are like that. Men too." She cocked her head toward the door. "I hear Sally coming. The less said about this, the better it will be. Just treat Sally like usual. By afternoon she'll be herself again."

That afternoon Sally asked if she could go with me to inspect the plot Parley had spaded for the new garden. As we walked outside, she hummed a little song under her breath, then she began talking about planting beans and corn, all of it done as if nothing had passed between us. We stood on the edge of the spaded plot, the late autumn breeze tangling Sally's thin brown hair, the smell of moist soil all around us. There was a definite bite to the air. I pulled my paisley shawl more closely around me, and Sally lifted the skirt of her white apron up over her thin arms.

"Next spring we'll plant peas first, then cabbage," I told her. "Potatoes should go in early too, if we want to have baby ones to go with the peas." I nodded, already anticipating the treat. "New potatoes and cream peas were my mother's favorite."

Sally didn't say much, but I could tell she was pleased to be included in my plans. She bent and laid a fallen leaf over a displaced worm, gently, a woman-child who wouldn't hurt the tiniest creature.

Later, after we'd eaten and the dishes were washed, we went up to the sitting room where Sally had made a fire. The cheery flames were welcome, for the wind had changed to the north and rattled the windows. In the circle of warmth by the fire we felt snug and safe. Sally had brought a footstool for Mary's legs, and I had made a fresh pot of tea. Sally's eyes lit with pleasure when she noted I'd brought sugar and a pitcher of rich cream, and some slices of angel cake too.

I don't recall what we talked about. There was silence intermingled with the clink of cups on saucers. It was a good silence, the kind that comes when people are comfortable with each other, when there's trust and caring.

When we'd finished our tea, Mary sent Sally upstairs for her Bible. "I'm not much at reading . . . hardly had any schooling and now my eyes are bad." A pause, and a look that was neither pleading nor embarrassed passed. "But I've always liked Proverbs."

I read the first chapter of Proverbs to the accompaniment of Mary's, "Now that's a good one," or "Isn't that the truth?" Having read more of Shakespeare than the Bible, I was impressed by its contents. Perhaps I read too long. More likely it was the combination of full stomachs and a warm fire. All too soon, I heard Mary snore and saw Sally's head droop.

We were a tired threesome as we climbed the stairs to bed, though Sally and I giggled trying to help Mary. We were like two scrawny sticks attempting to keep a wallowing tub afloat.

"You should have a room downstairs," I declared. "To expect you to climb these twice a day is ridiculous."

Neither commented. To do so would have been disloyal to Mr. Tremayne.

"I'm going to talk to Mr. Tremayne about it when he returns. You need a room down by the kitchen, not all the way up here."

Mary's loud breathing was her only reply.

"You should have Mr. Tremayne's study. It's big enough for your bed and would be warm in the winter and cool in the summer. There are plenty of rooms upstairs for his study." By now we had reached their room.

"It's good of you to think of me, but Mr. Tremayne . . ." Mary paused to catch her breath. "Mr. Tremayne's right partial to his study."

"He's partial to you too. Anyone with two eyes can see he dotes on you. You're like one of his family."

Mary sniffed at this and Sally smiled.

"I'm going to talk to him."

It was late by the time I was ready for bed, my hair brushed and an extra quilt brought from the cupboard for my bed. As I climbed between the muslin sheets, I felt a quiet rejoicing, something bordering on peace. I'm not certain how it had happened, for nothing had actually been said. But Mary and Sally—like a mother and daughter—had taken me into their circle and made me their friend.

—•—

Caleb didn't return until two days later. His return caused a subtle change in our routine. The dusting was more thorough, meals prompt, and everyone walked with a quicker step, even Mr. Brown. I wondered what he thought of the wagon's absence and quiet return, both departure and arrival taking place under cover of darkness. I did my share of thinking too.

I watched Caleb closely that first morning while serving breakfast, a meal that wasn't up to its usual standard since I didn't know he was back until he entered the dining room. Had I been more bold, I would have asked if he'd had a pleasant journey, though the pockets of fatigue under his blue eyes made me suspect he had not. I contented myself with commenting about the weather and that the hens weren't laying as well with the cold.

Caleb speared his fork into a fluffy German pancake. "The lack of eggs doesn't seem to have affected your cooking."

"Not as yet," I acknowledged, my cheeks warm from the compliment.

Caleb made short work of the four pancakes and reached for the platter of ham. Wherever he'd been, it had left him with a healthy appetite.

I brought a pot of fresh coffee and set it by his plate. With his stomach full, it would be a good time to broach the subject of a change of rooms with Mary. "I've been thinking," I began.

"Yes?" Caleb raised his head, his eyes suddenly wary.

The change in his expression gave me pause.

The corners of Caleb's mouth lifted at my indecision. "I'm sorry, Miss Yeager. 'I've been thinking' is my mother's favorite phrase, one she's wont to use just before she informs me of a new plan."

"I fear I have a plan too . . . one that involves Mary, not you, though in a way it does involve you." Caleb's amusement had grown into the beginnings of a smile. I hurried on, "Mary has a terrible time getting up and down the stairs. Last night it took both Sally and me to help her, so I was thinking . . ."

Caleb's smile grew, as if once he started he couldn't stop.

" . . . that if she had a room down here . . . perhaps your study."

Amusement fled Caleb's face. "No." As if he regretted his sharpness, his voice softened. "I'm concerned about Mary too. More concerned than you might think. But my study will remain where it is."

My mouth opened and quickly closed. How could the man who'd rescued Sally and Mary refuse to help now? Was having his study downstairs more important than Mary's well-being?

"Since the only other rooms down here are the kitchen and dining room," Caleb went on, "we must look elsewhere . . . perhaps the empty room next to the sitting room? That would limit her to just one set of stairs."

I wanted to ask why that room couldn't serve as his study just as well. "I'm sure you know what's best." My voice was flat, angry too. I removed Caleb's plate and started for the kitchen.

"Miss Yeager." His commanding tone stopped me. "Although you might doubt this, I'm as concerned about Mary as you are. Between us, I'm confident we can find a workable solution."

I did doubt it, though I was too timid to say so. I continued into the kitchen and set Caleb's plate down with a clatter. It was good that Mary and Sally were upstairs, else they'd have seen me in a temper. But more than that, I didn't want them to know I had failed.

November was upon us, the trees losing the last of their leaves, the days cold and so short we had to light the lamps before supper. There was a subtle shifting of rhythm, as if earth and sun and man were adjusting to the coming of winter. Sam and Parley spent the afternoons chopping wood and stacking it in the woodshed. Caleb sometimes joined them, his muscular arms swinging, the breadth of his shoulders stretching his brown woolen shirt as ax bit into log.

Two days before, Mary's bed and dresser had been carried down from the upstairs bedrooms to one of the empty sitting rooms on the second floor. Mr. Brown and Parley struggled to move the bulky items without scratching the carved oak banister. To say Mary and Sally were pleased would be putting it mildly. With a lovely view from curtained double windows, and only one set of stairs to climb, Mary thought herself not far from heaven.

I was not so easily pleased, but I tried to reconcile myself to the situation. Even so, I would have liked Caleb Tremayne better had he not been so selfish.

Now that there was not so much work on the farm, I half-expected Caleb to desert us for his uncle's home in Boston. Such was not the case. He seldom left the farm except to visit his mother.

I couldn't decide whether I liked this new arrangement, this abundance of Caleb when in the past there had been a drought. The impact of being so often in the company of someone who'd slipped past the barriers I'd erected after Jacob Mueller's defection and betrayal was like getting too much sun. Sometimes it even made me giddy.

Caleb still spent each morning outside, seeing to his animals or doing chores. But his afternoons were spent in his study with the door closed and a fire burning.

"Winter is the time he does all his figuring," Mary informed me. The two of us sat in the kitchen, Mary's black-shod feet propped up on the fender of the stove, a cup of tea in her hand. "He's always been one to figure. How much this costs. Should he plant more wheat? The kind of things men fill their heads with."

I knew Caleb did more than figure and go over the farm accounts. He did a good deal of reading too, as evidenced by the many books, magazines, and newspapers I found on his desk and scattered about the room. I allowed Sally to dust and polish all she liked in the other rooms, but I had declared Caleb's study off limits. I wanted the study for myself. By glancing through his magazines and papers, I hoped to gain better insight into the man.

There was a mystery about him, too many things unexplained. I, ever curious, and made more curious by my growing interest, was not above snooping. Good manners, not to mention good sense, told me I did wrong. Hadn't curiosity been the cause for Miss Cooper's dismissal? Still, I persisted. It was as if I had gained new purpose in life. I'd found something to fill the void left by Mother's death and the loss of Jacob and Clarissa.

On a stormy November morning, with wind driving droplets of rain and sleet against the windows, I entered Caleb's study. He'd left for the barn, hat pulled close over his head as he sprinted across the yard. He and Mr. Brown were repairing a wheel on the wagon, something that should take the entire morning.

I took a dust cloth and a container of beeswax with me, intending to give the furniture a good polishing. I set down the beeswax and let my gaze travel around the whitewashed walls; they were lined with stained oak shelves and hung with a map of the New England coast and framed paintings of the sea. I wondered that these couldn't have gone just as well in the empty parlor.

While I pondered this, I gathered up the scattered books and magazines and put them on a shelf. Then I turned to the newspapers—two copies of the *Boston Sentinel* and a copy of the *Philadelphia Gazette*. As I straightened them, I noticed a smaller newspaper, one whose headlines were smaller, the print less distinct.

The North Star, its masthead proclaimed. Intrigued, I saw that the paper was published in Rochester, New York, its editor one Frederick

Douglas. I continued to read—a denouncement of the Fugitive Slave Act and an appeal for funds to help runaway slaves reach Canada by use of the underground railroad.

I sat down on a chair. This was strong material, something I hadn't known Caleb read. Like many Northerners, I didn't hold with slavery. The concept of one human owning another was repugnant to me. Even so, I had never given slavery much thought. Perhaps the blame can be laid to my upbringing. My education had been private, the bulk of it administered by Mother or an occasional itinerant schoolmaster who'd roomed in our house. Since Mother disliked discussing anything unpleasant, the subject of slavery was barely touched upon. I had never seen a slave, and the majority of the freed blacks of the North congregated in cities rather than farms and villages.

Isolated? Naive? I could say yes to both. More than that, I was afraid—fearful of thinking new thoughts, seeing new places. To leave Mickelboro had taken every scrap of my courage. And now? Nibbling my lower lip, I scanned the front page of the newspaper, the storm outside and the dusting forgotten. The next caption was the personal account of a slave named Sarah Whitehead and her flight to freedom.

Feelings of horror gripped me as I read. How could something so evil be permitted to happen? How had this Sarah endured it? I followed the account onto the next page, my interest nailed to the woman's story, tears welling in my eyes when I learned that after suffering untold hardship, her only child had died before they could reach Canada.

"No," I whispered.

"Yes."

My heart leapt at the sound of a male voice, banging against my ribs with such force that for a second I thought I might faint.

"Mr. . . . Mr. Tremayne. I didn't know . . ." I meant to say I didn't know he'd come back inside. My mind had been so caught up in the poor woman's plight I'd lost track of place and time. I hastily wiped at my tears.

"Unfortunately too few of us know."

I stared at Caleb, noting the white feathers of snow clinging to his crisp, dark hair while I tried to understand what he was talking about. The slave woman, Sarah Whitehead. Of course.

"I didn't know," I repeated, this time meaning the Negro woman.

"Neither did I until my uncle enlightened me to their plight. Since then . . ." He glanced down at the floor and saw that his wet boots were leaving water on the oak floor. His expression turned contrite. "Mother would have my hide if she saw what I've done." He looked at me. "Most likely you'd like a piece of it too."

"No . . . it's your home. Your floor. If you've a mind to drip water on it, it's not my place to be offended."

"Mother would be."

"I'm not your mother." My voice was cross, whether because he'd likened me to his mother or because I'd been caught reading his papers, I wasn't sure.

Caleb didn't look too sure either—sure of what he should do about the snow melting on the floor, sure about me, sure about much of anything. An awkward silence settled around us. Instead of trying to overcome the silence, my mind skittered off in several directions— why being likened to Caleb's mother should bother me so, why he'd never married, and if there was a woman in his life.

Before, when anyone expressed hope that Caleb would marry, I'd considered it like one considers the weather: Will it be hot? Will it rain? Has the wind changed? I chose to distance myself from feelings that might cause pain. Today my heart wasn't so wise. I pictured Caleb in one of Boston's finely furnished drawing rooms surrounded by beautifully dressed women who smiled and danced with him, women with pretty faces and soft shining curls. I looked down at my plain cotton dress, saw my coarse leather shoes, and my knuckles, chapped from helping Sally with the laundry.

I wondered if Caleb were making a similar comparison. He was wiping the melting snow from his boots and the floor with the dust cloth. At times his bent head was so close I could have touched it. I wanted to. Even then I wanted to, imagining how it would feel to run my fingers through the dampness of his hair. Jacob Mueller's russet head was forgotten, diminished by Caleb's darkness; his hair was black like polished ebony, glistening from the snow.

"Are you Abolitionist?" I think my question surprised me as much as it did Caleb.

"Yes, I am," Caleb's reply came quickly, as if it were something to which he had given careful thought. "How can anyone not be an Abolitionist? I don't think God intended one man to own another, do you?"

"No." I glanced down at *The North Star* on my lap. "Isn't it dangerous? I mean, aren't there laws against it? From what I was just reading . . ." I pointed to the headline about the Fugitive Slave Act.

He went to the fireplace and jabbed a burning log with the poker. "There's no law in this country that prevents a man or a woman from thinking what they please. And as for being dangerous . . . it seems to me that if something is wrong, you can't let danger stop you from trying to change it. If men had done that, we wouldn't have access to the Bible and we'd still be English."

"I suppose so." My tone was doubtful.

"I know so." Caleb's answer was convincing, purposeful, as I imagined George Washington or Thomas Jefferson had sounded when they'd spoken to Congress.

"Would you mind if I finished reading this?" I indicated to the newspaper.

My request seemed to surprise him, but then he'd surprised me too, catching me when I should have been dusting, reading from a newspaper that likely wasn't on display in drawing rooms and society ladies' parlors.

"Not at all." His eyes went from the newspaper to the container of beeswax.

"I hope you don't think I make a habit of reading your things. I'd never seen this newspaper before."

"Not many people have. Frederick Douglas is a freed Negro you know."

"No, I didn't." I wondered if Mr. Douglas had gone to Cambridge like Caleb. Was a good education available to those of color?

"As for reading in here, I believe I gave you permission to make free with my books and magazines. If I failed to say newspapers, I was remiss."

"Thank you." A gust of wind sent a fresh spate of snow against the glass panes of the window. "It looks as if we're in for a storm."

"It does. Fortunately snowstorms don't last long this early in the season." Caleb's gaze was upon me instead of the snow. "Although you're free to read what you like in my study Miss Yeager, it would be unwise for you to let others know the nature of all you see."

"Such wasn't my intent."

"Good." His eyes continued to hold mine, blue and piercing. I felt that he was taking measure of my heart, perhaps even my soul. "Good."

For a moment I thought he was going to say more, his tall frame a silhouette against the fire, though his eyes and full mouth had never seemed more clearly defined.

I wondered what Caleb would say if I told him I'd seen him launch the boat from the cove, wondered how he'd react if he knew I'd watched him leave that night with his wagon. In that moment, something at the very center of me shifted, allowing my mind to walk down new paths, look at new shapes and patterns. Patterns which would alter my thinking and forever change my life.

CHAPTER 9

The conversation in the study caused a change in our relationship. Instead of just being a servant, I felt as if I were now a member of Caleb's family, rather like Mary and Sally, one he meant to care for and protect, someone he could trust. After all, he must trust me if he shared his views on slavery.

This thought carried me through the next day, making me smile more often than was usual, laugh, and once, when rolling out a pie crust, break into song. Mary's brows lifted and I took care after that, reminding myself that perhaps I'd made too much of our conversation. Country bred, I didn't know what people in Boston talked about at dinner; they might well discuss the pros and cons of slavery at every meal. Being an Abolitionist certainly wasn't against the law. Indeed, in parts of the North it was popular. But helping runaway slaves was still illegal.

This last thought gave me pause and set me to wondering even more about Caleb Tremayne. I watched him more than I'd done in the past and tried to decide if he were involved in helping runaway slaves. Back and forth I went, sometimes deciding he was a member of the underground railroad, the next minute thinking he was in love, the sudden trips traced to a woman, one he loved so much he couldn't bear to be away a second longer.

Caleb was watching me too. I'd look up from my plate and catch him gazing at me, a crease in his brow, his expression quizzical as if he were trying to decide about me. We were a pair, each covertly watching the other, both attempting nonchalance.

Sometimes, late at night when I lay in bed, I'd pretend Caleb's gaze held more than interest, that he saw me as a woman—admired my lips, my hazel eyes, my hair shining black in the lamplight.

About a week after our conversation, Caleb brought his chair over and joined us by the fire. Mary was knitting a pair of blue mittens, and I'd just finished helping Sally write her name. The cat purred softly on my lap. All of us were a little drowsy. He turned his chair around, straddling it, and folded his arms across the rail back. Sally stopped writing and smiled at him while I began to think the evening promised to be far more interesting than it had started.

Caleb talked to Sally, praising her for how well she wrote her name, asking how many eggs the chickens had laid that day, things he knew Sally enjoyed. Then he did the same with Mary, though it took longer with her, especially when he asked about her grandchildren.

I sat stroking the cat, whose real name, I had discovered, was Annie, not Ol' Cat—but she came no matter what we called her, liking good food and a warm fire as much as we did. While I ran my fingers through her soft fur, I wondered what Caleb would say when it was my turn for conversation. Probably something about my carrot cake or the garden.

"What did you think about the articles you read in *The North Star*?" he asked instead.

I strove to hide my surprise. "I found them most interesting."

"Only interesting?"

"Enlightening might be a better term. My mother made certain we read and understood Shakespeare, but we never subscribed to a newspaper. Truth is, we seldom spoke or read about anything to do with politics."

"Do you think slavery is but politics?"

"No . . . though it seems some to try to make it so. From what I was reading . . ." I paused to meet his eyes, wondering if his interest were genuine or if he were merely being polite. I liked what I saw, the directness of his gaze and the pleasant lift to his mouth. He looked like a man entirely taken with what I was saying. ". . . it seems to have been going on for many years—slave states, free states, the Mason-Dixon line, events I've given little thought to."

"And now you have?" Caleb prompted.

I nodded, aware that my pulse had quickened, that my earlier notion of drowsing by the fire had fled. "I didn't realize slave catchers are allowed to come and go as they please while decent folks who try to help fugitive slaves are considered criminals."

"My word." Mary's indignant tone perfectly matched my own. "How'd they come up with that kind of craziness?"

"The government passed the Fugitive Slave Law," I told her. "Anyone caught helping a runaway slave can be arrested and fined so heavily they could lose everything they own."

"Mercy." Mary shot Caleb a worried look.

"Unfortunately it's true," Caleb said. "Under this law, a man can lose his home, his farm or business . . . all that he has. On the other hand, federal officials are paid a reward for every runaway slave they apprehend. Some Northern officials are as bad as the slave catchers."

As he spoke, I could picture Caleb driving his wagon through the darkness, an important link in the underground railroad. I sensed that he was the kind of man who would risk his life, hide slaves in barns and cellars, help them go from station to station. And if so, what if he were caught and lost his home . . . the very room in which we sat?

I looked up and intercepted Caleb's gaze, his eyes as calm and placid as a summer morning. He didn't look like he lost sleep worrying about such things. Indeed, he looked as if he were enjoying himself, having hitched his chair closer to mine, his attention entirely engaged in our conversation.

"Similar injustices have gone on for centuries," Caleb said. "Touch a man's purse or property and he'll bellow clear across town. Slaves are the plantation owner's gold . . . his way of life. To his way of thinking, catching a runaway is no different than going after a stray horse or cow."

"They're not animals. They're men and women. When I think of what poor Sarah Whitehead went through . . . what all the slaves go through. Can't something be done to change the law?"

"Some are trying, but unfortunately the wheels of government turn slowly. The proponents of slavery are just as vocal as those who oppose it . . . perhaps more so, since their livelihood is at stake."

My mind was alive with stimulating new ideas, ones that made me speak with conviction. "A livelihood dependent upon the misery of others."

"Did you know George Washington was a slave owner? Jefferson too. Provisions for protecting slave owners are even written into the Constitution."

I realized how limited my education had been. "How can that be?" I demanded.

"The purse, again. One man and his family can't work and harvest the vast acreage of a Southern plantation. They require help . . . hundreds of field hands sometimes. The wages would empty that purse. Thus slavery: a solution to economics," he finished wryly.

"They put their purse above a human life . . . another man's freedom?"

"Unfortunately."

Annie's soft purr and the fire's popping shower of sparks were the only sounds. My thoughts turned to Father and the long hours he'd spent in the fields, proud suddenly that he'd never indulged in slavery, that he'd paid those who worked for him, laboring side by side with men who ofttimes became his friends, rather like Caleb and Mr. Brown.

Caleb. Just thinking his name filled me with a jolt of pleasure. I looked up and discovered he was still gazing at me, his elbows resting on the back of his chair, the backs of his hands a platform for his chin. His interest in me, for I knew with certainty it was interest, made me a little reckless. Without thinking, I smiled, feeling a soft warmth rise to my cheeks when the corners of his lips lifted in answer. I scarce believed the words that tripped from my mouth. "What do you want me to do?"

"Do?"

"Yes. Isn't that the point of our conversation? To discover my sentiments . . . perhaps enlist my aid?"

Silence filled the room. Then Caleb chuckled, a rich, rumbling sound of pleasure and wonderment rolled together. Mary looked up from her knitting and Sally smiled. Their actions reminded me that Caleb and I were not alone. Warmth came to my cheeks. What had come over me, speaking to him in such a manner, smiling at him, thinking I'd discovered a deeper meaning to our conversation?

"I'm sorry." Caleb made a valiant effort to control his laughter. "Mother warned me I shouldn't underestimate your intelligence."

"Oh?" I questioned, which was the same as saying nothing, but it was the best I could do, even as I wondered why Caleb and his mother had been discussing me. I felt his gaze, probing as though he could see me in the soft light of the lamp as clearly as in bright sunlight. There was eagerness in his expression, admiration too, as though he'd just discovered something that pleased him immensely.

His close surveillance made me jumpy. So did the realization that Mary and Sally were watching us as intently as if we were the main actors in a play. Mary's fingers were still, the half-finished mitten lying with the ball of blue yarn in her lap. My quick glance at them reminded Caleb of their presence and of Sally's penchant to repeat things.

Caleb cleared his throat. "I hadn't realized it was so late . . . well past your bedtime." He looked pointedly at Sally, who didn't look a bit sleepy.

In a matter of minutes the sitting room was empty, its fire banked for the night, and as I climbed the stairs the soft murmur of Sally's and Mary's voices as they readied themselves for bed drifted to me.

I did not hear Caleb's tread on the stairs until I was in bed, the lamp blown out, a thick patchwork quilt pulled up to my chin. I listened as his steps traversed the length of the upstairs corridor, heard the soft click as he closed his door. In my mind I pictured Caleb walking over to the bed I'd helped Sally make that morning, perhaps pausing to loosen his collar, then going to stand at the window to look down on the yard, heaped and bundled with new-fallen snow. I could see his waistcoat hanging in the wardrobe, the pillows plumped white and soft across the bed, his dark head now lying there. Would his breathing slow as he slipped into dreams? Or was his mind still alive like mine, thinking of runaway slaves and way stations, and how he might best enlist me to aid in his worthwhile cause?

I was a long time falling to sleep, my mind tumbling with half-formed pictures of those who helped unfortunate slaves flee to Canada and freedom. Through it all were whispers of excitement as I recalled how I'd spoken to Caleb and dared to smile at him, seeing his surprise when I caught him at his game. What would follow? Where would our next conversation lead?

"Dear God, let him use caution," I whispered into the darkness. "And please keep him safe."

Despite my hope that Caleb would seek out a more private moment to continue our conversation, the days slipped by uneventfully. There was too much to do to spend all my time speculating and worrying, especially now that Caleb seldom went further away than his mother's. He went several times a week, which made me question Mary's statement about his independence. When I voiced this, Mary shot me an indignant glance.

"That shows you don't know much about Mr. Tremayne. He's as independent as they come, but he's also got a soft heart. Can't bear to see anyone hurting or struggling without wanting to help . . . and there's plenty of struggling going on next door.

I looked at her in surprise. "His mother?"

"More than you might suppose, though I think it's Hannah he worries about. She's much changed. No spirit or life left in her, while before . . ." Mary paused. "I don't think I ever saw a happier woman. She made everyone else happy just being around her. Always singing and laughing and doing things for people, especially her husband. She fair idolized the man. Now that he's gone . . ." Mary looked up from her knitting and shook her head. "Makes me want to cry when I see her, and I know it's hard on Mrs. Tremayne and the children. I'm sure the master is concerned as well. Young David needs a man to keep a tight rein on him, the little girls too, since their mother can't seem to find the heart or energy to discipline them. So it all falls on Mrs. Tremayne who's not as young as she'd like us to think. Fair wear her out, they do. That's why she went to her sister's for a month and why we don't see as much of her here as we used to."

We were gathered by the kitchen stove, our usual place to sit now that cold weather had arrived. We didn't make the sitting room fire until afternoon, and the little Franklin stove in my bedroom wasn't kindled until evening. Although Melvina might sing the new house's praises, with only Sally and me to run up and down stairs, keeping several fires burning was both impractical and unsafe.

"Mrs. Tremayne used to come over here often?"

"My, yes. At least once a week, sometimes oftener. Like to drove Miss Cooper crazy . . . always making suggestions and looking things over like part of her wanted us to fail."

"Why would she want that?"

Mary's plump fingers raced to finish a stocking for Sally. She was so long in answering I thought she'd forgotten me. "I've thought on this many a time," she finally said. "I think Mrs. Tremayne believes that until Master Caleb takes a wife and sets up a family, he shouldn't keep such a big place. In her eyes there's too much space, too much waste of time and energy on our part for just one man."

"If he can afford it, why should she mind?"

Mary's brows furrowed. "Most likely she feels Mr. Tremayne didn't want to live with her, so he built the new house."

"Do you think that's true?"

A gust of wind rattled the kitchen window and echoed down the chimney. Mary's lips pursed and counted the stitches. "Partly."

"Are there bad feelings between them?"

"My, no. I just think Master Caleb needed to be independent and show that he's capable of making his own decisions. If he went back to live with his mother, it would be like he was turning back into her little boy."

"At his age?"

Mary shrugged. "That's just my opinion . . . like it's just my opinion that Hannah and the children played a part in his decision too. Master Caleb likes his quiet, and anyone with two eyes can see there's little of that at the old house any more. He likely feels guilty . . . believes he ought to be there helping, but chose to be here instead. Could be he thinks he's failed them."

"Do you think he has?"

"Mercy, no. He has a right to a life of his own, just like his brother had . . . his sister too. He can't go about trying to fix everyone's problems."

I thought about this while I peeled apples for a Brown Betty. I could understand Caleb's feelings of family responsibility and his need to make his own life, as well. Even so, I thought Mary and I had skirted the real reason Caleb had chosen to live alone, isolated from close neighbors, no curious or talkative children underfoot. The account of

Sarah Whitehead's flight to freedom tumbled through my head, and I couldn't shake the feeling that the new house might be a way station on the underground railroad and that Caleb was one of the conductors.

Much as I wanted to speculate and test Mary's thoughts about Caleb's frequent trips, I knew it was too soon. Mary and Sally might have widened their circle to include me, but our relationship was still too new and tentative to have entirely won their trust. I turned my mind to other questions. "Why doesn't Mrs. Tremayne come over anymore? Surely her grandchildren don't tire her that much."

"Maybe she's given up . . . seen it's not done her a speck of good to try to change things. Master Caleb's still here. We keep the house up for the most part." She paused and gave me a quick look. "Besides, you're here."

"Me? What have I to do with it?"

Mary's long, steady look reminded me that she'd been sitting with us when Caleb and I had talked about the Fugitive Slave Law, the night when I'd been emboldened to recklessness. "I'm not sure," she finally answered.

Sally, who'd been polishing a cooking pot, spoke up. "I know."

Mary looked at her. "What do you know?"

"Why Mrs. Tremayne don't come over no more. I heard Master Caleb tell her not to. Said it had caused problems with Miss Cooper and he didn't want the same happening to you. Said his sister, Melvina, was to stay away too."

"How come you didn't say nothing about it before?"

Sally shrugged, her bony arm moving in short strokes as she polished the pot. "Just never thought to."

Mary looked thoughtful. "That certainly explains things. Mrs. Tremayne probably thinks she was the cause of Miss Cooper's leaving and doesn't want to be blamed for doing the same with Miss Yeager."

I knew from Caleb himself that Miss Cooper's fondness for snooping had been the true cause of the housekeeper's leaving. *Be careful,* a voice whispered in my brain. *Remember what happened to Vilate Cooper.*

The warning gave me pause. Not just because I'd found a home and friends and the means to earn money. It was something more, something deeper, and wrapped around Caleb Tremayne.

The next week I visited Abigail Hamilton in Bayberry. The trip came about almost by accident, though Mary and Sally played a part in it—they, and my need for winter clothing. In my haste to leave Mickelboro, I hadn't thought to bring a cloak, only the thin paisley shawl. Wearing only that was rather like trying to protect myself with cobwebs in a New England blizzard.

"You should tell Mr. Tremayne," Mary admonished after seeing me wrap up in a blanket before going out of doors. The cold was with us in earnest—mid-December's gusting winds, snow and water frozen in the chicken troughs. When I came back inside, I knew Mary and Sally had been talking about me.

"How come you only have summer clothes?" Mary asked after Sally left the room. "Somehow, you don't strike me as a woman who'd come away unprepared . . . like you didn't expect to stay long." She gave me a sideways glance, one that said she knew she was prying, but wasn't about to stop. "Sally and I was just wondering," she added.

I wanted to say they would have to keep wondering, but friendship said it was time they knew something of my circumstances. At least part of them.

"It's not something I like to talk about," I said after a moment. "There was a man . . ." I thought I'd succeeded in burying the image of Amos Mickelson, but I had only to say, "There was a man," and all the sordid, frightening memories rushed back. I swallowed and cleared my throat, ". . . a man not unlike Sally's father, though it never got to that . . . but . . . close. I knew if I didn't get out of the house fast . . . that very night . . ." I swallowed and went on. "There wasn't any Master Caleb to rescue me . . . just myself. I was so frightened I grabbed what first came to hand . . . the few clothes you've seen and my mother's books."

Mary's mouth pulled into a straight line. "Beasts they can be if you run onto a bad one. But there's good ones too . . . like my John and Master Caleb." She looked me straight in the eye. "I think you ought to tell the master. He'll be glad to take you into Bayberry so you can buy a proper cloak and a few warm things. These days he doesn't have that much to keep him busy."

I shook my head, not wanting to ask Caleb to make a special trip into Bayberry. More than that, I didn't know if I could spare the money. Not if I intended to join Harriet and Mary Ann. I'd reckoned without Sally, however, who had no misgivings about asking a favor of her Master Caleb so long as it wasn't for herself. I don't know what she told him. Probably not much, her being of few words, but it was enough for me to find myself two days later ensconced in the carriage with Mrs. Tremayne and Hannah while Caleb drove the heavy vehicle over the rutted road to Bayberry for a day of shopping.

"There's a few things I'd like to buy for Christmas dinner," Mrs. Tremayne said. She had a list she kept consulting. "And Hannah's going to sew new dresses for Becca and Lydie, so we'll be looking at stuff goods."

I sensed she expected me to tell her what I intended to buy. I didn't want her to know of my circumstances, though I'm sure she suspected, for Mary had loaned me her brown cloak, one Mrs. Tremayne must have recognized.

"Do you like to sew?" I asked Hannah.

"Yes . . . at least I used to."

"You should see the dresses she's made," Mrs. Tremayne added. "Beautiful they are . . . every bit as finely sewn as anything you'll find in Boston."

She gave Hannah a fond look—Hannah, who sat listless and sunken into herself on the seat facing me, her voice wooden, her light blue eyes never quite meeting mine. I suspected she suffered from melancholia and I wished I could help her.

"What are the ages of your children?" I asked.

"David's nine. Lydie six. Becca just turned three. Becca was just a baby when John died."

"You must miss him," I said and earned a sharp look from Mrs. Tremayne.

"I do. More than I thought it possible to miss another person. Had you known my husband you'd know why. He was the finest man I've ever known. Kind, loving . . . ." Her voice broke.

Mrs. Tremayne took Hannah's gloved hand and squeezed it. "Courage, Hannah."

I felt I was witnessing a scene played many times before, Hannah buckling under grief while Mrs. Tremayne strove to shore her up.

"I'm fine, Mother. Really I am. I like to talk about John."

"Do you think it wise? You know how it always leads to tears."

"Is that so terrible? At least then I feel something besides this emptiness . . . this nothing." Two bright spots of color suffused her sallow cheeks. "I like to talk about John, but you never let me."

"Why, Hannah . . ." Mrs. Tremayne looked shocked. Her gray eyes filled with tears. She swallowed once, then a second time, as if she'd gotten something unpleasant out of the way. "I like to talk about John too, but I've been afraid to . . . scared you'd cry again, though if I'd known . . ."

Hannah squeezed Mrs. Tremayne's hand. "You know now."

During the two hours it took to reach Bayberry, I learned much about John Tremayne—of his steadiness and quiet wit, his good head for figures, his love of the soil, and that he'd always been considered the plainer of the two brothers, though Hannah thought him handsome. The two women talked to each other, sharing memories, recalling love, and I realized that I'd just as well be riding outside with Caleb.

When I understood an occasional smile and nod were all that were required, I fell to thinking about Caleb, wondering how he fared in the cold. Although he'd donned a heavy woolen cloak and beaver hat, I knew the wind was blowing out of the north. What kinds of things would I say about him if I were given the chance to talk as Hannah and Mrs. Tremayne were doing?

I leaned my head against the carriage door and closed my eyes. I'd say Caleb was kind, though I was still disappointed he hadn't given up his study for Mary. I'd say he was smart, though *intelligent* might be a better term for one so well educated. Evenings when Caleb sat immersed in his books and papers, I realized how limited my schooling had been. Knowing Shakespeare and quoting poetry were but a small part of being educated.

Next thing I knew, we were in Bayberry. Caleb dropped us off at Samuelson's Mercantile. His nose and cheeks were red from the wind, but other than that he looked no worse from the weather, in fact he seemed in uncommon good spirits when he opened the carriage door.

I was the last to descend. Caleb helped me over a puddle and onto the wooden walk fronting the store. *Your nose is red,* I wanted to tease. Instead I thanked him for bringing me to Bayberry.

"Mother and Hannah needed to do some shopping too." He glanced at the two women who were looking at a pair of slippers in the store's window. "When my sister engaged you as housekeeper, I think she neglected to tell you I pay a bonus as recompense for having to live so far from town." He pressed some coins into my gloved hand. "And for your efforts with Sally."

"But . . ."

Before I could say more, Caleb had climbed onto the carriage. He slapped the reins across the horses' rumps, not hard like some men do, but gentle, as if he were dealing with friends, which I guess they were since they pulled the wagon when he left on secretive trips in the dead of night.

I didn't want to be seen gaping after him, especially not by Mrs. Tremayne or Hannah. Nor did I want them to know about the money. "I'll be back in a few minutes," I called. "I want to say hello to Abigail."

I hurried away, eager to see Abby, uncertain of what to do about the money. I'd brought a small amount. But this . . . I opened my hand when I rounded the corner, stopped when I saw what it held. The two gold eagles and four half eagles were more than I could expect for an entire year.

By the time I reached Abby's door, I was fair to flying, buoyed by the prospect of buying a new cloak, elated with the coins. I hoped it would be proper to keep them. If not, Abby would know what to do.

"Tamsin!" Abby's greeting was all I'd hoped for—a hug and a quick kiss on the cheek while she laughed and demanded to know how I'd gotten there. "Are you all right? Why didn't you write and tell me you were coming?"

"I didn't know until last night . . . and I'm quite all right, thank you."

She pulled me inside out of the wind and stepped back to inspect me. "You're quite lovely with all that color in your cheeks. Eyes clear and bright. I can't imagine why some man didn't scoop you up long ago." She met my eyes head on. "It's every bit true, Tamsin Yeager. There must be something wrong with the men around here . . . though I hope you plan to do something about that horrible cloak. It's big enough for two of you."

While I explained about the loan of the cloak and my purpose in coming to Bayberry, Abby put the kettle on.

"I can't stay but a few minutes. This time of year I'm sure Ca— Mr. Tremayne is anxious to be on the road as soon as possible."

Mischief danced in Abby's eyes. "So, it's 'Caleb,' is it?"

"I've never called him that before. I don't know how it happened."

"I can. Half the women in the county would like to be on a first-name basis with that man." She paused and gave me a searching look. "How does he feel about you?"

Warmth came to my cheeks. "No more than any man feels for his hired help."

"Are you sure? Remember Caleb Tremayne is a deep man, one not given to compliments or the niceties of society. With such a man it's difficult to judge his true feelings," she said encouragingly.

"Perhaps." The room suddenly seemed over warm. I slipped out of the cloak's heavy folds, remembering Mary's concern, her sharing. They were good friends, she and Sally. So was Abby. "I was hoping you could break away to go shopping with me. I'd like your advice about color. Advice about these too." I laid the six coins on the table.

Abby's brows lifted. "How did you come by these?"

While I told her, Abby laid cups and saucers on the table. "I'm not sure what to do," I concluded. "Would it be proper to keep them?"

"Sounds to me like you've earned it . . . more than earned it with Mary not able to help but half the time."

"You think so?"

"I do." She reached and took my hand. "I've been praying for you, Tamsin. You're in my prayers every day. Hearts were touched. Doors were opened. Surely you can't think this was all a coincidence?"

"No." My voice was tentative but my tears weren't, pooling in my eyes and threatening to spill over. The knowledge of Abby's prayers was both unexpected and touching.

"Come, I want to show you something." Abby led me to the bedroom where she opened the wardrobe and removed a gown from a hook. Deep turquoise it was, like the ocean on a bright summer day, the skirt wide in keeping with fashion. A small bustle draped the fabric down the back. "This would be perfect for you."

"It's yours!" I exclaimed in refusal.

"Only under protest. Peter's grandparents brought it from Boston last year. I've only worn it twice . . . both times when they came to visit. The color's wrong. It makes me look like a drained turnip."

She held up her hand when I giggled. "Don't laugh. You'll know what I mean when you see it." Abby laid the dress against her, the deep color reflecting up onto her face and turning it a sickly blue-green.

"It doesn't suit you," I admitted.

"But it will suit you. You'll be magnificent. Look." She held up the dress and turned me toward the mirror. "Beautiful," she whispered.

The dress brought color to my cheeks and intensified the blackness of my hair. It suited me the way whitecaps suit sun-sparkled water. "Are you sure you want to be rid of it?"

"Yes. We're so near the same size I doubt it will need adjusting."

I gave her a hug. "I'll take it, but only if you'll let me pay you."

"Tamsin . . ."

"No. I insist. This will save hours of sewing. Besides I'm not that good with a needle. Clarissa always . . ." I closed my lips and looked away.

"Have you heard from her?"

"No. She has no way of knowing where I am. Since she never wrote before, I don't know why she'd start writing now."

"What about your other sisters?"

"They don't know I'm living with Mr. Tremayne, and I'm not sure where to send a letter so they'll know."

"He's back to being 'Mr. Tremayne,' is he?"

"That's all he can be. Besides, if one of the ladies in Boston hasn't managed to snare him, I doubt there's any hope for me."

"Don't be too sure."

We let the matter drop and talked of other things over tea. Later, we walked to the store, my turquoise dress wrapped in paper, one of the coins left on the table, Mary's bulky cloak billowing around me like a sail.

Luck continued to follow me. I found a cloak—fir green with a gold braid, warm stockings, and flannel to make serviceable petticoats to wear under my summer gowns. Remembering my two friends, I added a jar of liniment for Mary and a bag of peppermints for Sally.

By then the women had finished their purchases. Mrs. Tremayne kept looking out the window, her movement impatient. "What's keeping Caleb?" she demanded.

I wondered the same. He'd made no mention of buying anything. Perhaps he had business to attend to—banking, or ordering seed for spring planting. I tried not to dwell on the fact that it was perhaps female company Caleb had sought. But it was in the back of my mind, buzzing like a pesky fly that refuses to light, niggling at me until I joined Lucinda Tremayne at the window.

"It's getting late." Hannah's voice was tired.

Lucinda gave an impatient sigh and walked to the other window. They were concerned, just as I was, though whether it was for the same reason I didn't know.

"Shall I send Peter to look for him?" Abby asked.

"No, though it's good of you to offer. I'm sure Caleb will be along." She opened the door and stepped out onto the walkway. Hannah and I followed her, the sharp wind tugging at my green cloak.

Hannah pointed to a buggy down the street. "There he is."

I was glad to see Caleb in deep conversation with a man, not a woman—a man plainly attired in black. They stood next to a buggy, oblivious to all who passed them.

"A Quaker," Hannah whispered.

I looked at her in surprise, noting her pinched face, the lines of worry on her brow. Why did Caleb's speech with a Quaker cause her concern?

Mrs. Tremayne and Hannah stared at the men, then glanced quickly at each other. It couldn't have lasted more than a few seconds, the unease, the quick intake of breath.

"They're probably talking about farming," Lucinda said, as if Caleb's actions needed explaining. "The Quakers have the best farms in the county. One man has invented a new seeder that should cut down planting time by half."

"Oh my!" Hannah responded, nodding and looking impressed.

Unlike Hannah, my interest centered on the women's attempt to cover their unease, not the new seeder. Hadn't it been a Quaker who'd helped Sarah Whitehead to freedom? Did they suspect Caleb was involved with the underground railroad as I did?

Caleb looked our way and raised his hand in acknowledgment. Even so, it was several minutes before he came away.

"We'd begun to think you'd forgotten us," Lucinda said.

"You know I would never do that. I sent a boy to bring the carriage from the livery stable. I wonder what's keeping him?"

As if on cue, the carriage turned the corner, the team trotting smartly; a boy not much older than Sam held the reins. I turned to bid Abby good-bye, gave her a hug, and thanked her again for the new dress.

"It was my pleasure. All I've done for you has been a pleasure," she replied. I knew this was true. Abby was one who derived pleasure in helping and doing things for others.

"I'll keep you in my prayers." She leaned close so none could hear. "Take care, my Tamsin. There's a handsome man admiring you."

I felt my color rise. "More likely he's admiring my new cloak."

"Trust me, Tamsin. At my age, I recognize admiration when I see it."

Figuring Abby knew more about men than I did, I gave Caleb a shy smile when he helped me into the carriage. Was it admiration I saw? I thought so . . . knew so . . . for a tiny, dazzling moment when his hand closed around my elbow, when his blue eyes looked into mine.

"Your new cloak was an excellent choice." Caleb's voice was soft. I thought he might have meant more, but didn't know how to express it. At least that's what I told myself that night when I lay in bed, the darkness soft as a fine, woolen shawl, soft like my feelings as I repeated Abby's parting words, *At my age, I recognize admiration for a woman when I see it.* And I believed her.

CHAPTER 10

I shall always remember that winter of 1858–59 as a season of pristine whiteness. Mounds of snow covered the landscape in humped hills and windswept swells, while icicles hung like crystal pendants from rooftops and bare-branched trees. Mornings I'd stand at my window with my shawl wrapped tightly around my shoulders, marveling at winter's bright, sun-sparked whiteness, scarcely noting the cold.

I blessed the deep snow that kept Caleb close to home. Close to me. With animals to care for and wood to chop, there were times he ventured out, and of course times we all had to venture outside. I gave thanks many times for the warmth of my green cloak, for thick woolen stockings, and for my new turquoise dress.

Christmas afternoon was my first occasion to wear it. I didn't need a mirror to know both design and color suited me. I saw it in Mary's eyes, in Sally's smile.

"Oh, miss," Sally's voice was close to worshipful. For a fleeting second, I saw regret as she looked down at her ill-fitting brown dress. Just as quickly the look was gone, replaced by awe as she stretched out her hand and touched the bustle. "It's like a flower. One of them big cabbage roses that grows in the woods. And you . . ." What she thought of me seemed beyond her ability to express.

"You look quite nice," Mary said. There was no oohing and aahing from her. But there was a sparkle in her eyes as if she looked forward to an outing to the old Tremayne house as much as I did, and that my "looking quite nice" added to her pleasure.

We'd been invited the week before. Caleb had brought the invitation. "Mother wants all of us to come. Melvina and Hiram will be there. Mother hopes to make an occasion of it. She thinks we've seen too much gloom these past years."

Mary and I baked pies—pumpkin taken fresh from the oven, two mincemeat prepared the day before. I sensed Mary's reputation was at stake, and I experienced satisfaction as I looked at the pies. I didn't think we had anything of which to be ashamed.

Caleb didn't seem to think so either. He was all smiles as he wished us a merry Christmas at breakfast, whistling as he carried one of the pies out to the waiting sleigh, the collar of his coat turned up against the cold.

When we arrived, I wasn't sure if I should go to the kitchen to help Mrs. Brown or stay with the guests. Sensing my quandary, Lucinda Tremayne drew me into the sitting room and thanked me for the pies. Hannah also seemed glad to see me, but I sensed some restraint on Melvina's part.

"You must come and meet Hiram's cousin," she told Caleb as soon as he'd removed his coat. I watched Caleb's dark brows lift, saw the rueful shake of his head as if to say, *Not again, Melvina.*

Melvina paid no heed, her step and smile confident as she took his arm and led him to meet the cousin. I immediately saw the reason why. The cousin was pretty, though she looked barely old enough to be out of the schoolroom, her dark hair and blue eyes set off to perfection by the shimmering silk of her white gown.

Had I not been wearing the new dress, I might have taken a chair in the corner so no unflattering comparison would be made. Instead, I turned to Hannah and asked about her children and if she'd finished the new dresses.

"Mother Tremayne and I finished them yesterday." Animation sounded in her voice and her cheeks were flushed with color, giving me a glimpse of the woman she'd once been, attractive and brimming with life. "Here are the children. They've been showing their gifts to their cousins."

The three had just entered the room, Becca holding on to her sister's hand, David leading the way. They were comely children, and obviously glad to see Caleb, who lifted Becca into his arms and took Lydie's hand. Two older children followed, a dark-haired boy and a plain-faced girl who looked much like Hiram.

"What beautiful children," I said. "You must be proud of them."

"I am . . . at least most of the time, though you've only to talk to Mother Tremayne to know they're not always the best behaved. John's passing . . ." Hannah's lips trembled and she looked ready to cry. She took a deep breath. " I promised myself I'd be cheerful . . . and I have been. It's Christmas and . . ."

"You're doing splendidly. Will you introduce me to your children?"

Hannah brought the children over, the girls' dresses swishing above black slippers, pink ribbons pulling dark curls away from their faces. Becca gave a shy smile and Lydie attempted a curtsey. It was David who held my interest, dark hair and blue eyes set beneath thick brows. Was this how Caleb had looked as a boy?

"Have you met my children?" Melvina asked. If she were aware they were not as well favored as their cousins, she gave no show of it. "Martin will soon be thirteen and Amelia has just turned ten." The children murmured polite phrases before hurrying to sit on the couch amid whispers and giggles. "Hiram's cousin is with us too. Her name is Jennett. Jennett Drurry. Isn't she a pretty girl?"

Before I could think of a reply, Melvina went on. "I've been telling Jennett about Caleb . . . how he only needs to meet the right girl to end to his foolish reluctance to marry. Perhaps this time I've found someone to his liking. I hope so, for Jennett and I get on well." She paused to watch them.

Caleb's attentiveness to the young cousin pleased Melvina. It did not please me. Had it been in my power, I would have retreated to the kitchen with Mary and Sally. Better there than having to watch Caleb with Jennett.

Not wanting Melvina to suspect my feelings, I searched for something to say, which was a waste of effort for Melvina continued to talk, filling my ears with more praise for Jennett, her talent for painting, and of the prize she'd won in elocution. Scarcely pausing for breath, Melvina added, "I must say you're looking well, Miss Yeager. Judging from your appearance, I can only assume that living in Glen Oaks suits you."

"It does." I met her gaze, my hazel eyes holding hers.

Melvina smiled and her eyes filled with sudden warmth. "I'm glad." She touched my arm as if we were old friends. "I'm truly glad."

I didn't know what to make of her, let alone what to say, which went unnoticed with the garrulous Melvina Ashcroft, who went on. "Mother says you get on well with Mary and Sally. Caleb seems pleased with you too, though after Miss Cooper, I think anyone would please him." She laughed. "The woman was so set in her ways, poor Mary and Sally felt like they were always walking on eggs." She looked me full in the face again. "Perhaps providence played a part in our meeting at the fair." She smiled and nodded. "I know Mother believes it did. After today, I'm inclined to agree with her."

———•———

Twelve of us sat down to dinner that Christmas afternoon. Mary and Sally ate later after helping Mrs. Brown and her daughter in the kitchen. I don't recall much of what was said as we ate, only fleeting impressions, the foremost being my determination not to let Caleb's attention to Jennett bother me. *Melvina has a perfect right to wish her brother happily married,* I reminded myself. And Caleb had a perfect right to enjoy Jennett's company. But reason fled when Caleb came around the table to help me into my chair, fled each time his gaze chanced to fall on me as we talked and enjoyed the meal.

My emotions were as fickle as a kite without a tail, shooting skyward each time I felt Caleb's eyes on me, plunging when I heard him laugh at the witty Miss Jennett Drurry or lean close to hear what she said. Although Jennett might have won a prize in elocution, her voice came soft as a kitten's and forced Caleb to lean close.

You little conniver, I thought and wondered how one so young knew so much about ensnaring a man. Clarissa had been young, I reminded myself, with a warmth and spontaneity that attracted all who knew her—ensnared also, as well I knew. Thereafter, I carefully kept my eyes on Hannah or my plate and refused to be a spectator to the conquest of Caleb.

So great was my determination that I did not look at Caleb until he assisted me into the sleigh as we were leaving. His eyes appeared black in the fading light. Dusk was fast coming on, and white puffs of steam rose from the horses' nostrils. We brought out warm bricks for our feet along with the leftover pies and ham.

"The bricks should keep you warm until you get home," Lucinda said before stepping back to wave with the rest of the family.

Mary and Sally were in high spirits, though Mary said she was tuckered out and ready to put her feet up. "Did you bank the fires so the house will be warm?" she asked. Before Sally could answer she went on, "A fine day it's been." Mary's voice was almost covered by the whish of sleigh on snow and the jingle of bells. "It was good to hear laughter at the old house—the first I've heard in a long time."

"That girl what came with Mrs. Ashcroft was ever so pretty," Sally put in. "Maybe that's why there was so much laughin'."

Mary gave a sniff, her plump cheeks almost obscured by the woolen scarf wound around her head. "I doubt 'twas the girl what brought the change, though a pretty face does bring a lift to the heart. But there was more than one pretty face at the table this afternoon. Mrs. Brown and I both remarked on how pretty Miss Yeager looked." Mary nudged me with her elbow. "And I don't think we was the only ones noticing."

Just what Mary meant by that she didn't say, and I was too proud to ask. But I wondered and hoped, and felt my resolve not to bother myself with Caleb Tremayne fly off into the brisk December air. I studied his dark silhouette on the seat in front of us, noted the jaunty set of his tall beaver hat, the quiet way he had of speaking to the horses.

Later, as the four of us sat by the fire, Mary's feet propped on a stool, a pitcher of hot cider to warm us, I felt the familiar lift to my spirits that occurred whenever Caleb was with us. *The day isn't over yet*, the hopeful side of me whispered, but the realistic side—the side that still remembered Jacob and Clarissa—kept yammering about the need to be careful. With a shake of my head, I reached for the pitcher and poured hot cider into four cups.

Caleb raised his cup. "A toast to all of you. You've more than earned it these past months." His words made the color rise to Sally's cheeks. "You've earned it," he repeated, including Mary and me with his smile.

"Pawsh," Mary said, while I sipped the cider and looked at Caleb over the rim of my cup. I hoped there was no betraying show of color in my cheeks.

Mary put down her cup. "A grand day. The ham was done to perfection and the oysters too. Reminds me of when your father was alive. It was good to hear people laughing again . . . especially Hannah. I think she's turned a corner in getting back to rights. Wouldn't you say so?"

Caleb relaxed in his favorite chair, a booted ankle crossed over one knee, the cup in hand. "I think you're probably right," he said. "At least I pray so."

"That young cousin of Mr. Ashcroft's seemed to liven things up some too. Right pretty she is." She gave Caleb a swift look. "Had the look of the city about her. Is she from around these parts?"

"I believe so."

"Close enough for you to visit her, should you have a mind to?"

"If I have a mind to," Caleb agreed. Amusement, rather than irritation, sounded in his voice. "I hope you're not planning to be like Melvina and spend your time trying to marry me off."

"Why no . . . I only thought to ask if she lived far away." Now it was Mary's plump cheeks that took on color.

Caleb uncrossed his legs and stretched his feet toward the fire. "Did you enjoy the day, Miss Yeager? If I don't ask you first Mary will, as filled with questions as she is tonight." His smile took some of the sting from his words. Even so, I thought Mary would think twice before she made any reference to Miss Drurry.

"I enjoyed myself very much," I answered, and realized with surprise that despite Jennett's presence I had passed a pleasant afternoon. I had found a friend in Hannah, and if not the same in Caleb's mother, then at least respect. As for Melvina . . .

With a deep sigh of contentment, Mary spoke "'Twas a grand day even though we worked ourselves to the bone fixing such a large dinner. It's just as it used to be." She paused and stared at the fire lapping at the fresh log Caleb had added. "All we needed was for your father to read to us from the Bible. Do you remember how it was . . . him reading about the holy night and the babe in the manger?"

Caleb's expression was somber as if he pictured the bygone time with his family gathered and cranberries and popcorn strung on a tree cut fresh from the woods. He slowly got to his feet. "That reminds me. I've a little something for each of you . . . a Christmas remembrance." He left the room and went upstairs.

"He's never done that before," Sally whispered.

"Old Master Tremayne did," Mary confided. "Every Christmas he gave us a little something . . . usually a half-dollar and a bottle of Mrs. Tremayne's dandelion wine. I wonder . . ." She paused at the sound of Caleb's whistle as he came back down the stairs. "Something's sure put him in good spirits."

"Maybe it's that new lady," Sally giggled.

"Say that again and you're likely to get your mouth slapped," Mary warned.

Caleb returned with his hands filled with presents—a bright woolen scarf for Sally, a tin of sweets for Mary, and for me a book.

"Robert Browning," he said, handing the slender volume to me. "I know how much you enjoy poetry."

I was taken back. Sweets or a scarf maybe, but this? "Thank you."

"I asked my uncle to send it to me." His voice sounded anxious, as if he feared I might not like it. "Robert Browning is a favorite of mine."

"Mine also."

We looked at each other so long I forgot where I was, conscious only of warmth glowing in blue eyes, Caleb in a white linen shirt with a black cravat tied loosely at his throat. Sally's voice shattered the fragile silence. "Red's my favorite color."

I dropped my gaze to the slender book, brown leather with gold lettering in flowing script, then to my hands—white and trembling slightly—which held it.

"Won't nobody be wondering where I am when I'm with this," Sally went on. She wrapped the scarf around her bony neck and turned so we could admire it.

"You'll be a regular sight," Mary agreed. "Not to mention keeping warm on cold days." Mary's plump fingers worked at the fastening on the tin of sweets. Her eyes glinted in anticipation when she removed the lid. "Oh, my! You shouldn't have . . . but I'm glad you did," she laughed, passing the tin around. "Take some and don't hold back. After all, it's Christmas."

I watched and heard it all with but half a mind, wanting to savor the moment when Caleb had handed me the book, to wrap it around me and hold it tight. I ran my fingers over the gold lettering, as if by doing so I could give the book life, make it speak, and tell me what the gift meant.

January slipped by with harsh winds blowing in from the Atlantic, and ice so thick in the water troughs that Mr. Brown and his boys had to use an ax to break it for the animals. That winter I did not mind the cold, did not mind much of anything. I was content to be within the same four walls as Caleb Tremayne, to sit across from him at his table, to warm myself by his fire. Evenings were the best. The four of us would gather in the sitting room, the cold having driven Caleb to our end of the room.

Sally could now do simple sums and write all four of our names. *Master Caleb* and *Miss Yeager* marched in squiggly lines across the slate below that of *Sally* and *Mary.* Caleb didn't join in the lessons, but read from one of his newspapers. Sometimes he'd share them with us, chuckling as he passed along some amusing anecdote or made some crushing remark about the latest antics of Congress.

"Here's a man with spirit and courage." His voice crackled with excitement. "Listen to this."

I looked up from my embroidery, expecting to hear of some senator who'd disagreed with the president, for they were always disagreeing, if not about taxes, then about the need for national harmony.

"Thomas Garrett was arrested, tried, and found guilty of breaking the Fugitive Slave Law," Caleb read. "A fine of $5,000 took all of his money and forced him to sell his belongings at public auction. The sheriff who conducted the auction said to Garrett, 'Thomas, I hope you'll never be caught doing this again.' Garrett replied, 'Friend, I haven't a dollar in the world, but if thee knows of a fugitive anywhere on the face of the earth who needs a breakfast, send him to me.'"

"Mercy," Mary said.

Despite a tiny stab of unease, I managed to speak in a normal voice. "I wonder if I could be so brave . . . risking all I had for total strangers." I looked at Caleb and saw a spark of recklessness in his eyes, one I'd not seen for several weeks. It was about to begin. As soon as the weather warmed, it would start again, the sudden trips, the danger, the secretive look slipping back over his face. My mouth went dry and I had to wet my lips before going on. "One would have to be a true Christian to risk so much."

"Or hate slavery." Caleb's voice was hard. "To my way of thinking, Christianity can too easily be twisted to suit a man's purpose. You forget that the South abounds in churches too, though theirs are likely to preach of slavery."

"Yes," he said when he saw my doubt. "Ask most Southerners and they'll tell you slavery is ordained of God. Didn't Abraham and Isaac own slaves? Don't two of the Ten Commandments speak of men servants and maid servants . . . another term for slaves? If that's not enough to convince you, they'll gladly quote the Apostle Paul, who encouraged servants to be obedient to their masters. Masters, Miss Yeager. They're quick to emphasize the word *master.*"

"Surely it's not the same," I protested.

"I don't believe so." Caleb's voice held conviction. "At least the God I pray to doesn't condone such a practice."

"Mine neither," Mary said. "Hearing about that man makes me like them Quakers even more. The way they help runaway slaves. They do talk funny though. They call everyone 'friend,' whether they're friendly or not, and all that 'theeing' and 'thouing.' Puts me in mind of Quaker Oldroyd from over Bayberry way. My son used to work for him. Said he'd never met a finer man." Before either of us could comment, Mary hurried on. "Did I tell you about the time he and Sam got cornered by a bull?"

Mary was off, telling the story of Quaker Oldroyd and the bull, her tongue flying as fast as her needles. I only half listened. My mind couldn't let go of Thomas Garrett, how after losing everything he was still willing to help runaway slaves. What of me? What of Tamsin Yeager? Should the occasion arise, would I be willing to do the same?

My mind wrestled with this while Caleb poked at the fire, the sparks crackling and flying against the screen. His lips turned up in amusement as he listened to Mary's story. Even so, I sensed the restlessness in him. It was banked like the fire, waiting for the weather to warm up, for the thaw to set in. Then he'd be off.

Less than a fortnight later Caleb said he was going to visit his uncle in Boston, I wasn't greatly surprised. Neither was I surprised to note a spring to his step, a resurgence of energy that had been suppressed during the weeks he'd been forced to stay indoors. Our winter idyll was ending, the long evenings by the fire, the softness of Caleb's gaze as I read aloud from Robert Browning.

My fear changed to irritation when I witnessed Caleb's eagerness to go and heard his merry whistle when he came down the stairs each morning. Did those who sat with him by his fire mean so little? Or was it the lure of more stimulating company that enticed him? Matrons with pretty, marriageable daughters?

I began to pull inward, the instinctive need to protect myself stiffening my smile and squashing my usual animated responses to Caleb's questions. Now my answers seldom consisted of more than a word or two, my body stiff like my smile. My eyes sought the cat, or Sally, anyone except Caleb. Once, as my gaze flitted from gravy bowl to plate of biscuits, I caught Caleb looking at me. Frown lines wrinkled his brow and a puzzled expression was on his face. I didn't know whether to be glad or sad. The resulting uncertainty made me even more out of sorts.

"Bristly is what you are," Mary said one night after supper. "Might as well have a thorn bush sitting with us. Ain't your usual self at all."

I averted my gaze. "I'm sorry. I have a headache." Which was true, but it was not the real reason, as Mary well knew. Fearing she'd have the truth out of me, I walked to the door. "Would you and Sally please put things to rights? I'm not feeling well."

I left the kitchen and went to my room, which was as cold as my heart, even with the stove burning. The February wind moaned around the corner of the house. If I hadn't known that indulging in a good cry would only make my headache worse, I would have succumbed to tears. Besides, what did I have to cry about? Hadn't I found friends and refuge from Amos Mickelson? Wasn't my horde of coins increasing? By summer I would have enough to pay for the trip out west.

But even the prospect of joining my sisters held no charm. There'd be no Caleb Tremayne in the Great Salt Lake Valley. "How could you have been so foolish?" I asked my reflection in the mirror. I noted my untidy dark hair and my hazel eyes that now appeared muddy brown. Small wonder Caleb was so eager to be gone. There was little of beauty to keep him here.

The prospect of spending the evening by myself was daunting, but I had no wish to sit and witness Caleb's cheerfulness. In the end, I took pen to paper and wrote letters to my sisters, hoping that somehow they would receive them. By the time I finished, it was late.

I donned my nightgown, one Mary had finished the week before; it was soft white flannel with ruffles above the high collar and a gather of lace at the cuffs. The routine of brushing my hair was so ingrained that I did it without thought, absently running my fingers through the thick, dark waves. When I finished, I wandered in a desultory fashion around the room, absently touching Mother's books, then going to stand at the window. I pulled back the curtains and looked out at the night. The moon was but a slender sickle, the stars half obscured by clouds. I knew that if I climbed between the covers I'd only toss and turn as my mind chased after Caleb. Worry and chagrin warred as I chastised myself for losing my heart to a man who didn't return my feelings.

Don't forget the book of poetry he gave you, a small voice whispered. Not wanting to reopen the door to hope and feelings that might later cause pain, I ignored the whisper and went to the door. What I needed was a cup of warm milk. Such often calmed Mother when she was too restless to sleep.

The upstairs corridor was awash with shadows, and the candles burning at the top of the stairs gave off only a dim glow. It was enough to see me safely down the stairs where another branch of candles shed light at the landing. There was no crack of light showing under the sitting room door, none from Mary's bedroom either. Everyone had gone to bed. Except Caleb, of course. The candles wouldn't still be burning if he'd come upstairs to bed.

When I reached the lower level, I saw a slit of light under the study door. I padded past and on to the kitchen, my toes curling against the cold stone floor. The banked stove beckoned with light and warmth. The wooden match holder with sandpaper striking board hung on the wall by the stove. As I felt for matches, a noise came from the study. I held my breath, and wondered if Caleb had heard me. The sound came again—footsteps going past the kitchen to the back of the house.

Forgetting the matches, I looked out into the corridor in time to see the outline of Caleb's head as he descended the steep steps to the cellar. The lamp he carried cast erratic shadows onto the wall and ceiling—down into the cellar he'd forbidden us to enter because the ground was unsafe.

Liar, I thought as I followed him, keeping to the shadows. The cold of the unheated corridor made me shiver. I stopped at the top of the steps, my eyes riveted on the light illuminating Caleb. I watched him remove a can from a shelf by the door—the door that was always kept locked. This last information had come from Sally, who'd crept down the stairs to try it.

"If it's so dangerous, how come Master Caleb goes down there?" Sally had asked me. "Him being so smart, it don't make no sense."

I'd shrugged her question aside. But I'd wondered, just as I did now when he removed a key from the can and inserted it into the door.

I waited, the stones like slabs of ice, my feet numbed by the coldness. The angle of the stairs prevented me from seeing the room he entered. Only flickering shadows and the scrape of his boots told me of his presence.

The cold drove me back to the kitchen, where I struck match to sandpaper and lit the lamp. The scrape of the match sounded unnaturally loud, as did the clank of glass against brass as I replaced the chimney in the lamp's base. My hand trembled so badly I feared I might drop it. If I hurried, I could be back in my room, pitcher of hot milk in hand, before Caleb came up from the cellar.

Thoroughly chilled and shaking with cold, I poured milk into the pan. "Hurry, do hurry," I whispered. I impatiently stuck my finger into the milk to test for warmth.

Some unnamed sensor alerted me to Caleb's presence. How he came without me hearing, I don't know. He was suddenly there in the doorway, a tall figure with a lock of black hair hanging across his forehead. He watched me, not speaking. I lifted my gaze and met his, the cold forgotten. His eyes reflecting the light from the lamp held me so I could not move.

"You gave me a start," Caleb finally said, though he sounded more thoughtful than startled. "I thought everyone had gone to bed."

"We had . . . I had, but when I couldn't sleep, I thought . . . " I was conscious that I was in my nightgown, that my hair hung loose around my shoulders. I felt the color rise in my cheeks. "Warm milk used to help Mother sleep," I finished.

"My aunt uses the same remedy," Caleb acknowledged. He continued to watch me with a thoughtful expression on his face. It was one I'd seen often as we sat together in the evening, the warmth of the fire and our friendship making a little circle—Mary, Sally, Caleb, and me. Now there were just the two of us, but the warmth was there, like sun rays on grass in June, like hot tea steaming from porcelain cups in winter.

"Why couldn't you sleep?" Caleb asked.

I turned back to the stove as I searched for an answer. When none came, I made do the best I could. "Some nights are like that. Restless."

"I'm acquainted with restless nights. They . . ."

I glanced over my shoulder, aware that his eyes were looking at my hair.

"How long have you been downstairs?"

"Only a few minutes." I'd never been good at lying, so it was well Caleb couldn't see my face. I dipped my finger into the milk. "It's ready."

I reached for a cup and poured the milk, making a show of being busy in the awkward silence that fell between us. Neither of us knew what to say. I was glad for the warmth of the stove, relieved that I'd stopped shivering.

I glanced at Caleb before I blew out the lamp. He stood with one shoulder leaning against the door jam, a hand in his pocket.

"So you're going?"

He nodded. "I leave tomorrow. Parley will drive me to Bayberry. I'll take the train to Boston from there."

Still holding the warm cup of milk in my hands, I moved toward him. "How long will you be gone?"

"A week . . . maybe two. I haven't decided." His answer came slowly, as if his mind were on something other than what he was saying, like it had gotten tangled up in me.

The two of us stood close, the air seeming to breathe for us—pulsing and charged with feelings I could not put a name to.

Caleb reached and brushed a strand of hair away from my face, his fingers lingering as if to savor its texture. They moved to my face, tapered fingertips tracing one cheek, then down to my chin, his fingers soft as velvet. Warm.

My heart beat so hard it hurt. I thought he was going to take me into his arms. That's what I wanted, the milk put aside, me wrapped tightly in his embrace.

Caleb suddenly dropped his hand and stepped back. "I think you'd better go, Miss Yeager." There was tight-lipped control to his voice, as if he'd suddenly realized what he was doing, as if he'd reminded himself of what might happen if he let go of control.

"Good night." I managed a smile while disappointment swirled in the shadows. With the milk in my hand, I stepped past him into the hallway—until I heard my name. It was no more than a whisper, like a breeze playing with willow leaves, the quiet forming of the familiar word.

"Tamsin." I doubt he was aware his lips had formed it. But I heard—and knew—and took hope as I climbed the stairs to my room.

CHAPTER 11

The next morning I was in the kitchen early, the hours I'd managed to sleep but few. My mind was filled with one thought only—Caleb. Would he come for breakfast, or had he already had Parley harness the team, not waiting to eat, not wanting to see me after last night?

Last night. I tried not to think of Caleb's touch, the warmth of his fingers on my cheek. Best to get on with fixing breakfast, best to put my mind on practical matters like stoking the fire and cracking eggs.

As I poked the coals with a stick of wood, I heard the back door open—a step. I pretended not to hear as I jabbed the coals, sparks flying, my heart pounding. Would Caleb speak to me or pass through the kitchen as he sometimes did?

Unable to bear the waiting, I turned in time to see Caleb shrug out of his coat. His nose and ears were red from the cold, and he brought the smell of the crisp February morning into the kitchen.

Neither of us spoke, our eyes locked and held. Caleb's were appraising. Mine, against better judgment, were full of hope. The corners of his mouth deepened and stretched into an easy smile.

"Good morning." His voice was easy like his smile. "Parley just finished the milking. I told him I'd bring it in."

"Thank you." Using the poker, I put the lid of the stove into place with a clank. Caleb moved to my side and stretched his long fingers to the heat, widening them so the veins and tendons stood out.

"I told Sam and Parley to be sure to bring in plenty of wood for you while I'm gone. They'll do the milking too."

"We'll be fine."

"I know you will. You being here has taken much of the worry from my mind. Since Mary's not well and Sally . . ." He paused and shot me a quick glance. "I know you'll look after both of them."

"And they me."

"Yes . . . that too. With Mary around, it's certain you won't lack for someone to talk to."

That brought a smile to my face, something I'd wanted to do from the moment Caleb stepped into the kitchen.

"Did the milk work?" he asked.

"Milk?"

"The warm milk you were heating last night."

"Yes." In truth I'd been a long time falling asleep.

"I'll have to remember the remedy." His voice sounded absent, as if he'd recalled that I'd seen him go down to the cellar.

The easiness between us slipped away. In an effort to regain it, I reached for the frying pan. "What would you like for breakfast?"

Unease was wiped away with the quirk of his dark brows. "I'd like some pancakes. The kind you fixed the other morning."

"German pancakes. They were Father's favorite and one of the few things Mother learned to cook for him."

"Oh? I thought she taught you how to cook so well."

I shook my head, still holding the frying pan. "Mother preferred the pianoforte and reading."

"So you play the pianoforte, do you?"

"A little. My sister . . . Clarissa was much better then I was."

"Was?" Caleb's eyes probed as if knowing about me and Clarissa were very interesting. "Is your sister deceased?"

"No. She . . ." I looked away. "Clarissa eloped," I said with effort. "But that was after—" I swallowed and reached for a bowl. "After Father died, I was assigned to the kitchen. At first I was upset, but later I discovered I enjoyed it."

"And became one of the finest cooks in the county."

"I doubt that." Remembering how Susannah had harped at me for not graciously accepting a compliment, I added a tentative, "Thank you."

"You're welcome."

I stole a glance at Caleb and caught him smiling at me, the red of his woolen shirt reflecting up onto his cheeks. It was a good kind of smile, the kind you share with friends or someone you're fond of. I was also smiling—big and wide, probably foolish too. If a man were only half-smart he could see love glowing in my smile. Happiness too, even though he was going off to Boston with its pretty women, going off to danger and perhaps helping runaway slaves. But a part of Caleb would stay at the farm—with Mary and Sally and me. I could see it in his blue-black eyes, promising he'd come back and that he'd miss me. For now, that was enough.

Caleb left on Monday. We soon settled into our "when-the-master's-away" routine—sleeping late in the morning, leaving the dusting until afternoon. We babied Mary by insisting she stay upstairs, her black-shod feet propped on the footstool while she knitted and dozed by the fire. Annie, the cat, often joined her, as did Sally, who'd learned to knit. The sound of their voices floated down to me in the kitchen.

With less to do, I spent my time in Caleb's study, curled up in his leather chair, breathing in the lingering scent of his spicy shaving soap. I was besotted with Caleb Tremayne, a most unwise condition for a woman of my station. Then I'd remember Caleb's touch on my cheek, the softness in his voice when he'd whispered my name, and for a few minutes I'd catch hold of hope and dream.

Caleb had been gone three days before I ventured down to the cellar. The idea had been planted when Caleb lashed out at Sally, and nourished when I saw him go down the steps the night before he left. What was he hiding? Why the lie?

These questions followed me as I made my way down the steep, stone steps, a lamp in one hand, the other braced for balance against the cold masonry wall. I found the key hidden in the can among a jumble of nails and pieces of string and leather.

The key slipped into the lock and turned without difficulty, as did the latch. The heavy wooden door swung open at my touch. Holding the lamp high, I shivered, half expecting to see a rat.

What I found was surprisingly innocent—sacks of corn stacked in a corner, a wooden bin filled with wheat, and garden tools and a broken rocking chair. Other than cobwebs, that was all the room contained. I turned in a slow circle and inspected the room again "Why does Caleb keep it locked?" I whispered.

My question echoed in the room while the cold seeped through the soles of my slippers. I was anxious to be gone, but stubbornness kept me. I'd come, half expecting to find a hiding place for runaway slaves. Instead I'd found a granary, though why in the cellar, I didn't know. Nor could I think why Caleb had come here before he left for Boston. Unless . . . I shrank from thoughts that seeped like the cold into my mind, penetrating deep and making me shudder. Smuggling. Ill-gotten gain. Contraband.

I didn't want to think such things. Not of Caleb. An unbidden force widened and enlarged the thoughts until they verged on certainty. I'm not proud of what I did, but neither do I condemn my actions—the quickness with which I set down the lamp and plunged my hands into the wheat bin. I'm not certain what I searched for. Something that wasn't grain. Something that would unlock the mystery and explain Caleb's actions.

I found only wheat in the bin, only corn in the sacks, though my search of the latter was less thorough. The relief I experienced verged on physical pain—a release of icy bands of suspicion that pulled like a noose around my chest. Thank God there was nothing.

I locked the door and dropped the key into the can. Stopping myself from thinking about the room wasn't as easy. Why a granary in the cellar instead of the barn? Why the locked door and the lie about it being unsafe? I wrestled with the puzzle through the rest of the day and might have gone on wondering indefinitely had it not been for an incident that evening that wiped all thought of the cellar from my mind.

I spent a pleasant evening with Sally and Mary, reading aloud from Mary's Bible—we were going through Proverbs, then from Mother's book of Shakespeare. One page of *Hamlet* was all they could absorb before their eyes glazed over. Afterward we banked the fires and checked the doors.

After bidding them good night, I started up the stairs. In my haste, I tripped and almost fell, barely righting myself while I balanced the lamp. Mother's book flew from my hand and tumbled down the stairs.

"Are you all right?" Mary called.

"I'm fine. I just dropped Mother's book," I assured her.

I retraced my steps to retrieve it. I didn't notice until I bent to pick it up that something had fallen out. I thought one of the pages had broken loose, but on closer inspection I discovered a piece of folded paper with my name written on the outside.

"Clarissa." My heart pounding, I whispered my sister's name. Only Clarissa wrote my name that way—*TAMSIN*, with a smiling face in the *A*. She'd done the same with the *A*'s in *Clarissa*. "We must make our own happiness," she'd told me on a long-ago afternoon. Since then, she'd used the *A*'s in our names as a reminder, a pact, that we would be happy.

Sally opened the bedroom door. "You sure you're all right?"

"Yes . . . fine." In truth I could not think straight, my movements jerky as I groped for the paper and stuffed it back into the book. Distracted, I climbed the stairs, my body stiff and without grace. Why was a letter addressed to me inside Mother's book?

Once I was in my room with the door closed and the lamp on the dressing table lit, my breathing slowed. Even so, my fingers had difficulty unfolding the paper.

Dearest Sister,

I hope you can forgive me for what I am about to do. I would not do it if there were any other way—run away with Jacob Mueller, a man I do not love, the man promised to you, Tamsin.

I wish I could talk to you and explain, but time is of the essence. If I don't leave now, Deacon Mickelson will have me. No matter what others may think, he is an evil, wicked man. Of late, he has insinuated and hinted. But Wednesday night, while you and Mother were gone to prayer meeting, he came to the house. It was terrible . . . the fumbling and kissing. I wanted to vomit and scream. I only escaped by promising to meet him tomorrow.

Oh, sister, what am I to do? He says if I speak of what happened he'll stand up in church and say I am a whore. You and Mother too. We'll be cast out of the cottage. Cast out of the village.

Here words had been crossed out, and those that followed were so hastily scrawled they were almost indiscernible.

> *Jacob is my only hope. I know you care for him, but Jacob is not the one for you. He has a wandering eye. I've seen how he looks at me, how he looks at Elsie Hathaway and Pru Clayton. He cannot long give you happiness. Me either . . . but it's either him or Deacon Mickelson, and I'd rather die than submit to that.*
>
> *You said you could not leave us to marry and move away with Jacob. I am not as timid as you, but fear acts as my prod. I pray you will understand and someday forgive me.*
>
> *I am forever your loving sister,*
>
> *Clarissa*
>
> *P.S. I will write and tell you where we have gone.*

I sat and stared at the yellow flame of the lamp, my thoughts jumping erratically—Clarissa, Jacob, Amos Mickelson—no thought holding long enough to form or make sense. Willing myself to calmness, I read the letter a second time. I didn't notice until I reached the end that the *A*'s in Clarissa's name showed a frown and tiny tears.

My own tears came slowly at first, then in rivulets and sobs—sobs held back three years by bitterness and feelings of betrayal. "Oh, Clarissa." A stream of memories came: Clarissa barefoot at our cove, the waves crashing around her; sisters, giggling and sharing secrets; Clarissa scampering to safety from a bull while I watched from the hayloft . . . She'd dared when I hesitated, led when I held back—the golden, younger sister, and my best friend.

Had I loved her? Of course. But I had also hated her—for running away with Jacob, for striking at the fragile core of my confidence. All the dark, ugly feelings returned—my anger and embarrassment when it was discovered that Jacob Mueller was gone with his father's best team and wagon. I relived the pitying glances of Mother's friends, the whispers of my peers. The looks and whispers cut like jagged stone on soft flesh and drove me into myself, into the cottage and away from life. Over and over, the questions came. How could Clarissa deceive and betray? What had changed her? These questions sat at my table each day, turning my food tasteless and shriveling my insides.

Things which had gone unnoticed at the time—the deacon's knock on the door the next evening, his prattle to Mother about nothing as his eyes searched the room—came to me now. He'd been looking for Clarissa while he pretended solicitude for Mother's health. I remembered his agitation the second day, his anger on the third. My mouth tightened as I recalled his pudgy hands, his knowing eyes as he'd looked at me in the rainstorm. Clearly I wasn't the first. How had Clarissa borne his fumbling touch and kisses? Small wonder she'd run away. Understanding replaced bitterness, forgiveness overrode condemnation as I realized I might well have done the same, snatch as a drowning man would a log, despite the consequences. As for Jacob . . .

My smile turned rueful as I recalled the girl I'd been, smitten by first love, a first kiss. Now I recognized Jacob's weaknesses. Even then I had noted his wandering eye, his restlessness, how his father took him to task for his irresponsible behavior. Love-blind, youth-blind, I'd mistaken Jacob's, "Come with me, Tamsin. We'll marry and go someplace new," for Jacob's love. But fear of the unknown had bound me to Mickelboro, to Mother and Clarissa, who were my security. I'd made excuses to Jacob and convinced him to stay.

A month later Jacob and Clarissa were gone, my hopes and pride shattered, the pain almost past bearing. To be betrayed by anyone is painful. To be betrayed by one's own sister and the man you love had been devastating. Months had passed before I began to heal. Years had gone by before I could again enjoy life's pleasures.

Still holding Clarissa's letter, I pushed back my chair and went to stand by the stove. Why hadn't I received the letter? Why had it lain for years inside the book? I looked at it more closely. The worn creases told me Mother had read the letter many times. Why hadn't she told me? Why had she let me and the rest of the village think the worst of Clarissa?

The answer hit like a blow to the stomach. Mother knew about Deacon Mickelson. She'd known about him all those years. Why hadn't she shared her knowledge and warned me?

Wondering what else was hidden in the book, I shook it. Nothing fell out, but a closer inspection showed the close lines of Mother's handwriting crisscrossing the blank pages at the back of the book. As I read, more questions filled my mind. Why hadn't Mother trusted me? What had she feared?

May 7, 1852

What am I to do? I'm not certain I can even write what has happened. How I wish Frederick were here to guide me. But if Frederick were here, none of this would have happened.

Deacon Mickelson has begun to make improper advances toward me. The first time it happened I thought 'twas only my imagination. But after today, there can be no mistake. Dear God, what am I to do?

My throat tightened. Not Mother too. In my mind I pictured her pacing the floor of the parlor, clutching her shawl, blinking at tears that were prone to flow whenever she was upset. She had written this in 1852; I would have been fifteen, Clarissa fourteen. I tried to lock on to some event or incident that would bring the year of 1852 alive. Wasn't it then when one of the Mickelson kitchen maids had been discovered to be with child?

I recalled Hester Mickelson's angry voice in our parlor as she'd conveyed the news to Mother. "Six months along she is."

"Who is the father?" Mother had asked.

"That I don't know, but I mean to find out and send that girl packing."

Clarrie and I had looked at each other, our eyes wide as we listened from the next room. The unfortunate maid was gone within the week and we noticed that all who worked for Hester thereafter were middle-aged, with the exception of Becky, who was badly scarred from burns.

Had Amos Mickelson fathered the child? The answer came just as it must have come to Hester, who had taken steps to end his philandering. Was it then his unwelcome advances had turned to Mother?

I turned back to her writing with a sick heart. The next entry was dated two days later.

I've quarreled with my dear friend Susannah Partridge and fear there is no way to put it back to rights. I went to her for advice, not intending to tell her the deacon had attempted to kiss me. Somehow it tumbled out. As soon as it was done, I regretted it. Susannah does not have difficulty making up her mind. She sees what needs to be done and does it, while I go willy-nilly, first one way, then the other, as I'm doing now. To be precise, Susannah told me I must leave the cottage and live with them.

I do not wish to leave the cottage. It's all I have. Mine, as I have made it with my books and the pianoforte and my embroidery. Not by deed or title, only by Amos Mickelson's goodwill. That goodwill must be maintained, though how, I do not know. Susannah says I am the world's biggest simpleton if I do not leave at once. I cannot bear the thought of leaving—giving up my home for the second time, living as Susannah's guest. Perhaps I can find another solution.

I closed my eyes, recalling the day they had quarreled, the day when Susannah ceased to add her warmth to our lives. Poor Mother.

May 15, 1852

I am shaking so badly I can hardly keep a steady hand. The deacon has just left. He waited until the girls went to the cove, then quick as you please, he was at the door, a cunning smile on his face. Why have I never considered it cunning? Because until now my eyes were closed to his wickedness. I thought Deacon Mickelson only good—my benefactor, the one who rescued me from my dilemma over the farm, all kindness, as befits a deacon of the church.

He made no pretense this time, his purpose evident as soon as he closed the door. I tried everything I could think of, offering him tea, stepping around the table, trying to keep some object between us. Deacon Mickelson said he wanted no more of my games. A game he called it, as if I'd been leading him on. He said he'd take me by force, if need be, but he hoped such wouldn't be the case. Where was my gratitude? Didn't I owe him something for all he'd done for us? A small kiss perhaps?

'Twas then I blurted that I planned to move, that Susannah wanted me to live with them. I saw at once I had made a mistake. Amos is not without intelligence, and it didn't take him long to deduce that I had told my friend what had happened. Still as a rock he became. His breathing slowed and coldness settled over his features.

"I do not think it wise to move from the cottage," he said. "Nor do I think it wise for you to continue your friendship with Mistress Partridge. Do I make myself clear, Mistress Yeager . . . Ellen?"

The deacon does not mean to give up. And I have brought Susannah into it. What have I done? What will he do to Susannah and her husband?

I knew what he had done—the rumors about Susannah and her husband, doors closed and credit withheld. Susannah thought their friendship had ended because of differences over Amos. Instead it had been his threat. My dislike of the deacon increased until it bordered on hatred. Thank God I had escaped. But what of Mother?

May 24, 1852

Worry about the deacon has made me ill. Dr. Field says it is my nerves and that I must rest and daily drink four cups of a special tea he gave Tamsin to brew for me. I do not think either rest or tea will help. It is so much more than nerves. Just thinking of Amos Mickelson sets my heart racing in a frightening manner. Palpitations, Dr. Field calls it, a not uncommon condition for a woman of my age and delicate constitution.

It's fear that causes the malady, though perhaps fear and nerves are the same. It does not matter. What matters is that I do not lose my home and standing in the community. Having Deacon Mickelson as my benefactor bears great weight, as well I know. More than that, he promised to hold a portion of the money from the sale of the farm in reserve for Tamsin and Clarissa when they marry. Should I arouse his anger, he might refuse to give it to them. So I walk a delicate balance, hoping to keep my home and an inheritance for my daughters while still managing to hold the deacon at bay. My recent illness helps. Amos is all solicitude again, acting his part while I act mine; pretending nothing is amiss, always gracious. I try to close my mind to what happened—his grasping hands and attempt to capture my mouth with his. Pig! Hypocrite! I want to hurl the words at him while Dr. Field and Hester are present, let them know the manner of man the self-righteous deacon is. Perhaps Hester knows already. I've seen the way she looks at me. The jealousy. Can she think I welcome her husband's attention? I think Hester knows full well what manner of man she has wed.

June 16, 1852

I am still not myself, having come down with a fever of such severity that Dr. Field was called three times. He is not certain what to make of the fever, but is concerned, as I am, at the slowness with which my strength returns. My daughters are all goodness. Clarissa sings and plays for me on the pianoforte, and Tamsin tries to tempt me with warm scones and fresh-made jam. More importantly, the deacon keeps his distance. He fears to catch the fever, though it is abating. Hester comes almost daily. I dread her visits, for she is domineering and does not mince words when it comes to my daughters. I knew from the first she resented them. Now, only a thin shell of politeness shields me and them from her criticism. I bear it as long as I can before I pretend a headache and say I must rest. Then for a few hours I am free of both Hester and Amos.

I remember well the days of which she had written. Thank God Mother's illness had succeeded in sheltering her from the deacon, though at no small price for Clarissa and me. How we had worried, fearing we were about to lose our mother to the fever. Had we known the true cause, perhaps we would have worried less, though now that I knew the truth about Amos Mickelson, perhaps we would have worried all the more. Shivering, I drew my chair to the fire and turned my attention back to her writings.

October 10, 1852

Summer is gone and my health is still not recovered. Both malaise and headaches linger, as do the palpitations, though they come less often now. I find I do not regret the loss of my health as much as I expected, but I do miss my visits with Susannah. She was the dearest friend and my one regret at my change in circumstance. Considering what might have happened, I try not to count the price I pay for a home and fire and two lovely daughters with whom I share it. All is as it used to be, Deacon Mickelson once again our jovial benefactor. No hint of what he once felt or desired shows. It's as if my illness has wiped all beauty and allure from my person. Sometimes I examine my reflection in the mirror and wonder if my looks and vitality are no more. 'Tis true my face is pale and thin, my hair is less thick and lustrous, but no matter. I am content to spend my days with my books and leave Clarissa to make music, Tamsin to cook and mother. My health has never been strong, but now 'tis a ruse I deploy, like Napoleon or Julius Caesar. Instead of strength, I use weakness, and with that weakness I have unmanned my foe.

I closed my eyes, wincing at the pretense her words exposed, though it was not all pretense. I had felt the heat of her fever, seen her cracked lips, heard her whimpers of pain. Only the lack of full recovery had been pretense. Its cause I understood. But it did not explain why Mother had failed to give Clarissa's letter to me.

The next entry was dated three years after the deacon's unwanted advances. The month Clarissa ran away.

May 14, 1855

I am in a state of shock and great anguish. Clarissa has eloped with Jacob Mueller. I hold her letter in my hand, addressed to Tamsin, not me, though thank God I discovered it before Tamsin did. It would not do for her to know the true reason for her sister's leaving. Better that Tamsin think perfidy on Clarissa's part than know of Amos Mickelson's true character. 'Tis cruel, I know. Am I an unnatural mother to wish such pain on my daughter? Sweet Tamsin is all I have left. But if she is told the truth about the deacon, who knows of the repercussions? She might accuse him to his face or tell others to save pride, for they whisper cruel things about Tamsin, snicker at her loss of Jacob. If Amos's philandering is made known, he will make good his threat and brand us all as loose women who must be turned out of the village. Deacon Mickelson wields great power. Our word would stand as nothing against his.

There, I have written it—thoughts that rob me of sleep, my fear of losing our home and its small comforts. Tamsin must not know why Clarissa left. It is for her own good. She would not wish us to lose our home. Even as I write this, I know I speak untrue. 'Tis I who am terrified of the loss. I am as wicked and selfish as the man I loathe. I do not want the truth let out because it might take away my selfish comforts. I protect a man who tried to force himself upon both me and my sweet daughter. I cover his lust because I am too weak to stand against him. I once boasted that my weakness had unmanned my foe. I took pride in what I had accomplished with my invalidism. Now I see it was but paltry nonsense and that by silence I have brought near harm to my daughter and have not lessened Amos Mickelson's wickedness one whit. Dear God, why can't I be strong?

I was shaking—my legs, my hands, even my lips trembled as if I had a case of ague. The pain of the days after Clarissa left returned as if it had just happened. The passage of the years seemed as naught. Running through it like a burning brand was the fresh pain of learning that Mother had known the truth and had kept silent. She'd let me suffer and think the worst of myself as well as my sister.

August 23, 1855
Three months have passed since Clarissa ran away. I continue to sit and do nothing, watching dear Tamsin move from room to room, a mere shadow of herself. Both of us watch and wait for a letter from Clarissa which does not come. I do not sleep well, neither do I have appetite for food or the comforts for which I paid such a price. My soft mattress and sugar and cream with my tea have lost their savor. I am weighted down with guilt and

remorse. I should have warned my daughters about Amos. I should not have stayed in the cottage. Why didn't I take refuge with Susannah? Her husband and sons would have protected us. Susannah has come several times to see me. I waver, wanting to see her dear face again. Then I remember Amos's threat and know I must refuse her kindness and send her away.

This morning I tried to gather courage and tell Tamsin what happened. In the end I failed. I am too weak, not just in body, but in character too. Knowing all I have done and not done makes me want to cry each time I look at her. The light has gone from her eyes, her face is wooden, her hair dull and untidy. She's turned into a woman who does not care, a woman without hope, seldom speaking and never smiling. Dear God, what have I done to my cherished daughter?

I spend many hours reading my Bible, hoping to find a measure of peace and a release from my guilt. Selfish. Selfish. I write the words that are seared into my heart. Had I not been so fearful and selfish none of this would have happened. If only I had . . .

Unable to bear more, I closed Mother's book. Her pain was my pain. Her guilt too, for which of us has not done something we later regret? Weak. Foolish. Ellen Yeager was both. But she had loved me. Loved Clarissa too. I knew that just as I knew Mother had muddled along as best she could. She was a woman thrown loose on a world she wasn't equipped to fathom or understand. Father had protected and cosseted her, as had her parents. Soft and feminine, her books, music, a loving husband and children were all she desired. And her comforts, as she had called them. I must not forget her comforts. But could I fault her for them?

Love would not allow me to, neither would it let me harbor bitterness. At last I understood her sickness and demands. Ellen Yeager had been consumed with guilt and regret, a mother who believed she had failed her children. Such emotions do not make one happy. Small wonder Mother had been unpleasant and that her courage had failed her. As for Clarissa—

I picked up her letter and read it again, the tears in her name cutting at my heart. "You're forgiven," I whispered. "I know you wouldn't have gone with Jacob if there had been any other way. Besides, I've found someone better than Jacob." I smiled as I spoke, but my mind lingered on my sister. "Where are you, Clarrie? Why didn't you write like you promised?"

Comprehension came. "Deacon Mickelson," I breathed. "He took her letters . . . kept them." I recalled his offers to fetch our mail from the village, his jovial face smiling as he spoke. A false smile, I knew now, just as I knew he had feared what Clarissa might tell us, and fearing it, had intercepted the letters. What had poor Clarissa thought when she received no answer? That we hadn't forgiven her? That she was no longer sister and daughter? I must find her. It would be hard, but I must find her, I determined.

Carrying this thought with me, I took my nightgown from the peg behind the door and undressed. For the first time in many years, I knelt and said a prayer for Clarissa. "Please God, let her know that she's forgiven. And help me to find her," I prayed. With that done, I climbed into bed and pulled the heavy quilts around me. Not once did I think of Caleb Tremayne or what he might be doing in Boston on that cold February night.

CHAPTER 12

I was not myself for several days. My mind was too filled with Mother's writings to have room for much else. Poor Mother. How her heart must have lurched each time Amos knocked on our door. Innocent of the wiles of men, I had never once suspected.

If only I'd known. Each time the thought formed, it was closely followed by another. What would I have done? What could I have done? Very little. Deacon Mickelson's power was too large, his reputation for goodness too deeply ingrained. The only recourse was flight. As Clarissa had done. As I had been forced to do later.

These thoughts followed me down from my bedroom and into the kitchen. "Where are you, Clarrie?" My question swirled around the stove and Ol' Cat's ears twitched as she napped by the fire. Where had they gone? Missouri? California? "I must find her."

"What's that you say, miss?"

I looked up and saw Sally standing in the doorway. "I . . . I was talking to myself."

"Yes'm." Sally regarded me for a moment before her eyes shifted to the empty bowl on the table. *Why isn't the bread mixed down? How come the fire needs tending?* her look implied. A frown crossed her narrow features. "Are you all right?"

I gave a bright smile. "I'm fine."

"You don't act fine," Sally countered. Her hand sought a lock of her lank brown hair and began to wind it around her finger. "Me and Mary been talkin' about you. We're worried."

"There's no need to be." I opened the metal-lined flour bin under the cupboard and ladled flour into the bowl.

"Mary thinks maybe you're pining for Master Caleb."

"What?" I stared at Sally and forgot about the flour.

"That's what she said."

"Well . . . she's wrong."

Instead of answering, Sally left the room.

"She's wrong," I called. Hearing no reply, I dropped the scoop and hurried after her, entering the sitting room close on Sally's heels. "What's this you've been gossiping about?" I demanded.

Mary looked up from her knitting. "Gossiping?"

"Sally said you think I'm pining over Master Tremayne."

Mary shot a glance at Sally. "You know how Sally mixes things up."

"I don't think she got anything mixed up."

Mary continued to slip the brown yarn over her needles, and Sally had wound her hair so tightly around her finger I feared she'd pull it out.

"Well?" I prompted, aware I was tapping my foot as Mother had done when Clarissa and I misbehaved.

Mary sighed and set down her knitting. "We've been worried. You've hardly smiled or spoken the past few days. What's wrong?"

I had it in mind to tell her the only thing wrong was her thinking. Me pining for Master Tremayne—the very idea! But when I looked into Mary's face and saw Sally move closer, my throat tightened and my lips began to tremble. "Oh, Mary." My eyes filled with tears and I groped for my chair.

Mary laid a hand on mine and Sally's arm went around my shoulder. Taking a deep breath, I told them—about Clarissa's letter and Mother's journal, about Amos Mickelson. Pain and the terrible years of thinking I'd been betrayed by my sister mingled with my tears.

"I'm sorry . . . so very sorry." Mary took both of my hands in hers, patting them, stroking. "No wonder you've been so quiet."

"If only I'd known about Deacon Mickelson sooner . . . what Mother and Clarissa went through."

"But you didn't. I'm sure your poor mother did what she thought was best. That's all the good Lord expects of any of us."

"I know." I wiped tears on my apron. "But if I'd known, we could have borne it together. Things aren't as bad when you share them."

"Like we're doing now," Sally said. Her arm tightened on my

shoulder and I saw traces of tears in her eyes.

None of us could speak. The clock's soft ticking and the hiss of the fire filled the silence. For the first time in days I felt at peace. A heavy burden had been lifted from my shoulders.

"I'm going to try to find Clarrie," I told them that evening. By then I was in better spirits, my wet, crumpled apron replaced with a clean one. Fresh-baked sponge cake and hot tea awaited us.

"I thought you might." Mary stretched her feet toward the fire. "Where will you begin?"

"At the post office in Mickelboro. I'm sure Clarissa wrote to us. She always kept her promises."

"What about that man . . . that Amos feller?" Sally asked.

I poured tea into a cup. "I hope to do it without him knowing, though it will be difficult since the post office is in his store."

Mary grimaced. "Sounds like he owns the whole town . . . like as not the church too, him being a deacon and all."

"You've got to do it," Sally insisted. "Clarrie needs to know you don't hold it against her for running off with Jacob."

We spent the evening discussing ways for me to return to Mickelboro and talk to the postmistress. For a time we played with the idea of asking Abigail to go with me, the two of us traveling there in her buggy. But I didn't like the idea of putting Abby at risk.

"What if that Amos feller sees you?" Sally kept asking. The more we talked, the more agitated she became. Hoping to put her mind at ease, I suggested disguising myself as an old woman or even as a man.

Mary shook her head. "It won't do. None of this will do. There's too much chance of the deacon seeing you and trying to . . ." She left what he might do unspoken. Stifling a yawn, she added, "The best thing to do is sleep on it and pray about it. In a matter as important as this, you should make the Lord your partner."

———•———

A fortnight later, I stepped down from a hired buggy in front of Amos Mickelson's store. Caleb Tremayne's hand reached out to steady me, his blue eyes meeting mine for a second; questioning, dark brows raised. How I'd come to be here with Caleb still seemed like a dream, one I half expected to wake up from at any minute.

It was mostly Mary's doing, though Sally also played a part in it. The two of them conspired behind my back and enlisted Caleb to my cause within hours of his return from Boston. While I'd busied myself preparing his favorite dinner, they'd filled his ears with all that had happened and of my resolve to return to Mickelboro.

I didn't once suspect. I attributed Caleb's thoughtful expression during dinner to his business with his uncle, the frequency with which his eyes met mine to our encounter the night before he left. Later, when Caleb announced his intention to accompany me to Mickelboro, I could only stare with my mouth slightly agape. For a second I didn't comprehend that Mary had told him of my intention.

"Mary . . ." I turned on her in indignation.

She met my gaze with steady gray eyes. "Going alone is too risky. I've been praying about it, not knowing what to do. Then when I saw Master Tremayne, it came to me, like the circle of warmth I get when I sing a hymn. Master Tremayne must go with you and keep you safe."

"But . . ." I turned to Caleb and found him looking at me in that steady way he had, one that seemed to see to the bottom of my soul.

"She did right. Going alone is too risky. With me there . . ." Caleb's mouth tightened into a stubborn line and recklessness shone in his eyes. "I'm looking forward to meeting Mr. Mickelson . . . a deacon in his church, Mary tells me. It's time someone put him in his place. There are a few things I need to take care of here, but after that . . ."

"After that" proved to be a week. We traveled by rail car from Bayberry to Scobeyville, then hired a carriage, arriving at Mickelboro late on a blustery March afternoon. Mary had insisted on accompanying us, pointing out that it wouldn't be right for me to travel alone with a gentleman. Of course, Sally couldn't be left alone, so she came too.

I tried to see the village through their eyes, noting how Amos Mickelson's two-story store dominated the few shops that lined the street. The white church where we'd worshiped each Sunday was nestled behind a row of bare-branched trees.

"Are you all right?" Caleb asked as he helped me from the buggy.

I nodded even as my chest tightened. Now that I was finally there, the palms of my gloved hands went damp and my heart jumped and made it difficult to breathe. In my mind I saw Amos looking down at me from his buggy, his eyes greedy with desire. My ears heard the anger in his voice and the crash of the potted geraniums the night he'd broken into the cottage.

I closed my eyes to ward off memories. As I did, Caleb took my hand and placed it on his arm. The gesture steadied me and brought me back to the man standing firm and tall by my side, a man who looked ready to take on anything or anyone, not the least of which was Deacon Mickelson.

It's strange how these moments come, ones when you know something for a certainty, when things you've wondered about all of your life are suddenly clear. That's how love came to me—knowing that I loved Caleb. Not when I was consciously thinking about him or lying soft and dreamy in my bed. It happened as we stood in the dusty street beside Mickelson's Mercantile. The ribbons from my bonnet fluttered in the wind, and Caleb looked down at me with a look in his blue eyes that sent shivers through me. I wanted to hold the moment close, cling to it—his gaze filled with caring, my hand resting on his arm. This was what I wanted for the rest of my life—to have him at my side, to be able to touch him, to have his love and protection. I wanted this, even more than I wanted to find Clarissa.

I did not plan to stay long in Amos Mickelson's store. I intended to walk briskly past the well-stocked shelves of crockery, ladies' bonnets, spools of ribbon, and tins of beef to the small alcove at the back that served as the post office. We'd scarcely walked through the door when I heard a gasp. As my eyes adjusted from sunshine to dimness I saw old Mrs. Haines staring at me, one hand to her bosom, the other grasping a packet of pins.

"My laws, it's Tamsin, Ellen Yeager's girl."

I gave the elderly woman a stiff smile, aware that Phoebe Steadman was peering around a display of calico. Both women were friends of Hester Mickelson's and had often been cool to Mother. Let them gawk, I thought, aware of the fine figure Caleb cut. His iron-gray waistcoat and black trousers bore the mark of a tailor, his height and confidence proclaimed his breeding. Compared to him, Jacob Mueller was small potatoes and well I knew it.

With Caleb at my side and my friends following, I was able to quell feelings that in the past had kept my eyes fastened on my feet. Not wanting to see the pitying glances or hear the whispers after Clarissa eloped with Jacob, I'd pretended blindness and deafness on the few occasions I'd ventured into the village. Each outing drove me further into myself, into misery. In time I ceased to go there. Instead, I relied on Betsy to bring us the few things we needed.

Today, resolution and my friends brought firmness to my steps, kept my eyes straight ahead. We passed a row of tinware, my attention centered on the caged half-door where Lucy Oglethorpe dispensed letters and packages to the villagers. Overshadowing my newfound confidence was the fear that Deacon Mickelson would suddenly appear, that there would be a scene, perhaps even an altercation. I did not forget that Caleb Tremayne possessed a temper and that of late he seemed bent on being my protector.

Lucy Oglethorpe watched our progress from behind the bars of the post office, her small mouth pursed into an *O*, her gaze darting over the four of us. "Tamsin," she said. "We thought you'd left these parts and gone west . . . at least that's what Mistress Mickelson said."

"She was wrong." I tried to control the tremor running through my words. Although Lucy had always been pleasant to us, I knew she was clearly in Amos's pocket. Her position as postmistress made her dependent upon his goodwill. I licked my lips and attempted a smile. "Do you happen to have any letters for me or my mother?"

Lucy shook her head as she glanced at the cubicles lining her office. "Ain't nothing come for you or your ma in a long time. Not since she died and you left, in fact, though you folks was never ones to get much mail. Just those few letters from out in Utah Territory."

I'd been right. There had been letters, letters the deacon had intercepted. "My sisters Mary Ellen and Harriet."

"And then there was those that come from Clarissa."

My heart jumped and I felt Caleb stiffen. Caution warned me to choose my words with care, but the need to know forced the question before I had time to think. "Do you remember where they came from . . . the ones from Clarissa?"

"Why, no. 'Twern't nothin' on them but your name and hers smaller up in the corner . . . Mrs. Jacob Mueller." A frown puckered her features. "How come you're asking me where they came from? Didn't you read them?"

"I never got the letters."

"Never got? . . ." Lucy's frown deepened. "I gave them to the deacon. I recall plain as day how he said you and your ma was feeling poorly and that she'd asked him to pick up your mail. He asked every week, but then everyone knows how good he was to help your family."

"Mother and I never got Clarissa's letters."

Silence followed my words. After a few seconds Lucy found her tongue. "Are you sure? I mean, maybe you got them and forgot. I've done that, been so caught up in something I forgot what I was doing." She glanced nervously past my shoulder.

I expected to see Amos when I turned. Only the two old ladies hovered by the tinware, their ears alert to every word we exchanged.

"Where can we find Deacon Mickelson?" Caleb asked. Authority edged his voice. Anger too.

"He . . . he went home to eat. Left just before you got here."

"Thank you." Caleb nodded to her and with gentle pressure on my elbow steered me from the alcove and back through the store. Mary and Sally followed; Mary's loud breathing the only sound to mark our departure.

"Aren't you going to introduce us to these people?" Mrs. Haines asked.

"We're Miss Yeager's friends," Caleb answered.

"Good friends," Mary wheezed.

"Like family," Sally added. I'd never heard that proud tone in her voice before, as if she dared Mrs. Haines to say otherwise.

When we'd gained the outside of the store, Caleb paused to look at a poster tacked to the storefront. I stepped closer to read it as well.

$200 REWARD

RUNAWAY FROM THE SUBSCRIBER, A BLACK MALE SLAVE NAMED HENRY MILLER, ABOUT TWENTY-ONE YEARS OF AGE, FIVE FEET TEN OR ELEVEN INCHES HIGH. LONG SCAR ON LEFT

FOREARM, RATHER THICK LIPS, POLITE WHEN
SPOKEN TO AND VERY GENTEEL IN PERSON. AS
HE HAS ABSCONDED WITHOUT PROVOCATION,
IT IS ASSUMED HE WILL MAKE FOR PENNSYLVANIA
OR NEW YORK. I WILL GIVE $100 IF TAKEN IN THE
STATE OF MARYLAND, OR THE ABOVE REWARD IF
TAKEN ANYWHERE NORTH OF THAT STATE AND
SECURED SO I CAN GET HIM AGAIN, OR I WILL PAY
ALL REASONABLE EXPENSES IF BROUGHT HOME
TO THE SUBSCRIBER WHO LIVES IN THE NORTH
END OF THE CITY OF WASHINGTON.
                    THOS. C SCOTT

Scrawled across the bottom in equally large letters was the added message:

IF THIS SLAVE IS SEEN OR IF YOU HAVE ANY
INFORMATION CONCERNING HIS WHERE-
ABOUTS, CONTACT AMOS F. MICKELSON,
COMMISSIONER FOR THE FEDERAL COURT OF
THIS DISTRICT.

I stared at Amos's name. It and the poster went together, Amos's greedy hands reaching for the ten-dollar fee paid for each reclaimed fugitive. Had it always been thus? The posters and Amos acting as commissioner of the court? I searched my mind, but realized that because of my isolation from Mickelboro society, I couldn't rightly say.

Sally pressed against my side, her face screwed up as she tried to decipher the words on the poster.

"Two hundred dollars," she began.

"Two hundred dollars for what?" Mary interrupted.

"For a runaway slave." I didn't want to look at the poster.

Caleb's hand tightened on my elbow. His features were tight too, as if Henry Miller were someone he counted as his friend. "Read it to them. It's something they need to hear."

So I read it, my voice trembling as I did.

"Dear heaven," Mary whispered.

"'Tain't right," Sally said. "And that Amos feller . . ." She took my hand and squeezed it. "He's a bad 'un."

"Yes, he is," I agreed.

We made our way to the buggy without speaking. Caleb didn't remain silent for long. As soon as we were settled, he turned to me. "Where does Amos Mickelson live?"

"On a farm just south of town. But do you think we? . . ."

"I do," Caleb answered, seeming to know in which direction my mind had flown. "It's time Amos Mickelson accounts for his actions instead of pretending he's king of the county. Commissioner of the court." This last was said with disgust, as though Caleb were describing a pile of warm horse manure.

I don't remember how we got to the Mickelson farm, only my nervousness and the growing fear that we were riding straight into trouble. Although I didn't doubt Caleb's ability to protect me, I was aware he was at a disadvantage. There were no influential friends or uncle in Mickelboro, no lifetime neighbors or loyal farmers as there were in Glen Oaks. Here, Amos Mickelson held all the advantages.

Caleb's voice jerked me away from worry. "Is that where you lived?"

I looked across a newly plowed field to the white clapboard cottage, a border of yellow daffodils dancing in the March wind, the apple trees not yet leafed out. Emotion closed my throat. "Yes."

"I think we should stop and look for the letters." Seeing my questioning glance, he added, "In case Deacon Mickelson gave them to your mother."

"He didn't." My tone was emphatic.

"You never know."

I could tell Caleb's mind was made up.

"We got to do everything we can to find Clarrie," Sally said.

Caleb turned the buggy onto the lane to the cottage. I held onto the edge of my seat as we bounced over the uneven ground. A tin laundry tub leaned against a stump, and the clothesline strung between two trees hung limp as a becalmed sail. It and the listing wooden cover over the well gave an aura of neglect and abandonment.

"The cottage might be locked," I told Caleb as he helped me down from the buggy. "Though perhaps not. I can't remember what I did that night . . . only the need to escape."

"If it's locked I'll find a way to get in." Caleb leaned his weight against the locked back door and used his broad shoulder like a battering ram—twice, three times—until with a splinter of lock from hasp it flew open.

The kitchen was just as I had left it. Curtains at the window, blue-patterned cups and plates on the shelves, the table and three chairs. One of the chairs was tipped onto its side among the litter from the smashed geranium pot. Dust was everywhere. Cobwebs too. I wrinkled my nose at a stagnant smell that permeated the air—one of spoiled food and a room closed up too tightly and for too long.

"Careful," Caleb cautioned as I stepped around pieces of broken pottery. Mary and Sally followed, Mary shaking her head.

"Amos was angry when he couldn't find me," I explained.

I led the way to the parlor and stopped as my hand flew to my mouth. It looked as if a storm had raged through the room, throwing everything helter-skelter—crashing, breaking. Books and broken glass littered the floor and Mother's cherished deal table was upended, its legs missing or broken, as were those of the chairs. I cried out when I saw the pianoforte. Someone had taken an ax to it, chopping until the top had fallen in, the ivory keys twisted and scattered.

"Merciful heaven," Mary whispered.

Too stunned to speak, I moved trancelike through the litter. I bent to pick up a crystal candle holder which had somehow survived the onslaught, reached for a crumpled doily, then for a book with its back splayed open. A tiny sound escaped my lips when I saw my parents' portrait. It had been pulled from the wall and the beloved faces slashed until they were no longer recognizable. I gathered it to me and leaned my face against the frame Father had carved.

"Who? . . ."

"Mother and Father," I whispered.

"No . . . who done it?" Sally asked.

I shook my head, tears pooled in my eyes and my throat too tight to speak. Caleb's arm went around my shoulder, his touch bringing warmth and comfort. "I'm here," he said, just as Papa had done when I cried.

"Dirty booger . . . mean ol' dirty booger," Sally said.

"Sally!" Mary's voice was too weak to be indignant.

"Well, he is. Look what he done to Miss Yeager's home and her ma's pretty things."

Mary didn't seem to know what to say, the loud rasp of her breathing taking the place of words.

"It was the deacon, wasn't it?" Sally went on. "Ain't no one else would do it. Mean ol' booger."

I struggled for composure and nodded to Caleb when he asked if I was all right. When he left me to move around the room, it felt as if a warm cloak had been stripped away. He poked at the debris with the toe of his boot and bent to look more closely at one of Mother's books. Although I knew he looked for the letters, I could feel his anger pulsing like hot air ready to explode in a summer thunderstorm.

"Wait until I get my hands on the man!" The rage in Caleb's voice vibrated through the parlor. He'd moved to the bedroom, his tall frame filling the doorway.

"Has he been there too?" I asked as I picked my way through the litter of broken furniture to join him.

Like the parlor, the room was in shambles. Feathers covered the floor, the mattress ripped and flung over a bedpost, the armoire toppled onto its side. Bits of glass from the broken mirror mingled with feathers, and a hodgepodge of clothes spilled from the armoire.

"What if he'd done this the night I hid under the bed?" I whispered. "Took his ax to it . . . to me?"

"Let's go." Caleb's voice was harsh, his fingers tight as they closed around my arm and propelled me through the parlor and on to the kitchen. I had no chance to protest, though if the truth were known I was as anxious as he was to be quit of the place. Mary and Sally followed us, the sound of Mary's breathing and her ponderous progress amplified by the stillness.

"Wait!" Sally cried and ran back into the cottage.

Mary shrugged when I looked at her and Caleb acted as if he hadn't heard. He helped us onto the back seat before he unwound the reins, his movements impatient, as if he couldn't wait to be off. Luckily Sally wasn't long, not more than a couple of minutes. When she returned her brown skirt was gathered up into a basket.

"Here," she said, squeezing onto the seat. "You can't go without something to remember your ma and Clarrie by." While Caleb maneuvered the buggy around the well, she opened her skirt to reveal its treasures—the crystal candleholder and doily, several books, Mother's blue paisley shawl, some keys from the pianoforte. "I thought you'd like 'em."

"Oh, Sally." I touched the doily and the books, remembering how the parlor used to be. I hardly noticed when Caleb snapped the reins and we started up the lane.

"It's all right, my dear," Mary said. I thought she was excusing Sally for running back. Then I became aware of the tears running down my cheeks and knew she spoke to me.

"I know." I took a quivering breath and tried to smile. "Thank you, Sweet Sally."

Sally nodded, her pleasure in having done the right thing shining bright as stars on a clear summer night.

I doubt Caleb was even aware of what Sally had done. It was as though he'd gone someplace else—a place of dark thoughts and anger, one so deep and closed it had no room for anyone else.

All too soon we were there. The two-storied house stood tall and dignified like Deacon Mickelson when he walked down the aisle of the church. My pleasure in Sally's gift fled, replaced by fear. Anger too, when I thought of what Amos had done to the cottage.

We walked up the path to the white-columned porch of the house. Caleb lifted the brass knocker on the front door.

Betsy's surprise when she saw me was evident. Gladness showed on her poor, scarred face, twisting into the grimace that passed as her smile. "Tamsin . . ." Her voice came in a squeak. Embarrassed, she put a hand to her mouth. "We thought you'd left these parts. That's what the master said." She leaned close and whispered, "I was scared somethin' bad had happened to you."

"I'm doing very well. I've found a good position. Good friends too. And you?"

"Fine." Her gaze, bright with curiosity, went to the others.

"Is Deacon Mickelson in?" Caleb asked.

"Yes, sir. He just come home to eat. Him and the missus should be sitting down most any time."

"Would you tell him he has company . . . company that can't wait."

Betsy dropped a curtsy and hurried away. No one spoke while we waited, though Sally was busy taking in the polished oak floor of the entry and a large gilt-edged mirror that dominated one wall. How well I remembered it and the times Clarissa and I waited there while Betsy carried a message from Mother to one of the Mickelsons.

I took a deep breath and tried to be calm, but when I heard his heavy footsteps fear returned. His bulk seemed to take up the space in the entry, and his smile was forced as his gaze traveled from me to Caleb.

"Miss Yeager." The way he said my name made it both a question and a statement.

I nodded, unsure of what to say.

"Miss Yeager has come to get some letters . . . ones from her sister she never received."

"Letters?" One of Amos's pudgy hands tightened.

"We've just come from the post office. Mrs. Ogelthorpe said she gave them to you. I believe you told her you would deliver them to the Yeagers. Since they never received them . . ." Caleb paused and gave Amos a long, steady look. "We'd like her letters."

"Since I no longer have them, I can't help you." Amos's smile was more confident, stretching the fatty contours of his face. "I gave them to Tamsin's mother." His gaze shifted to me, his small blue eyes daring me to say otherwise. "Didn't she give them to you?"

"No." Even with Caleb by my side, I felt myself tremble.

"You never delivered the letters," Caleb said. "You kept them because they revealed your improper conduct with her sister."

Amos snorted as if Caleb had made a bad joke. I heard a small sound from the direction of the parlor and knew Hester was listening.

"Tamsin has long had a reputation for being a little strange," Amos said. "She hasn't been the same since her sister ran off with Jacob Mueller. Then after her mother died . . ." He spread his hands and sighed. "Some think Tamsin's mind came unhinged."

I stiffened and wanted to pummel him with my fists. Before I could do so, Caleb's arm went around my waist. "That's a lie."

Amos acted as if he hadn't heard. "A tragedy, for Tamsin was always such a bright girl. My wife and I tried to help her, but she wouldn't let us . . . ran off without so much as a by-your-leave." Amos fixed his gaze on me, his demeanor taking on the look he gave Mother when she'd displeased him. "That was hardly the thing to do, especially after all we did for you and your family."

"All you did for my family was cheat us out of the farm and act as if the money you doled out to Mother was yours." The words I flung at him were hard and cold and no longer afraid. "As for leaving . . ." I paused and looked him square in the face. "You know why I left. After you broke into the cottage to try to get your hands on me, how could I stay?"

Little beads of sweat appeared on Amos's forehead and bald head. "Broke into your cottage . . . that's preposterous."

"I don't think so." Caleb's voice was cold and hard like mine. "The night you broke in wasn't the first time you went there uninvited. We know what you tried to do to her mother and sister."

"I didn't do anything to her mother or sister."

"Only because her mother became ill and Clarissa ran away."

"Lies . . . all of it."

"I don't think so."

The two men eyed each other, their faces tight and angry. I half expected Amos to strike Caleb, or failing that, to order us out of his home. Before he could do either, Caleb went on.

"We would also like an explanation of what happened to her mother's furniture. We've just come from the cottage and found it all destroyed . . . hacked to pieces like some crazed monster had gone through the place."

"I don't know anything about it."

"I think you do. A man such as you wouldn't let his property lie vacant without checking on it from time to time."

"Well, I have checked it, of course, but I don't know who ruined it. Ruffians, most likely. We've had problems with vagrants."

"And they just happened to stop there and decided it would be amusing to break the furniture?" Caleb's voice held derision.

"Listen, you . . ." Amos shook a pudgy finger in Caleb's face. "I don't have to stand here and answer your questions. I don't have to listen to you or her, either. I've had enough of this nonsense. Stealing letters . . . destroying furniture. Do you have any idea who you're talking to?"

"Deacon Mickelson, I think you're called . . . a self-righteous man who goes to church every Sunday and takes his pleasure on defenseless women during the week."

Amos's barrel chest rose in indignation. "Get out of my house!"

Caleb didn't flinch or look the least afraid. "We'll be back," he promised. "I'm not stopping until I find out exactly what happened."

"You don't scare me." Amos's face showed otherwise. "She's got you duped, just like her mother duped me. Whores, both of them. Liars too."

The crack of Caleb's fist against Amos's jaw filled the room. Amos dropped like an apple flung from a tree and sprawled across the floor, his eyes registering surprise before his head lolled to one side.

"Let's go," Caleb said.

Amos's fleshy face had gone slack and one arm was splayed to his side. It took me a second to tear my eyes from him.

Caleb reached for Mary's arm. "Come."

I took Mary's other arm and we helped her out the door and across the porch. Sally followed us, her sallow face anxious.

"Heavens . . . merciful heaven," Mary gasped.

I tried to hurry, but Caleb sauntered along as if he were out for a Sunday stroll. I snatched a quick glance at Sally, then back at the house, expecting to see Amos coming after us with a gun.

"Hurry . . . please, hurry," I cried.

Caleb quirked his brows at me as we boosted Mary into the back seat of the buggy. "There's no need to be afraid."

"Amos will come after us. I know he will."

"Why would he do that? The deacon doesn't want us around to spread the truth about him."

"You don't know him like I do. He'll never forgive you . . . insulting him and knocking him down. I doubt anyone's ever challenged him before."

"Then it's high time they did."

"But he might come after you . . . after me."

"I'm not afraid of him. You shouldn't be, either. I'm here. Don't you understand?" Caleb's fingers closed around my arm and his eyes looked deeply into mine. "I'm here," he repeated. "So are Mary and Sally. You aren't alone anymore, Tamsin."

I stared up at him for a long moment. "I know . . ." All I heard was *Tamsin*. He'd called me Tamsin.

Caleb continued to look down at me, lending me strength as the corners of his mouth deepened. "But if it will ease your fears, I'll hurry."

Caleb slapped the horses with the reins, his beaver hat set at a jaunty angle. "You'll have to show me the best way out of here."

My fear began to dissipate as we pulled away. "Turn right at the next bend. It's more trail than road, but Clarrie and I sometimes used it with the cart. It cuts into the main road to Scobeyville."

Before I knew it we were bumping over the track where Amos had intercepted me on the day it rained. The grass of the meadow was still winter brown and the firs stood like green sentinels on the bluff. I glanced at Caleb, and wondered if he recognized it and remembered launching the boat from the cove. Then I looked back at Mary and Sally. Had I been in a mood to laugh, I would have done so. The two of them held onto their seat as if their lives depended on it, the ribbons from Mary's bonnet flapping in her face and Sally bouncing around like a sack of potatoes.

Caleb kept his eyes on the track, though occasionally he glanced at me. Twice he took a deep breath, like he wanted to say something. "I'm sorry," he said finally. His look was contrite. "I should have held on to my temper and left without hitting the hypocrite. But when he called you and your mother . . . what he did . . . I lost control."

"If you hadn't hit him, I would have," Mary declared.

The three of us burst out laughing—Caleb's rich and full bodied, Sally's high, as if she verged on hysteria. The laughter did us good, scouring out the fear and serving as a goad to confidence.

"We'll be fine," Caleb assured us. He took my gloved hand and held it as though it was something he wanted to keep forever.

I looked up at him and almost forgot where I was. I think Caleb did too, his eyes turning tender. "We'll be fine," he repeated.

Happiness and something wonderful and intangible washed over me—love mixed with soaring elation when I realized Caleb had said, "we."

CHAPTER 13

We reached home the next afternoon, taking the train from Scobeyville to Bayberry, then retrieving Caleb's carriage from the livery stable for the trip back to Glen Oaks. Caleb drove the team while we rode inside with a wool blanket spread over our knees. My disappointment at not finding Clarissa's letters was swallowed up in the memory of Caleb's fingers holding my hand, his use of the word *we*. Although I might be unsure of myself with men, I didn't think I'd misread the look on his face or the softness in his eyes.

Sally's voice jarred me away from thoughts of Caleb. "I wish we could've found those letters," she sighed. "I'm beginning to doubt Miss Yeager's ever gonna find her sister."

"You mustn't think that." Mary sat with eyes closed, her head jarring from side to side when the wheels went over a bump. "Now's the time to show faith." A smile touched her lips. "Didn't God prompt me to ask Mr. Tremayne for help?"

Sally and I nodded.

"And didn't He help us?"

"Yes." This from Sally.

Mary's eyes opened and fastened on me. "Well, didn't He?"

"Yes, though we don't have the letters or know where she is."

"You'll find her. I've been praying about it all morning."

"And?"

"It's time to trust in the Lord. To pray. Not just me, but you and Sally." Mary straightened and took my hand. "Trust Him, Tamsin. If you'll turn to God, He'll show you the way to find Clarissa."

As I looked at the light in Mary's tired gray eyes, I knew she believed every word she spoke. I wanted to believe too. I truly did.

"Trust him, Tamsin."

"I'll try."

Mary smiled and patted my hand. "Good."

For her the matter was settled, but it didn't come as easily for me. I had too much of my father's skepticism, too little of my older sisters' faith.

Caleb jumped down to help us from the carriage when we reached home. He took special care with Mary, who looked ready to collapse, then swung Sally to the ground beside her. He took his time with me, acting as though I were a fragile piece of fine china. His gloved hand grasped my elbow and his eyes looked steadily into mine—asking questions without him speaking and me not knowing how to answer except with a smile.

Sally and I didn't waste any time getting Mary into bed. This was no small task what with her bulk and removing shoes and stockings from swollen legs and feet. Mary was close to tears by the time we finished.

"I'm sorry," I lamented.

"For what?" Mary asked.

"Your pain. I shouldn't have let you come."

Mary's smile warred with a grimace of discomfort. "Small chance you'd have had at stopping me," she wheezed. "I wouldn't have missed it for the world . . . seeing Mr. Tremayne knock the deacon to the floor. Haven't had so much excitement in a long while, though I'll admit a time or two I was scared." Mary smiled and closed her eyes. "Can you imagine the tale we'd have to tell if we'd been chased out of town?"

"We almost was," Sally said. "I thought sure he was comin' after us."

"But he didn't." I met Sally's eyes as we smoothed the covers. "With Mr. Tremayne here we don't have to worry. We're safe."

Sally nodded. "Master Caleb's good at keepin' people safe."

My mind remained on Caleb as I made my way downstairs. I wanted to thank him for all he'd done. I'd tried, but each time I began, something got in the way—railroad schedules or the clamor of crowds.

Caleb's words at the railroad station came back to me. "I don't want you to ever worry about that man again."

Since then, I'd ceased to worry. Home. Just saying the word brought pleasure, aided by the memory of Caleb taking my hand, the crack of his fist against Amos's jaw. As soon as supper was over and Sally had joined Mary in their bedroom, I went down to the study.

My knock was soft and when Caleb didn't answer I raised my hand again. As I did, the door opened and Caleb's tall frame filled the doorway.

"Tamsin . . ." The gladness in his voice made my heart quicken. A slow smile lifted the corners of his mouth. "I was about to come looking for you." He stepped aside, pulling out a chair for me, then going to stand by the fire. He'd loosened the top button on his shirt and his white neck cloth lay on the desk. His dark hair was rumpled as if he'd been running his fingers through it. "What can I do for you?"

"I wanted to thank you for what you did . . . taking me to Mickelboro, standing up for me against Deacon Mickelson. It was good of you and greatly appreciated."

"Albeit unsuccessful," Caleb added.

"It *was* successful. I know now that my sister wrote to me. Perhaps in time she'll write again."

"There shouldn't have to be a next time. When I think how that man took your letters . . . what he did to the cottage."

Something in his tone brought me to my feet. "No matter what happens, I shall always be grateful." I paused at the expectant expression on his face that seemed to say he hoped I'd say more and come closer.

"Tamsin."

My name came in a half whisper, soft like the night and filled with longing. For a moment I felt as if I couldn't breathe. I'm not sure which of us moved first or how we came together, his fingers gently touching my cheek, his face bent close to mine. I felt his lips cover my mouth, felt their touch all the way to my toes, soft as satin as his hand encircled my neck.

My arms went around Caleb as naturally as if they'd been doing it for years, my fingers finding their way to the back of his neck to comb through the rough edge of his thick black hair.

"Tamsin."

Such a plain name, one I'd never thought beautiful until he spoke it. I clung to him and wanted to laugh and cry all together it was so wonderful.

"Do you know how many times I've wanted to do this? Kiss you? Hold you?"

I shook my head.

"More times than I can count." He released me and looked down into my face. "You're so very lovely."

"I . . ." The words died on my lips when I saw the look in his blue eyes, a look of such intensity it seemed to touch me just as his hands did, gentle as sun in springtime.

"I love you."

I wanted to cry, hearing the words I'd longed to hear all my life from the man I loved. "I never expected this," I whispered. "I thought there must be someone in Boston. You're always going there. I tried not to care."

Caleb pulled me into his arms, his lips demanding, mine answering and trembling. For the first time I understood the wonderful danger of kissing a man, what it does to one's bones, seeming to turn them to milk.

"We had best take care, my Tamsin."

"I know."

We laughed, which was wise, for it brought an air of normalcy back into the room, grounding us, and helping us regain balance.

Caleb placed two chairs by the fire, ones I'd polished earlier that week, tracing the carved arabesque backs and dreaming they were mine. That night I felt as if they were mine. Ours. Caleb and I sat so close our knees sometimes touched, the green fabric of my dress next to the black of his trousers. We talked of marriage while the fire crackled and the clock on the mantle ticked.

I'm not sure what prompted me to tell Caleb I'd seen him launch the boat from the cove. "I couldn't believe my eyes when Melvina introduced you to me," I concluded.

Caleb got to his feet. "Do others frequent that cove?" Lines of disquiet tightened his mouth.

"Only Clarissa and me. We never saw anyone else."

"Good." Caleb fell silent as he studied the map of the New England coast hanging on the wall. A frown creased his forehead and for a moment I thought he'd forgotten me. It was as if he had gone somewhere else—a place where danger and quick wits clashed and fought for position.

Determined to bring Caleb's involvement with the underground into the open, I went to him. I knew I risked his anger by what I intended to say. "I know what you're doing with runaway slaves."

Caleb stiffened and he gave me a long, steady look. "I was afraid you did." There was a strained look to his face. "How did you find out?"

"I was standing at my bedroom window one night and saw you go out to the barn with someone. A few minutes later you left in the wagon, but I couldn't see the man. When you weren't back the next morning . . ."

Caleb's expression stopped me—a tightness around his mouth, a look of irritation. "I tried to keep you from suspecting."

"Why? Didn't you know you could trust me?"

"It's not a matter of trust. It's . . . I want you safe, Tamsin. Mary and Sally too." He opened his mouth as if to say more, then pulled me to him, his voice low as I rested my cheek against his chest. "Didn't my warning that first night mean anything to you? By rights I should send you away like I did Miss Cooper." His arms tightened around me. "But I can't. Not now."

I wanted to capture that moment and frame it in the center of my heart: me in Caleb's arms, his face resting against my head. Our closeness—so close I could feel my own breathing and his.

"Tamsin."

I lifted my head. "Let me help you with the slaves. I want to help."

He shook his head and laid a finger across my lips. "Shhh."

"But I want . . ."

"Shhh . . ." His finger traced my mouth, but the unyielding expression in his eyes told me that for now the matter was closed.

I won't deny that I was disappointed by Caleb's refusal to share the details of the underground railroad with me, but I had only to think of our love and kisses, and my disappointment lessened. On the surface, life went on as it had before, but underneath there were vibrations of excitement each time Caleb and I met, our glances holding, shared smiles. We decided not to say anything to Mary and Sally for the present, but I was sure they suspected.

Spring was upon us, making large demands upon Caleb's time as he supervised and helped with plowing and planting—corn and wheat, not to mention potatoes. He spent long hours out of doors, as did Sally and I. My garden now took precedence over kitchen chores. We planted peas first, then potatoes and turnips, putting the seeds and tubers into the loamy soil, raking and tamping it.

I will always cherish those days of April, my love for Caleb brimming in my heart, the warmth of the sun radiating through the gray fabric of my dress, my face shaded by one of Mary's old bonnets.

"I wish I'd brought starts of flowers from Mickelboro," I said to Sally. She was always with me, seeming to enjoy the feel of sun and seed and soil as much as I did. "We had lovely peonies there. Flags too, and roses."

"Can't eat roses," Sally said, though she was as drawn to flowers as I was. Hardly a day went by that she didn't bring me dainty violets and trilliums from the woods. She was learning to arrange them for the table, sometimes adding stalks of dried grass and seedpods for variety.

The steep steps from the house prevented Mary from coming with us, but it wasn't uncommon for Caleb to join us. He stopped by on the slightest pretext, breaking away from work to be near me. I couldn't get enough of him either, forgetting what I was doing while I admired how his broad shoulders filled the fabric of his indigo shirt.

During those weeks I needed only to express a wish for something and it was mine. One day Caleb appeared with cuttings from his mother's roses; later he came with two lilac bushes, their leaves newly opened, the roots and soil carefully balled inside a burlap sack. Days like that, it was difficult for me to hide my pleasure, so I gave up trying and hummed and sang whenever I felt the notion. It was a time of pure happiness.

My confidence in Caleb's love was so great that when I couldn't find my hoe, I cast aside his warning about the cellar and went there in search of one. I lit a lamp in the kitchen, where a chicken roasted in the oven, and went down the stone steps to the cellar. Although the day was warm, the steps were cold on my feet. So was the floor.

Even with the lamp, the room was dim and eerily silent. I looked at the bin of wheat, the sacks of corn, the hoe and shovel. All was just as I remembered it. Nothing had changed. Except . . .

Tiny prickles of fear ran along my spine, and I sensed that someone was watching me, he or she as frightened as I was. Silent too. I pretended nonchalance and forced myself to stop and examine the old rocking chair. My fingers were clammy as they clutched the hoe. I would use it as a weapon if forced to. Use it and scream.

Easy, Mother's voice seemed to whisper, soothing and calming as it had been when I struggled in a nightmare. *Turn and go back upstairs. You'll be fine.*

I obeyed, as I'd done as a child. Trusting. I couldn't seem to close the cellar door fast enough. Part way up the stairs, a sound stopped me. I jerked around, heart hammering. My pent-up scream turned to unsteady laughter when Ol' Cat poked her gray head out of an opening next to some shelves in the stairwell. Since we'd been forbidden access to the cellar, I'd never had a close look at the shelves filled with pickle crocks and tinware. I scowled down at Ol' Cat, aware that my hand and the lamp trembled.

"Mercy . . . you scared me. What are you doing down here?"

Ol' Cat blinked her eyes and slipped back through the opening.

I called to her. But she ignored me, and with her gray tail sticking straight in the air, she disappeared into the darkness.

Instinct told me the shelves had been built to move. Setting down the lamp, I grasped one end and pulled. Nothing happened. I tried again, pushing this time. The unit of shelves slid several inches, like a rail car moving on a set of tracks. One end disappeared into the wall as the opening widened. I felt the coldness, saw the blackness and shivered, knowing I'd stumbled onto one of Caleb's secrets.

"Ol' Cat." My voice was as unsteady as my hand when I thrust the lamp into the opening. Something moved. I screamed and almost dropped the lamp, my heart hammering so hard I could scarcely breathe. Erratic lamplight danced over the features of a black woman's face. Cowering next to her was a little girl. The woman was hunched ready to spring at me. I cried out, "Don't! I . . . I won't hurt you!"

The Negress remained silent, her frightened eyes watchful while her hand clutched the hilt of a wide-blade knife.

"I won't hurt you . . . your child, either. I'm Mr. Tremayne's housekeeper."

Except for dark eyes, the woman might have been carved out of stone.

"I was outside and couldn't find the hoe. That's why I came here. Why I . . ." I knew I babbled. If only she'd put down the knife.

"Stand back, woman." Her voice was low and threatening.

"But I won't . . ."

"I say stand back." She raised the knife. "You come one step closer and I put this blade clean through yo' belly."

I stepped back, my legs weak, grateful for the support of the wall.

We eyed each other for a long moment—me holding the shaking lamp, the slave woman clutching her knife. I saw that the knife shook too. Maybe she wasn't as mean and dangerous as she wanted me to believe.

"Mammy . . ."

"Hush, Livie." The woman's eyes never left my face.

"If you'd listen, we could stop this nonsense. I truly won't hurt you."

"Ain't nonsense to me. It be called stayin' alive. That's how me and my man got this far. Bein' careful. Not takin' no chances. That be the last words Henry say to me before him and our boy go on ahead of us to the next place. *You be careful, Delilah.* So I mean to be careful."

"Your man . . . your husband gave you good advice."

Delilah shifted position, as if her legs were tiring.

"Mammy . . ." I moved the lamp so its light fell onto the little girl. She looked to be about four years old with woolly black hair and traces of fresh tears on her face. Judging from her appearance, she was as scared as I was. Probably cold too, hiding in the dark hole with nothing but a mattress and a quilt for warmth.

"What a beautiful child," I said.

"She be that, all right." There were traces of pride in the woman's voice, a slight relaxing of her body.

"It must be hard for her down here in the dark . . . the cold."

"Livie know it have to be. She brave like her daddy."

"How long have you been running?"

"Don't know for sure. Seem like forever, though probably only a few weeks. We done good so far." She paused and studied me, her eyes still watchful. Something in my face must have reassured her, for after a moment she went on. "How far yo' think we have to go?"

"Not far. I doubt there's more than a couple of hundred miles between here and Canada."

"Canada." Delilah's voice sounded like Mary's did when she talked about heaven.

"Where was your home?"

"Weren't no home." The fierceness was back. "It only a place were we kept like pigs and cows and chickens. Buy 'em, sell 'em, whip 'em, do what they please with 'em." Her voice grew louder. "I ain't no cow. Livie's not, neither. We people same as you."

"Yes you are."

My heart ached as I imagined the cruelty and hardship they'd endured. Along with the ache was admiration for their courage. I'd read enough accounts of runaway slaves to know what they risked if they were caught, not to mention the weeks of running and hiding, of being shut up in dark places like this for hours, sometimes days. "I understand your need to be careful . . . especially with Livie. But our home is safe. All the people here are kind. No one will hurt you."

Something flickered in Delilah's eyes, but she made no response.

"Would you like to come out and stretch your legs and use the . . . chamber pot?"

Delilah blinked. "Horatio say we not to come out 'cept at night."

"Horatio?" It took me a moment before I realized this must be Caleb's underground name. "You and Livie will be safe in the kitchen. Hardly anyone comes to visit." I could sense her wavering. "I'll pull the shade down over the window and have Sally watch the door."

"Please, Mammy. I got to go. Bad . . ."

Delilah's brow puckered. "Yo' sure it safe?"

"I'm sure."

She gave me another long look. "Livie here havin' a hard time since her daddy left. That why I opened the shelves. Gettin' out will help her." Delilah lowered the knife and slipped it into the pocket of her worn brown dress. Scrambling forward, she felt for the stairs.

I guided her bare foot to the step then offered my hand. She took it, meeting my eyes briefly before reaching for her daughter.

"You'll be safe, Livie. I'll bring you and your mama a chamber pot, then you can sit in the kitchen and have something to eat. Do you like chicken?"

Livie nodded as her thumb went into her mouth.

"I thought you would. Probably your mama does too." When I turned I saw the cat standing in the opening. "Come on, Ol' Cat."

"You lucky you still have dat cat," Delilah said. "I 'most slit her throat I so scared.

"I'm thankful you didn't. I'm very fond of her and so is . . . Horatio."

As soon as we reached the kitchen, I pulled oilcloth shades down over the windows. "Now no one can see you, though we seldom have visitors."

I could tell she still didn't entirely trust the situation. If the truth were known, I didn't either. The magnitude of what I'd done struck with force.

"Sit . . . sit down." I pulled a chair away from the table.

Delilah sat on the edge of it, back stiff, her feet flat on the floor, ready to run. "Where dat Sally who 'posed to watch the door?"

"I'll get her." A glance at Livie reminded me of the child's need. "I'll ask her to bring a chamber pot too."

I went to the dining room and called Sally. I'd spoken so confidently when I'd said she would guard the door. And she would—guard it with her life, she was that loyal. But could Sally be trusted with our secret?

Sally was humming as she came downstairs with the chamber pot. The humming broke off when she saw Delilah. "Who . . . who are they?"

"People who need our help."

Sally backed away, her eyes large and frightened.

I took hold of her arm. "It's all right, Sally." I could almost see the thoughts flitting through her mind—danger, trouble, Master Caleb's anger. "It's all right," I repeated. I took the chamber pot from her hands. "I'll be back and explain as soon as they've had a chance to use this."

I handed the pot to Delilah. "I'll take you into the next room so you can have some privacy."

Delilah's eyes were on Sally. "She goin' to keep watch?"

"She is." I directed my gaze at Sally. "I want you to stand by the back door and tell me the minute you see anyone coming."

Sally acted as if she hadn't heard me, and when I took her arm she tried to pull away. I looked at her hard to try to reach past her fear. "Sally." I used my firmest voice. "You must do what I say."

"Yes'm." I knew she answered out of habit. Her eyes darted to Delilah and Livie as she started for the back door.

Delilah's face spoke of unease. "She'll keep watch," I said. The whisper of bare feet as I led them to the study was Delilah's only answer.

After pulling the green drapery across the window, I left Delilah and Livie and went into the dining room. A sense of unreality followed me. I felt as if I were someone else instead of Tamsin Yeager, someone with courage who knew what she was doing. Merciful heaven, what had I done?

I looked out the window, having forgotten the warm spring afternoon, the blue sky and fluffy clouds with a breeze ruffling new leaves on the maple. For a second I wished I'd stayed in the garden and weeded the turnips by hand. If I had, I'd still be daydreaming about Caleb, good thoughts, not worry, clanging through my head.

No, I was glad I'd brought Delilah and Livie out of their hiding place. They needed sunlight and warm food served at a table, people to fuss over them and show they cared. Although I might not know much about the workings of the underground railroad, I knew with sudden clarity that I'd done the right thing.

When Delilah and Livie came out of the study, I noticed that Delilah walked with a limp. "Is something wrong with your foot?"

"Done hurt it on a rock a while back. Cut it some."

"After you eat, I'll look at it and see what we can do."

In between checking on the chicken and adding wood to the stove, I studied Delilah, noting her full lips and rich mahogany skin. She was pretty, with large expressive eyes and her head wrapped in a brown turban.

"You sure dat Sally watchin' the door?" Delilah asked.

I nodded, though I felt compelled to go to the alcove to check. Sally was there, but the look she gave me was far from happy. "Remember the poster we saw in Mickelboro?" I asked. "The one about the slave?"

"Yes'm." Understanding slowly came to her eyes—understanding and a desire to help. She stepped from the door to look at Delilah, who sat at the table with Livie pulled close against her. The child's thumb was in her mouth. "Don't be scared," Sally said. "I'll watch good for you."

Delilah nodded and there was a slight relaxing to her features. I put my hand on Sally's arm. "This is a secret. One you can't tell anyone. Not ever. If you do, men like Amos Mickelson might find Delilah and Livie and do bad things to them. Do you understand?"

"Yes'm." Sally's face was solemn and she looked me directly in the eyes. "I know when to keep my trap shut. Won't nothin' make me tell."

"Good." But it didn't feel good. I was worried about giving away Caleb's secret and taking risks with Delilah. Maybe I should have left them in the hiding place and taken food and the chamber pot down to them.

I heard labored steps coming down the stairs and hurried to intercept Mary. "Thought I'd come down and see what I can do to help with supper," she wheezed. "Want me to peel the potatoes?"

"That would be helpful, but first . . ." I felt like I was walking blindfolded. Should I include Mary in the secret or send her back upstairs? The need to trust won out. ". . . first, I need to tell you something." Mary's eyes widened as I explained. "They were scared, and it was so dark and uncomfortable I couldn't leave them."

"Of course not . . . but we'll have to be careful. It wouldn't do for Mr. Brown or one of his boys to stumble onto them." Mary shook her head. "We'd better hope Mr. Tremayne don't find out what you've done neither." Mary pursed her lips and a satisfied expression slipped over her round features. "I knew he was up to something . . . the way food disappeared. All his trips." Her face broke into a smile. "Don't surprise me a bit."

We ended up feeding Delilah and Livie leftovers. Livie was disappointed, but the chicken wasn't done and I was anxious to get them back downstairs. Delilah was uneasy too, especially since Caleb had told them not to come out except at night.

We found time to talk, though. Delilah spoke between bites of cornbread covered with molasses, telling how they rested during the day and traveled mostly at night. "We done walked miles and miles, taking turns carrying Livie when she get tired. Sometimes people hide us or give rides like Horatio done with my Henry and Jeremiah."

I poured warm water into a basin and soaked Delilah's foot. Her feet were so big they looked like they belonged to a man, rich brown on top, callused and as pink as my own on the bottom. The cut worried me. Part had healed over, but the rest was red and puffy.

"How did you know to come here?" I asked.

"Man at the last place told us to keep headin' north 'til we come to an unpainted barn with a white horse on top. Think he call it a weather vane."

I glanced up in surprise. I'd never suspected the weather vane was a signal for runaway slaves.

"Mr. Brown and Parley are comin' from the field," Sally called. She'd been calling out every few minutes: "No one's coming," or "Can't see no one."

"Must be milking time." Mary was spreading a thick layer of peach preserves onto a slice of corn bread for Livie.

"Now they're goin' into the barn," Sally called again.

The sense of urgency increased. It wouldn't take long to finish milking. "See if you can find a clean cloth to wrap around Delilah's foot," I told Mary. I looked at Delilah. "When will you be leaving?"

"Tonight, probably, though Horatio want to make sure it safe."

"What about your husband and son?"

"They be waitin' at the next place. Horatio say that man has a bigger wagon than he do. One big enough for all of us to ride in."

I mixed a poultice of flour and lard and warm milk for Delilah's foot. As I blended the ingredients, I heard footsteps and turned to take the bandage from Mary. When I saw Caleb I froze, one hand holding the bowl, the other hand outstretched. Delilah sprang to her feet so fast the basin tipped and sent water over the kitchen floor.

Caleb's mouth opened in surprise. "What the? . . ."

"Caleb . . ." That's all that came out—his name and my nervousness.

Delilah edged around the table to Livie. "I . . . we . . ." she stammered.

"I brought them upstairs." My voice was calm, as if I didn't know about Caleb's temper and I was in the sitting room reading poetry.

"*You* brought them?" Caleb's face tightened with anger. "What made you think you had authority to do that? Expose them to danger . . . yourself too. Do you realize the risk you've taken?" He took hold of my shoulders, gripping them so hard it hurt. "Do you, Miss Yeager? Do you?"

"Yes . . . no." I wished I'd never gone down to the cellar, never seen Ol' Cat. But the wish only lasted a second.

"What if it had been Mr. Brown that came in just now? Or my mother? Or God forbid, Amos Mickelson?"

"Sally's keeping watch. We'd have had time to get them back to the cellar." I glanced at Sally, saw the stricken look on her face and the strand of brown hair wound around her finger. I was also aware Caleb had called me Miss Yeager, not Tamsin. Using anger to cover my worry, I hurried on, "How did you get inside anyway?"

"Through the porch door. I thought you'd be in your garden and . . ." Caleb took a deep breath and his grip on my shoulders eased. "Never mind why I wanted to see you. The important thing is Delilah and her daughter. Do you know what will happen to them if they're discovered? The whippings? The family split up and sold to other plantations? These are people's lives you're playing with."

It took effort to control my anger. "I'm well aware of that. It's because they're people that I brought them upstairs. You can't just leave them down in the cellar like they're sacks of corn." I paused to swallow, meeting Caleb's gaze head on. "Did you ever think they might be frightened? They'd lain in the dark for hours, and Livie was crying and needed to use the chamber pot."

I hurried on before Caleb could reply. "What you're doing is wonderful and courageous . . . risking all you have to help these people. But Delilah and Livie need more than someone to take them from place to place. They need kind hands and caring people." I turned and met Delilah's wide brown eyes. "Don't you, Delilah?"

Delilah glanced at Caleb and her big hand went around Livie's slender shoulder. "Yes'm, we do. Specially Livie here."

The kitchen went so quiet I could hear the spatter from the roasting chicken.

Caleb released my shoulders. "They need to get back into the hiding place. They can come out again tonight, but for now . . ."

"Delilah hurt her foot. Mary and I need to bandage it."

"Mary?"

Mary stepped out of the dining room. "I'm right here."

Caleb sighed and grimaced. "I should have known."

"Yes, sir, you should have. And you should've known you couldn't keep what you've been doing from the rest of us. 'Tain't right. Couldn't you trust us?"

Her question seemed to hang in the air. I saw Caleb look at Sally, watched his lips purse. "Trust had nothing to do with my decision. I couldn't ask for more loyal servants and friends. But each person who knows increases the risk of discovery. A word can accidentally slip and some women tend to gossip."

Mary's lips tightened. "Some women, maybe, but not us. We know when to keep quiet, don't we, Sally?" Mary's expression was pleading.

"I already told Miss Yeager I know when to keep my trap shut."

"Then make sure you do." Caleb walked over to Sally and gently unwound the lock of hair from around her finger. "I'm depending on you, Sally. So are others like Delilah and Livie."

"I know."

Her words didn't entirely reassure him. We were all aware of Sally's weakness for speaking before she thought. The look Caleb turned on me was long and searching, contrite too. He crossed the kitchen and placed his hands on my arms.

"I'm sorry. I shouldn't have lost my temper, but the sight of you with Delilah . . . knowing the danger and . . ." He shook his head. "I want to protect you, Tamsin. Keep you safe, not expose you to danger. I . . ." Caleb gathered me into his arms and held me close, my head cradled against his chest, his lips like a whisper on my hair.

I closed my eyes and savored his arms around me, my anger melting under his touch. I was dimly aware we were not alone—Mary, Sally, even little Livie watched us as though we were on a stage and they the enthralled audience ready to voice their approval with applause.

Before anyone could do so, I lifted my head and met Caleb's gaze. "If we're to marry, secrets can't stand between us. I want to share your life, Caleb . . . to stand by your side and know you trust me."

For an instant, wariness warred with his smile. Then he nodded. "Yes." Another nod. "Yes." As he spoke he ran his fingers over my cheek, and with everyone looking on, he lifted my chin and kissed me.

CHAPTER 14

The next morning I found a note from Caleb slipped under my door, telling me he'd taken Delilah and Livie and that he'd be back as soon as he could. It was on his last words my gaze lingered.

Would you be so good as to accompany me to church on Sunday so I can introduce you to my friends? For more years than I care to remember they have been anxious for me to take a wife. It will give me great pleasure to present you as my future intended and one whom I hold most dear. I love you and cherish our time together.

Yours always,
Caleb

I smiled and held the note close as I made my way downstairs, my mind shifting to all that needed to be done. Busy as I was, I intended to air and make the hiding place more comfortable for those who came next. That would be my first priority.

After Sally had carried a tray upstairs for Mary, I lit the lamp and descended the stairs to the cellar. This morning the cupboard doors were closed, the dark wood contrasting with the gray of the wall, everything tight-fitting and snug. I studied it with new eyes, those of a federal deputy or slave hunter. Everything appeared innocent and commonplace. Even when I opened the cupboard doors there was nothing to hint that it was anything other than a place to store crocks of pickles, apple butter, and salted herring. The shelves slid into the wall with little noise or effort.

I shone the lamp into the darkness. "Godspeed," I whispered, wondering about Delilah's foot and if she and Livie were reunited with Henry and Jeremiah by now. Trying not to worry about Caleb, I set down the lamp and climbed inside. It was more a crawl space than a room, the ceiling no higher than the cupboard, the length no longer than that of a man. It went deep, though, probably six feet, large enough for several people should the need arise.

I blew out the lamp and lay down. The masonry floor pressed into my back and cold seeped through the fabric of my green dress. I tried to imagine how it had been for Delilah, for Livie—the darkness and the silence, and being closed up as if they were in a grave.

Shivering, I retrieved the lamp and slid the shelf into place. As I retraced my steps upstairs, I thought of all I took for granted— freedom and wonderful friends, a warm home with ample food. Though I'd had my trials, I had never been mistreated. Now that I'd found Caleb, I no longer had to be afraid.

———•———

When Caleb failed to return the following day, I grew uneasy. When he wasn't home by Saturday, I began to worry in earnest.

"Ain't like Master Caleb to go so long," Sally said. "Hope nothin' bad happened."

"Now don't start worrying," Mary said. We were in the sitting room, the house straightened, stew simmering on the back of the stove. "I remember a time he was gone for a week. When he got back, he was just fine. He'll be fine this time too." She nodded. "I've been praying, not just for Mr. Tremayne, but for Delilah and Livie and all the other poor people he's helping. They need our prayers."

I'd been praying too. Since I'd learned about Clarrie, praying came easier. Letting go of bitterness had let in faith. Loving Caleb helped. Love did that . . . softened the soul so faith could get inside.

"I try not to worry," I said. "But Caleb . . . Mr. Tremayne left a note asking me to go to church with him tomorrow. He wouldn't have invited me if he hadn't expected to be home."

Mary didn't say anything for a moment, her eyes intent on her knitting. "Invited you to go to church, did he?" Worry seemed to be the farthest thing from her mind. "Don't surprise me after what happened Thursday." She smiled and winked. "We've suspected for some months now. Since Christmas, in fact. Anyone with a noggin of sense could tell Master Tremayne was having a hard time keeping his eyes off you in that new dress."

"Mary . . ."

"It's true. Me 'n Sally talked on it a number of times."

Sally gave a shy smile. "When are you and Master Caleb gettin' married?"

"Soon, I hope. Probably this summer."

Sally's smile grew. "I was hopin' you would. Mary said maybe you'll let me carry flowers for you at the weddin'. I could gather roses and daisies and hand them to you when you leave the church."

"What a lovely idea."

That set Mary talking about Melvina's wedding and how she and Mrs. Brown had spent almost a week preparing all the food. She rambled on, but I had a hard time keeping my mind on her.

"How far do you think Caleb had to take Delilah?" I asked when Mary paused. "I read in a newspaper that underground stations are usually close enough to travel between them in one day."

"Or a night. Lots of times he travels at night." Mary's face softened. "Don't worry, my dear. He'll be home by morning."

I carried this thought with me as I prepared for bed. Even so, before I climbed under the quilts, I knelt and said a prayer for Caleb.

———•———

I awoke at first light, the thought that Caleb would be home soon still with me. I went to the window when I was dressed. Sun was everywhere, dappling the leaves on the maple and lifting misty dew from the grass. I took satisfaction in the sight of my vegetable garden, the dark green leaves of the turnips and potatoes marching in tidy rows along one side. A movement behind the granary caught my attention. It was a horse, legs half-obscured by mist—black instead of a bay like Caleb's, and saddled and without a rider.

The sight sent me down the stairs to Sally, who was stoking the stove. A rasher of bacon sat on the table.

"There's a horse behind the granary. Is someone here?"

Sally's brow puckered. "Didn't see no one when I brought in the wood. Didn't see no horse neither."

Unease sent me down the back steps and across the yard, Sally following as I skirted the garden and granary, our skirts and slippers soon damp with dew. I could see the horse now. Flecks of mud and lather spattered its dark coat, but there was no sign of a rider.

I was suddenly struck by our vulnerability—Mr. Brown and his sons were at their home since it was Sunday, leaving three women alone. Shading my eyes against the sun, I looked back at the house. My breath caught when I saw a crumpled body lying in the tall grass. I ran to it, recognizing the blue coat and dark hair before I dropped to my knees and turned Caleb over.

Blood covered his shirt and stained the dark fabric of his coat like a red satin lining. Even the ground was bloody. "Dear . . . God." My whispered prayer mingled with the sharp intake of Sally's breath.

Caleb's eyes fluttered open, their color dulled as if the blue were draining out with his blood. His voice was a hoarse croak. "Tamsin . . ."

"What happened?"

"Shot." He licked his lips and his eyes closed.

For a second I could only stare—cold, frozen—noting the deathly pallor of Caleb's face, his closed eyes sunk deep into their sockets. Had he died? Instinct shoved me into action. I checked for a pulse between the cords of his neck and took heart when I felt it.

"Help me, Sally. We've got to stop the bleeding."

Sally edged away, her face as pale as Caleb's.

"Sally!" I shouted.

Sally's head jerked up like a deer poised for flight—away from blood, away from death.

I grabbed her hand. "Master Caleb needs your help. So do I. Or he'll die."

Something snapped inside Sally, bringing her to her knees, little choking noises passing for speech. But at least she was moving.

I pulled back Caleb's coat and my fingers fumbled with the blood-slick buttons on his shirt. In desperation I finally tore them apart, gasping when I saw the wound below his right shoulder, jagged and gaping, and oozing blood each time he breathed.

"No," I whispered. I turned to Sally. "Untie my apron and fold it into a compress."

This time Sally lost no time in responding. I pressed the folded apron against the hole and pushed hard with the heel of my hand. "We've got to get him inside," I said when I could manage to speak.

"Is . . . is he goin' to die?" Sally whimpered.

"Not if I can help it." I looked down at Caleb's ghost-white skin and blue-tinged lips. His stillness reminded me of a corpse. I pressed down on the wound with new vigor. He needed a doctor—a doctor and warmth.

"Run and get a quilt."

I willed Sally to hurry as I cautiously lifted the apron. Blood still oozed from the hole. "Please, God, don't let him die." I repeated the prayer like a litany while part of me pleaded with God to show me what to do.

The damp from the grass on my dress and petticoat chilled me. Caleb's blue-tinged lips revealed the toll it had taken on him. How long had he lain here? Why hadn't I awakened earlier?

I heard Sally coming, her breathing ragged and her haste such that she almost tripped as she veered past the horse. "Here . . . 'tis," she gasped. "And I told . . . Mary."

"Good." I spread the quilt next to Caleb. "Help me roll him onto it."

"How about the bleedin'? Has it stopped?"

Blood still oozed from the jagged opening when I lifted the compress. "We've got to tie it tighter when we move him."

Sally helped me lift Caleb and bind the compress into place with the apron ties. His eyes opened and tried to focus.

"We're going to roll you onto the quilt. We'll try not to hurt you."

Sally and I gently rolled him onto the quilt and wrapped it around him. As we tried to lift Caleb I saw the impracticality of attempting to carry him. His weight was too much. It was Sally's idea to use the wheelbarrow—Sweet Sally whom Melvina thought simple, but whose love for her Master Caleb knew no bounds.

Getting Caleb into the wheelbarrow was no small task. Caleb had lapsed into unconsciousness, his stillness and pallor filling me with fear. Each time we stopped for breath on our wobbly journey to the house, I tested for a pulse and took heart when I detected a thready beat along his neck.

Sally helped me tug Caleb into a sitting position when we reached the back stoop. The movement jarred Caleb back to consciousness. His eyes were wild and frightened until they focused on me. He tried to help, scrabbling with his feet for leverage until he reached a half crouch.

"Put his arm over your shoulder," I told Sally as I grasped Caleb around the waist. "We've got to go up the steps. Can you walk?"

A nod passed for yes.

The three of us struggled up the steps, Caleb's weight like a log despite his efforts. His breath came in ragged gasps. "Now the door," I said.

We made it through the door and staggered past the kitchen. "We'll never make it up the stairs," I wheezed. "Try the study."

Sheer determination got us there. The three of us collapsed onto the couch, Caleb's dead weight pinning me beneath him. I struggled for breath, each gasp bringing the smell and taste of his blood into my mouth and nostrils. I gagged and pulled free, lurching across the room to lean against the bookcase as my stomach convulsed in dry heaves. The acrid smell of blood was so strong I felt as if I'd drunk it. I couldn't be rid of the taste or the stickiness. It colored my fingers and smeared the wood next to my hands.

When I'd gained control of my stomach, I returned to Caleb. The sight of him struck new fear in my heart. I touched the clammy white skin on his forehead and prayed the struggle to get him inside hadn't killed him. The rasp of a labored breath came like music to my ears. I was only dimly aware of my grateful tears and of Sally, huddled on the floor, her head and arms pulled close to her knees.

When I settled Caleb more comfortably onto the couch, I found fresh blood on the leather. Where had it come from? It was then I discovered that the bullet had gone through Caleb's shoulder and that blood oozed from a hole in back as well as the front.

"Help me get Master Caleb out of his coat so I can stop the bleeding."

"Bleedin'?" Sally's gray eyes looked frozen and her voice was a whisper. For a moment I thought I'd have to shake her, but she managed to get past the fear on her own, struggling to her feet and waiting for me to show her what to do.

We eased the sleeves of Caleb's coat and shirt from his arm. My brain hardly registered the whiteness of Caleb's shoulders half-covered with the apron bandage. My focus was on the hole in the back of his shoulder—small and dark and oozing fresh blood.

"Get towels from the kitchen, then run and get Mary."

As soon as Sally returned, I grabbed one of the towels and pressed it hard against the smaller hole. A moment later I heard Mary's heavy footsteps on the stairs, her labored breathing as she came through the door.

"Sally said Mr. Tremayne's been shot." She paused and gasped when she saw the blood. "Dear heaven."

Mary's heaving presence quieted some of my fear. She'd know what to do. With her years and experience she'd know how to stop the bleeding.

But she backed away and sat down heavily on a chair. "I don't know a thing about nursing . . . leastwise not when there's blood," she said weakly. "The sight of it makes me faint."

Pressing on the wound, I looked at her in dismay. Mary's skin was chalky and the lax expression on her face caused me concern. "Don't you dare faint," I cried. "Put your head between your knees."

Sally moved to help her. The two of them made a pathetic sight— Sally bloodstained and shaking, Mary hunched into a heaving lump on the chair. Who was going to help me? I closed my eyes as reality washed over me. There was no one to help Caleb except me.

Please God, show me what to do, I pleaded. And in the next breath, *If only Susannah Partridge were here.*

Just saying Susannah's name brought a measure of calm. What would she do if she were here? Suddenly I knew. Just as clearly as if it had happened yesterday I remembered how she'd saved Hans Anderson from bleeding to death by covering his badly cut leg with cobwebs. And everyone knew turpentine was good for cleansing.

"We need turpentine and cobwebs," I said. "There's a jug of turpentine in the woodshed. Most likely cobwebs too."

Sally looked at me out of tear-filled eyes, her mouth quivering as she fought for control.

"One of us must go and get them," I continued. "Since you're afraid of spiders, you stay with Master Caleb and hold the towel tight to stop the bleeding. Do you think you can do it?"

Sally wiped her eyes on her apron and took a deep breath. "Yes'm," she quavered.

After showing her what to do, I caught up my skirt and ran from the house. Pray God the cobwebs would work their magic. I used a stick to gather them from the corners of the shed, aware of the morning chill and wrinkling my nose at the dust. The cobwebs clung to my fingers as I wiped them off the stick and put them into my pocket. When I judged I had enough, I grabbed the jug of turpentine and hurried back to the house.

Sally was kneeling by the couch when I returned, her tears replaced by a look of quiet determination, as if she thought she was all that kept her Master Caleb alive. Perhaps she was. God and Sally.

I gently removed the compress from the front wound and swabbed the oozing blood away. Growing bolder I poured some turpentine into the hole. Caleb shuddered, the muscles of his stomach tightening, his eyes jerking open. When he quieted, I laid a film of cobwebs over the hole.

"Hand me another towel," I said to Sally, who now seemed eager to help. She watched quietly as I packed the towel into a compress over the cobwebs then did the same with the wound in back.

"Sally needs to fetch Mr. Tremayne's mother," Mary said. She paused and took a deep breath as if to clear her head. "The old missus is good at nursing . . . her and Dr. Hillman. Get one of the Brown boys to ride for the doctor."

At the mention of the doctor, Caleb stirred. "No, . . ." he whispered. "No . . . doctor."

"You've got to have help Caleb," I said.

His head moved back and forth on the couch. "Too dangerous." He took a shuddering breath. "Men who shot me . . . looking for me."

Fear pushed words out of my mouth. "The horse? What if they see the horse?" But Caleb had slipped back into unconsciousness, the rise and fall of his bandaged chest the only sign that he lived.

"Go, Sally," Mary said. "Hurry!"

I noticed the blood on Sally's hands and dress. "Wait! If men are looking for Caleb, no one . . . not even the Browns . . . can know he's wounded. Wash your face and hands and change your dress."

Sally nodded and ran up the stairs.

While she was gone, I brought the quilt from the wheelbarrow and tucked it around Caleb. When I hurried to intercept Sally, determination was back on her face and she looked as mature as her fifteen years.

I placed my hands on her thin shoulders. "You mustn't tell anyone except Caleb's mother what happened. Do you understand?"

"Yes'm."

"She'll know what to bring . . . what to do."

"I'll run as fast as I can and I won't tell no one 'cept the old lady why I came," Sally promised.

I watched her slight figure hurry across the yard and take the shortcut through the fields. "Hurry . . . oh, hurry," I whispered. Part of me wanted to go with Sally to put the right words into her mouth, partake of the strength and good sense of Lucinda Tremayne. But love and concern for Caleb pulled me back to the study where Mary sat, her hands clasped in her lap, her eyes closed in prayer.

The sight of Caleb sent a chill through my heart. He was so still. Too still, except for the occasional shudder that passed for breath. I placed my hand on his brow, hoping that by sheer will I could force him to stay with me. My fingers trailed to his closed eyes with their thick, dark lashes. Pain gathered in my throat when I realized I'd never kissed them, that perhaps now, I never would.

I dropped to my knees and laid my face against his. The stubble of Caleb's unshaven jaw raked my skin as I kissed his eyelids, his cheek, his lips. "Don't leave me," I whispered. "Please, Caleb. Stay. For me. For us."

As if he heard me, Caleb took a deep breath, followed by a shiver. I tucked the quilt more firmly around him and hurried to the kitchen for something more to warm him.

Mary heaved herself out of the chair and followed me. Her soulful expression told me more loudly than words of her guilt, that she thought she'd failed Caleb and me.

"Your prayers are more potent medicine than cobwebs," I said.

"I hope so." She slowly made her way to the stove, her steps as uncertain as her expression. "We'd best get something warm in him."

Mary put the kettle on and stoked the fire while I hurried to find bricks to warm in the oven. Warmth was what Caleb needed, and warmth was something Mary and I could provide.

As we worked, worry about the horse niggled at my mind. If men were searching for Caleb, the grazing horse would be a dead giveaway. What if they were coming even now, men on horseback, perhaps even a deputy marshal? My stomach tightened as I hurried outside, certain I'd see someone coming. Cows grazing in the pasture and the distant trail of smoke from Lucinda's chimney were all I saw.

Relieved, I searched for the horse and found it standing by the water trough, head hanging, tail swishing at flies.

At my approach the gelding lifted his head, his eyes wary. Fortunately he was more tired than skittish. On the second attempt I was able to grab his reins and lead him into the barn. Thankfully, Sam had already done the milking and hadn't noticed the horse. I needed to send it away, but for now it would have to stay in the barn, the girth to the saddle loosened, water and oats left in buckets.

Worry hurried me through the task and sped my feet back to the house. I saw Mary pouring water into a cup as I passed the kitchen, but my mind was on Caleb. Had the cobwebs stopped the bleeding?

Caleb lay with his eyes closed, his breathing so soft I couldn't see any movement. I gently pulled back the quilt, grateful to detect the soft rise and fall of his chest and see that the towel showed little blood.

"Thank you," I said. To God, to the cobwebs, to all who had stopped the bleeding.

Caleb's eyelids fluttered and he shivered. I tucked the quilt back around his shoulders and pushed a lock of hair away from his brow. Love urged me to take him in my arms and cradle his head against my shoulder, holding him close so the warmth of my body could penetrate into his. Fear of restarting the bleeding bade me wait, just as it bade me to wait to pull off his damp breeches and muddy boots. I would wait until Caleb's mother arrived and rely on her superior knowledge and skill.

———•———

Lucinda Tremayne and Sally arrived a half hour later, Lucinda driving the mare, the two of them in the buggy. By then I'd succeeded in getting a little hot tea into Caleb and had wrapped bricks inside sheets and slid them under the quilt for warmth.

My relief when Mrs. Tremayne walked through the door was such that I burst into tears. Seeing me, his mother stopped, the flush in her cheeks from the May breeze draining away so quickly I feared she'd faint. "Is he? . . ." she began.

I shook my head, unable to control my emotions. "He lives . . ." I finally managed to get out. "Please, oh please . . . help him."

Lucinda nodded, the color returning to her narrow features, her manner once again brisk. "Have you got the satchel?" she asked.

"Yes'm." Sally edged toward the study door as if she needed to see for herself that her Master Caleb still lived.

Instead of following her, Lucinda untied her bonnet and handed it and her blue cloak to Mary. Then she went to the basin and washed her hands. "Dr. Hillman is a strong believer in washing one's hands before attending to the sick and wounded. He claims it lessens the chance of fever."

I glanced at my hands, now cleansed of blood and grime, thankful I'd scrubbed them with lye soap and hot water after I returned from the barn.

I followed Mrs. Tremayne into the study, letting her shoulder my burden. For a second she faltered and an expression of terrible grief crossed her spare face. I imagined how it must be to gaze down at the only son she had left and him looking like he barely clung to life. As quickly as it came, her hesitancy passed, the vulnerable woman I'd ·glimpsed set aside by square, capable hands that gently pulled back the quilt and inspected the bandaged shoulder with no more emotion than if she'd been Dr. Hillman.

"Looks like you've stopped most of the bleeding."

"It's doing better. I heard cobwebs are helpful. I put them over the wounds and bound his shoulder as tightly as I could."

"Good. The warm bricks were a good idea too."

Hearing his mother's voice, Caleb's eyes opened but he made no effort to speak. Lucinda laid her fingers on his forehead. A flicker of a smile curved his lips before his eyes closed again.

"Sally said the bullet went through his shoulder," Lucinda said in a softer voice. "Since I don't have the skill to remove a bullet, we can be thankful for that. But suturing . . ." She nodded. "I've had plenty of practice at suturing."

Lucinda loosened the towels and studied the wounds, first the one in front; then gently moving Caleb, she looked at the one in back. "They both need sewing. But first we need to get him out of his damp breeches and boots." She paused and shot me a quick glance. "If you and Sally will see to Caleb's boots, I'll take care of the rest."

Sally and I struggled with the wet laces of his boots and left Lucinda to remove his breeches while we carried Caleb's boots and bloodstained shirt and coat out of the room.

The next half hour passed in a haze as I helped Mrs. Tremayne sew up the wounds with a needle and silk thread, her stitches as neat as those on a piece of embroidery as they pulled the skin back into place. Caleb flinched each time the needle entered, his mouth tightening as he strove to keep from crying out. I went hot and cold, and bile rose hot in my throat.

"Are you all right?" Lucinda asked, her brow drawn in concentration.

I nodded and swallowed, willing myself to think of my garden and the beautiful spring morning, anything but the needle piercing Caleb's smooth white skin.

Sally remained at my side, helping me hold Caleb's arms when pain penetrated the fog of unconsciousness, biting her lip and looking ready to cry the same as I did. During those tense moments the three of us were bound into a single entity of love for Caleb Tremayne.

CHAPTER 15

"We need to make plans," Mrs. Tremayne said after Caleb had been bandaged and dressed in a fresh nightshirt, and warm bricks and the quilt tucked back around him. Although Caleb wasn't fully conscious, his breathing seemed more regular and his color was better.

We sat in the kitchen with cups of fresh tea steaming on the table. Mary had made the tea and, difficult as it was for her to walk, I knew it was important for her to feel she was doing her part. I was glad for the chance to talk. There were too many questions, too much unspoken worry and fear. If we talked, maybe words would poke holes in my fears and put my feet squarely on the floor again.

Mrs. Tremayne's gaze went around the table, resting on Mary, then Sally, and finally stopping on me. "Do you know what happened, Miss Yeager? How my son was shot?"

"Yes . . . at least partly." I wondered how to explain without giving away Caleb's involvement with fugitive slaves.

"Just tell me what you know," Lucinda said. "And if you think you'll shock me by divulging that my son is helping to transport runaway slaves, you can put that fear aside. Although Caleb has chosen to exclude me from his confidence, I've known . . . or at least suspected for some months now."

Mary made a small sound and Sally looked stunned. I was relieved, her words having just laid to rest my concerns. "In that case, you know why he was shot. How or where it happened, we don't know . . . though he left with two slaves early Thursday morning. A woman and her child. We expected him back by Friday evening and when he didn't return last night, I . . . we began to worry."

Mrs. Tremayne didn't say anything for a moment, as if her suspicion had been just suspicion and hearing the truth had broadened her fear. While she sipped her tea, I told her where we'd found Caleb, about the black horse, and of Caleb's concern that men were still searching for him.

Lucinda sighed. "I was afraid such might be the case. That's why we must plan and do all we can to protect him."

Everyone nodded. "Something needs to be done about the horse," I ventured. "If it's found here . . . especially with a bloodstained saddle, it won't go well for Caleb."

"Gotta' hide Master Caleb too," Sally put in. She sat with her elbows resting on the table, her expression intent as if she were trying to think of where to put him.

"That too," Mrs. Tremayne agreed.

"His clothes and everything bloody need to be washed or hidden," Mary added. "If men come, they'll be looking for signs of blood."

I wondered how we'd act if men came to the house. Would we be able to conceal our fear so they wouldn't be suspicious? Could we rely on Sally not to blurt something out?

"The first thing is to get rid of the horse." Mrs. Tremayne's gaze made its way around the table again and rested on Sally. "As I recall Sally, you do right well on a horse. Ride it down to the river. That way it will have food and water until it's found."

Sally's eyes widened as she took in Lucinda's plan.

"No one must see you riding the horse, so keep to the trees and hide if you must," Lucinda went on. "Do the same on your way back so no one will recall they saw you walking so far from home."

"Yes'm." Sally's voice lacked conviction.

Mrs. Tremayne reached across the table for one of Sally's small hands. "You'll do fine. Remember how you found Becca last summer? And look how well you did coming to get me today?"

I watched Sally and tried not to worry. What if she stumbled onto the very men who were looking for Caleb?

"You'll need to take some food with you," Mary said. "Might be late by the time you get back."

Her words drew my eyes to the clock ticking on the shelf above the crockery, the hands showing just a few minutes before ten. Had only three hours elapsed since I'd looked out my bedroom window and seen the horse? It felt like an entire day had passed as we'd cried and prayed and frantically worked to pull Caleb away from death. Somehow we'd managed it. With nothing but sheer will and love and Mary's prayers, we'd succeeded.

A glance at Sally told me she felt the weight of her responsibility, and I tried to ease her burden. "While Mary gets food ready, I'll go with you to the barn."

Sally seemed grateful for my company. After we'd cleaned most of the blood off the saddle and tightened the girth, I helped Sally shorten the stirrups and gave her a boost onto the horse. She looked so small up there, smaller than her fifteen years with her faded dress bunched up around her spindly legs and a nervous look in her eyes.

Mary waited on the step with the food. There was no sign of Lucinda, nor thankfully, any sign of strange men or a marshal either.

"May the good Lord ride with you, Sweet Sally," Mary said. Her double chin quivered and there was evidence of tears in her eyes.

"I'll be praying for you too," I said and hoped Sally knew these weren't idle words, that I'd truly be praying.

"Most likely the old lady'll be prayin' for me too," Sally said. The smile she attempted was almost swallowed by fear and nervousness. I wanted to tell her not to go, that I'd take the horse the few miles to the river. Before I could speak, Sally straightened in the saddle and urged the horse across the yard. "I'll be home by afternoon," she called. "Don't worry none about me. Just worry about Master Caleb."

———•———

The next hours passed in a whirl of scrubbing and cleaning.

"We must do away with any evidence that Caleb's here or that he's been wounded," Mrs. Tremayne said.

We concentrated on the evidence first, scrubbing away all signs of blood and shoving Caleb's clothes and my and Sally's bloodstained dresses into the hiding place by the cellar.

In between scrubbing, one of us would check on Caleb or I'd run upstairs to the cupola that rose above the roof and offered a good view of the country. I looked north, south, everywhere—hoping and praying I wouldn't see anyone, which I didn't.

I thanked God so often that afternoon He probably got tired of hearing me. I couldn't stop myself. My gratitude and belief were so strong I wanted to thank Him and let Him know I had faith in Him.

"How about the place where you found Caleb?" Lucinda asked after one of my trips to the cupola. I hurried outside and pulled up most of the stained grass and poured water over the rest. Urgency pushed me along. I don't ever remember being so hurried.

As I worked, I kept thinking we had everything backwards. We should be hiding Caleb first. Then we could clean the house. But each time I went to check on him, I changed my mind. His paleness frightened me. The thought of moving him frightened me even more. There were too many stairs and we were but three women, two really when it came to moving Caleb. What if we restarted the bleeding?

Those weren't the only reasons for not moving him. The fact was, we didn't know where to put him. Although the hiding place offered protection, the steep stairs and the cold room would likely be the death of Caleb. When I voiced my concern to Lucinda, she agreed.

"He has to be kept warm so his lungs don't get inflamed. That's one of the risks of a wound like this . . . inflammation and pleurisy, not to mention fever. He'll likely be feverish by night . . . tomorrow for sure."

Just thinking about tomorrow frightened me. Would Caleb still cling to life? Would strange men be swarming over the place looking for him? The questions brought me to my knees beside Caleb. I reached under the quilt to find his hand and brought it to my cheek to let him feel my tears and my love when I kissed it.

I didn't concern myself with what Caleb's mother might think, though I sensed her presence by the door. Smart as she was, she'd probably figured things out. Maybe Caleb had told her of our plans to marry. There was much I didn't know then. About Lucinda Tremayne and about myself.

"We've got to get nourishment into him," his mother said.

Still holding Caleb's hand I looked at her. "Is he strong enough to swallow?"

Lucinda pursed her lips. "We've got to try. Beef broth is good to build up the blood. After all he's lost—" She paused. "Between the two of us we should be able to get something into him."

Accomplishing this was no small task. I'd spoon-fed Mother after her stroke, but she'd always been strong enough to swallow. Caleb was too far gone into unconsciousness to respond. In the end, I had to gently massage the muscles of his throat each time Lucinda put the spoon to his lips. Once, twice, four times until he turned his head away.

"It's a start," Lucinda said. "We can try again later." Her voice was calm, instead of worried, as if we had all the time in the world to find a hiding place for Caleb. As if no one more threatening than Mr. Brown might come looking for him.

In between quick trips to the cupola and helping Mary fix something to eat, I searched my mind for a safe place to hide Caleb. I pulled up another chair so Lucinda and I could both keep watch beside him. I felt her love flowing out to him in a warm, calm stream. Could love heal him just like faith could? My love and hers?

"Please, God," I prayed and knew his mother was praying too. We sat together, not speaking, nothing but Caleb's quiet breathing and the occasional rush of wind through the maple tree to break the quiet.

"I'm going to take a look outside," Lucinda said. "Sounds like a storm's blowing in."

I stayed with Caleb. I don't know what alerted me to the fact that he was awake, that sometime during the quiet his eyes had opened— cobalt blue and puzzled, like he was having trouble remembering what had happened.

I smiled from pure joy and he did too, though his smile was a little lopsided. His smile only lasted a few seconds before sliding into something like pain. His eyes darted around the room, past me, past Mary standing by the door, flying out of the house and across the miles to the place he'd been shot. Fear glinted in his eyes and I could almost hear the shouting, "Ride! Quick! Faster! Faster!"

"You're safe," I told him, though perhaps I lied.

"Men were chasing me. They might . . . still come."

"We know," I assured him. "We've been watching from the cupola. That's where your mother is now."

Caleb quieted and his eyes grew calmer. Suddenly he tried to rise. "The horse! . . ."

"Hush." I gently pushed him back. "The horse is gone. Sally's taken it away." I smiled, hoping the gesture would quiet him. "We've cleaned up everything so no one will know."

I reached under the quilt for Caleb's hand and took heart when he squeezed it. "We've been afraid to move you. I don't want to put you down in the cellar . . . it's too cold." I bit my lower lip to keep it from trembling. "We don't know where to hide you," I conceded.

"There's a hiding place in here . . . behind the bookcase."

"Here?" I wanted to cry with happiness.

Lucinda was as cheered by the news as I was when I called up the stairs to tell her. "Just imagine," she kept saying. When she reached the study, she paused in the doorway to look at her son and saw him smile. "Thank Thee, Lord," she whispered. Then she covered her face with her apron and burst into tears.

<hr />

The hiding room in the study was just as cleverly concealed as the one by the cellar. The design of the opening was also similar, the middle section of the bookcase sliding on a track into the thick outer wall of the house.

"Mercy," Mary whispered when she saw it. "I've been here all this time and never suspected." She looked at Caleb with something bordering on awe. "Your mother always said you were a clever one."

The ceiling of the hiding place rose to the same height as the study, but the space itself was long and narrow and just wide enough for a single bed, a small table and a chair.

Lucinda and I lost little time in readying it. We couldn't do anything to get rid of the musty odor, but we made up the bed and brought in hot bricks to warm it. We were so caught up in fixing the bed we forgot about danger until the back door banged shut.

"We gotta hide Master Caleb . . . fast," Sally panted as she burst into the room. Her hair fell in straggles from beneath her bonnet and the hem on her dress was torn. "Four men on horses was talkin' to Mr. Donnley down at the crossroads. Now they're comin' this way."

For a moment we could only stare. Lucinda was the first to recover. "Run upstairs and tidy yourself. Then go to the cupola and keep watch. Call down the minute you spy the men."

"Yes'm." Sally's eyes took in the secret room before they shifted to Caleb. "Is he goin' to be all right?"

"Yes," I answered. "Go now. And hurry."

Halfway up the stairs, Sally stopped and called back to us. "It's started to rain too."

All of my attention was focused on Caleb. "Can you sit up?"

He nodded and with my help he did, though the little bit of color that had returned to his cheeks left. The distance from the leather sofa to the bookcase was less than ten feet, but it seemed more as we helped Caleb over to it. Twice his knees buckled and I feared we wouldn't be able to get him there. At least not in time. *Oh, hurry! Hurry!*

When Caleb was finally settled in bed, his mother checked for fresh bleeding. Fear shoved me back to the sofa. Traces of blood were in abundance, dripped and smeared on the seat and across the arms. Anticipating my intention, Mary came with rags and a basin of warm water. I washed and dried the leather before I turned my attention to the floor.

"No one's comin'," Sally called. "But the rain's turned bad."

Mrs. Tremayne stepped out of the hiding room and left the sliding door open a few inches. "There's no fresh bleeding," she said with satisfaction. "And the rain will give us a good excuse to start a fire in here. Caleb needs all the warmth he can get." She nodded her approval when she saw the clean sofa. "Find an afghan to lay across the wet places"

I was returning with the afghan when I heard Sally clatter down from the cupola. "They're comin'," she cried. "Four of 'em turned off the main road." Her words seemed to come out of a nightmare. She stopped when she saw me. "What're we gonna do?"

I asked myself the same question, the need to hurry sending me down the stairs with Sally right behind me.

"What're we gonna do?" she repeated to Mrs. Tremayne.

"What you usually do when you have company." Lucinda's voice was matter-of-fact as she moved from the fresh fire and slid shut the opening to the room. "You and Mary keep yourselves busy in the kitchen, and Miss Yeager and I will pretend we've been gossiping in the sitting room. Hurry now . . . but you must act calm and natural. Mr. Tremayne's life will depend on how well we do."

We scattered in all directions—Mary and Sally to the kitchen, Lucinda toward the stairs. Fear had taken control of our minds. If I hadn't stopped to hang the afghan over the back of the sofa, I wouldn't have seen the basin of bloody water I'd left there. I picked it up so quickly some of the water sloshed onto the floor.

"Put it into the room with Caleb," Lucinda instructed when she returned to see what was keeping me.

I carried it to the bookcase without any more spills. Mrs. Tremayne slid the door open for me. "We'll be back," I told Caleb.

Before leaving, I stopped and hastily wiped the spilled water with the bottom of my petticoat. Heart pounding, I hurried after Lucinda. As I climbed the stairs I could hear the canter of hooves.

"Slowly," Lucinda whispered. "We can't be out of breath if we've spent the afternoon sitting and talking."

Trying to slow my feet proved almost as difficult as trying to slow my breathing. *Slowly. Slowly.*

As soon as we reached the sitting room, I picked up a book and sat down by the window. Caleb's mother took another chair. From there we could see four men dismounting from their horses. The rain had turned into a steady drizzle, dripping from the eaves onto my newly planted roses and wetting the men's coats and hats. I lost sight of them when they walked up the front steps.

The sharp rap of the brass knocker jarred through my nerves like a clap of thunder. I jumped and so did Caleb's mother, our eyes meeting like soldiers' eyes must do just before the first shot is fired in a battle. I got to my feet and took a deep breath.

"Slowly," Lucinda whispered. "Pretend it's just the neighbors."

I tried to follow her advice as I left, pausing to tuck back a stray lock of hair and smoothing the skirt of my dress before I crossed the wide foyer to the front door. All thoughts of pretense vanished when I saw the men's faces, grim and hard and full of purpose.

"Afternoon, ma'am," the tallest man said. "I'm sorry to bother you like this, but as deputy marshal, it's my duty."

"Your duty?" I looked at him in what I hoped was bewilderment.

"Could I speak to the gentleman of the house? We were told Mr. Tremayne lives here."

I slipped my trembling hands into the pockets of my apron before I spoke. "He does, but I'm afraid he isn't home."

The man's eyes narrowed. "Where is he?"

My heart quickened when I realized we hadn't planned what I should say. Before I could think of an answer, Lucinda called from the next room.

"Who's here, Miss Yeager? Have you invited them inside?"

"It's a deputy marshal. Deputy? . . ."

"Deputy Foster," the man interjected.

"He wants to know where Mr. Tremayne is."

This brought Lucinda to the door, holding Mary's knitting. She behaved in a manner I'd never seen her use before, like she thought she was better than they were, and didn't like mud tracked onto her polished floor. One of the men looked down at his feet and surreptitiously wiped the toe of his boot on the leg of his breeches. "I'm Mrs. Tremayne. Unfortunately my son isn't at home right now."

"Gone, is he? May I ask where?"

"That I can't tell you. My son often goes away on business. Besides being a farmer, he's also involved with his uncle in a shipping business out of Boston. He left several days ago. Thursday, I believe it was."

I gave Lucinda a quick look, wondering how she'd come up with her story and when she'd thought to pick up Mary's knitting.

"You're certain Mr. Tremayne's been gone that long?" Deputy Foster asked. I noticed he hadn't wiped his feet.

"I am."

"He said he'd probably be gone for at least a fortnight," I interjected.

The deputy studied Lucinda before he directed his gaze at me. I willed myself to meet his eyes. Nothing we had said had softened them. *Be calm. Act puzzled,* my brain cried.

"I see." The tone of the man's voice made me fear he saw too much. He scratched the stubble on his chin. "I don't want to alarm you, but we're lookin' for a man that's been shot . . . dangerous too."

"Mercy!" Mrs. Tremayne gasped and put a hand to her bosom.

"We found the horse he was ridin' down by the river," he went on. "We think he might be hiding here . . . in your barn or one of your outbuildings. Do you mind if we look around?"

"Why, no," I said. "In fact we'd be obliged if you did."

The men left, excusing themselves for troubling us, promising to be thorough in their search so we could rest easy come night.

My eyes flew to Lucinda the minute the door closed. She put a finger to her lips and shook her head. We listened to the sound of boots as the men walked down the steps, heard the marshal tell someone to check the granary, someone else to search the shed.

"Run upstairs and see what they're doing," Lucinda whispered. She took my hand and squeezed it before I hurried away.

From the cupola I had an unobstructed view of the barn and granary, the woodshed too. Seeing two men enter the barn with their guns drawn, I was thankful I'd rid the barn of any evidence of the black horse, putting the oat bucket back in its usual place and using a shovel to throw the fresh horse droppings into the pasture.

Hardly any time passed before I saw a man sprint from the granary to the barn, his head down and his hat pulled low against the rain. The storm was an answer to prayer. Not only would it prevent them from thoroughly searching the yard, it would wash away the blood on the grass and the wobbly trail left by the wheelbarrow.

"Thank you," I whispered when another man ran from the woodshed to join the others in the barn.

I stayed in the cupola until I saw them start back to the house. I scarcely had time to report to Lucinda before a knock sounded on the door. The sound set my heart hammering again. I willed myself to be calm as I went to answer it.

"Just wanted to let you know we didn't find anyone. Looks like you ladies can rest easy tonight." The deputy's cold, calculating eyes nullified pleasant features and polite words.

The thought of Caleb lying helpless on the narrow bed behind the bookcase acted as reinforcement for my courage. His very life was in my hands. "It was good of you to let us know." I made my voice as polite as the deputy's, then added like it was something I'd just thought of, "Could the man you're looking for have fallen off his horse and drowned in the river?"

The deputy blinked, as though it was something he hadn't thought of—something he didn't want a woman suggesting. "We're checking every possibility."

"Good." I smiled and continued my polite act. "Would you and your men like to come inside and warm yourselves? One of the servants can make hot coffee."

The marshal's dark eyes studied me for a long moment. My hands, which I'd thrust into my apron pockets, were trembling again, but the rest of me was surprisingly calm.

"No thank you, ma'am, though I appreciate the offer. There're a couple more farms we want to stop at before it gets dark." He looked toward the sitting room. "I noticed a horse and buggy tied up when I was on my way to the barn. Who do they belong to?"

"Mrs. Tremayne."

Hearing her name, Lucinda came to the door. "I live on the farm just east of here. My son farms both properties. I come by from time to time to see how Miss Yeager and the rest of the household are doing." Caleb's mother was using that voice again, the one that said she was the deputy's better and that she didn't appreciate all the questions he was asking.

"Raining like it is, you might want to move the buggy into the barn."

Lucinda smiled, all graciousness. "An excellent idea. Would one of your men be good enough to do that for me?"

For a second Deputy Foster looked like he didn't know what to say. "Certainly ma'am. We'll be glad to," he finally answered.

I looked past the deputy to the men standing on the porch, shoulders hunched against the wind blowing gusts of rain into their meager shelter. My satisfaction left when I saw the hardness in the deputy's brown eyes.

"We'll be going now." He gave a curt nod and slapped his wet hat against his leg, showering the floor and me with dampness. As he set it back onto his dark head he looked me square in the eyes. "If we don't find the man, we'll likely be back." The expression on his face was cold. Mean too. It sent a jolt of fear through me, but I made a point of meeting and holding his gaze.

"The man we shot is suspected of helping runaway slaves. Niggers." His voice lingered on the word, like it was one he enjoyed using. "I can't abide uppity niggers who try to take on white-folk ways. Can't abide whites who try to help them neither." He paused and smiled down at me. There was nothing smiling in his voice. It was hard and threatening. "Something don't seem quite right here, so don't be surprised if you see me and my men again real soon."

CHAPTER 16

It was late afternoon when Caleb's mother left. By then it had stopped raining and Sam had come to do the milking. After Sam brought in the milk, Lucinda sent him outside to bring the buggy to the front. As soon as he left, she pulled the green drapery across the study window and went to check on Caleb again.

Caleb stirred when I turned up the lamp on the table. He smiled weakly when he saw me, then his eyes shifted to his mother.

"I have to leave, but I'll be back tomorrow." She checked the bandages then felt his forehead for signs of fever. "I leave you in capable hands. Miss Yeager . . . Mary and Sally . . ." She paused to clear her throat. "They saved your life, you know. I couldn't have done better myself."

Lucinda leaned over and kissed him, something I suspected hadn't happened often in the past. Not with this restless son who'd run off to sea and liked to keep his feelings to himself.

Caleb's mother instructed Sally to keep the fire built up and burning through the night. Then she turned to me. "Dr. Hillman gave me some carbolic acid. I'll bring it tomorrow. It's better than turpentine for cleaning wounds. You have to be careful with turpentine or it will blister."

I recalled how Caleb had flinched when I'd poured it onto his wounds. Only great control had kept him from crying out.

I followed Lucinda out of the house to the back stoop. The long shadows of late afternoon stretched across my garden where the freshly hoed soil lay moist and black from the rain.

"I doubt Deputy Foster will be back tonight. But tomorrow or the next day . . ." She paused and gave me a steady look. "Should they come when I'm not here, I have every confidence you'll handle it. I know my son does too. Have Sally keep watch so you won't be taken by surprise."

"What about Caleb . . . Mr. Tremayne?"

Lucinda's expression turned pensive. "I think he'll live, if that's what you mean, though matters of life and death rest in God's hands, not ours. But still . . ." She pursed her lips and nodded. "The next two days will be the test, but I believe my son will live."

I clung to Lucinda's words through the long night as I kept watch beside Caleb. Although I managed to persuade Mary to go up to bed, Sally insisted on staying with me, the two of us sitting on chairs drawn close to the bed with nothing but the crackle of the fire and the hiss of the whale-oil lamp for conversation.

There was a conversation of sorts going on inside my head, the events of the day crying out in vivid flashes of memory. The sight of Caleb's crumpled body lying in the grass came again and again along with his blood and my fear and the frantic rush to save him. Each time the memory became too much, my eyes fastened on Caleb, who appeared as a shadowy series of lumps and hollows under the quilt. But he was alive. The barely discernable rise and fall of his chest whispered of the battle won, the pale triangles on the quilt our victory banner—at least for now.

I clung to that thought while the clock ticked and Sally dozed. She awoke with a start when I went to put fresh wood on the fire, her face a pattern of guilt when she realized she'd dozed through part of our vigil.

"Master Caleb?" she whispered when she saw me lean over and touch his forehead.

I nodded to let her know there wasn't any change. He breathed. He slept. There was no sign of fever.

Sally gave a sleepy smile and straightened in the chair, but it was only a matter of minutes until her head dropped forward again. My heart went out to the woman-child who had become my friend. Sally's straggly hair and ill-fitting brown dress made her all the more dear to me. They told the story of her past and all that life had forced upon her. But her brave actions today and the loyalty that kept her by Caleb's bed were the story of her future. There was strength and courage in that small body. Intelligence and great love too. I scooted my chair closer to hers and slipped my arm around Sally's shoulder. I heard her sigh, felt the weight of her head as it settled against me. Sally's heavy breathing told me that she slept. Caleb slept. And despite my firm resolve to do otherwise, I slept too.

———•———

I awoke with a start to a predawn chorus of robins singing in the maple tree. My eyes immediately fastened on Caleb. He lay as still as a corpse, his features but shadows and his eyes like two dark holes in the murky lamplight. Slipping my arm away from Sally, I felt for a pulse in Caleb's neck, my fear-caught breath easing out in a sigh when I found it. But my heart needed further assurance. I picked up the lamp and brought it close to the bed. The dark holes became eyes and the shadows turned into a three-day growth of dark stubble on his jaw and chin. Sweat gleamed on the pale skin of his upper face and trickled into the stubble. The fever had come—one that would set Caleb tossing and eat his meager strength.

The fever became our battle for the next two days as we bathed Caleb's burning skin with cool cloths and applied a poultice of milk-soaked bread to the wounds. When these failed to bring any change, Lucinda sent Sally to the creek to strip bark from willows. After boiling the bark, we spooned the bitter liquid between Caleb's protesting lips and held them shut until he swallowed. Through it all Caleb tossed in delirium, his eyes, when they opened, were glazed with terror or dulled, and showed no sign of recognition—not of Sally, not of me, not even of his mother.

When there was no improvement by Wednesday, I began to despair. The fever was taking a terrible toll from a body already weakened by shock and loss of blood.

"Don't let him die," I prayed. I wasn't the only one praying. We all spent time on our knees beside Caleb's bed or in the kitchen or cupola or wherever we felt ourselves falling into despair.

"The Lord is watching over him. Mr. Tremayne is in His hands," Mary reminded us, though there were times when even Mary's voice lacked conviction. Her waning faith frightened me almost as much as the fever.

On Wednesday morning Lucinda did not come. That in itself was a worry, and the note she sent with young Sam failed to lessen my concern.

> *Hannah and Mrs. Brown think I should send for Dr. Hillman if Mary is so bad she requires constant nursing. Rather than arouse their suspicion, I feel it prudent not to come for a day or two, especially since Deputy Foster and two of his men came by and asked more questions.*

My heart jerked when I read the deputy's name. Why hadn't he returned? What was keeping him? Concern for Caleb had almost driven the man's threat from my mind. Almost. Despite my turmoil, fear of the deputy hovered at the edge of my mind, like a shadow lurking in a dark corner that vanishes as soon as it's exposed to light— always there, but never seen. I shut my eyes for a moment, then with a shake of my head, returned my attention to Lucinda's note.

> *As I said before, I hold great confidence in your ability to nurse Caleb back to health. I have taught you all I know. Continue the cool cloths and poultice and a swallow of willow tea every few hours. Send Sally to get me if—*here words had been crossed out—*if he takes a turn for the worse. I have great faith in your nursing and judgment.*

"You won't die," I said to Caleb. "You're going to live." This phrase alternating with a plea for God's help became my beacon. "Hold on. Fight Caleb, fight." My spirits, like my faith, ebbed and flowed. One moment I fought death with both hands and every ounce of my energy, the next I felt as if my efforts were of no more significance than those of an ant.

That afternoon as I changed Caleb's bandages, I was at my lowest. Looking at the wounds always made me flinch—the flesh raw and puckered where Lucinda had made her stitches. This time they didn't seem as inflamed. Maybe the poultice was working.

I looked up to call the good news to Sally and encountered Caleb's gaze, his eyes blue and lucid, puzzled too.

Joy diffused through me, lifting my heart and making me want to cry out with happiness. Only strict control kept me from weeping. I smiled, my eyes filling with tears as I whispered his name.

Caleb returned my smile, though his eyes remained puzzled.

I lifted his hand and kissed it. "You were shot, and for three days you've run a terrible fever. But now . . ." I laid a tentative hand on his forehead, afraid I'd feel the dreaded heat. It was cool, or nearly so, the fever broken and our numerous prayers answered.

Mary and Sally helped me rebandage the wounds. Happy tears rolled down Mary's plump cheeks as she helped me tighten the bandages, and Sally's excited giggles when he took a few awkward sips of water were almost uncontrollable. Caleb slept the rest of the afternoon, his deep, untroubled slumber a stark contrast to the restless jerking and trembling which had filled it before.

As I rejoiced, I also sorrowed at the sight of Caleb's sunken eyes and gaunt cheeks. The bones were more prominent in his shoulders as well. But he lived. I took comfort in this and wrapped it around me like a warm shawl as I hummed and helped Mary stew a fresh-killed chicken for supper.

I greeted Sam with a smile when he came to the back door with the evening's milk. We took care to keep Mary out of sight since everyone from the old house thought she'd taken to her bed. I thanked him warmly for the milk and the extra chores he'd taken on while Mr. Tremayne was gone—the fresh-chopped wood and the spading he'd done in my garden.

"Mrs. Tremayne wanted me to ask about Mary . . . if she's still doing poorly and if there's anything else she can do to help."

I stared at him before I realized what Mrs. Tremayne was asking. "I believe Mary is doing better. The symptoms have lessened and she seems to be on the mend. Mary's still weak, though, and any suggestions from Mrs. Tremayne on a healing diet would be appreciated."

"I'll tell her," Sam promised.

I followed him into the yard, waving him on his way and watching his gangly frame leap the fence and take off at a run for his home and supper.

I took a deep breath, the first fresh air I'd breathed in hours, and hugged myself against the evening chill. I wanted to hurry back inside, but my heart begged to savor what remained of the day—the evening song of robins and the pearly shades of saffron and pink that painted the sky as the sun sank below the horizon. Gratitude washed through me as my soul drank in the evening's beauty. For the first time in three days I knew peace.

———•———

Following Lucinda's instructions, which were delivered in a note brought by Sam with the milk on the following morning, I spoon-fed Caleb a thin gruel made from oatmeal followed by a few sips of weak tea laced with willow bark tincture. The simple act of eating left Caleb exhausted, and after Mary helped him into a clean nightshirt he fell into a deep sleep.

"It's the best thing for him," Mary said as we left the tiny room. "Sleep and a little something to eat will do him a world of good." She paused and her round face creased into a big smile. "I think our Mr. Tremayne is going to be all right now."

"You and Sally have been such a help." I put my arm around Mary's plump shoulder and gave her a squeeze. "Thank you."

Mary shook her head. "'Twasn't nothing." She looked me full in the face, her eyes bright with mischief. "But I must say that for an old woman who's supposed to be so terribly sick, I've managed to do a fair amount of work these past few days."

Our laughter bubbled like a springtime brook, happy and tumbling. Cleansing too, as it washed away fear and worry and replaced it with spring-fresh hope.

"Oh, Mary," I gasped.

Mary laughed harder, her breath coming out in little whoops of delight that made her bosom jiggle. "Mercy . . . oh, mercy," she wheezed. Her face was pink and tears ran down her cheeks.

We were laughing so hard we didn't hear Sally run down the stairs. "Someone's comin'!" she cried. I turned to stare at her. "Seven men ridin' horses just turned off the main road."

Shocked silence replaced laughter. We'd been so busy nursing Caleb we'd scarcely given any thought to what we would do if the deputy returned. Thank heaven Sally had gone up to the cupola.

I took a long steadying breath as my eyes sought the opening to Caleb's hiding place. The door had been left open to let in the warmth from the fire. A dozen thoughts jangled through my mind and clamored for attention

"Get upstairs and into bed, Mary. Sally will help you."

They both looked at me as if I had gone out of my head.

"What about Master Caleb?" Sally began.

"I'll see to Master Caleb. It's your responsibility to help Mary."

"But . . ."

"Deputy Foster and his men went to the old house yesterday. They were probably told that Mary's been sick . . . so sick Mrs. Tremayne had to come over and check on her."

It took a second for my words to sink in. Then Sally took Mary's arm, the sound of Mary's heavy, frightened breath trailing after them.

"Since you'll be in bed, I doubt the men will be bold enough to question you," I called. "In case they do, pretend you've been so sick you have no notion of what's been going on."

"I'll try," Mary wheezed. "The Lord knows I'll do my best."

"Hurry back as soon as you're through with Mary," I told Sally.

"Yes'm." Sally's voice was so thin and harried I wondered if she'd be able to pretend—to conceal her fright.

I grabbed soiled linen from the sofa and thrust them into the room with Caleb. How he'd managed to sleep through the laughter and our fright, I didn't know. But he slept, his breathing deep and regular. Then I surveyed the study for any evidence of Caleb. I found it in a roll of bandages and in a tray with the remains of Caleb's gruel and the willow tea. These quickly joined the nightshirt and linen in Caleb's room. Reasonably sure I'd removed all the evidence, I slid the panel firmly back into place. There. It was done. The study was just a study again, the bookcase only a place for books.

Sally ran back down the stairs just as I reached the kitchen. "Mary said she could do the rest herself," she panted. "But we gotta hurry. I peeked out Mary's window and they're almost here."

"Almost," I said, trying to calm her. "Almost . . . which means we have time to collect ourselves and pray for God's guidance."

Sally's gaze darted around the kitchen like a frightened puppy that didn't know which way to run. "But we've gotta . . ."

"We've got to be calm," I finished for her. "If you show your fear, the men will guess you're hiding something."

"Oh, miss." Her lips trembled and tears welled up in her eyes.

Someone pounded on the front door. I put my hands on Sally's shoulders. "Measure flour into a bowl and start a batch of molasses cookies. You know how much Master Caleb likes them. He's counting on us. His very life will depend on how well we do."

Sally took a deep breath and nodded.

"Say a prayer," I whispered. Then I turned and made my way to the stairs. *Slowly. Slowly.* It was as if Lucinda were with me again, urging me to be calm and pretend it was only a neighbor.

As I climbed the stairs, the knock came again, its tone arrogant and impatient to my frightened ears. Despite my efforts to remain calm, my palms went clammy. *Slowly. Slowly.* I stopped and took a deep breath, expecting to see Deputy Foster when I opened the door. But it wasn't Deputy Foster's impatient eyes that widened in surprise. The eyes belonged to Amos Mickelson.

My first instinct was to run, but something kept me rooted to my spot as Amos's fleshy lips opened in astonishment. My tight hold on the door was all that kept my hastily prepared composure in place.

"Fancy meeting you here, Miss Yeager."

"Mr. Mickelson." I managed to keep my voice steady as I inclined my head and shifted my gaze to the deputy.

Deputy Foster removed his hat, and his voice was cold when he spoke. "We still haven't found the man we're looking for. The one helping runaway niggers."

"I'm sorry to hear that." I strove to give him my full attention, but my mind scurried back to Amos. Why was he with the deputy?

"This is my superior, Commissioner Amos Mickelson," Deputy Foster went on. "It seems you've already met."

"We have."

"Until last year, Miss Yeager resided in Mickelboro," Amos said. His eyes flicked back to me in a satisfied manner. "Deputy Foster thinks, and I'm inclined to believe him, that the man he's searching for has taken refuge here. His horse was found at the river."

I opened my mouth to speak, but Deputy Foster interrupted me.

"We need some straight answers from you. And we'll be searching the house. Three of my men are already looking in the barn."

My mind raced in circles of fear and indecision. "Mr. Tremayne won't be pleased when he returns and hears of your actions."

"It's about Mr. Tremayne that we want to question you."

My heart plummeted. Realizing that further protest would arouse more suspicions, I invited the men inside, willing myself not to tremble as I led Amos and Deputy Foster into the sitting room while the other two men remained in the foyer. I strove for calmness as I answered their questions. *Yes, Mr. Tremayne was still away. No, I didn't know when he'd be back. As his mother said* . . . I hurried on, "Mr. Tremayne is often from home and his return is determined by the amount of business in Boston."

Amos gave a little snort when I said *Boston*. "Deputy Foster has checked with the ticket agent in Bayberry. Mr. Tremayne did not purchase a railcar ticket to Boston or anywhere else last week."

I shrugged and hoped the action detracted their attention from my tightly clenched hands. "Of that I have no knowledge. I only know Mr. Tremayne left here last Thursday."

Deputy Foster shot a quick glance at Amos. They were sitting directly across from me. The deputy was frowning, everything bespeaking frustration. Not so with Amos. He lounged in the chair as if he sat there every day, his thick legs spread out in front like a man who has nothing on his mind except relaxing in a comfortable chair. His next words let me know that appearances can be deceiving.

"How many people are living here?"

"With Mr. Tremayne, there are four, though Mr. Brown and his boys are in and out all the time. None of us have seen anyone."

Amos gave another snort. "Get the others in here so we can question them too." I could tell he was enjoying himself.

Perversity made me take my time. I knew how much Amos enjoyed telling people what to do. "I can get Sally for you, but I'm afraid Mary is unwell and unable to get out of bed."

Amos's fleshy lips tightened. "Get her anyway."

"She's old, Deacon Mickelson. And her poor legs are so swollen from dropsy she can scarcely walk."

My words had the desired effect, though it was the deputy who responded instead of Amos. "Then we'll go in to her."

I waited for them to follow me, Amos scowling, Deputy Foster determined. Mary looked as if she'd been in bed for hours instead of minutes, her mousy hair hanging in an untidy plait over one shoulder and her night cap pulled low on her forehead. Mary's eyes widened for an instant when she recognized Amos, but the rest of her plump features remained slack like someone who'd just wakened.

"These men want to ask you some questions," I began.

"Yes . . ." Mary's voice quavered, and had I not known better I would have thought she scarcely had the strength to speak.

Deputy Foster did most of the questioning. "When did you last see Mr. Tremayne?"

"Mr. Tremayne?" Mary looked puzzled.

"Was it today? Yesterday?" The deputy's voice gave no hint that he was trying to trick her.

The furrow between Mary's brows deepened and she gave me an inquiring glance. "Didn't you tell them . . . the master's away?"

"I did."

"Then why? . . ."

"Just answer the deputy's questions," Amos cut in.

"Yes, sir." Mary paused as if to gather her breath. "Last week it was . . . though I've been so poorly . . ." She coughed and the rest of the sentence came out in a wheeze. ". . . I've lost track of time."

"You're certain it was last week when you saw him?"

Mary looked the deputy square in the eyes as she nodded.

"I see." Deputy Foster pursed his lips as his gaze wandered from Mary to the spoon and apothecary bottle on the table. Thank heaven Mary faithfully took the bad-tasting concoction. Otherwise there wouldn't have been anything in the room that bespoke illness.

Deputy Foster wasn't the only one looking. Amos went to the wardrobe and peered inside. Not satisfied, he pushed Mary's dress aside and felt the wood-paneled back. My blood chilled as I watched his pudgy fingers on the wood. What if he did the same in the study?

While Amos searched the wardrobe, Deputy Foster dropped to his knees and peered under the bed. "Nothing but the chamber pot and some dust balls," he muttered in disgust.

"Are you through with your questioning, gentlemen?" I queried in measured reserve.

"For now." The deputy paused and gave Mary a long, searching look. She met it with perfect equanimity, though I detected a slight quiver in the heavy flesh around her mouth.

Hang on, I prayed, and just as if she'd heard me, Mary's eyes fell shut. "Get the other woman," Amos said when we'd left her.

They returned to the sitting room while I called for Sally. My stomach tightened at the thought of what the next minutes could bring. Would Sally be able to skirt the deputy's questioning? In a sudden flash I knew I must protect her and by so doing protect Caleb. With God's help, I'd saved Caleb from his wounds and fever. I wasn't about to let them take away the man I loved. Instead of waiting for Sally, I rejoined the men in the sitting room.

"I want to thank you for not bothering Mary any more than was necessary." I forced myself to smile. "I hope you will be as kind with Sally." I paused, not sure of how to go on. "Sally's had a hard life and as a result she isn't quite right in her thinking. Mind you, she works hard. It's just that she gets confused sometimes and is frightened easily . . . especially by men." I turned my full gaze on Amos, who sat in the chair by the hearth. "Knowing of your close connection to the church, Deacon Mickelson, I have every confidence I can depend upon your kindness."

Amos looked uncomfortable and he shot the deputy a furtive glance. "Duty comes before kindness, Miss Yeager," he mumbled.

"Some may say that is the case, but a man of your high character can surely find a way to count them as equal."

I felt satisfaction when Amos refused to meet my eyes. Satisfaction in myself as well. It was as if someone older and wiser had suddenly taken hold of my thoughts and actions. My barely controlled trembling had given way to something close to calmness, and my brain, which had been partially numbed with fear, was now sharp and clear. Caleb's life might hinge on what transpired during the next few minutes, and I was determined that I, not Amos or the deputy, would come out the winner.

I heard Sally on the stairs. She entered the room short of breath and gasped when she saw Amos. Her frightened eyes flew to me and I could read her question: *What's that Amos feller doing here?*

"This is Deputy Foster and Deacon Mickelson," I told her. "They're concerned that a man who escaped from them might be hiding here." I turned to the men. "Gentlemen, this is Sally."

"Ain't no man hidin' here," Sally blurted. She'd found a lock of straggly hair and was winding it around her finger.

I watched as Deputy Foster arranged his face into a more pleasant expression—one that was kind and ingratiating instead of calculating. As he did, I tried to imagine what he was thinking as he took in Sally's gangly frame and too large dress. I was more concerned about what he might read in her frightened eyes, however. Would he take her fear to be only what I'd explained? Or would he search deeper until he found the true source?

"That's what Miss Yeager told me." The deputy smiled and continued to look pleasant. "But it's about Mr. Tremayne that I want to question you. Have you seen him lately, Sally?"

Sally shook her head and stared at a spot midway between Amos and the deputy. "Master Caleb ain't here neither."

"Where is he?"

Sally shrugged and continued to stare at the wall. "Just gone," she finally said. "He does that sometimes."

"I see." Deputy Foster exchanged a quick glance with Amos. I could sense their growing frustration, and I knew how much Amos would like to find and convict Caleb of aiding fugitive slaves.

I won't let you do that, my mind shouted.

"Are you sure you haven't seen Mr. Tremayne today?" The deputy asked. "We tracked the man we shot to a place not far from here. Found the horse he'd been ridin' down by the river. It appears he's hiding around here someplace . . . and since no one's seen a stranger, we're beginning to suspect the man we're looking for must be your Master Caleb."

Sally shook her head vigorously. "Master Caleb's a good man. He wouldn't do nothin' you should shoot him for."

Amos left his chair and moved so Sally was forced to look at him. "But suppose we did shoot Master Caleb. Suppose he was hurt and bleeding. Would you help him? Have you helped him?"

I moved my head ever so slightly. *Dear God, help Sally see the trap Amos has set for her.*

Sally stared at Amos with frightened eyes, the lock of hair wound so tightly it looked ready to break off. She suddenly turned and grabbed my arm. "Is he sayin' Master Caleb's been hurt? If it's true, we gotta help him, Miss Yeager. We gotta help!"

I was too surprised to speak. I knew the tears welling in her eyes were genuine. So was her fear. But the rest—then I realized Sally was playacting. Just as if God had handed her a script, she was following it and waited expectantly for me to take my cue.

I put my arms around Sally and pulled her close. Her heart hammered like that of a trapped bird. My voice was soothing as I smoothed her hair. "The deacon is talking nonsense. We know Master Caleb hasn't been shot. He's away on business and these men have confused him with someone else."

"I don't think we have," Amos said. But his voice lacked conviction. Sally cried in earnest, her shoulders shaking as she sobbed.

"I don't think we're going to get anything that makes any sense out of this one," Deputy Foster said. "The old woman neither."

Amos pushed past us and took the deputy by the arm. "Then we'll search the place. Get your men in here to help."

Remembering what Amos had done to the cottage, I hurried after them. "You'll have Mr. Tremayne to answer to when he gets back."

Amos turned, his eyes narrow and his puffy cheeks flushed with anger. "Mr. Tremayne can go to hell," he flung at me. "You and the girl too. You're all crazy." He shouted to the men in the foyer to search the rooms upstairs. "Look for anything suspicious," he said. "The abolitionists are clever at concocting places to hide niggers."

Sally and I stood by the door while the two men climbed the stairs to the bedrooms and Amos and the deputy checked the rest of the rooms on the main floor. I wanted to hug Sally and tell her how proud I was, but caution kept me silent while we listened to Amos rap on the walls. Since both of the rooms were unfurnished and empty, it only took them a couple of minutes to complete their search

"What's downstairs?" Amos demanded.

"The kitchen and dining room and Mr. Tremayne's study."

"Show us."

We preceded them down the stairs. I willed myself to remain calm as I showed them the dining room, the high-back chairs neatly placed around the table and a clean cloth awaiting our next meal. They gave the room no more than a cursory look, seeming to sense that nothing worth their attention was there.

The kitchen was next. A basket of eggs and the ingredients for molasses cookies sat on the table. My eyes searched the room. In my haste, had I left anything that might give away Caleb's presence? I saw it at once—bread soaking in a bowl of milk for a poultice.

Sally and I watched in silence as Deputy Foster looked inside the crockery cupboard while Amos pulled out the flour bin and thumped the back wall. Then Deputy Foster noticed the bowl of milk and bread. He stuck his finger in it and brought it to his nose.

"What's this?"

"A . . . a bread and milk poultice."

He shot me a look of disbelief. "Who's it for?"

"Mary. It eases the pain and swelling in her legs."

"Never heard of such a thing."

"I imagine there are several things you haven't heard of." I could tell the deputy thought I was getting uppity again. "Dr. Hillman and Mrs. Tremayne think highly of the treatment." The mention of the doctor mollified him some, but it didn't help Amos's mood. He wiped his hand across his cheek, smearing flour over it when he did. "Where's Mr. Tremayne's study?"

"Across the hallway."

Amos pushed the door open and stood there for a long moment. His bulk blocked the way and his stillness made my breath catch in fear. What did he see? Why wasn't he moving? Finally he spoke. "Why is a fire burning in Tremayne's study if he isn't home?"

"We often build a fire down here when he's gone," I answered, surprised at how easily the lie came. "It's more convenient to sit here than go all the way up to the sitting room."

"And Tremayne doesn't mind that you use it?"

"Not as long as we don't disturb his papers."

At the mention of papers, the palms of my hands grew damp. What if Amos or the deputy found the abolitionist newspapers?

My gaze flew to the bookcase as soon as the men stepped into the study. Would they suspect what it concealed? What if Caleb woke up and called me? I could feel Sally's fear. I smiled reassuringly and took her hand in mine. *Have courage!* I told her with a squeeze. She smiled and squeezed my hand in return. *I will.*

When I saw Amos open one of the desk drawers, I stepped into the room. "I don't think Mr. Tremayne's papers and private correspondence are any of your business or concern."

Amos looked up, his full lips lifting in a sneer. "They are if I choose to make them my business."

"You said you were looking for the man Deputy Foster shot. I hardly think that person can be hiding inside a drawer."

Sally giggled, and for an instant I thought I'd gone too far. Amos straightened, his features twisted in anger. I felt a prick of fear when he balled his hand into a fist. Deputy Foster saw it and cleared his throat. Muttering an oath, Amos slammed the drawer shut and began to rummage through the newspapers on top of Caleb's desk.

"We're looking for a man, not inspecting Tremayne's personal effects," the deputy reminded him.

Amos cursed and swept the newspapers onto the floor. My breath caught when I saw they'd landed so that the most recent issue of *The North Star* was in plain view.

Two quick steps took me to it, my shoes planted firmly over its banner and my gray skirt covering the rest. "Please, sir," I exclaimed. "We have enough to do without having you add to our work."

"It'll do you good." Amos snarled and threw one of Caleb's quill pens onto the pile of papers at my feet. The sound of the deputy's men coming down the stairs saved us from further display of his temper.

"Didn't find nothin' or nobody hidin' upstairs," one of them called. "Do you want us to help you down here?"

The deputy glanced at Amos. "We could use some help. See if you can find a cool room or cellar. I want every room searched."

One of the men stuck his head into the room and held up my lacy camisole, grinning as he did. "We did find a little somethin' up there." He twirled the corset by one of its ribbons. "How about havin' the little lady put it on so we can see how pretty it looks."

Sally lunged at him and tried to snatch it away. The man laughed, showing a mouth of crooked, yellow teeth.

Amos guffawed, but the deputy looked displeased. "Put it down, Pete. We don't have time for your tomfoolery today."

"Ah, come on. What's the harm in havin' a little fun?"

"I said put it down."

The man swore and threw the corset onto the sofa.

"Now see what you and Herman can do about helping."

Pete grinned when he saw the mess Amos had made with Caleb's papers. "We ought to be able to do that real easy."

I opened my mouth then closed it, sensing that any protest would only make matters worse. With Amos's attention taken with Pete and Herman, I glanced at the bookcase. I couldn't see anything to arouse their suspicion. *Please God, don't let Caleb make any noise, and help Sally and me to say and do the right things.*

As soon as Pete and Herman lit the lamp and started down the stairs to the cellar, Amos and Deputy Foster resumed their search, looking behind the green drapery at the window and rolling back the rug to check for a trap door. Amos dropped the rug in disgust when they failed to find anything.

Sally's nails dug into my hand when Amos moved to the book-case. He studied it for a long moment, his eyes going from shelf to shelf, past Caleb's leather bound set of maritime history and a minia-ture clipper ship. I closed my eyes, the clock's steady tick like an echo to my frightened heart. *Please God, please.*

"I think we found somethin'!" one of the men called.

Amos dropped a book and rushed passed me, throwing me a satisfied look as he did.

"Oh, miss . . ." Sally whispered. Her eyes were wide and fright-ened, and I feared her control was about to break.

"Hold on," I breathed. "Master Caleb is depending on us."

Sally took a deep breath. "I'm tryin'."

"I know you are. You've been magnificent."

I hurried after the men, afraid they'd found the hiding place. I stopped at the top of the stairs, my breathing a gasp of relief when I saw the sliding shelf was undisturbed and they were in the cellar.

"Seems awful strange for a man to store corn and wheat in a damp cellar," Herman was saying. "Don't make a lick of sense."

We heard the men rummaging through the sacks of corn and plunging their hands into the wheat bin.

"Maybe there's a secret room behind the bin," Pete suggested.

Sally smiled when we heard their struggle to move the heavy bin. Curses told of their failure. I pulled Sally into the kitchen before they came back upstairs. They were in a foul mood and one of them knocked a crock of pickled herring off the shelf as he passed it.

Thankfully Pete and Herman were too caught up in grumbling to see us, and the deputy was too busy apologizing to pay us any mind.

"I was sure we'd find Tremayne hiding here."

"You'd better think twice before you take me on another wild goose chase and make me look a fool," Amos cut in.

"But everything pointed to him . . . Tremayne gone and the horse found not far from his place."

"I don't want to hear your excuses." A tiny sound from Sally made the deacon stop. The look he shot me made my breath catch. There was a queer light in his eyes, like a man about to lose control.

"Whore," he spat. "You're just like your mother with nothing but a sick old woman and a crazy girl to help you. It won't last. Tremayne will tire of you and you'll be thrown out on your ear." He laughed, his face contorted and ugly. "Don't think you can come running back to me. I wash my hands of you."

"But I haven't washed my hands of you." Anger filled me with courage. "Mr. Tremayne is making inquiries into your mismanagement of Mother's affairs," I went on in a stronger voice, one that carried past Amos to Deputy Foster and the two men climbing the stairs. "Don't think you've heard the last of it, Deacon Mickelson. Or the last of me."

"Whore," he repeated. But little beads of sweat covered his upper lip and the queer look in his eyes had given way to concern. Instead of following the others upstairs, he stalked to the back door, slamming it behind him as he left the house.

Deputy Foster had stopped to listen to our exchange. Suddenly, it was as if a stranger jumped inside me, a woman with courage and backbone and a touch of recklessness. Instead of staying in the kitchen, I nodded to the deputy like I was a lady in Boston taking leave of her guests. "Let me show you gentlemen to the door."

Sally and I climbed the stairs. When we got to the foyer, the deputy stepped aside so we could precede him to the door, responding to my actions as though he'd suddenly recalled his manners.

"Would you give the gentleman his hat?" I said to Sally.

She flashed me a look of awe. Then as if she'd been doing it all her life, Sally took the deputy's hat from the peg by the door, dropped a curtsy, and handed it to him.

I gave an audible sigh of relief when the front door closed. A minute later I heard the clatter of hooves.

"Run up to the cupola and make sure they've all gone."

Sally nodded and hurried away. "They're gone," she called. "Seven of them riding down the lane." She laughed, her voice light and free of worry. "You should see that Amos feller. He's whippin' his horse like he wished it was you, and his fat behind looks ready to bounce right out of the saddle."

"Sally . . ."

"Sorry, miss." But I knew she wasn't. Sally was far too happy and pleased with herself for that. And I was far too happy to scold her. I gave her a quick hug, and we hurried down the stairs and slid the bookcase into the wall. We'd succeeded. More than that, the man we loved was alive and safe.

CHAPTER 17

Caleb's eyes were open when we rolled back the bookcase. Sally was laughing and I struggled not to cry as I knelt beside Caleb's bed and laid my face against his cheek while Sally held his hand.

"Thank God . . . thank God," I whispered.

"I was scared they'd start tappin' and find your hidin' place," Sally chimed in.

"So was I," Caleb said.

"Did you know they were here? Could you hear them?" I asked.

"Enough to know you and some men were in the study."

"Thankfully, they didn't find you."

"Amen . . . to that," Caleb whispered. "Did they say anything about finding my team and wagon?"

"No."

"Good."

Hearing the weakness in his voice, I got to my feet and turned up the lamp. "How are you feeling?"

"Weak." Caleb attempted a smile, the paleness of his skin a contrast to the dark stubble growing on his cheeks and chin. "If they'd found me, I couldn't have gotten out of bed . . . let alone run."

"Sally and I are here to take care of you until you're stronger." I smiled at the memory of Mary's performance in the bedroom and Sally's playacting. "I wish you could have seen Sally. She was frightened and yet she did so well. Mary too. You would have been proud of them both."

"What about you? Did you just sit in a chair and wring your hands?"

Sally giggled. "Miss done best of all, tellin' those men what they could and couldn't do. She acted like she wasn't one bit scared . . . not even of that fat ol' Amos."

"Amos?" Caleb's blue eyes sought mine.

I shot Sally a warning glance. "He's gone. And so are the deputy and his men." I leaned over and kissed Caleb's forehead. "We'll talk about Amos after you've slept and had something to eat. Your mother said you should have lots of broth. Sally and I will fix some while you sleep."

"Tamsin . . ."

I laid a finger across his lips. "Rest, Caleb. How do you expect to get your strength back?"

Caleb gave me a long steady look before he smiled and nodded. "All right." He took my hand and brushed it with his lips. "Thank you."

———•———

The next day Caleb seemed a little stronger, his color not so pallid, his voice less raspy. I knew the matter of Deacon Mickelson weighed heavily on his mind, so I told him all that had happened, playing down Amos's anger and concentrating on Sally's acting and the men's chagrin when they failed to find anything in the cellar. "After searching the house and barn yesterday," I concluded, "I think they're both convinced no one has taken refuge here."

Caleb frowned. "We still need to be careful."

"As we are." I reached and took his hand. "Sally and I continue to watch from the cupola. We've made plans too. Each of us knows what to do if Deacon Mickelson or Deputy Foster returns."

"Good." I could tell he didn't like it that Amos knew where we lived and suspected Caleb's involvement with runaway slaves.

I knelt beside Caleb's bed, a position I'd frequented over the past few days, arms and hands on the same level, our heads nearly so as well. "I'm not going to let Deacon Mickelson or the deputy find or harm you, Caleb." Determination emphasized my words. It must have shown on my face too, for Caleb looked at me in a strange manner as he squeezed my hand.

"What a fighter you have become."

I returned the pressure of his fingers. "Only when it involves the lives and happiness of those I love."

Moisture pooled in Caleb's eyes and he averted his gaze. I put my hand on his face, felt his tears as he turned his face into my palm and kissed it. "I hate this weakness," he rasped. "I should be protecting you, not you protecting me."

The sight of his tears made it difficult. "You'll soon be on your feet again," I whispered, not trusting my normal voice.

Caleb closed his eyes. "I doubt I'll be a good patient."

I brushed a lock of hair from his forehead. "We'll cross that bridge when we come to it. For now you need to rest."

Caleb slept all morning, waking only long enough to eat some broth and a few bites of bread at noontime. I used the time while he slept to catch up on neglected chores—helping Sally heat water for the washing, then going outside to check my garden. Everything, including the weeds, had grown. I spent a pleasant hour grubbing in the soil and admiring the new growth on the turnips and peas.

As I did, my thoughts slipped back to the previous week when I'd left my garden to search for a hoe. So much had happened since I'd discovered Delilah and Livie in their hiding place. Thank heaven Caleb had gotten them away. If only . . .

I wouldn't let myself dwell on "if only." Caleb was alive. He was getting better. In another week or two he'd be strong enough to stage his return. Careful plans must be made to accomplish this. I straightened and massaged my aching back. The mid-May weather was unusually warm, the sun burning into the gray fabric of my dress and making me glad I'd donned Mary's old bonnet. It was a lovely afternoon, the sky without clouds and not even a breeze to stir the branches on the maple.

Concern for Caleb wouldn't let me stay outside long. It also made me look over my shoulder to assure myself that no one was riding up the lane. The same concern had twice sent Sally up to the cupola, the clothes she'd been scrubbing draped over the edge of the tub while she checked for riders. Even Mary kept peeking out the back window, her round face drawn with worry as if she expected to see Amos dismount from his horse.

"Where is our faith?" I asked that night at supper. "We can't be looking over our shoulders all the time. The strain will wear us out."

"I know," Mary said. "I'm not sleeping well and neither is Sally . . . not to mention running to the cupola and peeking out the window like we do."

"We got to look, though," Sally said.

"Maybe not," I said.

They both stopped eating and looked at me. "If we have faith then we must also have trust. I don't think God spared Caleb's life only to let him fall into the hands of Deputy Foster. The work Mr. Tremayne is doing is right and good. God needs him."

Mary and Sally nodded, Sally's elbows resting on the table and Mary absently crumbling a piece of biscuit between her fingers.

"I've been thinking about it," I went on. "Trusting God doesn't mean we don't do our part. But once we know our part, then we can turn everything else over to Him and stop looking out the windows."

"I thought keeping watch was my part," Sally said.

"So did I," Mary added.

"I think we all did. But after today I realized that so much watching puts a terrible strain and worry on us. So . . ." I paused and looked at Mary. "Your part is to know what you'll do if someone knocks on the door. Do you remember what that is?"

"If I'm upstairs, I go to bed. If I'm here, I lie down in the study and pull the afghan up over me like I'm resting."

"And you?" I looked at Sally.

"Make certain everything we're using for Master Caleb is shut away with him in his room."

"And I'm to do the same." I smiled in satisfaction. "The key is trust."

So we tried it. The trusting. Since Mary had had more practice, she did it best. After that conversation, I never once saw her look out the window, but Sally and I still made occasional trips to the cupola. The strain eased. We trusted as best we could and our efforts brought a measure of peace. We all shared in the benefits. Sally softly hummed as she ironed a dress, Mary chuckled over a joke, and my step became more brisk.

Caleb also seemed to benefit from our trusting. His appetite improved and he became more alert. By Saturday he declared he was sick of resting, sick of sleeping too. "I never knew lying in bed could be so unpleasant."

Hoping company would make him less fretful, we took turns sitting with Caleb when he was awake. We gathered in the study in the evenings after supper too. I shall always look back on those evenings with fondness—our chairs forming a half circle by the opening to his room, the click of Mary's needles and the murmur of voices. Even Ol' Cat joined us, curled on my lap, her soft purr adding a pleasant note to our conversation.

"How did it happen? How did you get shot?" Sally asked the first evening.

"Road block," Caleb said after a moment. "Coming back I happened on a blockade, totally unprepared. I should have known better, but everything had gone so well. Delilah and Livie were with their family, the people at the next station were optimistic."

I wondered if the next station was a farm like Caleb's and if it had a hiding room too.

"We waited until dark to start back," Caleb continued.

"We?" I lifted my head, having thought Caleb traveled alone.

"The man I work with. He and his son had Delilah's whole family in the back of his wagon. We planned to travel together until we reached the turnoff north of Clarkston." Caleb paused and licked his lips. "I should have been more careful. That wooded area just out of Hanksville is an ideal place for a blockade. I came upon it going at a fair pace . . . barely had time to pull in the horses."

I pictured Caleb sawing on the reins, the horses' whinnies, men milling around, logs dragged across the road, his worry about Delilah and Livie in the other wagon.

"They ordered me to get down. Since I had at least six guns pointed at me, I didn't argue, though I was tempted to . . . anything to keep them from searching the wagons."

Sally's brow furrowed. "Since no slaves was ridin' with you, why didn't you want them to search your wagon?"

"I was afraid they'd find the false bottom where I put the slaves."

I repressed a shudder as I pictured Delilah and her family lying in a place so cramped the top must almost brush their noses.

"Two men searched me for weapons and the rest climbed into the wagon and rummaged through the sacks of seed in the back. Delilah's wagon was right behind me and I knew the men would search it next." Caleb's expression was grim, like he was there again, experiencing the worry—the fear. "I let them know I didn't take kindly to being searched, but they said if I didn't have anything to hide I'd be allowed to go on."

Caleb gave a humorless chuckle. "Of course, I did have something to hide and the men in the wagon were bound to find it. They knew their business. This wasn't their first blockade."

Mary's needles grew still. "How did you get away?"

"I shoved past the men and ran, hoping the diversion would let the other wagon get away. I scrambled onto a horse. A man grabbed my leg and almost pulled me off. It was nip and tuck . . . him pulling and me trying to stay on, the horse shying and plunging."

Silence engulfed the room. Even Ol' Cat stopped purring.

The rasp of Caleb's faltering voice broke the stillness. "Somehow I managed to kick the man down . . . and we took off . . . the horse as scared as I was. I held on and laid low over its neck so I wouldn't be a target. Bullets were flying everywhere."

Caleb licked his lips. No one spoke, all of us holding our breath while in our minds we saw it—Caleb and the horse flying through the darkness, dodging bullets and trees. My heart quickened as if I were there, hearing the men's curses, the crack of guns and the smell of gun powder and fear.

"Luckily it was me . . . not the horse . . . they shot. Otherwise I couldn't have gotten away. Knowing where I was helped too. I'd hunted and ridden those parts since I was a boy."

"Thank the good Lord for that," Mary murmured.

Caleb nodded and fell silent.

"How did you keep from falling off the horse?" I asked.

Caleb's voice was weak. "It wasn't easy . . . though trying to keep a clear head was even harder with the men close on my trail. That was my plan . . . that they'd come after me so the other wagon could get away. It worked, though I had to hide a time or two until I lost them. After that . . ."

Caleb looked at me for a long moment. I saw his love, his weariness too. "I guess you know what happened after that better than I do."

"Yes. Mary and Sally too." I wondered how he'd borne the pain and fought the weakness until he reached home.

"God was with you," Mary said.

"He was," Caleb replied.

Silence settled around us in gentle folds. Ol' Cat soon tired of it and jumped down to groom herself.

"I took a big chance in leaving my team and wagon. They could be traced to me." He paused and closed his eyes. "Since the deputy didn't mention them, I'm hoping Mr.—the other man's son drove them away."

My heart was too full of gratitude to speak. So much more could have gone wrong—the wagon found and traced to Caleb, Delilah and her family captured. *Thank you. Oh, thank you.*

Silence settled around us again, one born of trust and caring. I could see Caleb had tired himself with so much talking. Not wanting to risk a return of the fever, I got up as if to leave. Mary and Sally followed my example.

"Stay," Caleb whispered to me.

I eased his head onto the pillow and took his outstretched hand.

"Stay with me," he repeated.

"I will."

"Tamsin . . ." His voice dropped away and he looked at me for a long moment, his eyes brimming with love, his face soft with it. He lifted his hand and touched my face, traced my lips. "I love you."

Hearing the words almost undid me. "And I you," I whispered. I kissed him, not worrying about the fever or his weakness, needing the touch of his lips, the warmth of his face against mine.

I sat with Caleb for almost an hour, the tightness of his clasp telling me he was reliving those terrible moments at the blockade. What if he hadn't shoved past the men? What if the horse had been shot? What if I hadn't found him in time?

But he did. And you did, a quiet voice whispered.

The thought warmed me as surely as the clasp of Caleb's hand did. He wasn't alone. We weren't alone.

When Caleb's hold on my hand finally relaxed, I continued to sit with him, the need to be close outweighing my need for sleep. Caleb's quick thinking and God's help had brought him back to me. I wanted to savor the knowledge. After that I would sleep.

———•———

"Somethin' ain't right, Miss Tamsin," Sally announced the next morning. Her arms were filled with wood and she sounded out of breath, like she was scared or had been hurrying.

I looked up from the griddle cakes I was stirring. "What's wrong?"

"I don't rightly know. Maybe somethin'. Maybe nothin'." She dropped the wood into the bin and went on. "It was just a feelin' I had when I was in the woodshed . . . like someone was watchin' me. But when I turned 'round to look, no one was there."

I stopped stirring the batter and looked on Sally, noting her frown and that her finger was playing with her hair. "Are you certain no one was there?"

"Not all the way certain." She paused and threw a quick glance at the back door. "I looked some . . . but I mostly wanted to run."

The optimism I'd wakened with dissipated. Had Amos or the deputy sent someone to spy on us? Or was it just Sally? I immediately dismissed the latter. Sally might be flighty, but her instincts were usually correct.

"You acted wisely," I told her. "If someone's there, you . . ."

"That's just it. I ain't sure. It was just a feelin' I had. It made the back of my neck prickle."

I left the spoon in the batter and wiped my hands on my apron. "We'd better have a look."

"What if someone's there? What if they have a gun?"

I stopped with my hand on the door. "Then you must run and get Mr. Brown."

Sally looked at me for a long moment, her lips parted as if she wanted to say more. With a shrug she followed me out to the shed.

The morning was overcast and a breeze blew and tugged at my green dress. The woodshed walls were whitened like the stucco on the house, the interior poorly lit for lack of a window. Caleb and Sally were the ones who usually carried in the wood, but I'd been inside enough to be familiar with the layout, wood stacked along three walls and a bin for kindling.

My eyes made a slow circuit of the inside, my senses alive for any sensation of another presence. I felt it almost at once, the air seeming to quiver with suppressed fear. Sally had been right. Something or someone was hiding in the woodshed.

I lifted my gaze to a shelf by the rafters where Caleb kept the turpentine and tools for sharpening the ax and saw. Realizing the items had been jostled about, I narrowed my eyes to penetrate the shadows. Two eyes peered down at me, eyes too large to belong to a cat or small animal.

I drew in a quick breath and stepped back. "Who's there?" My voice sounded high and unnatural. Scared.

Buzzing flies and a song of a robin were the only answer. I cleared my throat and voiced the question again. Still no answer. By then I knew the person on the shelf hadn't been sent to spy on us. Except for two white rings around the iris of the eyes, the person was black. My fingers closed around a heavy stick of kindling. "Are you looking for someone?"

The silence stretched on. Even the fly ceased buzzing. "I am," a deep male voice finally said.

Sally grabbed my sleeve. "Should I run and get Mr. Brown?"

"No." I kept my gaze on the man. He was watching me as closely as I watched him, his muscles tensed and ready for attack should he think us a threat.

The deep voice came again, resonant and deep like a drum. "I lookin' for someone by the name of Horatio."

Remembering Caleb's code name I spoke back to the shadow. "Horatio is hurt. He can't come right now."

"Hurt?"

"He was shot trying to help a runaway slave."

Silence again as the man adjusted to the news of Caleb's injury.

I cautiously backed away. "You're safe here. Wait while I go and tell Horatio you're here."

Sally's steps matched mine as we hurried to the house. "Who's Horatio?" Worry sounded in her voice. "How's Master Caleb goin' to help that black man when he can't even get out of bed?"

"I don't know," I answered as my mind grappled with the worry of how the slave's arrival would affect Caleb's recovery and what would be required of the rest of us.

Mary was feeding Caleb, her face a little stern as she tried to coax him to eat another bite.

"Someone's hidin' in the woodshed," Sally blurted.

Caleb brushed the spoon aside and tried to sit up. "A runaway?"

I nodded. "He said he was looking for Horatio."

Caleb muttered something under his breath.

I stepped closer. "What should I tell him?"

"I don't know." He frowned and eased himself up on the pillow. "He shouldn't be here. There wasn't any lamp in the window, so he shouldn't have come in."

"Lamp?"

"I put a lamp in the sitting room window when it's safe for runaways to come in. If there's no lamp, they know to go on or wait another night."

I remembered the nights when Caleb had made a point of seeing us to our rooms before he went to bed. Was it then he'd put the lamp in the window? My mind grappled with more questions. Why had the slave come when there wasn't a signal? Could it be a trap set by Amos or the deputy? And if he was truly a runaway, what were we going to do with him? My eyes sought Caleb's. I saw similar questions running through his head. "Have slaves ever come when there wasn't a lamp in the window?"

"Once."

"Why?"

"A man and his wife. She was sick and they were desperate."

"This man don't sound sick," Sally said.

Worry settled around us—Mary still holding the bowl, Sally and me standing just outside the tiny room, all of our eyes on Caleb who stared at a point just above the door and frowned.

"It might be a trap and the man a decoy," Caleb finally said.

"I know." My stomach tightened when I remembered how I'd acknowledged Caleb's code name and said Caleb had been shot. Dear heaven, what had I done?

"Tell me exactly what happened . . . what was said."

So I did, watching Caleb's mouth tighten when I said I'd told the slave he'd been shot. "I'm sorry," I concluded. "It never crossed my mind it might be a trap. Since he knew your code name, I thought he'd come for help like Delilah and Livie."

"Most likely he did." Caleb smiled in an effort to reassure me.

"What do you want me to do?"

Caleb's eyes narrowed as if he sought the answer from the air above my head. "Ask who sent him and why he came when there wasn't a signal. Find out if he knows what the signal is."

I nodded and moved to go.

"Tamsin."

I turned and saw the love and concern in his blue eyes. Frustration at his weakness was there too. "Be careful. Take Sally with you and both of you be careful."

"We will." I tried to smile. For Caleb's sake. For Mary's too.

Sally gave me a nervous smile when we reached the back step. Everything was just as it ought to be. My bonnet still hung on the fence by the garden, and chickens scratched in the dirt by the barn. Straightening my shoulders, I took Sally's hand.

"Did you get a good look at him?" Sally whispered.

I shook my head.

"Me neither. But his voice sounded big. Big and strong."

Her words hovered in the air, filling my lungs with tension and urging me to take care. The door to the woodshed was partly open, stillness and stacks of wood seeming to be its only occupants.

My gaze immediately jumped to the shelf. For a moment I couldn't see anything, the slave's darkness melding with the shadows—silent and without movement, except for his eyes.

"You'll have to stay in here until it's dark," I told him. "It's too dangerous to come out now."

"I know that."

I glanced at Sally, who peered up at the slave like she was trying to judge his size.

"How did you know to come here?" I asked.

His answer was slow in coming. "Man sent me. Told me to look for a barn with a wood horse on top."

Recalling what Delilah had told me, I breathed a little easier.

"He say hide 'til dark and watch for a lamp in the upstairs window . . . third from the right, he tol' me." The slave changed position, an elbow angled over the edge, his head a dark silhouette above it. "I wait mos' of the night, but I never saw no lamp."

"That's because it's not safe. It hasn't been safe for over a week."

"Figured as much."

"Then why did you come?"

"Dogs," he rasped. "Sounded like more'n one . . . maybe a whole pack." He paused as if selecting his words. When the resonant voice came again, it was tight with anger. "Dogs done terrible things to my pappy. Massah set a whole pack on him."

Sally's fingers tightened on mine and stillness settled over the woodshed. In my mind I could see it—dogs tearing at the slave, his screams mingling with the savage snarls of the dogs.

"When I heard dogs last night . . . I run."

"How awful," Sally whispered. Then in a louder voice, "I'll bring you a quilt and pillow."

"Rather have somethin' to eat and drink. Haven't ate for two days now." The slave's voice was impatient, as if he thought we didn't have much sense.

"We'll bring your breakfast in a few minutes." I put a few sticks of wood into my apron. Sally did the same. I glanced up at the shadowy form of the slave. His body stretched the entire length of the shelf. He was tall. Scared too. And hungry. Maybe that explained his impatience.

"We'll bring you something to eat," I repeated. After I closed and latched the shed door, I hurried into the house to tell Caleb.

———•———

The slave's story allayed our fears of a trap, but it didn't solve the problem of what to do with him. After Sally and I took him a plate of griddle cakes and bacon and a jug of water, I sat down with Caleb to discuss the matter. We talked at length, agreeing the black man must be brought into the cellar, but disagreeing about how he should get to the next station.

"He'll have to get there on his own . . . like he got here," Caleb said. "It'll be risky though. Especially after all that's happened."

"How long do you think it will take for him to walk there?"

"Probably three days . . . more if he has to stop and hide." Caleb sighed and rubbed the dark stubble on his chin. "If I weren't so weak . . ." His voice trailed away in frustration.

"Don't even consider it." My mind kept thinking of dogs, the blockade, and the added danger to the slave if he attempted to get there on his own. "What if I took him? I . . ."

"No"

"I could take him in the buggy."

"No." Caleb's voice was tight with authority.

I sighed and took his hand.

"No," he said before I could say more. "I won't expose you to any more danger. What you've had to deal with is bad enough."

Sally's arrival prevented us from further discussion. "I took the slave a blanket and pillow. And I found out what his name is." She swallowed and hurried on. "It's Julius."

"Don't go out to him again," Caleb warned. "Is that clear? It's not safe. And I don't want you talking to him. You might let something slip. The less you know, the safer it is."

"I know how to be careful, Master Caleb. 'Cept for the four of us, I don't aim to say nothin'."

"Make sure you don't." Weariness trailed through his words.

Seeing how worry about Julius had tired Caleb, I kissed his cheek. "We can talk about the slave after you've rested."

Caleb gave me a long steady look. "The subject of taking him in the buggy is finished."

I studied Caleb after he closed his eyes, noting the dark circles still shadowing his eyes, the gauntness in his cheeks. In spite of our care and love, he was still weak and far from well. Caleb needed quiet, not worry. Peace instead of more problems.

Anger at the slave washed over me. He shouldn't be here. His coming was already interfering with Caleb's recovery, and it would continue to do so until he was safely away. Why hadn't he gone on when he didn't see the lamp?

Then I remembered the dogs and what they'd done to his father. Feeling guilty, I tried to think of how I could help the runaway without disobeying Caleb. If only I knew the identity of the others who were involved, the signals, and the location of the next station.

I grappled with the situation for the rest of the day, even questioning Mary and Sally. They were as much in the dark as I was. Caleb's work with the underground was something he'd kept to himself.

By early evening, I was no closer to finding a solution than I'd been that morning. Frustrated, I sought relief in the garden. I could always depend on the touch of soil and plant to soothe me. I spent a few contented minutes digging around the peas and potatoes. As I straightened to ease my back, I saw young Sam coming from the barn with a pail of milk.

"Evening, Miss Yeager," he called. "How's Mary?"

"Doing a little better."

"Good. Mrs. Tremayne wanted me to ask about her." Sam set down the pail of milk when he reached the gate, his eyes bright with excitement. "Have you heard the news?"

My heart jumped. "What news?"

"Men with dogs are lookin' for a runaway slave. They came all the way from Maryland." His freckled face brightened when he saw my interest. "Old Mr. Ross talked to them this mornin'. Told us to take care and watch for him. He's a big black feller named Caesar."

"Heavens," I exclaimed, as my mind took off at a race. Was it Julius they were looking for? Julius, who was really Caesar?

"Mrs. Tremayne wanted me to be sure and tell you. Said for you to take care and not take no chances." Sam paused and shot a quick glance at the house. "You tell Sally to 'specially take care. She's always goin' off by herself. See her all the time . . . traipsin' off to the woods or the river. She needs to be careful." Color spread over Sam's freckled cheeks when he saw how closely I watched him.

"I'll tell her," I promised. "And I'll make sure the doors are locked before we go to bed tonight." It took control not to look at the wood-shed. What were we going to do about Julius?

"Did Mr. Ross say how many men and dogs there were?"

"Two men and two dogs. And they're offerin' a five-dollar reward to anyone who helps catch the nigger."

"Negro."

"Negro." Sam's cheeks grew pinker, but it didn't spoil his enthusiasm. "Think of that, Miss Yeager. Five whole dollars."

"That's a lot of money," I agreed. Anxious to send Sam on his way, I thanked him for the news and told him to set the milk on the back step.

"Want me to chop more wood while I'm here?" he asked. "You're probably startin' to run low."

"We're fine, Sam. But thank you anyway. Be sure to tell Mrs. Tremayne that Mary's still making progress."

"I will." Giving me a smile and a wave, he hurried off at a run. I looked after him, watching his gangly form meld with the lengthening shadows, my mind in a quandary as to what I should do.

CHAPTER 18

When Sam was out of sight, I leaned the hoe against the fence and walked to the woodshed. I needed to know if Caesar was Julius, and Julius needed to know about the men and dogs.

Throwing a quick glance over my shoulder, I unlatched the door and eased it open. "Did you hear what the boy said about two men looking for a runaway slave?"

"I heard," the deep voice answered.

"And the five-dollar reward?"

"That too."

"Are you the man they're looking for? Is your name Caesar?"

The slave didn't say anything for a moment, the seconds spinning past in taut threads of tension. Then the answer came, the resonant voice brimmed with pride. "My name used to be Caesar . . . but it ain't no more. I call myself Julius now."

"Julius." I repeated his name and reached for a length of wood to put into my apron. "As soon as it's dark, we'll bring you into the house. Make sure you don't try to leave the shed before then."

When I got no reply, I frowned up at the shelf. "Did you hear?"

"I did. Might leave anyhow."

My frown deepened and I sensed that Julius was scowling back at me.

"Didn't you hear what Sam said about the dogs?"

"I did. Heard about that reward too. How I know you ain't plannin' to collect it?"

For a second I was too indignant to speak. When the words finally came, they were clipped tight with anger. "The man I love almost died trying to help a slave woman and her child. I wouldn't touch the reward money and neither would he."

I left the shed, kicking the door shut and wishing the door was Julius—wishing the men and dogs would find him. Guilt came fast. I knew nothing about Julius's life or what he'd been through or how he'd suffered. What if I was Julius and had to depend on strangers—and white ones at that? Could I trust them after what had been done to my father? Pity slowed my steps and dissolved my anger. By the time I reached the house, I knew what I must do.

When I told Caleb about the men with the dogs, his mouth tightened. "Dogs . . . they're the very worst. Especially tracking hounds."

"What if they track Julius here?" Sally asked.

"You've got to let me take Julius in the buggy," I interjected.

The lines around Caleb's mouth deepened. He glanced at Mary, then at Sally. "I need to speak to Miss Yeager alone."

Mary gave him a long, measured look. "Do you still think you can't trust us?"

"Trust has nothing to do with it. Common sense should tell you that."

Their gazes remained locked. Finally Mary grimaced and heaved her bulk out of the chair. "All right," she grumbled.

Caleb put out his good hand. "Thank you."

At first Mary pretended not to see it. Then she smiled and gave it a squeeze. But her face was troubled when she and Sally left the room, and I noticed that Sally's finger was in her hair again. All of us would rest easier when Julius was safely away.

———

I learned much from Caleb—where the next station was and of the subterfuge Caleb used for getting the slaves there. Besides the false bottom in the wagon, there were hollow seats in both the carriage and buggy with hinged padded lids that formed a soft cushion for unsuspecting passengers to sit on—as I and Hannah and Lucinda had been.

"I had no idea," I said.

"That was my intention."

"Was someone hiding there on the day you took us to Bayberry?"

Caleb shook his head. "Few seek help once the cold comes."

Safe places, fugitives, hollow seats. My head whirled with the terms and information. Clamoring through it was concern for Caleb. Worry about Julius was taking its toll.

"Tell Sally to get some burlap sacks from the granary," Caleb went on. "Have Julius wrap them around his feet before he comes inside. The sacks should hide his scent if the dogs come here."

At the mention of the dogs, my stomach tightened. I wanted to get Julius away just as soon as possible. "Can we leave tonight?"

"No, it's too dangerous." He paused and sighed. "I don't like putting you in danger. When I think . . ." His voice broke off and he cleared his throat. "If it weren't for the dogs—"

I leaned over and pushed a lock of hair from his forehead. "We'll be fine. With Mary's prayers, things are sure to go well."

We decided I would say I was going to visit Abigail, and Sam would go to drive the buggy and offer protection.

"Sam's uncle lives just this side of Bayberry. You can drop him off there and pick him up on your way home."

Sally ran over to the old house with instructions for Sam. When she got back she found the sacks for Julius's feet. It was late before we brought Julius inside. I'd known from his voice and silhouette that he was big—big hands, big feet, massive shoulders, and a body that must have towered above Caleb by a good four or five inches.

We snuffed out the lamps as a signal for Julius to come into the house. Sally and I waited by the back door to help him remove the sacks and show him the way to the hiding place in the cellar.

"First you need to eat," I said. Sally had set a place for him at the kitchen table, the shades were pulled down, and our only light came from the stove. With Sally gone to help Mary into bed, I gave Julius a brief outline of my plan. Now that I'd seen him, I worried about his long frame fitting into the hollow seat of the buggy.

"I done worse things," he said between bites of potato and gravy. "Yo' just worry 'bout gettin' me there." He paused and looked me over, shaking his head as he did. "Yo' ever do this before?"

"No . . . but I'm all you have." I plunked the butter onto the table and stepped back and looked Julius squarely in the face. I watched his eyes narrow, felt his antipathy, his doubt. I knew he didn't put much stock in my ability to get him there. "Remember, beggars can't be choosers."

Julius concentrated on eating after that. His dislike of the situation was evident as was his dislike and mistrust of me. It emanated from his powerful frame when I relit the lamp and he followed me down to his hiding place. The slave's close proximity sent skitters of unease up my neck and made me wish Caleb were with me. I could hardly wait for Julius to climb into the hiding place so I could roll the shelf back into place.

Julius looked inside the space, his silent inspection as thorough as that of a man making an important purchase. When he finished he turned and looked down at me, his coffee-colored eyes assessing me just as he'd done with the hiding place. I stared back, noting the breadth of his nose and nostrils, his full lips, and the coarse, kinky hair that grew back from a wide forehead. Everything about Julius was alien to me—alien and frightening, especially his eyes. Something hard and cold glinted in their depths. Sudden fear caught in my throat and I wanted to drop the lamp and run. It seemed forever before Julius finally climbed into the hidden room and I rolled the shelf into place.

My breathing was ragged and uneven when I reached the kitchen. I was glad Sally wasn't there to see me. I didn't want her to know of my unease. Caleb either. It wouldn't do at all.

—•—

"Julius is so big I don't know how he's going to fit inside the buggy seat," I told Caleb when I'd composed myself enough to go to him. The lamp on the table had been turned down and I hoped the shadows hid my worry. Caleb reached for my hand as I sat down.

"There's no other way." He looked at me before he went on, his voice hesitant when he finally spoke. "There's something else I need to tell you. The family at the next station is Quaker. The wife hangs a quilt on the clothesline if it's safe to bring someone there." He paused and his fingers tightened on my hand. "If you don't see a quilt, you'll have to go on."

"Go on?" My voice cracked with dismay. "Where? How far?"

"Lobster Harbor. One of my uncle's ships often puts in there." He paused to let the words sink in. "It's usually safe at the Quakers. I've only had to go to Lobster Harbor a few times. A man named Barney lives there. He has a lobster shop by the wharf. I've worked with him before. He'll hide Julius until the next ship comes. His shop is called *The Lobster Pot.*"

In my mind I pictured the harbor as I'd last seen it—the ramshackle buildings lining the wharf. Shanties, Deacon Mickelson had called them on the day he'd taken Mother and me and Clarissa on an outing. My eyes had been drawn to the men mending nets or emptying bright-colored lobster pots. Never once had I suspected that anything other than lobster trading might be going on.

"I wouldn't let you do this if I didn't believe you could. You've managed so well with me and with Deputy Foster. And Amos." Caleb's voice tightened when he said "Amos."

"I can do it." My voice held more conviction than I felt. "Lobster Harbor is just a few miles from Mickelboro. I have friends there if I need them."

"There's something else you need to know." Caleb paused and ran a finger along the back of my hand. "Once Barney wasn't there and I had to take the slave up the coast to Mickelboro. That's when you saw me."

I remembered Caleb's strength as he'd walked toward the boulder where I'd hidden that morning, his purposeful stride and handsome features. I'd known nothing of love then, nothing of the complex man who was now holding my hand.

"My uncle's ship is called the *Eudora*. If Barney isn't there, send word out to the skipper that the shipment from Lowe will be a day late. He'll know what you mean."

I repeated the phrase and tucked it away in my mind along with the names of Barney and the *Eudora*.

"I'd give all I possess if I didn't have to put this on you." Anger edged his words. "When I think of what it could require of you, I want to send the slave on his way. But then I remember what those poor devils have been through . . . what they've risked to get here."

"It's all right. I can do it," I whispered. "Since you can't help Julius, I'm here to take your place. That's how I want our marriage to be, Caleb. The two of us working together."

Caleb brought my hand to his lips. "What a lucky man I am."

I savored the touch of his lips and wished I didn't have to leave— wished it could always be like this, the two of us close, our love pulsing between us like a warm, steady flame. My thoughts leaped to the years ahead, Caleb strong again, long evenings by the fire while we talked and read and laughed. Of late, there hadn't been opportunity for this. But there would be. I wouldn't let myself think anything to the contrary.

———•———

Instead of retiring to my room, I spent the night on the couch in the study, my ears tuned for the first sleepy chirp of the robins. I needed to be up before dawn to take Julius out to the barn. Despite my exhaustion, my mind was too full of concern to sleep well. The little sleep that came was brief and interrupted by jabs of worry and anxiety. I might pretend bravery for Caleb's sake, but as I lay alone in the darkness I knew fear.

I awoke as soon as I heard the first robin. Putting on my shoes, I lit the lamp and made my way down the stairs to the cellar. Julius was awake and sitting up when I rolled back the shelf, his shoulders hunched beneath the low ceiling, his face pulled into an unfriendly scowl. Determined not to let his antipathy spoil the day, I wished him good morning and handed him his breakfast tied in a towel.

"Sam will be here to milk the cows as soon as it's light. You'll need to be inside the box before he comes." I wondered again how Julius was going to fare during the long ride inside a box that was probably a foot shorter than he was.

Julius nodded and followed me up to the kitchen where he tied the burlap around his feet. As I stepped out into the predawn shadows, Julius's big arm shot out and pinned me against the door, the sound of his breathing loud in my ear. "Don't never step out in plain sight without lookin'," he hissed. "Thas how folks get caught."

My heart's frightened pounding made it hard to speak. "I'm sorry."

"Bein' sorry don't keep you alive. It make you dead."

Julius made a careful survey of the yard and outbuildings, his body tensed and alert like a hunting dog studying its quarry. With Julius's warning still hissing in my ears, we slipped across the yard to the barn, the slave looming like a black silhouette a step or two ahead of me. My irritation at his taking over was such that I didn't notice the dampness of the grass on my slippers until we'd almost reached the barn. A wave of gratitude washed over me when I realized it had rained—the rain Mary and Sally had likely prayed for to wash Julius's scent away.

Julius pulled the door to the barn open. The sound it made as it scraped across the hard-packed dirt was as stealthy as our footsteps had been. We listened, straining to detect any sign of danger in the black interior. No sound came. No movement, either, only the pale gray of approaching dawn seeping through the cracks. I felt along the wall for the lantern that hung from a hook next to the door.

"Close the door," I whispered. I struck a match and lit the lantern.

It was by lantern light that Julius inspected the hollow box that served as the back seat of the buggy. Nothing in his expression changed when he looked inside and saw the quilt lying in the bottom and a space between two boards to let in light and air. If I'd been showing the seat to Delilah or Livie, I'd have apologized for the cramped quarters. I knew my apology would only be a waste of breath with Julius.

"Sam won't be here for a while, so if you want to wait until you hear him coming to get in, you can."

"I'll do what feel right," Julius said. He bent down and inspected one of the wheels, the raised tendons on his fingers gleaming in the lantern light as he tested one of the spokes.

Realizing I'd been dismissed, I hung the lantern on the wall and snuffed it out. Irritation covered regret for leaving him in the dark. More and more I didn't look forward to taking Julius to the Quakers.

Sally was making her sleepy way down to the kitchen by the time I got there and Mary wasn't far behind. "Me'n Mary want you to have a good breakfast before you leave."

I gave her a quick hug. What would I do without those two, dear friends? But dear as they were, my primary thoughts were with Caleb. He was awake when I rolled back the bookcase, sitting up with his legs hanging over the side of the bed.

"Caleb." Happiness carried his name from my lips. "What a wonderful surprise." And in the next breath. "Should you be sitting up? How are you feeling?"

"Better than yesterday. I can feel my strength starting to come back. If Julius could wait another week—"

"But he can't." I wouldn't let myself think of Julius and what might lie ahead. I savored the sight of Caleb sitting up, noted the healthy color returning to his face. Love pulled me to him and Caleb's good arm went around me. I heard the whisper of his breathing, felt the softness of his beard. Then his lips found mine, warm and filled with love. I closed my eyes and cradled his face with my hand. As the kiss lengthened, Julius and my worries ceased to exist.

We left Glen Oaks with Sam sitting in the front of the buggy and me in back with my claret skirt spread wide across Julius's hiding place. If Julius were uncomfortable or changed position, I wasn't aware of it. The rattle and crunch of the wheels and Sam's merry whistle masked all but the loudest sounds. I welcomed this and was glad Sam showed no inclination to fill the miles with conversation.

Concern about Caleb was never far from my thoughts. I knew Sally and Mary would do their best and I'd made them promise they'd send for Lucinda if any problems arose. As for the men and the dogs—I could only hope the storm had washed away Julius's scent from the yard.

There was no sign of rain that morning, only sun and blue sky dotted with a few fluffy clouds. I took this as a good omen. It and Mary's prayers were certain to get us to Bayberry without problems.

We arrived at Sam's uncle's farm just after noon, the family dog announcing our arrival as Sam's cousins ran out of the house to welcome him. Sam was reluctant to let me drive the buggy into town.

"I've been doing this since I was a girl," I assured him. "I'll probably be back for you tomorrow . . . Friday at the latest."

Four miles brought me into Bayberry. The sight of Samuelson's Mercantile reminded me of the day I'd climbed out of the freight wagon, Peter's suggestion to go to his mother, and Abby's subsequent friendship and love. Eager as I was to see Abby, my first concern was to get Julius safely through town and out to the Quakers. After that I could relax and enjoy Abigail's company.

I took the road north, the one Caleb said led to Clarkston and Springville. "The farm is about a mile from the crossroad," he'd said. "A sign with a basket of apples painted on it hangs by their gate."

It took me longer than I'd expected to get there. The sun beat down onto the top of the buggy with such intensity that I began to have concern for Julius. I'd heard a scraping noise just before we got to Sam's uncle, but nothing since. Had he fallen asleep or was he impervious to discomfort?

Since there were no travelers on the road, I pulled on the reins and spoke. "We don't have much farther to go. Are you all right?"

I began to think he hadn't heard me. "Get goin'," the deep voice said.

I spoke to the horse and we continued on. As we rounded a bend I saw the sign with the basket of apples. Just seeing it lifted my spirits. We were finally there. Soon I could be back with Caleb.

I flicked the reins to hurry us along, noting the neatly fenced fields and orchard, the barn that dominated the home. As we drew closer, my eyes searched for the clothesline and quilt. Finally I saw it—ropes stretched between poles by the house. But no quilt. Dear heart, where was the quilt? Even as the question formed I knew the answer. After the close call with Delilah and Livie, not to mention Caleb being shot, the Quakers felt their station was no longer safe.

The mare slowed and turned into the lane leading to the house. I pulled on the reins, realizing as I did that she'd been here before. I glanced around, unsure of what to do and saw a plainly dressed woman come out of the house and walk toward us, her gray-clad arm raised against the lowering sun. "Can I help thee?"

"I . . . I seem to have taken the wrong turn." I glanced back at the sign, then over to the clothesline. "Horatio's directions weren't very clear. He's soon to become my husband, but he's not well, so he sent me in his place."

She grasped onto the buggy, her eyes darting from me to the road. When she spoke her voice was urgent. "We can't help thee. Thee must go."

When I didn't immediately respond, she grabbed the mare's lines to help turn her. "Go quickly," she urged. She kept glancing at the road, her movement like those of a nervous sparrow.

The Quaker's fear was contagious. I pulled on the reins to complete the turn. The woman followed us for a few paces. "Tell Horatio we have his team and wagon," she said in a low voice. "My husband hid the wagon under a pile of hay. The horses are pastured with ours." Giving a quick wave, she hurried back to the house.

———•———

Disappointment and worry followed me back to Bayberry. Knowing it would be safer if we arrived close to dark, I kept the mare at a slow pace. Even with all the extra time to think, I didn't know what to do. Julius needed to get out of the box. The horse needed rest and water. It would take a full day to reach Lobster Harbor.

I'd planned to spend the night with Abby and return to Glen Oaks on the following day. But that had been with Julius safely delivered to the Quakers. Where was I going to hide him at Abigail's?

The question weighed on my mind. I was so caught up in finding an answer that I almost drove past Abby's house. As I reined in the horse, Abby came around the side of the house, her arms filled with clothes.

"Tamsin!" Her voice was threaded with surprise, and the corners of her pretty mouth lifted into a welcoming smile.

Just seeing Abigail cheered me—that and the knowledge that she was my friend. Still, I hesitated to involve her. What if Julius were discovered and traced to Abby?

"What a pleasant surprise," she went on. Seeing my forced smile, she paused. "Are you all right? Has something happened?"

"I'm fine," I said. I was slow to get down from the buggy.

When I reached into the buggy for the portmanteau I'd borrowed from Abby, her face filled with concern. "Are you sure everything is all right?"

Fearing we'd be overheard, I nodded and walked toward the house. Neither of us spoke until we were inside.

"Peter's off with his friends. He should be back soon," Abby said as she carried the clothes into the bedroom and laid them on the bed. "He can take the horse and buggy to the livery stable when he gets here."

"We need to talk before he does."

Abby gave me a searching look. "I thought as much." She crossed the room and hugged me. "You look exhausted. Let me fix you a cup of tea."

I removed my bonnet while Abby heated water and set cups and saucers and a wedge of apple pie on the table. "I'm not running away," I said when she eyed the portmanteau. "But I do need help."

"You know you have it."

"Listen to what I have to say first." And I told her—about Caleb, about Amos, and finally about Julius. Abby's eyes widened as the story unfolded, urging me with the press of her hand to sit down, pouring my tea. "The slave is inside the back seat of the buggy," I concluded. "I know I ask much, but I didn't know what else to do. Is there someplace here to hide him?"

"I . . . I think so." Abby frowned and I could almost see her mind flying from thought to thought. "The wash shed. There's a room at the back of it for tools and storage. He can stay there."

"Are you certain you want to do this, Abby?" I reached across the table and took her hand. "If the slave is discovered, it could mean serious trouble for you and Peter."

"I know. But I also know this is what God wants me to do. He'll look after us. Still . . ." She smiled and gave my hand a reassuring squeeze. "It will be best if Petey doesn't know about the slave. He has a tendency to brag and say too much to his friends."

Just as if he'd heard us talking about him, Peter called from the backyard. "Ma . . . there's a team and buggy out front. Is someone here?" The back door slammed and Peter burst into the room. He stopped and grinned when he saw me. "Evenin', Miss Yeager."

I returned his greeting and took heart when I saw his pleased reaction to the news that I was staying the night. "Ma was sayin' the other day she wished you'd come visit." He paused to catch his breath. "Can I take your horse and buggy to the livery stable?"

"That would be most helpful," Abby said. Intercepting my look of alarm, she hurried on. "But first I need you to run over to Mrs. O'Conner's and see if we can borrow a quilt. I loaned our extra one to Milly Thompson while they have company this week."

Peter frowned, clearly frustrated at the delay. "Now?"

"Yes, now. The nights are chilly and I don't want Miss Yeager to get cold."

"But, Ma—"

"Now, Peter."

"You can take the buggy to the livery stable as soon as you get back," I promised.

Encouraged by my promise, Peter left the house. Abby and I were not many seconds behind him. With Abby keeping watch, I climbed into the buggy and released the latch.

"You can come out," I said. I threw a nervous look over my shoulder as I lifted the heavy padded lid. I heard Julius's quick intake of breath as he eased himself into a sitting position. Despite myself, I felt a wave of pity as I imagined his long uncomfortable ride.

"Hurry," I whispered. "We haven't much time."

Julius rolled out of the box, his breath escaping in a little whoosh as he eased himself to the edge of the buggy and lowered his legs. They almost buckled when he tried to stand. He muttered something and rose to his full stance, his large head turning as he studied the night.

It was likely Julius's pride as much as his strength that got him to the side of the house where Abby kept watch. Keeping to the shadows, the three of us slipped around to the backyard.

"You can stay in my wash shed," Abby whispered. "There's a room at the back big enough for you to stretch out in."

The shadows were too deep to tell if Julius nodded.

"I'll get food and something for you to drink," Abby went on. She stretched out her hand in a gesture of welcome. Julius shrank away so quickly he stumbled against me. There was a startled silence before Abby slipped away to the house.

"You ought to be ashamed of yourself," I hissed. "That woman is a widow. She's risking her security and that of her son to help you." I waited for Julius to apologize or respond. When he didn't, my anger rose. "The least you could do is thank her."

I felt rather than saw Julius straighten to his full height. "No white folk ever thank me," he shot back.

"Just because some white folks don't have good manners doesn't excuse you," I retorted. "Have I been rude or unkind to you? Has my friend?"

Julius didn't say anything to that. We stood in an uncomfortable silence until I remembered the need to explain about Peter. Julius remained silent throughout the telling. He let out a long sigh when he learned we had to go on to Lobster Harbor. "Maybe it would be wiser to rest for a day before we go on," I concluded.

"No." The word was a deep rumble.

I scowled up at the shadow that was part Julius, part the trunk of the sycamore. "Why not?"

"We gotta keep movin'. Those men and dogs likely be right behind."

The fear in Julius's voice bolted across the space between us. I glanced at the road, half expecting to hear the bay of hounds. Had I made a terrible mistake by stopping at Abby's?

CHAPTER 19

Early the next morning we left for Lobster Harbor. Abigail had insisted on going with me. Petey sat tall and proud on the front seat of the buggy and drove the little mare. Abby sat in back with me, our skirts spread wide over the seat—claret next to indigo—two sentinels guarding the slave's hiding place.

Each time I heard a dog bark or spied a man on horseback, Julius's fear jumped onto the seat and sat beside me, tensing the muscles in my chest and causing the palms of my hands to grow clammy. I was grateful for Abby's calming presence and for Peter's cocky grin as he nodded and lifted his hat to those we passed on the road. Abby's argument that a woman traveling alone was more likely to attract notice than the three of us riding together was soon evident. But her wisdom did not absolve my guilt. I tried not to think of what might happen to Abby and Peter if we were discovered. The worry diminished my enjoyment of the spring-fresh fields and pastures, the Queen Anne's lace that hugged the roadside and bordered the fences.

Peter's presence prevented us from mentioning Julius, and Julius's close proximity put a damper on some of the things we said. Even so, we found much to talk about, the most important being the love Caleb and I shared.

"Didn't I say I could tell when a man admires a woman?" Abby chuckled. She looked particularly charming that morning, her blue dress accenting her eyes and wisps of curls escaping from her bonnet.

While the miles slipped by, I told Abby about the trip to Mickelboro, of our visit to the post office and cottage, and about Caleb's confrontation with Amos. Abby's "Oh, my!" and "Mercy!"

interspersed the narrative, her expression as incredulous as it had been the night before when I'd told her about the slave. Although I made it a point to speak softly, Peter looked back from time to time, his face bright with curiosity. From Julius there was only an occasional muffled scrape as he tried to make himself comfortable. Each time I heard him, I felt a wave of pity. Even though Julius had made his opinion of white people clear, his present circumstances had to be pitied. How his legs must long to stretch.

Abby had brought her parasol, and during the morning it and the fringed top of the buggy provided welcome shade. By afternoon, the sky turned cloudy and a brisk breeze sprang up. As the miles slipped by, my worry over pursuit gave way to concern about getting Julius safely aboard the Tremayne ship at Lobster Harbor. I wished Caleb were with me. What if I couldn't find Barney? What would I do if the ship weren't there?

In an attempt to rid my mind of worry, I talked about Lucinda Tremayne's gift for nursing, Mary's improved health, and how I suspected that Sam had developed an interest in Sally.

When Abby failed to respond with her usual questions and enthusiasm, I turned and saw that her eyes were closed and that her head rested against the back of the seat.

"Are you all right?"

"Yes . . . no." Abby sighed and raised a gloved hand to her forehead. "I fear I'm coming down with a headache. Sometimes they're so bad I have to go to bed. Dr. Wheeler calls them migraines."

"Oh, Abby."

"It's not your fault."

"But it is. You shouldn't have come with me. See what happened."

Abby roused enough to attempt a smile. "It could just as easily have happened at home. Sometimes they come for no reason."

"Today there was a reason," I declared. I looked at her more closely. Her skin was pale and the lids of her eyes drooped. While I searched my mind for something to help her, Petey called out.

"Looks like someone had a breakdown."

A wagon was pulled across the road. I knew at once it wasn't a breakdown. Abby reached for my hand, her fingers tightening when three armed men stepped from behind the wagon.

"Bring it in slow," one of them called.

Peter glaced at his mother as he complied with the man's orders.

Oh, Peter, what have I done? my mind cried even as my thoughts flew to Julius. Should I try to warn him? Recalling his keen hearing, I realized he already knew.

One of the men grabbed the harness before Peter could bring the mare to a halt. "Sheriff's orders," he said. "We've been told to search all vehicles going north."

"Sheriff?" Petey's voice cracked with excitement and fear.

Two men approached the buggy, their guns ready. "Good afternoon, ladies," one of them said. Although he wore a pleasant expression, his watchful eyes and tensed muscles reminded me of a cat about to pounce upon an unsuspecting bird. I strove to make my expression just that. Unsuspecting. Innocent. A woman who could easily be brought to tears.

"Please, sir . . . what's wrong?" I asked.

"A runaway slave's been tracked this way. His owner is offering a big reward and we've . . ."

"A runaway slave?" My hand flew to my mouth in pretended shock. The tremble in my voice was genuine. "You can see we have no such person."

"We don't know that for certain," the heavyset man cut in. "All sorts of people help niggers." He crouched down to look under the buggy. "Some build a false bottom under their wagon for the runaways to hide in."

"Mercy," I exclaimed.

The other man thumped the bottom of the chassis. "Ain't no false bottom on this one."

I gave the man a bright smile when he straightened. "Can we go?"

"No, ma'am. We got orders to make everyone get out so we can make a thorough search. Sorry, but I'm afraid you ladies will have to step down."

Fear curled from my stomach and caught in my throat as he reached to help me down from the buggy. Only the strongest will kept my eyes from flying to Julius's hiding place. *Don't move. Don't even breathe.*

When Abby took the smaller man's proffered hand, her smile looked as if it had been pasted on, and she was so pale I feared she might collapse. I put my arm around her waist.

Peter looked more excited than frightened, as if he were looking forward to sharing his adventure with friends. "Do you think a runaway could be hiding around here?" he asked. "Seems like they could tell there's no place big enough for anyone to hide in this buggy."

"They're only . . . doing their job," Abby managed to say before she retched and stumbled to the buggy. As she grasped a wheel for support, the remains of her lunch spewed onto the ground with such force that some of it splattered the toe of the stocky man's boot.

"Oh . . . Abby." I held her shoulder as she strove to bring her rebelling stomach under control, her deep breaths and little gasps mingling with Peter's concerned, "Are you all right, Ma?"

Abby straightened finally and wiped her mouth with my handkerchief. "I'm so . . . sorry," she whispered. "I could feel it coming and . . ."

"You couldn't help it," I assured her. I glanced at the men. They'd backed away, the stocky one vigorously wiping his boot on a patch of grass while his companion looked on with distaste. Our way clear was suddenly apparent to me. "Please . . . won't you good gentlemen help us? My friend is unwell and needs to get to Lobster Harbor without further delay."

The man wiping his boot looked at his friend who gave a slight nod. They both looked at the man holding the mare.

I held my breath and waited, watched him frown as he looked at Abby. "Niggers have been known to hide in all sorts of places," he finally said. "But it don't look like one's hidin' here." He slipped his gun back into the holster and urged the mare and buggy forward a step or two. "Jake, help that poor lady back into the buggy."

Both men were quick to comply, their manner all solicitude. "I apologize for the inconvenience we've caused you," the smaller man said. "We was just followin' the sheriff's orders."

"And you did it most admirably," Abby said in a weak voice.

"You did, indeed," I added. The smile I gave them was genuine. "You have all been most kind. Thank you, gentlemen."

In no time Peter was back in the buggy and we were on our way. "I'm sorry," I whispered when Peter had ceased to exclaim about the incident and express his concern for his mother.

Abby squeezed my hand. Her eyes told me of her relief and that she didn't regret her decision to accompany me.

I did what I could to make her more comfortable, folding my shawl into a pillow for her head, fanning her too-pale cheeks. "Do cold compresses help your migraines?"

"Sometimes."

I instructed Peter to watch for a stream so I could dampen my hankie for his mother's forehead. As sorry as I was for Abby's misery, I was grateful too. Had she not become ill, we might still be at the blockade with the men's guns trained upon us, the lid to the seat flung open, poor Julius with his arms and legs bound. *Thank you, dear Lord. Oh, thank you.*

When Peter finally pulled the mare to a stop beside a small creek, I got down from the buggy to wet Abby's handkerchief while Peter watered the mare. The peaceful sound of water on stone soothed my mind, and the dainty wood violets growing along the grassy bank cheered my spirit. I wished Abby were with me. Julius too. He, if anyone, had a right to a few moments of peaceful respite.

Abby's drawn features concerned me when I laid the damp cloth on her forehead. Peter was concerned too, frequently looking back at his mother as he urged the mare to a faster pace.

"How much farther to Lobster Harbor?" he asked.

Nothing in the passing landscape looked familiar. "I'm not sure," I finally admitted. "I was under the canvas on the freight wagon when I came from Mickelboro to Bayberry, so I didn't have a chance to see much."

The corners of Peter's mouth drooped. His handling of the mare and buggy had made me forget how young he was. The long day had eaten at his earlier exuberance so that now he was just a slight-built twelve-year-old who was worried about his mother.

The heavy clouds brought the evening on quickly, the sun becoming a shadowed prism as it sank behind a distant farmhouse. The resulting chill and the lengthening shadows filled me with concern. What if we failed to reach Lobster Harbor before darkness?

Peter's voice intruded into my worry. "I think I see a signpost."

I peered into the dusk as the signpost emerged from the shadows.

"What does it say?" Abby asked.

"Can't tell yet." Peter urged the mare to a faster pace, both of us sitting forward.

"Mickelboro," Peter exclaimed in a voice heavy with disappointment. He cast an apologetic glance at his mother.

My heart filled with relief rather than disappointment. "Turn here. Mickelboro is where I used to live. A good friend has a farm not far from here. We can spend the night with her and go on to Lobster Harbor tomorrow."

It was past dark by the time we arrived at the Partridge farm. Their dog announced our arrival just as it had the last time I'd visited Susannah. Seeing his ears laid back, muzzle lifted, I feared he would spook Julius and wished I dared say something to reassure him.

"We're friends, Mick," I called to the dog. "Remember me?"

A man came to the door, his lanky body silhouetted against the lamplight. I recognized Susannah's oldest son, Matthew.

"It's me . . . Tamsin Yeager."

"Tamsin?" He called off the dog and turned to speak to someone. "Did you hear that, Mother? Tamsin Yeager is here."

Susannah was out of the door and hurrying to meet me by the time I could alight from the buggy. "Tamsin . . . my laws." Susannah engulfed me in a hug, patting my back then releasing me so she could kiss my cheek. "I've been worried about you. No one knew where you'd gone. Why didn't you let me know you were going?"

"I didn't dare. Deacon Mickelson might have found out."

Susannah's wide shoulders tensed. "I was afraid such might be the case. Did he? . . ."

"No."

"Thank God," Susannah whispered and hugged me again. "I can't tell you how glad I am to see you. Mercy, I've missed you."

It felt good to have Susannah's sturdy arms around me, to feel her love. I wanted to stay there and drink in her common sense, to be a child again, safe and secure.

"Is it possible for us to stay with you tonight?"

Her answer came without hesitation. "Of course."

I introduced Abigail and Peter to Susannah. By then her husband had joined us, but there was no sign of Matthew's wife and children.

"Mrs. Hamilton is suffering from a migraine," I explained. "Do you have anything to help her? I've tried a cool compress."

"Cool compresses are good, but I have something that's even better." Susannah put her arm around Abby's drooping shoulders. "Come, my dear. I have the very thing for you."

"Thank you." Abby's reply was a whisper and she leaned gratefully on Susannah for support.

Concern for Julius prevented me from following them into the house. Worry swirled around me as I watched Peter and the two men lead the mare and buggy back to the barn. Did they suspect anything? How was I going to find an excuse to go out to the barn after the family went to bed?

Abby gave me a wan smile when I entered the kitchen. She sat at the table while Susannah measured the contents of a tin into a cheese cloth.

"Susannah can help you if anyone can."

"I hope so. I haven't had a headache this bad since my husband died."

Susannah poured hot water over the herbs and set them to steep. As she worked, she filled me in on the news of her family. Matthew's wife and children had gone to spend a fortnight with the other grandparents, and Benjamin still worked at the wharf in Lobster Harbor. "You and Mrs. Hamilton can use the children's room, and the boy can sleep on the sofa," she concluded.

After Abby had drunk the herb tea and was tucked into bed, Susannah set out the remains of supper for Peter and me—oyster stew and bread and apple cobbler. While we ate she and her husband plied me with questions. I told them of Abby's goodness, my meeting with Melvina and subsequent position as Caleb Tremayne's housekeeper. My voice lifted when I mentioned Caleb, and Susannah's broad face broke into a smile. Through it all, my eyes kept straying to the window. Much as I loved Susannah, I was anxious to check on Julius. How had he fared? What was he thinking?

Even after Peter was asleep on the sofa and the men safely in bed, Susannah continued to ply me with questions. "What brings you back to Mickelboro?"

My answer was slow in coming. Abby had told Peter I was taking an important message to the captain of one of the Tremayne ships at

Lobster Harbor. I feared Susannah would see through this story and ask questions I was unprepared to answer. But I didn't want to tell her about Julius either.

Susannah's voice broke into my thoughts. "Do you need more than a place to stay, Tamsin? My help? Are you in trouble?"

"No." My answer came quickly. Too quickly.

Susannah pushed back her chair and brought it around the table next to mine. "What's wrong?" she asked.

"Nothing is wrong."

"Tamsin." Her tone was one she used when Mother tried to avoid her questions. "What's wrong?" she repeated. "And don't try to tell me nothing. I could tell something wasn't right as soon as I got a good look at you. Worry and tension are written all over your face." She paused and studied me like she was trying to see inside my head, my heart. When she went on, her voice was softer. "You're so very like your mother, Tamsin. Please, let me help you."

Fatigue played a part in my capitulation. But practicality was there too. I needed help to get to Julius without arousing suspicion.

Susannah's expression showed both astonishment and concern when I told her about the part I was playing to help the slave get to Canada. "My . . . oh, my," she whispered when I finished. She didn't say anything else for a moment, her hands folded in her ample lap, her eyes intent on the crockery cupboard as if it held the solution to all our problems. "You take great risk in bringing that man to Mickelboro. Amos Mickelson has no liking for abolitionists. His greatest passion right now is tracking down runaway slaves. Greed plays a part in it, I'm sure. He's paid ten dollars for every runaway he sends back. The sad part is, he's swung others to his thinking. Even my husband believes we should stay well out of it."

"Then perhaps we should go."

"No . . . no." Susannah laid her hand on mine. "You must know by now that I go my own way. Much as I love and respect Mr. Partridge, there's much that goes on here that he's unaware of." She gave a smile, one that was smug and certainly well pleased. "Don't you worry about my Percy. It's Deacon Mickelson that concerns me."

"I know." I told her about the day Amos came with Deputy Foster and searched the house.

"The old hypocrite," Susannah breathed. "Talking to you like that and calling you and your mother those names." Susannah pushed back her chair and got to her feet. "Let me fix a plate of food to take out to that poor slave. I'd better stay inside in case Mr. Partridge wakes up and decides to see what's going on." Mischief twinkled in her eyes. "After thirty years I know how to keep my husband distracted." She handed me the filled plate and a jar of milk. "I'd better bring the dog in too."

The creak of hinges cried through the stillness when I opened the barn door. I held my breath and looked back at the house for any sign that Mr. Partridge had wakened. Everything remained dark and silent. Even the dog was quiet. Taking heart, I eased the door the rest of the way open and peered into the darkened barn.

The buggy was parked close to the door, its presence a black outline among the gray shadows. Needing all the light I could find, I left the door open and felt my way across the uneven dirt surface of the floor with my feet. I hadn't taken more than a few steps when the door suddenly swung shut behind me. I jumped and almost dropped the food, a terrified scream trapped in my throat, my heart hammering so hard I could scarcely breathe.

"When is yo' goin' to learn to be careful?" Julius's deep voice hissed. "The whole world be watchin' us with that door open."

"You . . ." I croaked. My voice fought with the scream and for a moment I feared I might faint. Anger surged passed the faintness to stiffen my spine and pour strength into my trembling legs. "Don't you ever scare me like that again."

"Scare you?"

"Yes . . . scare me. What did you expect when you closed the door?" Not giving him a chance to answer, I hurried on. "What are you doing out of the buggy?"

"Couldn't stand it in there no more."

I stared in the direction of the slave's voice. The inky blackness made it impossible to see him, a darkness so complete I was afraid to move. There was no sound or movement from Julius either. His still-ness unnerved me, my fear of pursuit and discovery swallowed by the realization of my own vulnerability. Panic flicked at the edge of my mind as I recalled Julius's height, the breadth of his muscled shoulders, his dislike of white people. Even Susannah's helpfulness with her husband and the dog could work against me. A stealthy noise by the door made me cry out in alarm.

"What the matter with ya', woman? Ya's skittery as a chicken."

"I . . . I can't see."

"Well, neither can I."

The stealthy noise came again—Julius's feet feeling their way in the darkness.

"I brought you something to eat."

"Good." Not "thank you." Just "good."

"The least you can do is say, 'thank you.'"

"Thank you."

His expressionless voice sounded like a child reciting something by rote. I took a deep breath and tried not to let Julius's surliness bother me. I realized then I could see the buggy, the outline of the hayloft, even Julius carefully feeling his way from the door.

I was still put out by his lack of appreciation. I set down the food with a thump. "Mrs. Partridge sent a jar of milk with your dinner. They're here on the step of the buggy."

Julius didn't say anything for a moment—not until I'd almost reached the door. "For all yo' helpin', yo' no better than the white women on de plantation."

I stared at Julius's shadowy outline. "What do you mean?"

"I mean yo' afraid yo' might soil dos pretty white hands by touchin' my black ones when yo' hand me the food."

I was so angry I couldn't speak. When I did, the words came out in a tight, cold rush. "It was your rudeness, not the color of your skin, that made me set your food on the buggy." I paused to catch my breath. "Maybe it's you that needs to change your way of thinking, Mr. Black Man. The chip you carry against white people is so big and mean it won't let you see that most people . . . and that includes both black and white . . . are basically good. They get gladness and joy out of helping others. But helping you . . ." I paused to swallow. "Your rudeness and lack of appreciation makes me mad, not glad."

Silence fell between us—me standing with my arms close to my sides and my hands tightly clenched, Julius a burly silhouette with his head slightly bowed as if he were studying the floor or his feet or something. I don't know what I expected to happen next. Maybe him saying something rude again. Or me stalking off with my indignation wrapped around me. Neither of these things happened.

"I'm sorry," Julius said gruffly.

His voice was so low that at first I thought I hadn't heard right. I was about to say, "What was that you said?" when he spoke again.

"Clydie was always gettin' after me for being rude . . . though she called it ornery."

"Who's Clydie?"

"My woman."

"Your wife?"

"I guess you call her that. We done jump over the broom together. And we done made ourselves some babies."

"How many?"

"Two. A boy and a little girl."

His voice when he said "little girl" went soft and mellow, like warm cider slipping down the throat on a fine, fall evening. It warmed me just listening to him, warmed me so there was no anger left. Just compassion and curiosity.

"Where are they now? Clydie and your babies?"

"Gone."

The hard, flat tone in Julius's voice when he said, "gone" made me afraid to ask more. Had they been sold? Were they dead? Oh, the poor man.

"I'm sorry." It was me saying the words, not Julius, my throat choked up with unshed tears.

Neither of us spoke, but the mood of the night had changed, the darkness softened just like my heart was. My senses too, soft yet sharp at the same time so that the sounds and smells of the barn seemed clearer and more alive. The chorus of chirping crickets became sweeter and so did the aroma of the hay. Even the tiny slits of moonlight seeping through the cracks seemed brighter.

"When we be leavin' for that boat?" Julius asked.

"In the morning. Peter will drive us into Lobster Harbor. There's a man there who'll hide you and help you get onto the ship."

"Thank you." The words came without hesitation, as if perhaps Julius even took pleasure in saying them. "And thank you for doin' somthin' 'bout that dog."

"You're welcome." I smiled into the darkness, feeling a gladness I thought I'd never experience with Julius.

I cautiously pushed the barn door open before I turned for one last word. "You'll need to get back inside the buggy before morning. Mr. Partridge and his son are early risers."

I didn't expect a reply, and when I heard a soft, "yes'm" my shoulders lifted. Instead of hurrying back to the house, I paused to look up at the stars, to savor the faint smell of the sea, and to say a silent prayer for Caleb. If Julius could bring himself to say, "I'm sorry," and "thank you," then surely other good things would follow.

CHAPTER 20

We arrived in Lobster Harbor while the morning was young. Since Abby was unwell, there was only Peter and Julius and I. With just a few miles to go, I judged we would be fine. The mare was fresh, and Peter looked forward to seeing the ocean.

His eyes grew large as we started down the incline to Lobster Harbor and the sea.

The sight of so much water seemed to overwhelm him. "It's so big," he exclaimed. "I never thought nothin' could be that big." He pulled in the mare while he took it in—the sparkling water and foaming breakers. I couldn't help but contrast Peter's excitement with Julius's plight, his enthusiasm with my fear. I wished Julius could be sitting up front with Petey, wished he could be drinking in the sight with his liquid brown eyes, free and unafraid instead of scrunched up and scared inside that dreadful black box.

Lobster Harbor wasn't much bigger than Bayberry. But it seemed bigger, mostly because the houses were clustered close to the harbor, the white clapboard cottages built into the hill like small step stones. The odor of fish and lobster permeated the air along the street to the wharf. I looked at the scene with new eyes—Peter's eyes—burly men wheeling carts of fish into a warehouse, a circle of women gutting fish, their colored kerchiefs lending a festive air to the morning. Housewives with baskets waited in line for the morning catch of fish. Thank heaven all were too busy gossiping to pay us any mind. Now if I could find Barney. I looked out at the harbor and saw a ship. Was it the *Eudora*?

"Where do you want to go?" Peter asked.

"Watch for a shop called *The Lobster Pot*. The man who owns it is a friend of Mr. Tremayne. I need to stop there first."

We passed several shops built of weathered wood and fronted with signs. Then I saw it, words painted in bold letters with a drawing of a red lobster taking up most of one corner.

"There it is," Peter called. It took him two tries to pull the buggy into place. After looping the reins over the post, he hopped down and offered me his arm.

I knew Peter was eager to explore the wharf and talk to the fishermen, but Julius's safety took precedence. I glanced over my shoulder; tension and the knowledge of why I was there made everyone seem suspicious. "Stay with the buggy and keep a sharp eye out. Unsavory men sometimes hang around the harbor."

At the mention of unsavory men, Peter's disappointment fled. He was a man again, one entrusted with the protection of the buggy.

A bell tinkled when I opened the door to the shop. The interior was small and humid from boiling pots of lobster. A balding man with a luxurious moustache held a lobster for a matronly woman to inspect while a lanky man adjusted the fire under one of the pots. I wondered which one was Mr. Barney.

"Can I help you?" the lanky man asked. "We've got a dandy catch of lobsters this morning. One of the best all season."

"I was told you had the best in Lobster Harbor," I answered. I searched the man's long face and blue-gray eyes for signs of a soft heart and a willingness to risk himself for a runaway slave. I found only curiosity. Why hadn't I thought to ask Caleb to describe the man?

"A friend recommended your place to me. Are you Mr. Barney?"

"No, ma'am. The name's Tom James. Barney isn't here today."

"Not here?" I tried to hide my dismay. "Do you know where he is . . . or when he'll be back?"

"His father-in-law died and he's gone to the funeral. Won't be back 'til the end of the week . . . maybe longer. But his absence don't change our lobsters. Like your friend said . . . they're the best."

"I'm sure they are." My answer came without thought. What was I going to do?

"Would you like to see what we have?" Mr. James asked.

"Yes . . . yes, of course." Somehow I managed to give the right answers, say the right thing even as my brain whirled back to the night Caleb had told me what to do in case Mr. Barney wasn't there. I needed to get a message out to the captain of the *Eudora*. But how?

After the lobsters were weighed, paid for, and dropped into a burlap sack, I carried them out to the buggy.

"Here, let me take that," Peter said. He took the sack and looked inside. "Lobsters." His freckled face broke into a big grin. "Ain't nothin' better than fresh-caught lobster drizzled over with butter and dill. Can we take it back to Mrs. Partridge to fix it for supper?"

"That's why I bought it. But first . . ." My mind was clearer now, my thinking straighter. "First, I need to get a message out to the captain of Mr. Tremayne's ship. It's important that he gets it before he pulls anchor."

"Ma said you had an important message." Peter's hazel eyes were bright with interest. "Mr. Tremayne must be rich if he owns a ship."

"It's his uncle's ship," I corrected. "Let's go down to the wharf and look for it. It's called the *Eudora*."

"Do you want me to drive the buggy there?"

I nodded and let Peter assist me up into the buggy. He threw the burlap sack with the lobster onto the floor and climbed up to join me.

From the wharf we had a clear view of the harbor and three ships anchored there. One was slightly bigger than the others. All had slack sails and little sign of activity.

I shaded my eyes against the sun's glare and studied the hull of each ship. "Can you read any of the names?"

Peter's answer was so long in coming I began to lose hope. Was the *Eudora* out to sea? What if I had to take Julius back to Susannah's?

"There it is," Petey exclaimed. "The big one on the right. I can barely make out the letters."

For a fleeting moment I felt as if my problems were solved. But all too quickly they settled back on my shoulders—how to get a message out to the captain, the best way to take Julius to Mickelboro and the cove. I remembered the basket of food Susannah had sent with me to give to her son. Benjamin would know how to get a message out to the *Eudora*.

After several false starts, we found the shipyard where Benjamin worked. Susannah had told me of her son's love for wood. Benjamin was in the midst of it—long ship beams and awls and hammers and wood chips. Several years had passed since I'd seen Benjamin and at first I didn't recognize him—the broad-shouldered man with beard and hair liberally sprinkled with wood shavings.

"Tamsin Yeager?" Benjamin stared at me, seeming to find me as greatly changed as I found him. As he looked me over, he smiled in appreciation. "Mother always said you'd grow up to be easy on the eye." He nodded and his face broke into a grin. "She was right, of course. Mother always is."

Had the circumstances been different, I would have enjoyed the compliment. Today, my only thought was to get a message out to the ship without arousing suspicion. I handed Benjamin the basket. "Your mother sent a few things for you . . . some pound cake. A bottle of fruit."

He took the basket and peeked under the napkin. "So what brings you to Lobster Harbor?" he asked after he'd inspected the basket's contents. "Mother said you'd left these parts."

"I did . . . have. My employer needs to send a message out to one of his uncle's ships. Since he's unwell, he asked me to get the message to the captain for him." I smiled in an effort to hide my nervousness. "Could you tell me the name of a reliable man with a boat? One I could hire?"

Benjamin's smile faded. "You're not thinking to have him row you out to a ship, are you?"

"No. I have a boy with me. He can take the message."

"Good. Wouldn't be safe or proper for you to go. But if you have a boy with you . . ." Benjamin studied me, his eyes more searching than before. Could he sense my fear? Pray God he would help me. "Tim Murphy's the man for you. He's got a good boat, one I built myself. He'll take the boy and not try to overcharge you if you tell him I sent you."

"Thank you." I heard the relief in my voice. Most likely it showed in my face too, for without me asking, he took my arm and led me to the front of the shipyard. "Wait here," he said and left me while he went inside.

I glanced at Petey who'd been left with the buggy again. He was so engrossed in a man climbing the scaffolding that at first he didn't see me. "Are you ready?" he asked.

"Not yet." I wasn't sure what Ben had in mind, but I hoped it would be good. Wasn't he good, like his mother?

By now the sun was high and a little breeze was blowing off the water. I worried about Julius with the sun beating down onto the back seat of the buggy. There wasn't any breeze inside the seat, and no way for him to see what was going on. What was he thinking? I glanced anxiously toward the shipyard office. What was keeping Ben? Was something wrong?

As the minutes slipped by, my nervousness increased. Finally Ben came out of the office. "Mr. Thompson said I could leave work long enough to help you." Ben handed me up into the buggy and told Peter the best way to get to Tim Murphy's.

In no time at all, both Tim and his boat had been procured and the sum for his services agreed upon. "I'll be off now," Ben said. "I told Mr. Thompson I'd only be gone a few minutes."

"Thank you, Ben. You've been a godsend."

"Think nothing of it. Mother would have my hide if she heard I hadn't helped you." He paused and grinned. "Besides, I've never been able to resist a pretty face."

Ben left me then, but only after he instructed me not to leave Tim Murphy's cottage. "His wife and daughter said they'd look out for you. They're good people. If I know them, they'll invite you in for a cup of tea and some of Mrs. Murphy's soda cake."

Peter's eyes brightened with excitement when he learned he was to take the message. "Tell the captain the shipment from Lowe will be a day late . . . that it will come in the morning," I told him. "You mustn't give the message to anyone except the captain. If he asks you who the message is from, tell him Mr. Caleb Tremayne."

"Yes'm." Peter was looking out at the ship, not at me, his mind more on his adventure than on the message.

"Peter." My voice was sharp as I gripped his shoulders and turned him to face me. "Repeat to me what you're going to say to the captain."

Peter gave me a questioning look as he repeated the words, "Lowe—in the morning—Mr. Caleb Tremayne," before he set off with Tim Murphy. I knew he could scarcely believe his good fortune at being rowed out to the ship. I said a silent prayer for his safety and that he'd remember the message.

The Murphys were just as hospitable as Benjamin had predicted. They invited me inside out of the sun while Tim, a stocky, blue-eyed Irishman with a delightful brogue, rowed Peter out to the *Eudora.*

I threw a quick glance at the buggy, my mind filled with worry for Julius's plight—and the heat and a need for explanation. "I bought some lobster this morning. Let me move them and the buggy into the shade," I said to Mrs. Murphy. I took the mare's harness and led her to a shady place next to a shed. While I pretended to check on the lobsters, I spoke to Julius. "I'm sorry, but there's been a delay."

"What's wrong?" his deep voice rasped.

"Nothing . . . just a delay," I said, not wanting to alarm him. "I'll explain when it's safe for you to get out of the buggy." My heart impelled me to add, "Don't give up, Julius."

When Peter and Tim returned, the boy's freckled cheeks were reddened by the sun, and his walk as he came into the yard was almost a swagger. "Captain Nichols said one day's delay won't be a problem . . . though he wanted to know why Mr. Tremayne hadn't come with the message himself."

"As he should have. Captains and ships have important schedules."

Peter nodded as if he knew all about such things, his shoulders squared and his feet planted firmly on the floor in what I suspected was a close imitation of Captain Nichol's stance. For a second, fear lost its hold on my mind and I wanted to tousle his dark hair and hug him.

Peter's steady stream of conversation filled the miles back to Susannah's. I tried to match his enthusiasm as he described the ship and the sailors and the captain, but my comments sounded forced even to my own ears. Instead of listening and responding to Peter, I wanted to explain the delay to Julius—to tell him not to lose heart. What would he say to spending another night in the Partridge barn? And what about tomorrow? Just thinking about it made my stomach tighten with tension.

"Didn't I do good at takin' the message to the captain?" Petey suddenly asked.

"Do good?" I looked at him in bewilderment.

"You ain't sayin' much . . . so I thought maybe I'd done somethin' wrong."

"No, Petey. You did wonderfully . . . like someone much older than your age. I can't thank you enough." I attempted a smile and placed a hand to my head. "The trouble's with me. The sun has given me a headache."

The mention of a headache reminded Peter of his mother. "I hope Ma's feelin' better." He paused and looked back at me. "If she's feelin' better, will we start back to Bayberry in the morning?"

"Probably . . . though I have something to deliver to a friend in Mickelboro first. It will depend on how quickly I can make the delivery."

"Oh." Peter's tone didn't tell me what he thought about the delay. But it wasn't Petey I worried about. Had my answer given Julius a hint of what was going on? Did he understand?

It was afternoon by the time the buggy pulled into the Partridge yard. Julius's legs banged against the side of the seat when the dog started barking.

"It's all right," I said to both the dog and Julius.

Susannah wasn't many steps behind the dog. "I'm so glad you're back." Then in the next breath, "How did it go?"

"Not as well as I hoped, but I'm confident things will work out."

Peter's dark brows lifted as he jumped down and came to help me. Not wanting to give him a chance to ask questions, I instructed him to put the buggy in the barn and see to the mare. As I watched him go, I wondered again about Julius. He knew our plans had gone awry. Surely he would understand and not try to get out of the buggy until after dark.

"Did you get the slave out to the ship?" Susannah asked.

"No."

Her mouth tightened as she led me to the wooden bench under the hickory tree. "What happened?"

I was only vaguely aware of the dog stretched on the ground at Susannah's feet, the play of leafy shadows on her broad face as I recounted the morning's events. "Do you think the cove will be safe?" I concluded. "How closely does Amos watch for such things?"

Susannah shook her head and considered the matter. "It's hard to say. If it were just Amos, I'd say your chances were good. One man can't be everywhere. But you know the extent of the deacon's influence. He's persuaded many to his way of thinking. Mind . . . they don't have patrols or anything, but they do keep their eyes and ears open." Her concern was evident when she went on. "When do you plan to go?"

"First thing in the morning. I've already told Peter I have to go into Mickelboro." My mind skittered in circles of worry. How to keep Peter from suspecting? When would the ship get there? And what about Julius?

The thought of Julius increased my unease. By now he must be ready to jump out of his skin. Such a man might do something foolish.

"Peter can't go with me in the morning," I said. "I'll have to rely on you to think of a reason to keep him here. And the slave . . ." I took a deep breath against the rising sense of desperation. "I need to talk to him and explain what's happened." I glanced at the barn, then at Susannah. "Where are Mr. Partridge and Matthew?"

"They've gone over to Nate Trunbill's. He's down with the grippe and needs help with his farm work." Anticipating my next request, she added. "When the boy comes back, I'll keep him busy while you go to the barn."

Susannah asked Peter to read to his mother while I slipped out to the barn. The wooden structure was wrapped in afternoon somnolence. Dust motes danced in the slant of light cast by the half-open door. Hens scratched and clucked near the ladder going up to the hayloft. The buggy was parked close to the door, but there was no sign or sound from Julius.

I didn't speak until I'd climbed into the buggy and released the latch. "It's safe to come out now."

Julius's hands and head lifted the lid with such force I expected it to fly into the hayloft.

"Whaaaa," was all that came out of his mouth. That and the cant of heavy breathing, like he'd been running and was about to explode. One hand wiped his sweaty face while the other grasped the side of the seat. His eyes seemed to go in five different directions, wild and desperate.

"Where's the ship? Why'd yo' come back here?"

"The man who was supposed to hide you is gone. He won't be back until next week."

Julius closed his eyes and his massive shoulders seemed to sag under the weight of his head. "I ain't waitin' here no week."

"Only another night," I promised. "The ship is going to sail up the coast and meet us at a cove not far from here."

"Yo' sure?" Julius opened his eyes and stared at me hard, as though he was trying to read my face . . . my mind.

"I'll take you there myself. I know the place well. It's safe."

Julius's eyes flicked toward the door. "What about the people here?"

"The men are gone and my friend is keeping the boy occupied. You can get out and stretch your legs a bit." I reached into my pocket and handed him a biscuit. "I'm sorry for the delay."

"Ain't yo' fault." I knew his mind wasn't on making conversation. It was on staying alive and being free and getting to Canada without being caught by men with dogs.

"I'll be back later with water and more food."

Julius did no more than nod, his eyes on the hayloft instead of me.

I got out of the buggy and walked toward the barn door. Julius's lack of anger, his stillness made me uneasy. What was he thinking? What was he planning to do?

"Please, don't do anything foolish."

Julius's head snapped around and his gaze locked with mine. "Some folk might say foolish is trustin' a white woman . . . 'specially one who ain't had no practice at runnin' and hidin'."

Anger rose in my throat. "But I know how to drive the mare," I said in a hard, cold voice. "And I know where to meet the ship."

Instead of replying, he just stared, his black face contrasting with the coarse fabric of his once-white shirt, his features stiff and mistrusting. For a second it was as if the events of last night hadn't happened. Then Julius smiled. "I guess yo' right," he conceded. He nodded and his eyes softened.

My anger left. So did my fear. I remembered Mary and Sally were praying for me. Caleb was too. Returning the slave's smile, I straightened my shoulders and walked back to the house.

CHAPTER 21

As soon as Mr. Partridge and Matthew left for the fields the next morning, I set out with Julius in the buggy. A day of rest and Susannah's kind ministrations had resulted in Abby's full recovery. They saw me off from the dooryard while Peter gave a halfhearted wave from the garden where he'd been set to weed the potatoes.

"It's the least we can do to repay Mrs. Partridge for her kindness during my illness," his mother told him at breakfast.

I knew Peter would far sooner be driving the buggy, and if the truth were known, I would have preferred to have him with me too. Though he might be young and small, his presence had given me a sense of security on the previous day. Now there was just me and the weight of Julius's safety riding on the buggy's front seat.

I'd traveled the winding road between the Partridge farm and our cottage dozens of times with Mother and Clarissa. That morning I traveled it with fear, my eyes searching past the familiar fences and fields and trees for any sign of danger. Strange that I should now brand old neighbors and acquaintances as dangerous. I couldn't risk talking to anyone lest they spread words of my presence to Amos.

I kept the mare at a brisk pace, hoping to cover the three miles to the cove as quickly as possible. The fields of young corn were scarcely noticed; likewise the spotted cows grazing in an adjoining pasture. My senses were alerted for people, not beauty. *Please God, help me get Julius to the ship.*

God seemed to be with me. The only person I passed was one of the Meyers boys herding a cow and her calf along the roadside. I gave him a quick nod and hoped the shadow cast onto my face by the brim of my bonnet would prevent him from recognizing me.

Soon I caught a glimpse of the twin chimneys and brown roof of the Mickelson home. I slowed the mare. Even though I planned to use the back way across the meadow, I didn't like being that close to the man. What if he saw me? What if he came after me and Julius? Fear coursed through me as I pictured Amos ordering me down from the buggy and lifting the lid of the seat. I saw his satisfied smirk as he pulled out his gun. "No . . ." I whispered.

The sound of my whisper jerked me away from the scene. Instead of Amos there was only me and the mare and the buggy. And if I wanted to keep it that way, I must hold my wits about me.

After that it was easier. Before I knew it we'd reached the lane that ran along the Mickelson farm. I clucked to the mare to hurry us past the apple orchard, using it like a screen. The wooded bluff above the cove was now visible on the other side of the rolling meadow.

Despite my resolve not to do so, I looked back over my shoulder. Once, twice, three times, holding my breath as I scanned the yard for any sign of Amos, letting it out again when I failed to see him. But what if he were looking out the window?

Then I was past and there was just the meadow, the lane angling off to the right and the deacon's farm, the way ahead not the best for a buggy.

"Brace yourself for bumps," I warned Julius as we set out over the uneven terrain. The bright patches of wild flowers were scarcely noticed, nor were the grassy humps and rocks, except as obstacles to be avoided.

We finally reached the first of the trees that stretched their boughs out over the meadow. Sanctuary—a safe place to conceal the mare and buggy. I tethered the mare to a tree several yards inside the woods. Its low branches and lush spring foliage would give excellent cover.

"We're here," I said as I released the latch on the seat.

The lid rose slowly followed by the slave's large hands, then his head. Julius paused and made a quick survey of the woods as though he still didn't put much stock in my judgment. The night before I'd told him about the woods and the bluff and the steep path down to the cove so he'd know what to expect. By the looks of him, he expected danger, mistrusting the sudden whir of a cicada and starting at the scolding of a jay.

We struck out to our left until we found the path Clarissa and I had followed when we'd first explored the area. Before we'd gone many paces, Julius picked up a large stick and carried it like a cudgel. Neither of us spoke. I was worried our voices might carry outside the woods and I think Julius was too caught up in looking for danger. When we reached the top of the bluff, we stopped to rest.

"How far now?" Julius asked.

I pointed to a large tree up ahead. "From there you should be able to look down on the cove . . . maybe even see the ship."

Julius moved past me, all thoughts of resting gone. His powerful legs and dilapidated shoes covered the distance in long hungry strides. Eager as he was, he remained cautious, half-crouched, the cudgel ready.

When he reached the oak, Julius rose to his full height, his shoulders as wide as the massive trunk of the tree, his legs as thick as its lower branches. Everything about him stilled as he held the cudgel at his side, his face to the Atlantic and the sight of freedom.

I gave him a moment to take it in—the cove and the unending sea. What were his thoughts? Was the ship waiting? This last thought hurried me to the tree. What if the ship wasn't there? But it was, the gray hull with slack sails rolling and bobbing with the waves.

"That be freedom," Julius breathed. He turned his head to look at me, a satisfied smile curving his thick lips. "I was scared it wouldn't be there."

"Me too."

His smile stretched even wider. "Guess we both got a surprise."

I laughed, my relief so intense I could almost see it. With the ship there, the rest should be easy.

Julius led the way down the path to the cove—a tall silhouette in white and brown among the trees with the stick braced against the steep incline and me following in my claret dress. I wished now I'd worn my green dress—green to blend with the trees.

Julius slowed when he neared the bottom of the path. He'd turned watchful again and I sensed his mistrust of the open stretch of beach.

"Wait behind one of the big rocks. I'll let the ship know we're here."

Julius nodded and watched as I walked onto the sand and waved my shawl. The breeze caught and billowed it above my head; the shawl and my skirt fluttered like flags to signal the ship. I waved the paisley shawl until my arms ached. Was someone watching? Would they see me? Finally I saw a dingy being lowered over the side of the *Eudora*. With my shawl still clutched in my hand, I watched its slow progress toward us. *Hurry, oh, hurry!* I could see two men rowing rhythmically, the dingy skimming the blue waves and swells. I turned and walked back to Julius.

He'd left his hiding place and stood with legs spread wide as he watched the approaching boat.

"It's come. It's here!" I called.

I saw the flash of his teeth as he started toward me, pleasure and relief evident in his loose stride. When he reached me we turned to watch the dingy. It was close enough that I could see the color of the sailors' hair.

"You'll need to wade out to meet them."

Julius nodded. "Figured as much." He left me then, walking with an easy stride toward the breakers. He hadn't gone more than a dozen paces before he turned and came back.

"Can't leave without thankin' yo'." He paused and looked at his feet. "Yo' a fine woman. 'Sides my Clydie, yo' the finest woman I ever met."

The "thank you" and "fine woman" hovered around my heart and made it difficult to speak. I extended my hand. "You're welcome."

Julius looked at me, then at my hand, his black face a study in indecision.

"You're free, Julius. This is part of freedom."

There was hesitation before my hand was engulfed by his calloused palm, black on white, and only the faintest pressure.

"Godspeed," I said.

Julius nodded and walked toward the boat. When he reached the water, he bent to remove his shoes.

"Watch out!" a boyish voice screamed.

The crack of a gun followed his cry. Sand spurted to the side of Julius. I whirled and saw Peter grappling with a stocky man with a pistol—Amos, I realized—Peter's small body clinging to the deacon's back, skinny legs flailing at burly arms. I knew Peter would be flung to the ground and the pistol raised for another shot.

Lifting my skirt, I ran toward them, my hightop shoes scrabbling for footing in the soft sand, my only thought to reach Amos before he could free himself and fire the gun.

My lungs were burning by the time I reached them. I hurled myself at Amos just seconds after he'd thrown Peter from his back, the boy an inert figure near his feet, the pistol still in hand. I heard Amos's surprised grunt, felt his stocky body waver, stagger—before we crashed to the sand in a tangle of skirt and arms.

For a second I couldn't breathe—couldn't see—Amos's weight crushing like a vise, the odor of his sweat filling my nostrils as I gasped for air. I struggled to grab the pistol and found my hand pinioned by pudgy fingers that twisted mine with such ferocity I feared they'd break.

"You . . ." Amos's teeth ground as he scrambled to his feet. His hard breathing came like an echo to his word, the pistol pointed down at me.

I pushed myself into a sitting position.

"Don't move," Amos snarled.

I expected him to pull the trigger. Instead, he stared at me, his puffy lips pulled into a sneer. "Scum," he said. His enjoyment of the situation was evident—in the use of the word, in the advantage given him by the pistol. *What did he intend to do? Oh, Caleb.*

I swallowed past my fear and tried to think, to plan. I could see Peter lying crumpled and silent. What of Julius? Pray God he and the sailors were on their way.

But he wasn't. As I looked past Amos I saw Julius stealthily making his way towards us, half-crouched and alert as he'd been in the woods, the stick retrieved and held like a cudgel.

I pulled my gaze back to the deacon and hoped he couldn't read my sudden hope. I must watch Amos, not Julius. I tried to think of ways to keep the deacon's attention focused on me.

"What do you plan to do with me?" I asked.

The quaver in my voice added to Amos's pleasure. He smiled and I saw the same hungry look that had frightened me that day in the meadow.

"I've had plans for you for a long time. But first . . ."

Black feet whispered on the sand, followed by the crack of the cudgel on Amos's skull. Shock fleetingly registered on the deacon's face before he crumpled to the sand. I heard him grunt, felt the whish of suddenly released breath when his head lolled next to my hand.

I stared at the puddle of blood near my hand only dimly aware that Julius had grabbed Amos's pistol and stood over us, the cudgel in one hand, the gun pointed at the deacon.

"Did he hurt yo'? Is yo' all right?"

Not trusting myself to speak, I nodded.

"What 'bout the boy?"

I crawled over to Peter and laid my fingers on his limp wrist, felt its steady pulse. "He's alive."

At my touch, Peter stirred and his eyes flew open. "What? . . ." Fear crossed his face when he saw Julius with the gun.

"He came back to help us . . . he saved us."

Still keeping a wary eye on Julius, Peter rubbed the back of his head and got to his feet. "How'd he get here? Was he hidin' in the buggy? Does my ma know?" Then Peter noticed Amos. "Oh . . ." He backed away, his eyes widening in horror. "Is he dead?"

"Prob'ly. I done hit him hard." Julius's bare foot nudged Amos's leg. When that brought no response, he handed me the gun and felt for a pulse along the deacon's thick neck. "Nothin'," he said after a moment. "Dead."

I slowly got to my feet. The heaviness of the gun felt alien to my hand. I wanted to fling it away. Although I'd often wanted the deacon out of my life, I'd never wished him dead. I averted my gaze from his lifeless form and found Julius watching me.

"What yo' want me to do with him?"

Before I could answer, one of the sailors hailed us from the dingy. I'd forgotten about them—forgotten everything except wresting the gun from Amos and staying alive.

"The ship can't wait, Julius. You've got to go."

"And him?" Julius nudged Amos's leg again.

"Don't worry . . . just go."

Julius gave me a long searching look. I could see the questions racing through his head. What would I do with the body? The gun?

He turned back to the breakers, saw the dingy bobbing offshore. The ship and freedom were waiting. He gave me one last look and nodded.

Peter and I watched Julius wade into the ocean, the water swirling around his calves, then his thighs. I reluctantly turned back to Amos. With my gaze carefully on his middle instead of his face, I slipped the pistol back into his belt. Then I grabbed hold of his foot. "Help me, Peter."

We dragged the body to the edge of the water, looking at Amos's feet instead of his staring eyes. The tide was turning. It and the waves would carry him out to sea.

Peter and I stayed on the beach until the little boat reached the ship. We waved and Julius waved back. Then we started back across the sand.

"In another hour this will be covered with water," I said.

"Yes'm." Peter surreptitiously wiped at his nose. "I didn't plan for this to happen . . . him dead. I was just tryin' to keep him from shooting you or . . . or that black man."

I put my arm around his shoulder. "It wasn't your fault."

"But I . . . feel like it was."

"It wasn't. That man was evil. If you hadn't attacked him, he would have killed Julius . . . maybe me. You saved our lives, Peter."

"Truly?" His face brightened.

I nodded. "Truly."

Peter pulled away, the mention of his bravery restoring his confidence.

"How come you're not hoeing Mrs. Partridge's potatoes?"

Peter's head came up. "I was worried about you driving the buggy by yourself." He paused and looked me square in the face. "'Sides . . . I knew you wasn't entirely tellin' the truth. A hundred people 'sides you could a taken a message to Mr. Tremayne's ship. And I saw how scared you and Ma was at the blockade." He paused the second time, pleased and proud at his correct deductions. "Then this morning I got to thinkin' about what that man at the blockade said 'bout ways to hide runaway slaves . . . so I decided to follow you—cut across the woods mostly—and see what you was really doin'." The grin Peter gave me shouted his pleasure. "I found out what you had to deliver, all right."

"I'm so grateful you did. If you hadn't . . ." My voice trailed off as I realized how it could have ended. Julius dead, me held as an accomplice, Caleb's involvement with the underground railroad traced back to him.

We were silent as we started the steep climb from the beach, the sound of the wind and the breakers a steady accompaniment to the scrape of shoes on stone.

When we reached the top, I turned and looked out at the ocean. The ship was hoisting its sails and moving. I knew Julius must be smiling, that the air he took into his powerful lungs would be coming easy. He was safe now. Safe and free.

CHAPTER 22

I led Peter across the wooded bluff and down to the meadow. A dozen questions followed me on the descent. How had Amos seen me? What had aroused his suspicion? I voiced these concerns to Peter.

"Maybe it was your bright dress that caught his notice. Twice when I was following you, I thought I'd lost you until I saw your dress."

I hoped this was so—that it was chance, not some plot of Amos's that almost caught me in his net. Never again, I thought. Never again would I have to worry about or fear Deacon Mickelson.

Susannah and Abby were standing at the door when Peter turned the mare and buggy into the yard.

Susannah's voice was anxious. "Did everything go all right?"

"It's done." I attempted a smile—attempt was all I could do. Amos's death had cast a pall on my success and Julius's freedom.

"Thank God." Abigail's hand went to her hips and she turned on Peter. "Where did you take off to, young man? Didn't I tell you to hoe Mrs. Partridge's garden?"

"Yes'm, but . . ."

"Peter saved the slave's life. Perhaps mine as well."

The women stared at Peter, Susannah's mouth agape and Abby's drawn into a circle of astonishment.

I glanced at the road and lowered my voice. "As soon as Peter tethers the mare, we'll tell you about it."

The four of us gathered in the kitchen and I related how I'd taken Julius to the cove. "Then Amos came."

"The deacon?" Susannah's question was a horrified whisper.

Peter told them how he'd followed me, of the gun and the struggle.

"Peter was thrown to the ground and Deacon Mickelson was holding his gun on me. That's when the slave crept up and hit him . . . killed him."

"Mercy . . . oh, mercy," Susannah whispered.

Abby pulled Peter to her, her hand on his head. "Oh, son." Peter looked like he wanted to cry. Taking a deep breath, he squared his thin shoulders. "I never want to see no one dead again. Not like that."

I knew the blood and Amos's staring eyes would stay in our minds for a long time. I wished Peter could have remained shielded from such harsh things. Wished I could have too.

Susannah went to the door and looked outside. "What did you do with the deacon's body?"

"We dragged it to the water and left it." Seeing her grimace, I added. "The tide was coming in. He'll be carried out to sea."

"Let's hope so." She turned to face me. "The sooner you get away from here the better it will be. Not that I expect trouble. It will be a while before they discover Deacon Mickelson is missing. Still and all . . ."

I recognized her wisdom and nodded. Susannah quickly wrapped slices of bread and leftover chicken in a cloth for us to eat while Abby went to retrieve her parasol and bonnet. With Susannah waving us on our way, we were gone in a matter of minutes.

Little was said for the first few miles, our minds filled with Julius and Amos and all that had transpired on the beach.

Abby broke the silence, her words addressed to the back of her son's head. "You can't ever tell anyone what happened this morning. Helping a runaway slave is against the law. So is murder."

"I know." Peter's voice was scarcely audible.

"You can tell your friends about the blockade, but that's all. The rest . . . even the trip to Lobster Harbor must be kept secret."

"But Ma . . ." Peter's face was a study in disappointment. "Can't I tell them about rowing out to the ship and talkin' to Captain Nichols?"

"No, Peter." Abigail's voice was firm and decisive. If something went wrong, she didn't want her son's name linked to a Tremayne ship.

Peter's dejected slump struck at my heart. "What if Peter said a friend arranged for him to be rowed out to one of the ships?"

The look Abby gave me wasn't pleased. "Do you want me to give permission for my son to lie?"

"It's not a lie. Benjamin is my friend. He arranged it for Peter."

"Tamsin." In the time it took for Abigail to say my name, her expression changed from displeasure to amused chagrin. "I suppose it will be all right." She took a breath and her mouth turned stern again. "But that's all, Peter. Just the blockade and an excursion to Lobster Harbor so you could see a ship. But the rest . . ." She shook her head. "The rest can never be spoken of."

We were a subdued little group by the time Peter pulled the mare to a halt in front of Abby's house. The long journey played a part in it, but the strain of the past few days had taken its toll, as well. One cannot remain in a constant state of apprehension without paying a price.

By morning the subdued feeling was gone. I was up early, eager to hurry back to Caleb.

"Won't you stay for a bit?" Abby asked after finishing breakfast.

I shook my head. "Caleb will be worried and wonder what happened."

While we waited for Peter to bring the mare and buggy around, Abby helped me sponge and freshen my travel-stained dress and bonnet. She followed me out front when Peter arrived. I put my arms around her and held her close. "I don't know how to thank you for what you did . . . all you risked. I couldn't ask for a better friend."

Abby's eyes were bright with tears when we parted. "We're friends, Tamsin. I know you'd do the same for me."

I turned and hugged Peter, ignoring his self-conscious squirm. "Thank you, Peter. I couldn't have done it without you."

"It wasn't nothin'," he mumbled, but there was pleasure on his face. "You take care," he said as he helped me into the buggy.

I wanted to snap the reins and set the mare to a trot, but when I remembered the miles she'd covered the past four days, I let her choose her own gait. My mind was so filled with Caleb that I scarcely saw the green fields and farmhouses. How was he doing? Was he able to sit up in a chair? By afternoon I'd be able to see him, hold him.

I'd only gone a few miles when I heard someone calling. My heart jerked when I recognized Sally driving a carriage from the opposite direction. I pulled the mare to a stop, my heart at a frightful clamor as I took in Sally's ill-fitting brown dress and scraggly hair. What was wrong? Then I saw Caleb open the carriage door, heard him call my name.

I was down from the buggy in a thrice and running toward the carriage. I reached it just as Caleb climbed out.

"Tamsin . . . thank God." I'll never forget the joy and relief in Caleb's eyes. His gaunt face was alive with it, and he pulled me to him, his panic and relief all tied up in one strong kiss while Sally prattled on.

We climbed inside the carriage—away from Sally's prying eyes. I felt him shaking, felt both of us shaking as his lips moved over my face.

"I was so afraid," he whispered. "I love you, Tamsin. Dear heaven, but I love you." He lifted his head to look into my eyes when he said it—the part about loving. Then he pulled me back into his arms.

For a moment there wasn't a world, no escaped slaves, no Sally. There was only Caleb and me, only the two of us and our love.

A slight jolt told us that Sally had gotten down from the driver's seat to join us. She looked a trifle embarrassed when she saw me snuggled close to Caleb. "I'm so glad you're safe. How about Julius? Did he get away all right?"

I reluctantly turned from the circle of Caleb's arms. "He did. He's aboard a ship on his way to Canada."

"Thank the Lord," Sally sighed. She placed a shy hand on my arm. "Me'n Mary said lots of prayers for you."

Caleb's hand tightened on my shoulder. "I did too,"

"We was all of us prayin'," Sally put in.

"I knew you were. I could feel them." Sally's eyes filled with tears and mine did the same. Scared as I'd been, I'd known God was riding in the buggy with me.

The mare's whinny reminded us that the carriage and buggy blocked the road and that a convalescing man needed to get back home.

I reluctantly left Caleb to drive the buggy as far as Sam's uncle's farm. From there Sally drove the buggy and Sam took over the driving of the carriage. I sat inside with Caleb, enjoying his closeness and feasting on the sight of his face with its high cheekbones and new beard.

"What took you so long? What happened?" Caleb asked after he'd assured me his shoulder was doing much better.

Caleb listened while I explained. I didn't tell him about Amos. There'd be time for that later. Then Caleb told me of his decision to look for me, and how after a near fall from the gelding, he'd given in to Mary's remonstrations and ridden in the carriage.

Although it pained me to hear of Caleb's worry, in a strange way it fed my heart. The magnitude of his concern opened another facet of his love.

"We spent yesterday scouring the countryside for you," Caleb went on. "No one was home at Abigail's . . . the house closed up." His arm tightened on my shoulder. "I won't tell you my thoughts . . . my fears. They grew stronger at the Quakers'. None of us slept last night worrying about you."

"I wish I could have let you know." I reached up and touched his cheek. "Where were you going this morning?"

"Lobster Harbor."

Caleb kissed me then, a kiss that was long and satisfying. We did not mind that the horses plodded. There was much to catch up on, more kisses to exchange—once, twice, most likely a dozen, each one savored like the first red, ripe strawberries plucked after a long, cold winter.

———•———

Two weeks later our engagement was announced from the pulpit of the village church at Glen Oaks. The wedding itself would take place in July. The night before our wedding, after Mary and Sally had gone to bed, Caleb led me to my favorite chair in the sitting room, the one next to the fire. He pulled his own chair close to mine and reached for my hand. "I have something for you. A gift."

My mind flew upstairs to the watch I planned to give Caleb the next day—one with a long gold chain and our initials and the date of our wedding engraved on the back. I wondered fleetingly what he had gotten for me and pictured a small box with a locket or perhaps a necklace.

Instead of a box, he handed me a long, flat parcel tied with a piece of ribbon. I looked at the packet, then at Caleb, saw the love and pent-up anticipation on his face.

"Open it," he instructed.

Not knowing what to expect, I untied the ribbon and pulled back the folds of brown paper. A stack of letters lay inside—ten, perhaps a dozen. Letters addressed to Tamsin Yeager in the handwriting of my sister.

"Clarrie." Her name was a whisper on my lips. "Oh, Caleb." The force with which I threw my arms around him made him chuckle. "Thank you. Oh, thank you."

"The only thanks I want is for you to stay with me for the rest of our lives."

"As I shall." My arms tightened around his neck and I kissed him, a short happy kiss that soon lengthened into something more. "Where did you find them?" I asked after a moment.

"Amos Mickelson."

"Amos?" His name came out in a rush of apprehension. Susannah had written that Amos's body had been discovered three days after we left, too battered from the sea to determine the cause of death. In the end they had put it down to a tragic accident. Though I knew he was dead, his name still had the power to disturb. "How?"

"I went to his home last week . . . figured that with him dead his wife might be persuaded to let me have them. That is, if she knew where they were." A pause and a satisfied smile. "His wife didn't, but the servant—the one with the scars—ran out to the buggy with them. She'd been trying to think of a way to get them to you."

"Dear Becky," I whispered. "It's an answer to all my prayers." I lifted the letters, felt them, counted. Almost a dozen to span the three years Clarissa had been gone.

We left the room and climbed the stairs together, Caleb and I and the letters. The good-night kiss he gave me at my bedroom door was reserved, as if he didn't trust himself to display any more feeling than that.

One would think that as soon as the door closed and the lamp was lit, I would sit down to read Clarissa's letters. I did not. Much as I loved my sister, I loved Caleb more. I didn't want anything to detract from my love for him that night, nor did I want anything to dilute my anticipation of my wedding day. The letters could wait. My love for Caleb could not.

The day of my wedding dawned warm and fair, a mirror of my heart. Although Caleb was not completely well, he presented a fine figure in a dark blue coat with a starched white collar and a dark cravat. My opinion that he was the handsomest man in the church wasn't wholly the product of love-prejudiced eyes. Seeing the admiration in the other women's eyes, I counted my good fortune as I have done numerous times since then.

Nor do I think my own appearance was lacking. My new sister-in-law, Hannah, had sewed my wedding dress—yards of white organdy and lace trimmed with tiny rosebuds she embroidered herself.

"It's much like my own wedding dress," Hannah confided. "My dearest wish is that you and Caleb will find as much happiness in your years together as John and I did."

"Thank you, Hannah."

Hannah's pleasure in having a new sister-in-law was as great as mine was. I wasn't as certain of Melvina. I think part of her was put out that her brother had chosen a wife without her help. But she was all graciousness as she and Abigail wound my dark hair into a coil and arranged little wisps of hair to curl around my face.

"Lovely," Abby said when she surveyed their work. "You're lovely."

Mary nodded her agreement from a chair. The sitting room had been turned into my dressing room—Caleb having been banished to the old house to dress for the wedding—and it was just the women, Mary, Sally, Abigail, Hannah, and Melvina. And, of course, Lucinda Tremayne—Mother Tremayne as I would call her. I did not doubt her regard, or she mine. We had bonded while we cared for Caleb. Her son, my future husband. It was a happy day for us both.

As it was for Sally. In her opinion there was no bride more beautiful, no groom more handsome. A long talk with Mary had convinced her that if she were going to carry flowers for the wedding, she needed to wear something besides the ill-fitting brown dress. This day she wore a soft shade of blue, one that brought a similar color to her gray eyes and made her skin look less sallow. I was not the only one who found her much improved. Young Sam could hardly keep his eyes off her.

The sound of the organ filled the church as I walked to the front to stand with Caleb.

"Do you take this man?"

"Yes . . . oh, yes."

Caleb answered the same. Man and wife. Mr. and Mrs. Caleb Tremayne. The look in his blue eyes spoke more. Of a love that almost passed bearing. What a glorious day!

When the minister finished the holy words and we turned to face the congregation, it was Sally's face I saw, her sallow cheeks flushed with pleasure as she handed me the bouquet of flowers she'd gathered.

"For luck," she whispered. Her lips grazed my cheeks with a kiss. Could this almost- woman be my Sweet Sally?

Other friends were also there to wish me well—Susannah and Benjamin, Abigail and Peter, and of course, Mary—all sitting in the same pew, friends almost as dear to me as my family. Almost.

My eyes misted over when I thought of my parents and sisters. Especially Clarissa. I longed for their love to reach over the years and across the miles. For a moment I felt it, fragile as the tiny white petals in my wedding bouquet. Fragile, yet strong, like love is.

Then I felt the gentle pressure of Caleb's fingers on my waist. I turned my head and met his gaze, saw his smile. Thoughts of family and friends receded and there was only Caleb and me, with the rest of our lives stretching before us. The two of us and love.

EPILOGUE

Salt Lake City—2002

Tears pooled in Jessica's brown eyes as she looked at her husband kneeling across the altar from her in the temple. A month had passed since her sweet experience with Tamsin Yeager in the temple—a month when thoughts of her ancestor had frequently filled her mind. How she wished she could have known this woman, walked in her shoes, glimpsed her hopes and dreams.

Just three days short of her twenty-second birthday, Tamsin Yeager had married Caleb Tremayne. Had her heart overflowed with love for the man she'd chosen? Had he loved and cherished her too? She hoped so, believed so.

And the children—six of them, two boys and four girls: Jonathan, Clarissa, Abigail, Theodore, Julia, and little Sally, who'd died before she turned three. How had Tamsin borne the loss of the small child? But today they were together, sealed, never to be parted—an eternal family.

Jessica's gaze turned to her brothers and sisters, who'd gathered with her in the temple. All were dressed in white, proxies for the six children, she and Greg kneeling as man and wife as proxies for Tamsin and Caleb—who'd waited 150 years for this day. The witness of their presence came with such force that for a second Jessica found it difficult to breathe. The gentle pressure of Greg's hand on hers told her he felt it too. Reverent tears made a slow trail down her cheeks as she shared her ancestors' joy. They were there . . . father, mother, and children . . . rejoicing.

ABOUT THE AUTHOR

Carol Warburton has always enjoyed writing and reading. Her love of reading led her to work for the Salt Lake County Library for thirteen years, while her love of writing has led to the publication of several books; this is her third published novel and another is currently in progress. Carol's other hobbies are gardening and genealogy. She has served in many ward and stake Church callings, both as a teacher and leader. At the present she is involved with the Church Name Extraction Program and the Stake Family History Library. Carol and her husband, Roy, live in West Jordan, Utah. They are the parents of six children and ten grandchildren who contribute greatly to their happiness.